"But you co **wasn't able t** **in my arms—**

"No, Sami," he countered in a husky voice. "I'm right here."

She was so staggered to hear him use her nickname she clutched the crib railing with both hands. A small cry escaped her lips.

"You're Ric?" She shook her head, causing her hair to swish against her pale cheeks. "I—I can't believe this is happening. I—"

The room started to swim. The next thing Sami knew, she found herself on the bed, with the man who'd made her pregnant leaning over her. He sat next to her with his hands on either side of her head.

"Stay quiet for a minute. You've had another shock."

He spoke to her in the compassionate voice she remembered—exactly the way he'd done in the avalanche. With her eyes closed she could recall everything, and she was back there with him in spirit.

But the minute her eyelids fluttered open she saw a stranger staring down at her. In her psyche Sami knew he was Ric. But she couldn't credit that the striking, almost forbidding male who'd swept past her at the police station was the same Ric who'd once given her his passion and the will to live.

Dear Reader,

Born at the foot of the Wasatch mountains, my family has always enjoyed winter sports in our Rockies, which rise ten thousand feet. In my travels to Europe I've also enjoyed the winter ski areas in the Alps. Perhaps there's no place more breathtaking than Austria, where charming villages are tucked in at the base of the mountains, all covered in snow. Innsbruck is one of my favourite places.

When I read an article about an avalanche that swept through a street in one of those Austrian villages, killing five people, I shuddered. We're familiar with avalanches in our Utah mountains too. The tragedy stayed in my mind and wouldn't let me go until I'd written a novel about it.

When a man and a woman are trapped in a similar Austrian avalanche, their outcome beats the odds. I hope their story will thrill you.

Enjoy!

Rebecca Winters

THE COUNT'S CHRISTMAS BABY

BY
REBECCA WINTERS

MILLS & BOON

First published in Great Britain 2012
by Mills & Boon, an imprint of Harlequin (UK) Limited,
Eton House, 18-24 Paradise Road, Richmond, Surrey TW9 1SR

© Rebecca Winters 2012

ISBN: 978 0 263 89485 1
ebook ISBN: 978 1 408 97159 8

23-1212

Harlequin (UK) policy is to use papers that are natural, renewable and recyclable products and made from wood grown in sustainable forests. The logging and manufacturing processes conform to the legal environmental regulations of the country of origin.

Printed and bound in Spain
by Blackprint CPI, Barcelona

Rebecca Winters, whose family of four children has now swelled to include five beautiful grandchildren, lives in Salt Lake City, Utah, in the land of the Rocky Mountains. With canyons and high alpine meadows full of wildflowers, she never runs out of places to explore. They, plus her favourite vacation spots in Europe, often end up as backgrounds for her romance novels, because writing is her passion, along with her family and church.

Rebecca loves to hear from readers. If you wish to e-mail her, please visit her website: www.cleanromances.com

To my darling son John, a wonderful husband and father, who started skiing at four years of age and can ski like a champion. His experience and expertise both in the Utah and Colorado Rockies have helped me to add authenticity to the many mountain scenes in my books.

CHAPTER ONE

"PAT? It's me."

"Where are you?"

"At the Grand Savoia eating lunch in my room. You were right. It's a lovely place with every amenity. Thanks for arranging everything for me."

"You're welcome. How my gorgeous baby nephew holding up?"

"He's taking another nap right now, thank heaven. That's giving me time to pick up where I left off last evening."

"Couldn't you have phoned me before you went to bed to tell me how things were going? Your text saying you'd arrived in Genoa was hardly informative. I waited all day yesterday expecting to hear more from you."

"I'm sorry. After I reached the hotel, I began my search. But the telephone directory didn't have the listing I was looking for. When I realized I wouldn't find the answer there, I talked to the clerk at the front desk. He hooked me up with one of the chief phone operators who speaks English who was more than happy to help me."

"Why?"

In spite of the seriousness of the situation, her suspicious sister made her laugh. "It's a *she,* so you don't need to worry I'm being hit on. When I told her my dilemma, she couldn't have been nicer and tried to assist me any way she could. But by the time we got off the phone, I was too exhausted to call you."

"That's okay. So what's your plan now?"

"That operator suggested I should call the police station. She gave me the number for the traveler's assistance department. She said there'll be someone on duty who speaks English. They're used to getting calls from foreigners either stranded or in trouble and will help me. I'm going to do that as soon as I hang up from you."

"And what if you still don't have success?"

"Then I'll fly home in the morning as planned and never think about it again."

"I'm going to hold you to that. To be frank, I hope you've come to a dead end. Sometimes it's better not to know what you don't know. It could come back to bite you."

"What do you mean?"

"Just what I said. You might be walking into something you wish you could have avoided. Not all people are as nice and good as you are, Sami. I don't want to see you hurt."

"You're not by any chance having one of your premonitions, are you?"

"No, but I can't help my misgivings." Pat sounded convinced Sami had come to Italy on a fool's errand. Maybe she had.

"Tell you what. If he's not in Genoa, then I'll be on the next plane home."

"I'm going to hold you to that. Forgive me if I don't wish you luck. Before you go to bed tonight, call me. I don't care what time it is. Okay?"

"Okay. Love you."

"Love you, too."

Sami hung up, wondering if her sister was right. Maybe she shouldn't be searching for the grandfather of her baby. If she did find him, he might be so shocked to find out he was a grandfather, it could upset his world and make him ill. Possibly their meeting could turn so ugly, she'd wish she'd never left home.

That's what worried Pat.

If Sami were being honest, it worried her, too. But as long as she'd come this far, she might as well go all the way. Then maybe she could end this chapter of her life and move on.

She looked at the number she'd written down on her pad and made the phone call. The man who answered switched to English after she said hello. "Yes?"

His peremptory response took her back. "Is this the traveler's assistance department?"

"Yes—"

"I wonder if you could help me."

"What is it you want?"

Whoa. "I'm trying to find a man named Alberto Degenoli who's supposed to be living in Genoa, but he's not listed in the city phone directory. I've come from the United States looking for him. I was hoping y—"

But she stopped talking because the man, whom she'd thought was listening, was suddenly talking to another man in rapid Italian. Soon there was a third voice. Their conversation went on for at least a minute before the first man said, "Please spell the name for me."

When she did his bidding, more unintelligible Italian followed in the background. Finally, "You come to the station and ask for Chief Coretti."

Chief?

"You mean now?"

"Of course." The line went dead.

She blinked at his bizarre phone manners, but at least he hadn't turned her away. That had to account for something.

Next she phoned the front desk and asked them to send up the hotel's childminder. Sami had interviewed the qualified nurse yesterday and felt good about her. While she waited for her to come, she refreshed her makeup and slipped on her suit jacket.

Only four people knew the private cell phone number of Count Alberto Enrico Degenoli. When the phone rang, Ric assumed it was his fiancée, Eliana, calling again to dissuade him from leaving on a business trip in a few minutes. She was her father's puppet after all.

Now that Ric was about to become the son-in-law of one of the wealthiest industrialists in Italy, her father expected to control every portion of Ric's life, too. But Ric had crucial private business on Cyprus no one knew about, and it had to be transacted before the wedding.

Love had no part of this marriage and Eliana knew it. The coming nuptials were all about money. However, once they exchanged vows, he planned to do his part to make the marriage work. But until Christmas Eve, his time and business were his own concern and his future father-in-law couldn't do anything to stop him.

When he glanced away from his office computer screen long enough to check the caller ID, he discovered it was his private secretary phoning from the palazzo.

He clicked on. "Mario?"

"Forgive the interruption, Excellency." The older man had been in the service of the Degenoli family as private secretary for thirty-five years. But he was old-fashioned and insisted on being more formal with Ric now that Ric held the title. "Chief of Police Coretti just called the palace requesting to speak to you. He says it's extremely urgent, but refused to tell me the details. You're to call him back on his private line."

That would have irked Mario, who'd been privy to virtually everything in Ric's life. In all honesty, the chief's secrecy alarmed even Ric, whose concern over the reason for the call could touch on more tragedy and sorrow for their family. They'd had enough for several lifetimes.

"Give me the number."

After writing it down, he thanked Mario, then clicked off and made the call. "Signor Coretti? It's Enrico Degenoli. What can I do for you?"

He hadn't talked to the chief since the funeral for his father, who'd died in an avalanche in January. The chief had been among the dignitaries in Genoa who'd met the plane carrying his father's body. The memories of what had happened that weekend in Austria would always haunt Ric and had changed the course of his life.

"Forgive me for interrupting you, but there's a very attractive American woman in my office just in from the States who's looking for an Alberto Degenoli from Genoa."

At first his heart leaped at the news, then as quickly fizzled. If this American woman had been looking for him, she would have told the police chief she was looking for a man named Ric Degenoli.

Ric and his father bore the same names, but his father had gone by Alberto, and Ric went by Enrico. Only his siblings ever called him Ric. *And the woman who'd been caught with him in the avalanche.*

"Does she know my father died?"

"If she does, she has said nothing. To be frank, it's my opinion she's here on a fishing expedition, *if* you know what I mean." He cleared his throat. "She's hoping I can find him for her because she says it's a matter of life and death," he added in a quiet voice.

What?

"Since she's being suspiciously secretive, I thought I should let you know before I told her anything."

The intimation that this could be something of a delicate nature alarmed Ric in a brand-new way. He shot out of his leather chair in reaction. Up to now he'd done everything possible to protect his family from scandal.

Unfortunately he hadn't been able to control his father's past actions. No matter that Ric was a Degenoli, he and his father had differed in such fundamental ways, including the looks he'd inherited from his mother, that the average person wouldn't have known they were father and son.

One of Ric's greatest fears was that his father's weakness for women would catch up with him in ways he didn't want to think about. With his own marriage coming up on New Year's Day, it was imperative nothing go wrong at this late date. Too much was riding on it.

His father had been dead less than a year. It wasn't a secret he'd been with several women since Ric's mother's sudden and unexpected death from pneumonia sixteen months ago. He recalled his mother once confiding to him that even if his father were penniless, he would always be attractive to women and she had overlooked his wandering eye.

Ric couldn't be that generous. If the woman in Coretti's office thought she could blackmail their family or insist she had some claim on his deceased father's legacy, then she hadn't met Ric and was deluding herself. "What's her name?"

"Christine Argyle."

The name meant nothing to him. "Is she married? Single?"

"I don't know. Her passport didn't indicate one way or the other, but she wasn't wearing a ring. She called the traveler's aid department and they turned it over to me. At first I thought this must be some sort of outlandish prank, but she's not backing down. Since this is about your father, I thought I'd better phone you and learn your

wishes before I tell her I can't help her and order her off
the premises."

"Thank you for handling this with diplomacy," Ric
said in a level voice, but his anger boiled beneath the
surface. To go straight to Genoa's chief of police to get
his attention was a clever tactic on her part. She wouldn't
have taken that kind of a risk unless she thought she had
something on Ric's father that the family wouldn't like
made public. *How convenient and predictable.*

She'd probably met Alberto at a business party last
fall when he'd decided he didn't want to be in mourning
any longer. More often than not those dinners involved
private gambling parties. Many of them were hosted for
foreign VIPs on board one of the yachts anchored in the
harbor where the police had no jurisdiction.

There'd be plenty of available women, including
American starlets, to please every appetite. But it would
be catastrophic if this last fling of his father's was the
one that couldn't be hushed up and resulted in embarrassing the family morally and financially.

Not if Ric could help it!

Anything leaked to the press now could affect Ric's
future plans in ways he didn't even want to think about.
He saw red. Before the wedding, the negotiations in
Cyprus *had* to go through as planned to safeguard his deceased mother's assets so Eliana's father couldn't get his
hands on them. Ric refused to let anything get in the way.

"*Per favore*—keep her in your office until I get there.
Don't use my title in front of her. Simply introduce me
as Signor Alberto Degenoli and I'll go from there." This

woman wouldn't have gotten involved with his father if he hadn't had a title, but Ric intended to play along with her ruse until he'd exposed her for a grasping opportunist.

"Understood. She went out for a while, but she'll be calling me in a few minutes. If you're coming now, I'll let her know you're on your way."

His thoughts were reeling. "Say nothing about this to anyone."

"Surely you don't question my loyalty to the House of Degenoli?"

"No," Ric muttered, furrowing his hair absently with his fingers. He stared blindly out the window of the Degenoli Shipping Lines office. For well on 150 years it had overlooked the port of Genoa, Italy's most important port city. "Forgive me, but when it comes to my family…"

"I understand. You know you can rely on my discretion."

"Grazie." Ric's voice grated before he hung up.

Whatever was going on, Ric didn't want wind of this to reach his siblings. Claudia and Vito lived with enough pain and didn't need to take on more, especially with Christmas only a week away. It was absolutely essential this be kept secret.

After he told his driver to meet him in the side alley, he rang security to follow them and left the office with his bodyguards. He needed to take care of this matter now, before he left for the airport.

For the second time today, Sami paid the taxi driver and got out in front of the main police station in Genoa with trepidation. The police chief had told her one of his staff had found the number of the man she was looking for and had contacted him.

It was a miracle! She couldn't have done it without the phone operator's help. After searching for Alberto Degenoli without success, she'd almost given up hope.

No telling what would happen at this meeting, but she had to go through with it for her baby's sake. His existence would come as a total surprise to Mr. Degenoli, but her son deserved to know about his father's side of the family.

Of course, the baby was too little to know anything yet. It was up to Sami to introduce them and lay a foundation for the future, *if* Mr. Degenoli wanted a relationship. If not, then she'd go back to Reno and raise him without feeling any attendant guilt that she hadn't done all she could do to unite them.

Once through the doors, she realized it was just as busy at four o'clock as it had been earlier. Besides people and staff, it was filled with cigarette smoke, irritating her eyes and nose. The nativity scene set up on a table in the foyer reminded her how close it was to Christmas and she'd done nothing to get ready for it yet. But she'd had something much more important on her mind before leaving Reno than the upcoming holidays.

Having been in the building earlier, she knew where to go. She'd just started to make her way down the hall when a man strode swiftly past her and rounded a corner at the end. He was a tall male, elegantly dressed in a tan suit and tie. Maybe he was in his mid-thirties. For want of a better word, he left an impression of power and importance that appeared unconscious and seemed to come as naturally to him as breathing.

Sami passed several men and policemen who eyed her in masculine appreciation before she turned the corner and entered the reception area of the police chief's office. With the exception of the uniformed male receptionist she'd met before, the room was empty. Where had the other man gone?

After she sat down, the receptionist picked up the phone, presumably to let the chief know she'd arrived. Once he'd hung up, he told her she could go in. After removing a few blond hairs from the sleeve of her navy blazer, Sami thanked him and opened the door to the inner office.

To her shock, the stranger who'd passed her in the hall moments ago was standing near the chief's desk talking to him. Obviously the chief of police was busy, so she didn't understand why his secretary had told her she could go in.

At a glance she took in the other man's lean, powerful physique. Her gaze quickly traveled to the lines of experience etched around his eyes and mouth. Maybe she was mistaken, but beneath his black brows, those dark eyes pierced hers with hostility after he'd turned in her direction. That wasn't a reaction she was used to receiving from the opposite sex.

Of medium height, she had to look up to him. His unique male beauty fascinated her, especially his widow's peak formed by hair black as midnight. Swept back like that, it brought his Mediterranean features and gorgeous olive skin into prominence.

The chief spoke in heavily accented English, drawing her attention away from the stranger. "Signorina, may I present Signor Alberto Degenoli."

Sami's spirits plunged. *This isn't the man I'm looking for.* But perhaps he is a relative? "How do you do?" she murmured, shaking the hand of the striking Italian male who'd extended his. He had a strong, firm grip, like the man himself.

"How do *you* do, Signorina?" His polished English was impeccable with barely a whisper of accent. But it was the depth of his voice that sent a curious shiver through her body, recalling an echo from the past. Maybe she was mistaken, but she thought she'd heard that voice before.

But that was crazy. They'd never met.

"You've gone pale, Signorina. Are you all right?"

"Yes—" Sami gripped the back of the nearest chair. "I-it's just that you're not the person I'm looking for and I'm disappointed," she stammered before gazing at him again. "You have his name, but you're...too young. Obviously there's more than one Alberto Degenoli living in Genoa."

He shook his head. "No. There's only one."

"You mean *you?*"

"That's right."

"Perhaps instead of Genova, you meant Geneva in Switzerland, Signorina," the chief inserted. "Many

Americans become confused by the two similar spell-ings."

She frowned. "Possibly I misunderstood. Mr. Degenoli's in shipping."

"So are others on Lake Geneva."

"But he's Italian."

"Thousands of Italians live in Switzerland."

"Yes. I know." Maybe because of the differences in pronunciation, she'd gotten the name of the city wrong. How odd. All this time… "Thank you for the sugges-tion." She looked at Mr. Degenoli. "I'm so sorry you've made this trip to the police station for nothing. I've put both of you out. Please forgive me."

"Perhaps if you gave me a clearer description of him?"

"Well, he'd probably be in his sixties. I'm not sure. I feel terrible about this. Thank you for coming here on such short notice." She glanced at Chief Coretti. "Please excuse me for taking up your time. You've been very kind. I'll leave now so you can get on with your work."

At her comment, he squinted at her. "You sounded desperate when you came to me, Signorina. Therefore I will leave you to get better acquainted with this gentle-man you've inconvenienced, and the two of you can dis-cuss…business."

Business? "What on earth do you mean?"

"Surely you're not that naive?" the chief replied.

Upset by the distasteful insinuation, she felt heat rush to her cheeks. "You've evidently questioned my motives, but whatever you're thinking, you'd be wrong—" she blurted.

At this point she felt oddly reluctant to be left alone with the intimidating stranger studying her with relentless scrutiny. "I haven't found the person I'm looking for, so there's no point in this going any further. I truly am sorry to have caused either of you any inconvenience."

Chief Coretti gave her a nasty smile. "What is going on, Signorina? You said it was a matter of life and death."

"It is." She hated the tremor in her voice.

He threw up his hands. "So explain!"

"I know I've been secretive, but I'm trying to make this inquiry as discreetly as possible to protect all concerned. When my other searches failed yesterday, I came to you for answers and hoped nobody would get hurt in the process. But the fact remains I'm looking for an older gentleman. I suppose he could even be in his early seventies."

Time seemed suspended as Mr. Degenoli swallowed her up with those jet-black eyes of his. "Signor Coretti—if you'd be so kind as to leave us alone for a moment."

"Of course."

After he left, the room grew silent as a tomb except for the thudding of her heart. It wouldn't surprise her if the stranger could hear it.

His lips twisted unpleasantly before he moved closer. "You've been secretive long enough. I'd like to see your passport." Sami had the strongest conviction he was curious about her, too. At this point she knew she'd heard his voice before. But where? When she'd come to Europe a year ago, she hadn't visited Italy.

While she rummaged in her purse, her mind was

searching to remember. He stood there waiting, larger than life with an air of authority much more commanding than any police chief's. She handed the passport to him. After he read the information, he gave it back.

"I've never heard of you." His eyes glittered with barely suppressed anger. "The Alberto Degenoli I believe you're looking for is no longer alive, but I think you already knew that. How well did you know him?" he demanded.

Ah. Now she understood the police chief's earlier remark about "business." Both men assumed she'd been involved with the man she was looking for. Sami lifted her head. "I didn't know him at all. In fact I never met him, but I'd h-hoped to," she stammered. Sadness overwhelmed her to realize she'd come to Italy for nothing.

"What did this man mean to you?"

Wouldn't he just love to know, but he'd be so wrong! She took a fortifying breath. "Since he's dead...nothing."

"How did you hear of him?"

Sami had heard of him through his son, but he was dead, too. If this man was the only living Degenoli in Genoa, then what the chief of police had said was probably true. She should fly to Geneva to start her search there before flying home.

"It no longer matters." She tried to swallow, but the sudden swelling in her throat made it difficult. "Forgive me for bothering you." She spun around and made a quick exit.

As she flew down the hall to the entrance of the police station, she suddenly realized what had been bothering her. The man she'd just left had the same kind of voice as her baby's deceased father. That's why it had sounded so familiar and disturbing…except for one thing.

This man didn't have that tender, caring quality in his voice. His tone and manner had been borderline accusatory. Her body gave a shudder before she stepped into the first taxi in the line-up in front of the building.

Ric had caught only a glimpse of tear-filled green eyes before she dashed from Coretti's office. Could there be two American women in existence who sounded that identical? He supposed the coincidence was possible, since he'd never seen this woman in his life.

For months he'd looked for the woman he'd been trapped in the snow with, hoping she would come looking for him, but by summer he'd decided she must have died in that avalanche.

He closed his eyes for a moment, remembering the way this woman's husky voice had trembled. Much as he hated to admit it, a part of him had felt her emotion was genuine. The classic features of her pale blond beauty, so different from his own countrywomen, already bothered him in ways he was reluctant to admit.

But great as her acting had been, Ric was convinced Signorina Argyle had lied to him, or at least hadn't told him the whole truth. Whatever her secret, he was determined to find it out.

Running on pure adrenaline at this point, he buzzed Carlo, his head of security, and told him to follow the twenty-six-year-old blonde American woman leaving the police station. When she reached her destination, he wanted to know exactly where she went from there, so he could arrange a private meeting.

Now hadn't been the time to stop her. The conversation he intended to have with her needed to be someplace where they could be strictly alone with no chance of anyone else walking in on them.

With his visit to the chief's office accomplished, he went out to the limo. Within a few minutes he learned she was booked in at the Grand Savoia—one of the best, if not *the* best hotel in Genoa. It was expensive any time, but especially over the holidays. He told the driver to take him there. Carlo indicated Ric would find her on the third floor, to the right of the elevator, four doors down on the left.

Before long he alighted from the limo and entered the hotel. Deciding to take her by surprise, he dispensed with the idea of phoning her and took the stairs two at a time to her floor. When he reached her door, he knocked loudly enough for her to hear.

"Signorina Argyle? It's Signor Degenoli. We need to talk." He got no response, so he decided to try a different tactic. "Why were you trying to find Alberto? I would like to help you if you'd let me."

Carlo had told him she'd gone into her room and hadn't come out again, but she might be showering. He gave her another minute, then knocked again. "Signorina?"

A few seconds later the door opened as wide as the little chain would allow. He saw those green eyes lifted to him in consternation, but they were red-rimmed. By the look of it, she'd been crying. That much was genuine.

The champagne-gold of her collar-length hair gleamed in the hall light. She'd discarded her jacket. From the little he could see, a curvaceous figure was revealed beneath the silky white blouse she'd tucked in at the waist of her navy skirt. Every inch of her face and body appealed strongly to him.

"I didn't realize the police chief had had me followed." The natural shape of her mouth had a voluptuous flare he'd noticed back at the station. But right now it was drawn tight. She hugged the door, as if she didn't trust him not to break in on her.

Ric lounged against the wall. "Don't blame him. I asked one of my men to keep an eye on you until I could catch up with you."

"*Your* men?"

"My bodyguards. If you'll invite me inside, I'll be happy to explain."

A delicate frown marred her features. "I'm sorry, Mr. Degenoli, but as I said at the station, there's nothing more to discuss and I have other plans."

"As do I." He was already late leaving for Cyprus. "But we have unfinished business," he rapped out. To his disgust, he wondered what her exact plans were. Deep inside, his gut twisted to think that he could be this intensely attracted to a stranger. His interest in her made no sense, but the sound of her voice and the way she talked still played with his senses.

A sound of exasperation escaped her lips. "Please believe me when I tell you how badly I feel that you were called into the police station for nothing. If you'd like me to pay you for the inconvenience, I could give you fifty dollars to cover the gas money. It's all I can spare."

If that were true, then she'd chosen too expensive a hotel to stay in. "I don't want your money. To be frank, I knew you were upset when you left the station." He cocked his head. "I can tell you've been crying. Now that we don't have Chief Coretti for an audience, you can speak freely with me."

"I probably could, but there'd be no point." She wiped her eyes with the back of her hands. "I've come to the end of my search. I have to say goodbye now."

There was no question in his mind she was holding back something vital. He put his foot in the door so she couldn't close it. "Not until I get more answers. For one thing—" He only got that far because he heard a baby fussing. The sounds came from the other side of the door. *I knew it!*

"Not so fast." Ric put his weight against the door so she couldn't shut it on him. "Whose baby is it?"

"Mine."

"And Alberto's?" With his mind firing, all Ric could think was that his father had made love to this woman and she'd come to present him with the fruit of that union, but it was too late.

"No—" she cried.

"Then prove it to me."

CHAPTER TWO

In HER mind Sami could hear Pat's dire warning, but she hadn't heeded it.

This situation had hit rock bottom and was exactly what she'd hoped to avoid, but this man wouldn't let it go and had followed her to the hotel. Since she'd started this, she decided that if she didn't want to deal with Chief Coretti again, she'd better let him in.

After undoing the chain, she hurried across the room to the crib. Once she'd picked up the baby, she cuddled him against her shoulder in a protective gesture. Kissing him, she said, "You heard noises and they frightened you, didn't you, sweetheart? Don't worry. It's okay." She flicked Mr. Degenoli a curious glance. "Our visitor will be leaving soon."

The arresting-looking Italian had already come inside the room and locked the door behind him. She shivered a little as he drew closer to look at her baby.

Sami decided *this* Mr. Degenoli *had* to be a relative of her baby's father. That's why his voice sounded so familiar to her. Back at the station he'd been as cagey as she'd tried to be in her effort to protect people and reputations, even to the extent of possibly lying about his name, but with both father and son dead, there was no worry now. The only thing to do was answer his questions, then go home to Reno in the morning.

"Excuse me while I change him." Reaching for a towel, she spread it on top of the bed and put the baby down.

"Where did you leave him while you were at the police station?"

Sami undid the baby's stretchy blue suit. "Here, of course. Don't you know the last place for a baby was that smoke-filled building? This hotel happens to have an outstanding child-minding service." Sami's sister had made the reservation for her. "That's the reason I booked in here. They sent a qualified nurse to watch over him while I went to the police station."

He didn't look as if he believed her. "I didn't kidnap him. If you're so skeptical, call the front desk and ask them yourself. They'll verify who I am."

At this point his eyes were riveted on the baby. "How old is he?"

Sami used the baby wipes and discarded everything in a plastic bag. After powdering him, she slipped him into a fresh diaper. "Two months, but that information wouldn't have any relevance for you. I couldn't bring him to Genoa to meet his grandfather before now."

"Grandfather—"

"Yes. Why do you seem so shocked? Most children have them. I'm heartbroken that my son is never going to know him or…his father." Her voice faltered.

She kissed the soft baby hair that was dark and too

beautiful for a boy. His handsome face was all flushed, but he stopped crying long enough to notice the intruder who was thoroughly inspecting him.

After fastening the snaps on the stretchy suit, she wrapped him in his quilt and picked him up to snuggle him. "I think you're ready for your dinner, young man." She walked over to the dresser for a fresh bottle of ready-mixed formula and sat down on a chair to feed him.

"Your voice sounds familiar to me, Signorina."

So she wasn't the only one imagining their connection. "Yours does to me, too. Strange, isn't it, when I know we've never met?"

His dark brows furrowed. "More than strange. Were you in Europe on holiday recently?"

"Not for close to a year, but I've traveled to Europe before."

"I'd like to see your passport again."

"Let me feed my son first, then I'll get it for you."

He was a good little eater, but he'd been awakened before his nap had been over and was ready to go back to sleep. She burped him, then put him back in the crib and covered him with the quilt.

Aware of Mr. Degenoli's eyes watching her every move, she walked over to the dresser and pulled the passport from her purse. "In case you were wondering, I applied for this passport several years before my baby was born."

Her visitor took it from her and studied the pages with the various entry stamps. "This last one dated in January says you visited Austria—"

"Yes."

"*Where* in Austria?" The inflexible male sounded in deadly earnest.

"Innsbruck."

At the mention of it, his complexion took on a definite pallor. "Why that town?"

"Because my sister and her husband own a travel agency, and I was checking out some hotels for them there and in the surrounding areas. They're always looking for new places to book their clients into."

Mr. Degenoli appeared so shaken, she decided to end their inane question-and-answer session. Without hesitation she reached for her purse and pulled out a brown envelope. "Here—" Sami handed it to him. "I brought this to show my baby's grandfather. It will explain everything."

He eyed her suspiciously before he opened it and pulled out the birth certificate.

"As you can see there, I named my baby Ric, after his daddy. Ric Argyle Degenoli. You see, b-both Ric and his father, Alberto, were caught up in the same avalanche I was buried in last January." Her voice faltered. "I assume Alberto was a relative of yours. Maybe your uncle?"

Her uninvited guest didn't make a sound. It led her to believe he was finally listening to her. "I'd just stopped in one of the hotels for a minute to check it out and get a hot drink in the dining room. As I was about to go outside again to do a little sightseeing, the avalanche swept through the three-story hotel like a supersonic freight train.

"Ric and I were entombed for several hours. I knew he'd died before I lost total consciousness, but until you told me at the police station, I didn't realize Alberto had been killed, too.

"After I woke up in a clinic, I assumed Ric's father had survived, because only one male victim named Degenoli was listed among the fatalities. That was Ric, of course. His father must have died later from his injuries, after the list was put out."

Sami couldn't stop the tears from spurting. "It was a nightmarish time. My sister came to Innsbruck to get me and fly home with me. I didn't realize until six weeks later that I was pregnant. At that point I determined that one day I'd look up Alberto and let him know he had a grandchild. But as you've let me know, this trip was in vain."

The man listening to her story had gone eerily quiet.

"My sister calls my son Ricky, but I love the Italian version. I named him after his heroic father to honor him."

"Heroic?" he questioned in a gravelly voice.

"Yes. One day when Ric is old enough, I'll tell him how courageous his father was."

"In what way?"

"You would have to have been there to understand. Ric was an amazing man. After the snow buried us, he kept me from losing my mind. You see, I suffer from claustrophobia. You can't imagine what being trapped did to me. I wouldn't be alive if it hadn't been for him.

"We were total strangers sealed in a black tomb together. We heard each other moan, but had no idea what the other one looked like. I know I was on the verge of a heart attack when he started talking to me and urged me to relax, because he believed we'd get out of there if we didn't panic. He pointed out that by some miracle, we were trapped by beams that kept the whole weight from falling on us, providing us a pocket of air and room to wiggle.

"At first I thought I was dead and that he was an angel the way he took care of me and never let me panic. But when he reached for me and held me in his arms, promising me we'd be all right, I knew he was mortal.

"His only thought was to protect me. At first his kisses on my cheek held back my terror. I returned them, needing his comfort while we lay there slowly suffocating. We talked a little. He told me he'd just come from a wedding with his father, Alberto. I explained I was on a trip, but we didn't go into details.

"As time went on and no help came, we realized we were going to die. At that point we drew warmth and comfort from each other's bodies." She took a fortifying breath. "We made love. It happened so naturally, it was like a dream. Then I heard a shifting sound. The next thing I knew a piece of wood had pierced his forehead."

A sob caught in her throat. "It knocked him unconscious and his warm blood spilled over both of us. I couldn't get a pulse and knew he was gone. When I woke up in a clinic, the last thing I remembered was that he'd died in my arms.

"We'd been literally tossed together with the broken

walls and furniture in the darkness of a catastrophic avalanche that hit the hotel. But for the time we were together, hanging on to life because we knew they were our last moments on this earth, I felt closer to him than to anyone I've ever known.

"When I look at my adorable Ric, I know I'm seeing his father. My only hope now is to raise him to measure up to the great man who gave him life. I know he was a great man because he was so selfless in the face of terror. He never once thought of himself, only of me. So now I hope that explanation answers your questions, Mr. Degenoli."

She stared at the tall figure still standing there. His face had gone ashen. The birth certificate had fallen to the floor. How odd he'd left it there...

"If you still don't believe me, then I don't know what more I can say to convince you. Maybe now you'd answer a question for me. Was Alberto your uncle?"

"No," he answered in a voice as deep as a cavern. "He was my father."

"Chief Coretti introduced you as Alberto, but that really isn't your name, is it? He did it to protect you. I can understand that."

He moved closer to her. "Let me explain this another way. My father was christened Alberto Enrico Degenoli, and was called Alberto. I was also christened Alberto Enrico Degenoli, but I go by Enrico. However my immediate family calls me...Ric."

As Sami stared at him, the world tilted.

"But you *couldn't* be that Ric. I wasn't able to waken him. He died in my arms—"

"No, Sami," he countered in a husky voice. "I'm right here."

She was so staggered to hear him use her nickname, she clutched the crib railing with both hands. A small cry escaped her lips. "*You're* Ric?" She shook her head, causing her hair to swish against her pale cheeks. "I—I can't believe this is happening. I—"

The room started to swim. The next thing Sami knew, she found herself on the bed with the man who'd made her pregnant leaning over her. He sat next to her with his hands on either side of her head. "Stay quiet for a minute. You've had another shock."

He spoke to her in the compassionate voice she remembered—exactly the way he'd done in the avalanche. With her eyes closed, she could recall everything and was back there with him in spirit.

But the minute her eyelids fluttered open, she saw a stranger staring down at her. In her psyche Sami knew he was Ric. But she couldn't credit that the striking, almost forbidding male who'd swept past her at the police station was the same Ric who'd once given her his passion and the will to live.

Sami's hair spilled onto Ric's fingers. If he closed his eyes, he could recall the same silky mane he'd played with in the darkness. The strands had been as fragrant as every part of her face and body. It was the same now, but at the time he'd had no idea its coloring resembled spun gossamer.

Still noticing her pallor, he got up from the bed to get her a cup of water. When he returned from the bathroom, she sat up. He handed it to her and she drank thirstily. "Thank you," she whispered in a tremulous voice before lying back again like a spent flower.

Ric put the empty cup on the side table, then sank down next to her once more. "Our survival was a miracle," he began.

"Yes. I'm still trying to deal with the fact that you didn't die and are here where I can see you."

She wasn't the only one. "When we were trapped together, I would have sold my soul to know what you looked like," he confessed emotionally. "Feeling you told me that you were a lovely woman, but I must admit that no dreams I've had of you could measure up to your living reality."

Like someone shell-shocked, she lifted one of her hands to his face in wonder. She traced his features, bringing back memories he would never forget. "Ric—" Her fingers traveled over his lips. "Maybe I'm hallucinating again."

He kissed the palm of her hand. "It was never an hallucination. We were mortal then and now."

Tears trickled out of the corners of her eyes, eyes that were alive like the green of a tropical rain forest. "When I thought you were dead, I wanted to die. While you were still breathing, I could hold on. But after that beam hit you and I couldn't get a response, it was the end of my world."

Ric heard the same pain in her voice he'd carried around for months afterward. He studied her facial features, overlaying his memories of her through eyes that could see the throb at the base of her slender throat. Tears trembled on the ends of long dark lashes so unusual on a blonde.

She kept looking at him with incredulity. "I feel just like I did after the avalanche struck. Maybe I'm hallucinating and none of this is real, but it *has* to be real because I'm touching you and it's your voice. You're actual flesh and blood instead of the stuff of my dreams."

"You were the flesh and blood I clung to while we were entombed," he confessed. "You saved my sanity, too, Sami. Like you, I felt I was in this amazing dream. When we made love, I remember thinking that if it was a dream, I never wanted to wake up from that part of it. Everything about our experience had a surreal quality."

Sami wiped the tears off her face. "I know. Until I found out I was pregnant, there were times when I thought I'd made it all up." She stared at him. "What happened to you after you were rescued?"

He grasped her hand. "I was told that another few minutes and the medics wouldn't have been able to revive me. I knew nothing until I woke up in a hospital in Genoa. I was in a coma for two days. When I came out of it, I was surrounded by my family. My first request of the doctor was to find out if you were one of the victims.

"He came back with the message that you must still

be alive because there was no name of Sami or anything close to it on the list of fatalities. After hearing that news, I determined to go after you once I got better. After our family held funeral services for my father, then I started looking for you."

"I can't believe it."

"Why are you so surprised? What we'd shared together was something so unique, I'll never forget. But when your name didn't show up on any established tour-group lists in the area, I had to look further afield. I remembered you'd told me you were from Oakland, California. That's all I had to go on. I put my people on it while we searched for you for several months."

"Oh, Ric—" she cried softly before sliding off the other side of the bed to come around.

He got to his feet. "You were my first priority, but you weren't listed in the Oakland phone directory. No flights leaving Austria for the States with your name. No planes arriving in Oakland or San Francisco had a name that could be traced to you. It was as if you'd disappeared off the face of the earth."

"That's because you didn't know my real name," she cried out in dismay. "I was nicknamed Sami because my father's name was Samuel. After my parents died, my grandparents took over raising me and my sister, and my grandfather said I reminded him so much of his son he started calling me Sami, and it stuck."

"I thought it had to be short for Samantha, but your passport says otherwise."

"That's what everyone assumes who doesn't know

me. To think you searched all that time for the wrong name. I can't bear it."

He couldn't either, considering the promise he'd made to his father when they'd gone to Austria for an important family wedding. Ric had done everything humanly possible to find her. When he'd exhausted every avenue to no avail, he'd got on with his life and eventually fulfilled that promise.

"It's true I was born and raised in Oakland," she went on to explain, "but after I went back to college, I started to feel ill and went to a doctor. When he told me I was pregnant, I couldn't believe it. My sister, Pat, insisted I move to Reno, Nevada, to be with her and her husband. Their travel agency is growing all the time. They're the ones who gave me a working vacation during my break from college."

Nevada... The avalanche had changed both their lives in ways Ric was only beginning to understand. "Were you ill the whole pregnancy?"

"No. After the morning sickness passed, I didn't have other problems. Since Pat's my only family and I wanted to be close to her and their children, I moved to Reno and started classes there. Without my legal name, no wonder you couldn't trace me."

He rubbed his chest absently while he was digesting everything.

Her anxious gaze fastened on him. 'Do you have any ill effects from your head wound?"

"Only the occasional headache," he answered, touched by her concern.

"I'm so glad it isn't worse. That was the most terrifying moment." Her voice shook.

"Thankfully, I don't remember."

"I don't like to think about it. Throughout my pregnancy I decided that after Ric was born and I'd had my six-weeks checkup, I'd take him to Genoa and look up his grandfather. My own parents had already died, and I thought it would be wonderful if Ric grew up knowing he had at least one grandparent who was still alive." She hugged her arms to her waist. "How tragic you lost your father."

"Yes," he whispered, but right now everything else seemed very far removed.

"I thought about him all the time," she said. "Naturally I feared how he would take the news. It might have been the worst thing he could hear, but I hoped it might comfort him a little to know you weren't alone when you died."

Ric's breath caught. "*Ringrazio il cielo* you looked for him! Otherwise I would know nothing! Be assured my father would have wanted to be a grandfather to our son." *Once he'd gotten over the shock of learning the circumstances of his grandson's conception.* Ric was still having trouble taking it all in.

She bit her lip. "I didn't know the right thing to do. That's the reason why I was so secretive with the police chief." Ric warmed to her for her desire to be discreet. "I didn't want to embarrass your father or cause him pain in front of anyone else. I really thought if I could find him, he'd refuse to believe me and that would be the end of it. But for the baby's sake, I felt I had to try.

"When the police chief suggested maybe I had the wrong city, I didn't know what to believe. I thought you'd told me you were from Genoa. The thought of flying to Geneva and starting another search sounded overwhelming, but I was prepared to do it for your son's sake. Oh, Ric—"

The woman he'd been trapped with had to be one in a billion.

His eyes strayed to the crib. The baby sleeping so peacefully was his son. It was unbelievable! Throwing off his own shock, he walked over to the crib and looked down at the baby—*his baby*—lying on his back with his arms outstretched, his hands formed into fists.

"In spite of all that death and destruction coming for us, we managed to produce a son!"

"Yes." She'd joined him. "Incredibly, he's perfect."

Ric had thought the same thing the second he'd laid eyes on him. In that moment he'd suffered pain thinking his parent had fathered such a beautiful child with *her*. Ric had been so convinced of it that he was still having trouble getting a handle on his emotions.

But it wasn't his father's— It was his own!

His elation was so overpowering, he reached for the baby and held him against his shoulder, uncaring that he'd wake him up again. Ric *wanted* him to wake up so he could get a good look at him. Warmth from the little bundle seeped into his body's core, bonding them as father and son.

The baby must have sensed someone different was holding him. He started wiggling and moved his dark silky head from side to side. He smelled sweet like his mother. He was such a strong little thing that Ric was forced to support his head and neck with more strength. He lowered him in the crook of his arm so he could pick out the unique features that proclaimed him a Degenoli and an Argyle. Both sets of genes were unmistakable.

"*Ciao, bambino mio.* Welcome to my world." He kissed his cheeks and forehead. His olive-skinned baby grew more animated. Ric laughed when those arms and legs moved and kicked with excitement. The *first* Degenoli in this generation to live.

His sister, Claudia, had barely learned she was pregnant before she'd suffered a miscarriage. It had happened soon after she'd heard their father had been killed in the avalanche. His sorrow for her and her husband, Marco's, loss would always hurt, but as he looked down at his son, there wasn't room in his soul for anything but joy.

When Ric looked up, he caught Sami's tear-filled eyes fastened on the two of them. After wondering what she'd looked like, he couldn't get his fill of staring at her.

"I can't fathom it that you're alive, that you're holding him," she cried. "When I left the police station, I was heartbroken. If I didn't find Alberto in Geneva, it meant going home knowing my baby would never know the Italian side of his family. What if you hadn't followed me here?" she cried.

"Nothing could have stopped me. I had to find out who

you really were because I couldn't believe there was another woman alive who sounded like you."

"I know what you mean. The second you spoke to me, I should have stopped trying to be cautious and just called you Ric to see what you'd do. It would have saved us both so much trouble."

Ric would have responded, but his cell phone rang. It jerked him back to reality. He had a strong idea who it was.

"I'll take the baby while you answer it." Sami plucked the baby out of his arms and walked the floor with him.

He watched his little boy burrow his head in her neck. The action brought a lump to his throat before he wheeled away from her and checked the caller ID. Though he'd finally come to the end of his search for the woman named Sami, time had passed during that search and other dynamics had been set in motion.

Ric groaned when he thought of how this news was going to affect negotiations with Eliana's father, let alone with Eliana herself. Theirs was no love match, but news of an unknown baby would be difficult for any bride-to-be to handle. He'd need to deal with her carefully. As for his own family, they would be in shock.

"Eliana?" he said after clicking on.

"I thought you would call me before you left the office, but your secretary said you weren't there."

He rubbed the back of his neck absently. "I'm on my way to the airport and planned to phone you before my jet took off." It would have been the truth if something else hadn't come up. Something that had changed the very fabric of his life. The Sami he'd been entombed with was alive and had just presented him with his *son!*

There was a distinct pause. "Are you all right? You sound…different."

Different didn't begin to cover what was going on inside him.

"It's…business. I'm afraid I'm preoccupied with it. Forgive me." It was the kind of business Chief Coretti had referred to at the station. But it had everything to do with Ric, not with his father. When he thought of the way his suspicious mind had worked trying to get answers…

"Of course I forgive you, Enrico."

Ric took a steadying breath. Before they were married, those words were going to be put to the test in the cruelest of ways.

Sami had called him a great man. How honorable did it make him if he kept this revelation from Eliana? But he couldn't tell her yet. It wasn't possible when he could hardly comprehend it himself. With this news there would be so many ramifications, he needed time to think how he was going to handle everything.

"I'll phone you from Cyprus tomorrow."

"That had better be a promise."

He gripped the phone tighter. "Have I ever broken one to you?"

"No, but I'm still angry you've let business interfere so much. After we're married I intend to keep you occupied for a long time. For one thing, I want to give you a baby. Hopefully a male heir."

Ric closed his eyes tightly. *Someone got ahead of you in that department, Eliana.*

His fiancée was a beautiful, polished product of her aristocratic upbringing. He couldn't fault his future wife for voicing her womanly expectations. But neither could he do anything about the new state of affairs. Fate had blown in with the avalanche, altering his world forever.

"Forgive me, Eliana, but I have to go. We'll talk tomorrow."

"A domani, Caro."

He ended the call and turned to Sami.

The baby had fallen asleep against her shoulder. She eyed Ric steadily. "While you were on the phone, I've had time to gather my thoughts. Maybe I'm wrong, but I sensed a woman was on the other end of that phone call. Judging by the tone of your voice, she's either your wife or your girlfriend."

During those hours they'd been trapped, they'd crossed all the boundaries waiting for the end. It didn't surprise Ric she wasn't only intuitive, but forthright. "My fiancée, Eliana."

Not one dark eyelash flickered. "Were you—"

"No." He knew what was on her mind. "I didn't get engaged to her until long after I'd lost all hope of ever finding you. I kept the thought alive that since I'd told you my last name, you might come back to Genoa to look for me. Now that I understand you were carrying our son all that time, I know why you didn't come until now."

"Did you ever tell your fiancée about us?"

"Not her, not anyone," he whispered before moving closer. "Are you involved with someone? Married?"

"No." Her single-word answer shouldn't have filled him with relief, but it did. "I'd just broken up with a man I'd been dating before I left for Europe on my trip in January. As you can imagine, I wasn't the same person when I returned.

"When Matt found out I was back, he called me and told me he hadn't given up on us." Ric could understand why. "I told him it was over for me, but he said he was going to keep trying to get through to me. When I discovered I was pregnant, I told him the truth of what happened to me in Italy so he'd give up."

Ric bit down hard. "And did he?"

"No. He said he'd marry me and help me raise the baby as if it were his own."

The idea of another man parenting Ric's son didn't sit well with him. "He must love you very much."

"Yes, I believe he does. I love him, too. He's really wonderful, but I'm not in love with him. There's a huge difference. That why I broke up with him in the first place, because I didn't want to hurt him.

"He's been very good to me, but I know it hurt him horribly that I would make love with a stranger, especially when he and I hadn't gotten to that point." Her voice faltered. "No matter how I tried to explain the circumstances, I realized it sounded incredible."

"It still does," Ric confessed. "Even to me, and I was there."

Color crept back into her cheeks. "It would be asking

too much of him to forget it. I know he's still hoping I'll change my mind, but I can't see that happening." She kissed the baby. "How soon is your wedding?"

The wedding to Eliana...

"January first."

"New Year's—that's coming soon."

With Sami standing there cuddling his son, Ric found it impossible to think about his upcoming nuptials. The shock still hadn't worn off.

Her eyes searched his. "I realize it isn't every day a man is confronted with a situation like ours—" she said anxiously. "If I'd known you were alive, I would have handled everything differently. But now that you know you have a son, I'm aware you need time for the information to settle in before you can tell how you really feel about everything."

"How I feel?" he questioned, not understanding the remark. "You've just presented me with my child. I didn't know that being a father would bring me this kind of happiness."

Neither Ric nor his siblings had ever been close to their father. He was gone so much, they rarely saw him. Though he'd ruled over their family, he left the child-rearing to their mother and the house staff.

Not until college did his father take an interest in Ric. Even then it was all about duty and money. When Ric thought about how his father had always ignored Vito and Claudia, his insides twisted into knots. Early on he'd decided that if he were ever to become a father, he'd get totally involved in his children's lives from day one.

For Ric, today *was* day one. He eyed the mother of his child. "I didn't know learning I was a father would make me feel reborn in a whole new way."

"Nevertheless, you're getting married before long and have all this to talk over with Eliana," she said in a pragmatic tone. "It's a good thing my flight for the States leaves in the morning. Ric and I will go back to Reno while you let this sink in. Now that we know of each other's existence and can exchange phone numbers, there's no hurry."

He frowned. "No hurry? I've missed the first two months of my son's life and don't intend to miss any more."

"But with Christmas and your wedding almost here, this isn't the time to—"

"To what?" He cut her off. "Decide how to fit our baby into my life? He wasn't conceived on your schedule or mine, but he's a living breathing miracle. Unlike my father, who hardly acknowledged the existence of his children until they were grown, I want to be with my son all the time that you and I can work out."

Her face closed up. "There's nothing to work out the way you mean. We live on separate continents. He's my reason for living. After you and Eliana are married, I'll bring him for visits the way I would have done if your father had been the one who was alive. My sister will help me so the flights won't be expensive. When it's possible, you and your wife can fly to the States to see him."

Ric was listening, but the woman who'd given birth to his child was still a stranger to him in ways he had yet to understand. However, that was about to change, because he had no intention of letting her fly out of his life with their son.

CHAPTER THREE

"WE'LL talk about that later. For now we need to get better acquainted." Already he sensed she would require careful handling first. "I'm on my way to my second home on Cyprus to do vital business, so I'm taking you there with me tonight."

Her eyes widened in surprise.

"You said you wanted Ric to know about the Italian side of his family. My mother came from Cyprus. I spent most of my childhood there. As Ric grows older, it will be his second home, too. I want you to be with me for the next week and see my world in relaxed surroundings. It has the warmest climate in the Mediterranean during the winter months. Tomorrow it's supposed to hit seventy degrees, warm enough to go swimming."

She let out a small cry. "I couldn't do that, Ric. I only intended to be here a few days."

His body stiffened. "But you didn't know you'd find *me*. Now that you have, everything's changed for both of us. Our baby needs to be with his family. If your sister can't rearrange your flight for a different day, *I* can."

"I've no doubt of it," she conceded, "*if* you didn't have a fiancée who won't understand."

"She isn't expecting me back until Christmas Eve day. Until then, what I do with my time while I'm not in Genoa is my business. You and I have to talk things through. For you to go home tomorrow is out of the question."

"But—"

"Sami—" he broke in. "You wouldn't refuse me this time with you and the son I didn't know I had. We need time together to process the fact that the three of us are alive." He sucked in his breath. "We were given a second chance, not only to live life but to rejoice together in our beautiful son."

"Still—"

"There's no *still* about it. After what happened to us at that resort in Imst, I'm not taking any chances of another unexpected disaster. Anything could go wrong on your way back to Reno. Don't say it wouldn't happen, because we know better. I need this time with you and Ric. Be honest and admit you need it, too, now that you know I'm alive."

Sami looked away. "Even so, your fiancée will be devastated when she finds out the truth. How long do you plan to keep her in the dark?"

His eyes narrowed on her features. "For as long as it takes. I don't have a better answer."

"I'm afraid for her, Ric. I saw how the news affected Matt and we weren't even dating anymore. The revelation about the baby will be so terrible for her, she might never recover from it, especially if you don't tell her right away. I know if I were in her shoes and—"

"Let's not anticipate what might or might not happen," he interrupted her. "Your boyfriend heard the truth and told you he still wants to marry you."

"Maybe, maybe not," she answered honestly. "I told him I needed time and haven't seen him in months. But if we did get together for the sake of the baby, I'm afraid that over time he would learn to resent me for what I did. He wants children one day.

"If we married, it would be normal for him to love a son or daughter of his own body more than he loved Ric. I couldn't bear for that to happen. That's been one of the things holding me back from getting involved again. I won't let anything hurt Ric if I can help it."

"I hear what you're saying, Sami." He loved it that she guarded their son's happiness so fiercely. "I have those same protective feelings. That's why I have to be careful before I tell Eliana anything. She'll be hurt in ways I can promise not even *you* have thought of yet."

She shook her head. "This is such an incredible situation."

"But not insoluble. Ric's been your first priority or you wouldn't have flown to Genoa to find his grandfather. Now that I know of his existence, he's *my* first priority. I want to get up in the night and feed him. Over the next week I want to bathe him and do all those things a new father does. In that amount of time I'll know better how to approach my fiancée."

"I—I'd feel better if Eliana knew I was with you," she stammered. "What if someone tells her?"

"Who? My staff and pilot are all loyal to me. Chief Coretti knows better than to discuss my business with anyone."

"Even so, I—"

"Even so nothing— Unlike you, I haven't had the advantage of nine months to think things through while waiting for the arrival of our baby. Once I've spent time with you and Ric, I'll be better equipped to know how to deal with Eliana and anticipate her questions. For you to turn around and fly back to Reno in the morning would be a knee-jerk reaction that will only complicate our situation."

She still wouldn't look at him. He admired her for wanting to protect Eliana, but the baby was a fact of life. While they'd clung together in the claustrophobic darkness, he'd made her pregnant. Little Ric was their creation. Despite the fallout when the news surfaced, the knowledge filled him with a wonder and excitement he'd never known before.

He darted her a glance. "The remarkable woman I was buried with wouldn't begrudge me those privileges. Has she changed so much in eleven months?"

That brought her head up. "But you're not prepared for a baby."

"Is anyone? If you're talking about his physical needs, you've brought everything he requires with you for the moment. Whatever is missing, I'll take care of it. With one phone call, a crib and bedding can be delivered."

"I don't know, Ric." She still wasn't convinced.

"Don't tell me you're uncomfortable with me, not after everything we've been through?"

A faint flush filled her cheeks. "No. Of course not."

"Then there's nothing to stop you from agreeing to come with me. I'll have one of my men check you out of the hotel."

She eyed him in confusion. "Who are they exactly?"

"My bodyguards."

"I remember you telling me you were in shipping. What I don't understand is why you would need that kind of protection."

"I'll explain later."

"But you're not ready for guests," she argued, "especially not an infant."

"Guests?" he exploded. "Ric's my son, and you're his mother. That puts you in an entirely different category from anyone else in the world. Would you rather I stayed here with you for the next week?"

"You mean at the hotel?"

He heard panic in her voice and realized with satisfaction that she wasn't any more indifferent to him than he was to her. "I mean in this room. After all you've gone through to find my father, do you honestly think I'd budge from here without you?"

"I thought you had vital business on Cyprus," she said quietly.

"My son is the only business more vital. I thought I'd made myself clear. But keep in mind that on the island you'll have your own bedroom with the Mediterranean only steps outside your suite. We'll set up a crib next to you where you and Ric can live in total comfort. But we can stay right here if that's your wish. The decision is up to you."

She pressed her lips together, further evidence she didn't like either option. "When were you going to leave?"

"Two hours ago. A limo is parked for me in front of the hotel."

He waited while she mulled everything over in her mind. "I'm frightened," she finally whispered.

"The woman who sought help from Genoa's chief of police to find Ric's grandfather was a warrior. It pleases me more than you know to realize my son has inherited that trait from you."

"You don't know that," she answered shakily.

Ric shifted his weight. "What do you think are the chances of a fetus to survive what you lived through both emotionally and physically?"

Her haunted gaze collided with his, giving him his answer. "If you'll get your things together, I'll take them down. It's a few hours' flight to Paphos. Once we're in the air, we'll have dinner. I don't know about you, but I'm famished."

She looked at the baby, then glanced back at him. "If you're sure about this," she murmured.

"I've never been more sure of anything in my life."

After another long hesitation, she walked over to a closet for her suitcase. With that action, the tautness left his body. He pulled out his cell phone to call his house-keeper in Paphos and give her some instructions. While he waited for Sami to finish her small amount of packing, he spoke to Carlo and the driver, alerting them to his plans.

Earlier, on the drive to the hotel from the police station, he'd entertained the thought that his father had indulged in an affair with this woman. No way on earth could he have known that Christine Argyle would turn out to be *Sami*. Even more astounding was the knowledge that the baby he'd heard crying from behind the door was none other than his own son.

Sami's legs felt shaky. The mixture of shock and hunger had reduced her to this state. For Ric to be alive didn't seem possible, yet here he was, this tall, hard-muscled Italian male who held the baby to his shoulder with one arm, and carried her suitcase in his other hand.

But he had a fiancée! The news of it flickered off and on like a giant neon sign. How could she just go along with him like this knowing he belonged to someone else? She'd tried to reason with him, but he'd refused to listen to her fears.

"This is heavy," he said in an aside, oblivious to her state of mind. "What's in here?"

"Baby formula. I had to bring a lot in case of an emergency."

He broke out in laughter, causing people to stare. She walked alongside him holding the car seat and diaper bag. For all the world the three of them looked like a married couple staying at the hotel for the Christmas holiday, yet the woman he intended to marry was somewhere in Genoa, not knowing what had happened.

Sami's guilt was so overwhelming, she barely noticed that the hotel had been festively decorated for Christmas. All she sensed was Ric's pride as hotel guests and staff alike smiled to see him carrying his baby.

She also saw the envy in the eyes of women young and old who found Ric drop-dead gorgeous. That's what he was. A thrill darted through her to realize their son would grow up to look like him. It was followed by another stab of guilt to be thinking about him like this when he had a fiancée.

When he ushered her through the main doors to the outside, he'd said his car was waiting. But there were no cars parked in front, only three black luxury limousines. The center one had special smoked glass and a hood ornament with a unique gold figure of what looked like an ancient seaman.

Two of Ric's bodyguards opened the doors to help her inside and deal with the luggage, including securing the car seat into place, with little Ric firmly settled into it. Their deference to him caused her to stare into his inky-black eyes once they were seated across from each other. The limo started moving. "Ric? What's going on?"

"We're heading to the airport." His deep voice oozed through her body, kindling her senses without her volition.

"But in *this?*"

"You're not comfortable?" Behind his hooded gaze she thought he might be smiling in amusement.

"That question doesn't deserve an answer. Why did the driver address you as Excellency? I may not understand Italian, but I heard him distinctly, so don't tell me I misunderstood. Are you an important government official?"

He kissed the top of the baby's head. Ric was still sound asleep. "My business is shipping, remember?"

She expelled the breath she'd been holding. "You do a great deal more than that! Who are you? Please tell me the truth." He could be a terrible tease, something she hadn't expected. Though they'd shared the most intimate experience between two people, she knew next to nothing about him…except the most important thing.

He was a man of character who'd welcomed his son without hesitation, even though he was engaged to be married. How many men would do that?

"I'm Alberto Enrico Degenoli the thirteenth."

"All of your predecessors had the same name?"

"Yes."

She made a sound that came out more like a squeal. "That's very interesting, but I know you haven't told me everything. When we were buried, you never said a word about any of this."

One black brow lifted. "You never mentioned you were a student or where you were enrolled. If you'd told me, I could have found you months ago."

If by those words he meant that their lives might be different, it was too late now! Her body trembled. "If you recall, we decided we shouldn't talk much."

"True. Instead we communicated in a more fundamental way under the most death-defying circumstances.

I believe making love in total blackness added a thrilling element that increased our pleasure, thus producing our son."

With those words, the memory of what had transpired caused her body to break out in feverish heat.

"One day," Ric continued, "he'll be indebted to us for giving him life against those odds, don't you agree? I know I'll be undyingly grateful to you for taking such meticulous care of him in my absence, Sami."

Though she was warmed by his compliment, the implication that his absence was now over rocked her to the core. She'd heard the steel behind it. Chief Coretti had jumped the moment Ric had suggested he leave the room. His own office! Come to think of it, the police chief had been able to locate Ric immediately. On the verge of asking him one more time who he really was, Sami was distracted by the limo coming to a stop.

"We've arrived," he murmured. On cue the doors opened for them.

She climbed out to see a gleaming green-and-white private jet with the word "Degenoli" printed in gold on the side with a logo of a mariner beneath it. Before she knew it, one of his staff escorted her to the jet with her luggage. She started up the steps with Ric right behind her holding the baby.

The steward showed her to one of the posh white leather seats in the club compartment. Ric strapped the car seat into the seat between them, then settled the baby, who'd fallen asleep again. As soon as she sat down, the

Fasten Seatbelts sign flashed on. Soon the engines started up and the jet began to taxi out to the runway.

Though she knew she wasn't living in a dream, the revelations of this day were still unreal to her. When she really thought about her and Ric being alone together again for a whole week, her body shivered with a barrage of new sensations.

She should have phoned Pat in Reno to tell her everything, but Ric was like a force of nature. Everything had happened too fast. Now wasn't the time to get into a conversation with her sister while Ric sat nearby, able to listen. But when they landed in Paphos and got settled, she'd make the call.

Pat was in for the biggest surprise of her life. She would have fits when she heard Ric had a fiancée who still didn't know about the baby.

When the jet reached cruising speed and the seatbelt light went off, the steward served them a delicious pasta and chicken dinner accompanied by a sweet white wine. After Sami took a sip, Ric eyed her intently. "I take it you aren't nursing."

Sami put the glass down. "I tried it, but my milk jaundiced him, so the pediatrician told me to put him on formula. He loves it at room temperature and has been a good eater from the beginning."

His gaze wandered back to the baby. "I noticed he drank every drop of his bottle back at the hotel. I'm eager to feed him when he wakes up again."

Little Ric must have heard his father's voice because it wasn't a minute before he opened his eyes and started making sounds. That was all Ric needed to release the baby from the seat and nestle him in his arms.

Having finished her dinner, Sami got up and searched in the diaper bag for a new bottle of formula and a clean burping cloth. "It sounds like you're hungry again, sweetheart." She leaned over to kiss his cheeks before handing Ric the bottle. "Just put it in his mouth and he'll do the rest." On that note she placed the toweling cloth over his right shoulder, then sat down again.

Ric laughed as he played with the baby before feeding him. When the steward came in, Ric lifted his son for the other man to look at. They both smiled and spoke in Italian before he took away their dishes.

Sami could see Ric was a natural at being a father. She was the slightest bit jealous their baby seemed content for his daddy to do the honors, but it also touched her heart. Little Ric was wrapped up in his silky blue baby quilt with the white lace around the edge. He made a beautiful picture against his father's tan jacket.

No doubt he wore a custom-made suit produced for him by a famous Italian designer. When they'd clung to each other in the darkness, he'd been wearing a shirt. But whoever said that clothes made the man hadn't met Ric.

Whether in the light or the dark, *he* made the man.

Stop thinking about him like this, Sami. He was about to be someone else's husband.

She felt his eyes flick to hers. "Our son is perfect."

Sami had been thinking the same thing about Ric. Out of all the men in the entire world, how had she happened to be caught in the same avalanche with *him?* "He reminds me of a baby prince in one of my old books of fairy tales."

"Not a prince," Ric corrected her before kissing his son on the cheek. "A count."

She blinked.

"The first Alberto Enrico Degenoli went to sea and amassed a fortune he brought back to Genoa. For that, the ruling power made him a count. Through various ventures in shipping, that fortune grew over the years. Our family history dates back to the thirteenth century."

Sami hadn't thought she could be shocked a second time in one day. Now, when she thought about it, the gold seaman ornament on the hood of the limousine made sense, but too many revelations in just a few hours had her reeling.

Her hands gripped the sides of the chair. Ric was literally Count Degenoli. In a few more weeks his fiancée would be *Countess* Degenoli. Good heavens!

"When you had the baby, you didn't realize you'd given birth to Alberto Enrico Degenoli the Fourteenth. He's my firstborn son. By rights he should be the next count after me."

Sami understood what he meant. That honor would go to the son he and Eliana would produce. Little Ric could never be the next count because he was the *illegitimate* son.

"After my father died, the title passed to me," Ric continued in a conversational tone, "but the title means nothing in this day and age, so forget it, Sami. To his friends, our son will be Ric Argyle Degenoli."

The ramifications of what all this meant made it hard for her to swallow. "Ric—I'm not naive. Knowing you're a count means your engagement is of public importance. Any move on your part will produce a ripple effect with serious consequences."

"You're right, but you agreed to come with me, so no one else knows yet. Later on we'll talk everything over. For the present I intend to enjoy this time with you and our son. Can you let your reservations go that long?"

Some nuance in his tone got to her. Sami bowed her head, attempting to come to grips with this latest revelation. She didn't know if she could do what he asked. But when she tried to put herself in his shoes, she could understand why he needed emotional time away from responsibilities and duties to deal with being a brand-new father.

"There's no precedent for what has happened to us," she admitted at last. "I'm sorry to keep fighting you on it. You're right for reminding me I had the whole pregnancy to realize I was going to be a mother. You only found out this afternoon that you're a father. I'll try to control my anxiety for a few days."

In the silence that followed, he leaned forward and put his hand over hers. She felt heat travel up her arm and through her body. "That sounded like the woman who helped me get through those first horrifying moments when we figured our time was up."

Tears filled her eyes. "I'm so glad it wasn't— Ric's the sweetest, most wonderful thing that ever happened to me."

"We did good work, didn't we?" he said in a husky voice before lifting his hand from hers.

She half laughed. "Yes. My family and friends go crazy over him." Pat had said more than once that the baby's father had to be some kind of Italian god to have produced a child as handsome as Ricky. As Sami eyed Ric covertly, she thought she could tell her sister that Ric was more sensational than any statue. She had to remember that soon he'd be another woman's husband.

"Tell me something. Are you rich?" she teased with a smile.

He kissed the top of Ric's head. "That depends on one's definition."

With a gloomy answer like that, he'd sidestepped the issue. Their son had a father like none other. "Is Eliana's family rich?"

A shadow crossed over his attractive face. "Yes."

Suddenly Ric did a loud burp and they both laughed hard. She was glad to see his father's frown had disappeared. There was nothing like a baby to reduce everything else to the unimportant.

"Forgive me for being curious. I've never known a count before."

"I don't like to be reminded of it, Sami. It's meaningless."

She rolled her eyes. "Not to the men who called you Excellency."

He grimaced. "Old habits die hard."

"I'm glad you told me how you feel. I'll never make

the mistake of calling you count. It will be up to you to tell Ric one day."

Sami heard his sharp intake of breath. "Since you're his mother, I'm going to let you in on a secret no one knows about yet. After my father died, I took the steps to have the title officially abolished. I made it legally binding so that it can never be bestowed on anyone else again, which means Ric's life is going to be free and his children after him."

She studied him anxiously. "Has it been such a burden?"

He flashed her a bleak glance. "You'll never know."

"Tell me about it." *Help me get my mind off the woman you love.*

"The title is always bestowed on the first male heir. It was all I heard about from the moment I can first remember. All the attention was focused on me—my education, my social life, my duties, my future wife. But my siblings were ignored.

"Vito and Claudia were fixtures in the background of our lives. My brother became a shell of himself with no confidence or sense of accomplishment. Claudia was a girl and virtually forgotten in the scheme of things.

"Every time I received an honor from my father, I flinched inside, knowing my brother and sister were left behind and in some cases forgotten."

"How awful," Sami whispered.

"You have no idea. It sickened me and I swore that the day I became count, I'd have the whole reign of terror obliterated. That day came after we buried our father."

Sami thought long and hard about what he'd just told her. Titles were still de rigueur in certain societies, but apparently Ric abhorred the whole idea of them so much, he'd taken steps to rid himself of his title. That took an unusual man with the strength of his own convictions. She admired him more than he would ever know.

His siblings wouldn't have believed at first that he could do such an extraordinary thing, but since he was still the count, he had the right to do as he pleased.

Sami had to admit the title had a certain ring. She secretly treasured the knowledge that when they'd made love, another Count Degenoli had been conceived. A very little one. For the short time left, she could fantasize about how romantic it all sounded.

But that was shameful of her when she knew how diabolical the system clearly was in Ric's eyes. Since the drive to the airport, Sami had felt as though she was living in a fairy tale; she was the young maid—being spirited away by the handsome prince to live in his castle. But there were two important caveats to this tale.

By Christmas Eve the spell would be broken and Sami and her baby would return to Nevada to get on with the rest of their lives. By New Year's Day, Ric would be married.

She sat up straighter in the chair. "What do you think Eliana will say when she finds out your title is gone?"

His answer wasn't a long time in coming. "She'll have to handle it. That's what she's been raised to do."

"Not if it wasn't her dream." For no good reason, her

heart rate accelerated. "When are you planning to let her know?"

"As soon as I receive word. I expected to hear a week ago, but the courts are slower here than in the States."

"I didn't know that was possible."

Another chuckle escaped his throat. "It's my Christmas present to myself, but your gift trumps anything I could have conceived of in this world or the next."

"You can think of Ric as your Christmas baby."

"*Our* baby," he corrected in a thick-toned voice before switching him to his other shoulder. She could see he was totally enamored by his son. Sami could relate. "I believe our little *bimbo* is sleepy."

"Bimbo?"

"It's another Italian endearment."

"That's sweet," she murmured. "He's easy right now because all he basically does is eat and sleep. In another month everything will change."

Ric nuzzled the baby's neck. "Did you hear that, *figlio mio?* How about we change your diaper before you sign out again?"

Sami chuckled as she laid everything out for him. "I know the diaper looks tiny, but it does the job." They smiled at each other before he got down to business. After a little too much powder, and a couple of tries to attach the tapes right, he'd managed to change their son's diaper. "Bravo," she exclaimed.

He picked up the baby and eyed her over his head. "I'll do better next time."

"I can't tell you the number of times I put the diaper on the wrong way. Ric was so patient."

By tacit agreement they both sat down with Ric hugging the baby to his chest. "Tell me about the delivery. Were you in labor long?"

"About eighteen hours."

His eyes grew serious. "Were you alone?"

"No. My sister and her husband took turns staying with me. I owe them everything."

His jaw hardened. "I should have been there. Did you know you were going to have a son ahead of time?"

Her lips curved. "Oh, yes. I called him Ric the second the technician handed me the ultrasound pictures. She told me I had a boy in there and everything looked great. I'll admit I wished you'd been in the room to hear the news with me. While I lay there, I had this fanciful notion that maybe you were watching from above or somehow knew, and I hoped it would make you happy."

"I think you know exactly how I felt when you handed me his birth certificate. It was the supreme moment of my life." The throb in his voice gave evidence how deeply his emotions were involved.

"Ric? Tell me the truth. Was the reason you looked for me because you wanted to know if you'd made me pregnant?"

His gaze wandered over her. "No. To be honest, I was afraid you might have died in the hospital you were taken to. You could have lost consciousness the way I did and never come to. I had to be sure."

"Why?"

"Because if you were alive, I wanted to meet you face-to-face. I wanted to understand why two strangers could connect the way we did. I thought if we talked, maybe I'd get answers to questions that have plagued me ever since."

She made an assenting sound. "I have the same questions, but am no nearer to an explanation. For us, it wasn't a physical attraction in the literal sense of the word. Maybe you'll think I'm crazy, but the only way I can describe it is that our spirits spoke to each other."

"Or recognized each other on some other level?" he inserted.

"Yes, as if we were bidding each other a final farewell which we did with…our bodies."

"I've had the same thoughts, Sami. They're not crazy."

"I'm glad you feel that way because I've gone over and over it in my mind and it's the only conclusion that makes sense." She stirred restlessly. "When I first got back to Oakland, I felt so empty inside. I knew you'd died and I felt this great loss. It alarmed me. It wasn't just the fact that we'd made love. What we did wasn't for the normal reasons. I mean—"

"I know what you mean." He read her mind with ease.

"While we were trapped, I'd assumed we would die. The thought of getting pregnant never entered my consciousness."

"Nor mine," he murmured. "The thought of using protection was the furthest thing from my mind."

"All we knew was that we were facing the end."

"But during those hours, I felt I'd lived a lifetime."

He'd taken the words right out of her mouth. "When I was released from the hospital, at first I thought what I was feeling had to be sadness over the way my father had died. But after a time, I still had that same heaviness. No matter how deeply I searched for the source of it, *you* were always at the bottom of it."

"That's how it was for me, too," she volunteered. "Matt thought I was having some symptoms of post-traumatic stress disorder because of the avalanche. He knew I'd been trapped with you, but I didn't tell him everything at first. I was hoping I'd pull out of whatever was going on inside me. Then I found out I was pregnant."

She glanced at their baby sleeping so trustingly on Ric's chest. "Maybe I shouldn't have been overjoyed by the news, but I was. Of course I had to tell Matt everything. But he never truly understood." After a pause she said, "I can promise you now—Eliana won't understand either."

"No. And once she learns the truth and meets you, she'll assume you're the reason why the physical side of our relationship has been unsatisfactory."

Sami squirmed in her seat. "I shouldn't have come to Genoa."

"You know you don't mean that."

No. She didn't... "For you to be engaged, I'm sure your love can weather anything."

"Sami—I'm not in love with Eliana."

What?

"We're marrying to secure the financial welfare of our two families. Don't get me wrong, Eliana has many admirable qualities and I care for her, but I don't love her. Unfortunately, when I asked her to marry me, I didn't know the 'for worse' part of the ceremony would precede taking our vows."

Sami stirred restlessly. Maybe he didn't love Eliana, but she couldn't imagine Eliana not being head over heels in love with him. What woman wouldn't love him? The knowledge of a baby would tear his fiancée to pieces. Sami was about to question him further when the Fasten Seatbelts sign flashed on. "We're in Cyprus already?"

Ric was on his feet in an instant to secure the baby for the descent. "I told you it's not a long flight. When we step off the plane, you'll notice a difference in the temperature. Whenever I breathe that air, it reminds me of my youth and carefree days. Do you know I haven't taken a real vacation here in a long time?"

"Not even with your fiancée?"

"She's never been here. Eliana's not fond of the water. But now that you're with me, I'm ready for one."

"But you've come on business."

"I'm capable of doing both."

CHAPTER FOUR

SAMI had barely paused for breath since meeting Ric again. Who would have thought a few short hours could have changed so much in her life? Now she and little Ric had flown on Count Degenoli's private jet to an exotic island in the Mediterranean. Whether right or wrong, she was too physically and emotionally exhausted to think about the wisdom of her decision to come with him. Tomorrow would be soon enough to face the consequences of her actions.

The drive from Paphos airport hadn't taken long before the car entered a flower-lined private estate isolated on a point overlooking the water. Within ten minutes Ric was showing Sami through a fabulous, white, two-story Grecian villa. The colorful Mediterranean furnishings against white walls caught her eye everywhere she looked.

A cushion of blue here, an urn of yellow with an exotic plant there, an unexpected Greek icon in predominantly red and gold colors around the corner. So many choice armoires and tables placed around on tiled floors with a definite flair revealed a luxurious treasure trove.

Beyond the villa was the sight of the water through the window and doorways. Ric's second home was paradise. Sami could only imagine the elegance of his first home.

She marveled that his staff had managed to buy a crib so fast and have it set up in one of the guest rooms on the second floor. Besides fresh flowers, they'd provided everything needed to make her and the baby comfortable. To her delight each room of the villa contained a charming Christmas crèche surrounded by lighted candles. Ric explained that Christmas trees weren't amongst their local traditions.

He introduced her to Mara and Daimon, an older couple, probably in their sixties. He told her they'd been living here taking care of the villa and grounds for years. They'd worked for Ric's mother's family and spoke good English.

When Ric showed them the baby, the dark-haired couple cried out in delight and took turns holding him. Whatever they thought about Ric bringing home a foreign woman and a child, they didn't let it show and honored him like the favorite son he evidently was.

Mara smiled at Sami. "Anything you want, you ask me."

"I will. Thank you."

"The little one is beautiful, like you. He has your mouth."

"You're very kind. I think he looks like his father."

Daimon nodded. "I knew he was a Degenoli the minute I saw him."

"I see Vito in him," Ric inserted.

"A little," Mara said. "He also has Claudia's shell-like ears, but his shape and size and those brilliant black eyes are all yours, Enrico."

Daimon nodded. "He's well named."

Sami glanced at him. "What does it mean?"

"Ruler of the household."

Ric's black orbs kindled with warmth as he studied their son. "For now he's our *piccolo*."

"There's another word I don't understand."

"It means little one."

"That's a darling endearment for him," she exclaimed, "especially the way you say it in such beautiful soft Italian. Your language has lots of words I love to say, like *ciao* and *cappuccino*." She'd emphasized the *chee* sound, causing him to chuckle.

Sami noticed an aura had come over him since they'd entered the house, as if he'd dropped his worries outside the door. She couldn't deny he looked happier. In truth he no longer resembled the intimidating male at the police station in the tan silk suit who'd glared at her with barely suppressed hostility the moment she'd walked in.

All of a sudden his gaze swerved to hers with concern. "It's almost midnight. You must be dead on your feet. If there's anything you'd like to eat or drink, Mara will bring it to you before we say goodnight."

She shook her head. "After that meal on the plane, I couldn't, but thank you anyway."

"What you and the baby need is a good sleep after your flight from Genoa." Mara kissed little Ric on the cheek before she and Daimon disappeared to their room at the back of the villa on the main floor.

Sami turned to Ric. "They're wonderful."

"They're like family to me. I trust them with my life. Our baby will be pampered and spoiled while we're here."

"What a lucky little boy. I'll just bathe him and put him down, then get ready for bed."

"I'd like to do the honors if you'll show me how." He led them upstairs to her guest room.

"You're not too exhausted?"

He gave her a speculative look. "I'm so wired, as you Americans say, I don't know when I'll be able to sleep."

She let out a gentle laugh. "Then bring the diaper bag into the bathroom and we'll get started. He loves the water."

"That's because he's a true Degenoli. The first one went to sea and now seawater runs through all our veins." His comment made her chuckle. As for the pride in his voice, it was something to witness.

"We'll have to be careful not to keep him in too long or his fingers will start to look like dried grapes." Ric's burst of laughter rang throughout the villa. "Go ahead and undress him while I fill the sink."

They worked in harmony. When the temperature felt right she said, "Lower him in the water and let him enjoy it."

It tugged at her heart to see the care he took with the baby, who got terribly excited. He wiggled and moved his arms and legs with sheer enjoyment as the water lapped around him. In the middle of so much pleasure, the baby urinated, creating a fountain that had Ric's shoulders shaking with silent laughter.

She couldn't hold back her own giggles. "As you can see, his plumbing works just fine. We'll have to start this again." While Ric held the baby in a towel, she let out the water and put some more in. His little chin quivered from leaving the warmth. He was so adorable. Soon he was lowered back in.

"This is glycerin soap to wash his hair and body. It's gentle. He needs his hair washed. Be sure and get into the creases around his neck and behind his ears where the milk runs."

While he did a pretty masterful job for a beginner, she set out a fresh towel ready to dry the baby.

"He's strong, Sami."

"Of course. He's what we Americans call a 'chip off the old block.' Not that you're an old block, but you know what I mean."

His eyes glinted as they shared a silent look of mutual understanding. This time he powdered his son just the right amount and diapered him without any problem. Sami got out a yellow stretchy suit. Ric fitted him into it and fastened the snaps.

"He's almost finished." She handed Ric the little hairbrush. He took it from her and played with the baby's soft hair for a minute.

When he was through, he lifted Ric and turned him to her. "What do you think, *mamma?*"

The use of the Italian version of *mommy* caught her by the throat. Everything felt so natural, she'd forgotten she was a guest in his house. She'd almost forgotten he had a fiancée who had no idea what was going on.

"No one would know you'd only learned you were a father today. He loved his bath with you. I have a feeling he's going to want you to do it all the time. Our baby likes the masculine touch, don't you, sweetheart?"

Sami had already gotten past her jealousy into an area where she was enjoying this way too much. Judging from the emotion streaming from Ric's eyes, he had the same problem. However it was one thing to bathe the baby with Sami looking on, and quite another to imagine Eliana helping him after they were married. Pain filled her chest at the thought of it.

Little Ric was so loveable, but it would take a super-human woman to love him when she hadn't given birth to him. Eliana's resentment toward Sami would always be there because she wasn't the mother of Ric's firstborn child, count or no count. It would boil beneath the surface and the baby would pick up on the tension.

Over the years Sami had met women who were making successes of their second marriages. But it was a struggle combining two families to form a new one. Sami's situation couldn't be compared to theirs. For one thing, she and Ric had been strangers, not husband and wife.

For another, Eliana hadn't had children yet. Her whole life had been lived in preparation for marriage to an aristocrat, a marriage in which the bearing of children was bound to be of the greatest importance, especially the first one. Ric might not want to be Count Degenoli, but

Sami knew in her heart it was part of who he was. Eliana was in for a double shock when she heard the title had been abolished. Sami felt horribly sorry for her.

Deep in thought, she handed Ric a fresh bottle of formula. "While you feed him, I'll clean up the bathroom and take a shower before bed."

Ric stood where he was, snuggling the baby, who was looking for his bottle. "Where did you go just now?" His voice may have been quiet, but she heard the demand in it.

Maybe it was a case of both of them having an extra dose of ESP in their makeup. He was keyed in to her thoughts far too easily.

"I'm pretty sure you know," she answered in a dull tone. "But as you said earlier, let's not get into it right now. This is a time to enjoy the baby. Do what you want with him. Since your room is across the hall from this one, you'll probably hear him cry in the night. If you want to feed him, feel free to come in my bedroom and get a new bottle out of the diaper bag. I'll leave the door open."

His veiled eyes played over her features until her legs shook. "Sleep well, Sami," he murmured before leaving the bathroom with the baby. She shut the door after him and leaned against it, waiting for the weakness to pass. To her alarm, it never did.

Ric had only seen Sami in her suit and blouse. When she walked into the breakfast room at ten the next morning dressed in jeans and a chocolate-colored top, he caught himself staring. Slowly his gaze dropped from her green-eyed blond beauty to the gorgeous mold of her body. His intimate knowledge of her eleven months ago would always be fresh in his mind, and made the visual reaction to her now a hundred times stronger, forcing him to look away.

"Well, look at you two!" She made a nosedive for the baby, who was lying in the carrycot Ric had set on the breakfast table so he could play with him.

"I just fed him his morning bottle, but he hasn't fallen asleep yet. It's giving us time to get better acquainted."

She came around to kiss the baby's face. "Are you having fun with your daddy? Is he already reading the newspaper to you while he enjoys his coffee? If he could talk, he'd probably be calling you *Daddy*. How do you say it in Italian?"

"Papa."

"That's what Pat and I called our grandfather!"

Her enthusiasm caused the baby to grow more animated and made Ric smile. While he watched her poke his son's tummy gently, he inhaled her peach fragrance. She'd just come from the shower. It took all the willpower he possessed not to grab hold of her womanly hips and pull her down on his lap.

"He loves mornings and usually stays awake for a while," she chatted. "No doubt being with you has stimulated him so much, he might not close his eyes till much later." She glanced at Ric. "Has he been good?"

"I think you already know the answer to that question."

She looked away first and sat down on one of the

chairs opposite him. He got the impression she was nervous about getting too close to him. How ironic after what they'd experienced in Austria. "I didn't hear him cry in the night."

"You were exhausted. When I saw you lying there, I realized you'd had the whole care of our son these last two months and no one to wait on you or give you relief."

"I could never complain. Having a baby has been the joy of my life."

"Not all women feel that way," he muttered. Sami was so hands-on with little Ric, he couldn't help but wonder what kind of a mother Eliana would be.

"Do you and your fiancée plan to have children?"

"Definitely. It's what I've been looking forward to most."

"Some men don't want to be fathers."

Ric knew a few like that, but his own father fitted into a different category. He'd wanted an heir, but didn't want to do the fathering that should have gone on. As Ric played with his baby's toes, he realized his father had been the loser on every count.

His mind wandered to Sami. What if this ex-boyfriend Matt stayed so persistent, she ended up marrying him? What kind of a stepfather would he be to little Ric? More and more he didn't like the idea of it.

"Did you get up with him?" she asked.

Her question jerked him out of his dark thoughts. "I did. Around four I thought I heard him fussing. He needed a complete diaper change."

Sami grinned. "Uh-oh. How did your first solo experience go?"

"We made it through, didn't we, *piccolo?*" The baby's tiny fingers still clung to his little finger. They were the same shape as his. He realized no force on earth was as strong as the pull of that miniature hand on his heart. Ric found he didn't want his son to hold on to any other man's finger but his. Until now he hadn't understood how possessive he'd already become over what was his by fatherly right.

Mara walked into the room to refresh Ric's coffee. "Good morning, Sami. Now that you're up, I'll serve breakfast. Coffee for you, too?"

"Just juice if you have some. Please don't go to any trouble."

"How could you be trouble?" she cried. "You won't let me do anything for you, and the *bambino* never cries. I've been waiting for the excuse to hold him!"

"Don't worry," Sami said. "Before long you'll hear him loud and clear. You have my permission to grab him. Just remember his cries can be quite terrifying."

The housekeeper laughed before going out of the room.

"She likes you, Sami."

"That's because she loves you, and therefore loves your son, who I must admit is irresistible."

So is Sami. The unexpected things she said and did had the alarming ability to charm him. Maybe that's why he'd found himself making love to her in the blackness of the avalanche.

At the time he hadn't thought of what she might look like. She was young and afraid, and all he knew was gratitude that he didn't have to die alone. They'd needed each other and taken comfort from each other before they'd both lost consciousness.

It wasn't until he awoke in the hospital and remembered everything that he wanted to find her, talk to her. He was naturally curious to see what the woman looked like who'd helped save his sanity. But it never occurred to him she would be so physically appealing.

When she'd walked into Chief Coretti's office yesterday, he'd found himself attracted to the blond stranger beyond a normal interest in a good-looking woman. Ric had known and been with a number of beautiful women in his life, his fiancée being one of them. But this attraction was different.

The fact that she'd instigated the meeting with the police chief while being so secretive about his father should have been a total turnoff for Ric, but the opposite had held true. She had that spark not given to many people.

As they sat there at the breakfast table, Ric realized the chemistry he felt for her was growing stronger, something that wasn't supposed to happen. Bringing her to Cyprus might have been a mistake after all.

He still needed to phone Eliana, but had been putting it off. Once he heard his fiancée's voice, the magic of this time with Sami and his infant son would evaporate. He wasn't ready for that yet.

Already the baby was his whole life. It had happened the instant he'd walked over to the crib in the hotel room and had seen him lying there so small and helpless. The Degenoli likeness had only increased his wonder.

While he was immersed in thought, Mara had served them. By the time they'd eaten, he'd come up with a plan to stay busy. It would prevent him from thinking too much. Ric refused to think right now and wanted simply to relish this fleeting time.

"Sami? How would you like to take a boat ride in the cabin cruiser?"

"That sounds wonderful!"

"Good. You'll be able to see Paphos from the water. The sea is calm and the air is getting warmer by the minute. Ric will love it. We have swimming costumes and wetsuits on board for your enjoyment. We'll take Daimon and Mara with us."

She lowered her glass. "Did you hear that, sweetheart? We're going on an adventure. We'll have to dress you in your little green sweater and overalls."

Just like that, she'd gone along with Ric without voicing a reservation. Her eagerness to fall in with his plan could mean several things. If she'd wanted a distraction to push her fears away, then he'd just provided an outlet. But if she was nervous being around him for any length of time because she found herself attracted to him, too, he was curious to find out, even though it was the last thing he should be thinking about.

He phoned Daimon and asked him and Mara to join them, then he carried Ric upstairs into her bedroom to get him dressed. Afterward he went to his room and slipped on his bathing trunks and a T-shirt.

Between them, they gathered everything they'd need and headed out of the house for the boat dock. While she held Ric, he found life preservers for all of them. After putting them on, they climbed in. Daimon helped push off before joining Mara at the back of the boat.

Ric's cruiser had a galley and a roof. Both provided shelter for the baby. To his satisfaction Sami sat next to him on the padded bench while he took the wheel. Once he undid the ropes, he idled out to the buoy, then opened up the throttle and they whizzed through the peaceful blue water. Ric kept looking at his son who was wide-awake.

"Do you think he likes it?" he asked her.

Sami smiled at him. "You're asking me when he already has seawater running through his veins?" Ric's white smile turned her heart over. "I'm sure the sound and the vibration have him enthralled."

"How about you?"

"I adore the water, but it's been a long time. This is pure luxury. I've been to Europe several times with Pat and her husband, but never this far south. Cyprus is beautiful."

"It's full of history." He pointed to the city in the distance. "This is the new Paphos. My mother's family home is there."

"Who lives there now?"

"My uncle and his family. It may interest you to know there's an old city there, too. It dates back three thousand years to the Mycenaean period. One of the big attractions is the Temple of Aphrodite."

"The Greek myths! We had to study them in my high-school English class. I loved them. But *you* grew up with them. What a playground you've had here and in Genoa. As I told you before, my grandparents raised Pat and me. Growing up in Oakland we had a view of San Francisco Bay, but here the sea is at your doorstep."

"I confess I love being able to walk out of my house to the water."

"Who wouldn't?" Her voice trailed.

"Tell me what happened to your parents?"

"They were on the freeway driving home when an earthquake hit. We were little girls and don't remember them, but our grandparents kept them alive for us."

"I'm sorry for your loss. Tell me about them." He cut the engine before turning to her.

"Dad was a chemical engineer and Mom stayed home to raise us. I grew up thinking I'd like to follow in his footsteps, but discovered I like computers, too. A year ago last fall I started graduate school to become a computer engineer. If there's been any one thing lacking in my life, it's been the loss of parents I never knew.

"Growing up I envied my friends who had moms and dads. Don't get me wrong. I adored my grandparents, but in a just world, nothing takes the place of a loving, caring parent."

"*Loving* and *caring* being the operative words," Ric mused aloud. More than ever he was determined to be there for his son no matter the obstacles.

He rubbed the side of his jaw. "When you first mentioned your studies, I assumed you were talking about your undergraduate studies. I'm impressed you're pursuing your career while being an exceptional mother at the same time. You have fire in you, Sami, a very rare thing."

She broke into an unguarded smile. "Flattery will get you everywhere."

"It's the truth," he came back. "What brought you to Europe that last time?"

"During the winter break in January, Pat gave me a free pass for a short trip to Innsbruck. I knew if I didn't go, I wouldn't get another vacation for a long time and I'd just broken up with Matt. She wanted me to check out several hotels in the area and give them feedback. They send a lot of ski-tour groups to Austria.

"On the day of the avalanche, I'd taken the train on a side trip to see some of the villages. While I was in Imst, I stopped at the hotel to check it out and wait for the storm to pass." She paused for a minute. "You know the rest."

He watched her through veiled eyes. "While you were waiting, I'd just left my father's room. He felt like a nap, so I decided I'd walk around the village to stretch my legs. After grabbing my jacket from my room, I headed for the stairs to go down to the lobby.

"Before I had a chance to put the jacket on, it felt like a bomb had gone off in the hotel. The next thing I knew, I was trapped in the darkness. I heard someone moaning and was grateful I wasn't alone. That person turned out to be *you*. The chances of our coming together on that day, at the moment, are astronomical, Sami."

"I know."

"It seems I have your sister to thank for our baby's existence. Have you told her you found Alberto Degenoli?"

She broke eye contact. "Yes. I was on the phone with her before I came in to breakfast."

"What was her reaction?"

Sami's head reared. "What you'd expect. Shock and shock."

"Did you tell her everything?"

"Yes."

"And of course she doesn't approve of you being here with me."

"No, but she's a mother, too, and knows Bruce loves their children desperately. In that regard she understands you and I are in a very precarious situation with no precedent."

"So she didn't give you advice?"

"No."

"I like her already."

"You'd love her. She's selfless…like you."

"Before you give me credit, remember I have yet to tell Eliana anything. My own siblings would call me a selfish swine for putting off the inevitable while I enjoy my son in private."

"They aren't in your shoes. I understand that now." After fighting him about coming here, her defense of him came as a gratifying surprise to him. She looked around them. "Why are all those boats out there?"

"People are scuba diving. Below them is the wreck of *Dhimitrios*. This is a popular area of the island."

She eyed him curiously. "Do you dive?"

"I did a lot in my youth. What about you?"

"No scuba. I've done some snorkeling and surfing in the summer in Carmel, but Matt's the expert."

Matt again. "Why don't we take a dip? Mara and Daimon will watch Ric. You'll find a locker below with all the swim gear including my sister, Claudia's, wetsuit if you need one. There should be flippers in there, too."

"Does your fiancée dive?"

"No. She's a horsewoman at heart. When I can get away, we go riding on their estate, but I must admit I prefer water sports. What about you?"

"I'm a jack of all trades, but excel at none."

"None?"

"Maybe table tennis."

He squinted at her. "Let's find out what kind of a swimmer you are."

"You're on. I'll be up as soon as I change."

After she kissed the baby and went below, he walked back to talk to his staff, who were clearly delighted to have charge of Ric for a while. Sami resurfaced faster than he would have supposed, wearing a wetsuit that hugged her body, revealing the lines and curves he'd memorized long ago. Desire for her overwhelmed him.

She sat on the end of the bench to put on the flippers. Trying to look at anything but her shapely legs was an impossibility. "I'm ready whenever you are."

Excited, Ric discarded his T-shirt. "Let's go." He helped her over to the side of the boat so she could jump in. He went in behind her. When her wet head appeared, he thought he'd never seen anyone so naturally alluring.

"We'll swim to that big rock. It's not far, but if you get tired, let me know and Daimon will bring the boat along. The sea gets rougher there."

Sami was glad they'd started swimming. In the boat she'd noticed his long powerful legs stretched out in front of him while they'd talked. The gorgeous sight of him almost made her lose her train of thought.

He paced his strokes so they stayed abreast of each other. The flippers gave her the momentum she needed to keep up. The closer they got to the rock, the bigger the swells became. When they were quite near, she could appreciate the beauty of the setting sun against the stunning blue of the sea.

Ric reached the rock first and caught her hand to pull her in so she could cling to it. "What is this place?" She was a little out of breath, but that had a lot to do with him being shirtless. His well-developed body made her mouth go dry. She'd had the same reaction when they'd been trapped. Without seeing him, she'd felt him and knew he was exceptional in many ways.

"The Goddess Aphrodite's birthplace. She was born out of the foam breaking on this rock. If you wore your blond hair long and flowing, you'd personify my own image of her."

Even though her heart was thudding, she laughed and threw her head back. "Oh—you Italian men are priceless."

"I'm half Cypriot," he declared, "raised on the stories of Zeus. Afraid her beauty would create jealousy among the other gods and cause war, he married her to Hephaestus."

Her smile deepened. "I know that story, too. But to his chagrin she was unfaithful to her husband and had many lovers."

One of them was the young god Adonis. With his wavy black hair and olive skin warmed by the sun, Ric could be a more adult version of him. However, she'd never seen Adonis depicted with hair on his chest. She decided she didn't dare tell Ric her thoughts to his face. He was engaged to be married. *Remember?*

"She had many children as a result," Ric teased.

A chuckle broke from her. "I've just had one. I'm afraid he's all I can handle."

Ric's black eyes grew shuttered. "Our baby's so perfect, he would make the gods jealous." The tone of his voice gave her gooseflesh.

"Then let's be thankful Zeus doesn't exist." It was frightening enough that Eliana didn't know about the baby. Sami feared her reaction when confronted with Ric's child.

Sami shouldn't be out here alone with him like this. Much too aware of him, she looked around her, noticing the pebbled beach in the distance. "It's all so natural here. Nothing's spoiled it."

"Perhaps not right now, but later you'll see tourists come here to the café above the beach. They believe these waters have mystical powers to soothe the troubled soul. You'll notice them clustering in the evenings to watch the sunset. That's the beauty of arriving by boat. When we want, we can slip back out to sea away from everyone else to witness the sun falling into the sea."

She believed that growing up in these waters had cultivated a poetic side to him. "Are you telling me you're a loner?"

"Sometimes. With the right person, you don't need anyone else," he said in a remote tone.

He'd said he wasn't in love with his fiancée. Maybe he was missing some woman from his past who'd been important to him. Sami had no idea. "Thank you for bringing me to this famous spot. How lucky am I? When I came to Italy, I couldn't have conceived of being at Aphrodite's birthplace two days later."

"Then you can imagine my incredulity that the woman I was trapped with is holding on to this rock with me."

She averted her eyes. "I think we ought to get back to the boat. Even if Ric is fine, I don't want Mara and Daimon worrying about us being gone so long."

"Never fear. My bodyguards are keeping watch."

"From where?" she asked in surprise.

"The shore and that sailboat out there."

Sami hadn't really noticed. Ric's masculine presence dominated everything. "They're very unobtrusive. It must be hard to watch you when you're having fun. I hope you pay them a good salary."

His laughter filled the sea air, mesmerizing her. Their gazes met in shared amusement. "I can't wait to tell them what you said."

She felt her cheeks grow warm. "Are they the same ones you told to follow me from the police station?"

"I'm not sure. They trade off shifts."

"Do you think they're scandalized to see you with someone other than Eliana?"

"Maybe. The only thing important is that they've been told that Ric is our son. They're too busy guarding us with their lives to do much else."

Though the sun was shining, she felt a dark shadow pass over her. "Have you had many threats on your life, Ric?"

"Enough to warrant protection, but I don't want you worrying about it."

"I'm not. I felt perfectly safe with you in the avalanche and feel the same way now."

"I'm relieved to hear it. Shall we go?"

"I'm ready."

"I'll race you back to the boat."

Her brows lifted. "Since you fly through the water like that striped dolphin you pointed out on the way here, what chance do I have?"

His lips twitched. "Those flippers give you an edge."

"Hmm. We'll see." Filled with adrenaline from being this close to him, she shoved off, determined to give him a run for his money even if the water was more difficult to handle. She thought she was doing fine until three-quarters of the way, when she lost power. Weakness had taken over.

Ric took one look and told her to get on his back. "Hold tight to my shoulders."

She obeyed him and let him do all the work. The sensation of swishing through the water on top of him gave her another kind of adrenaline rush. When they reached the ladder to the boat, she let go of him, afraid for him to know how much she'd enjoyed the ride. She'd never thought to be that close to him again.

He turned around. The motion tangled their legs. She let out a tiny gasp.

"Are you all right, Sami?"

"I—I'm fine." What a great liar she'd become.

"I'll remove your flippers so you can climb in."

No... She didn't want him touching her, but it was too late. He worked too fast. Like lightning he eased them off and tossed them in the boat. With no more impediments, Sami was able to heave herself up the rungs. Ric was right behind her. Their limbs brushed as they both got in.

Daimon was there to hand her a towel. "Welcome back. Did you enjoy it?"

"Yes, thank you. It was a wonderful trip, but before I do it again, I need to get in some conditioning. Poor Ric had to save me at the end." It was nothing new. He'd saved her eleven months ago.

"Surely you realize that was no penance?" he whispered near her ear before he headed for the front of the boat to check on their son. She felt the warmth of his breath against her skin in every atom of her body before following him.

Mara sat beneath the roof feeding the baby. She smiled at both of them. "He's been an angel. I hoped you would stay out longer."

"Please keep doing what you're doing. I'm going to run downstairs to shower and change."

"Take all the time you want."

What heaven to have a babysitter like Mara, but Sami didn't dare get used to such luxury.

Once she was out of her wet things, the warm shower felt good. She washed her hair. Afterward she put her jeans and top back on and walked out of the bathroom with a towel. As she started to dry her hair, a pair of strong hands took over.

She'd thought Ric would have stayed upstairs by the baby.

No man had ever dried her hair before. With Ric, she'd experienced all the wondrous aspects of being a woman. She was loving this too much. When she couldn't bear his touch any longer because she wanted more, she took a step back and pulled the towel from his hands. Unable to look him in the eye she said, "Thank you. I can manage now."

He was blocking the way. She suspected it was on purpose. "You were fantastic out swimming," he said in his deep voice. "After having little chance to swim since giving birth to our son, you're in amazing shape. That's no swimming pool out there. I'm impressed."

Sami needed to lighten the moment before she threw herself into his arms. She smoothed the hair out of her eyes. Being by the water had made it curlier. "I think I'm impressed, too." Or at least she had been until her energy had run out.

"I've enjoyed today, Signorina Argyle."

"The feeling's mutual."

"When you're ready, join me in the galley and we'll fix dinner for all of us."

She flicked him a glance. "You like to cook?"

"It's in my blood."

"I thought it was filled with seawater," she quipped.

"It's all part of the same thing." He kissed the end of her nose. "When we've dined to our heart's content, we'll pull up anchor and head back."

CHAPTER FIVE

AFTER eating a Greek smorgasbord of his favorite foods, Ric felt replete and glanced at the baby in his carrycot. He'd finally fallen asleep. Just he and Sami were on deck to watch the sunset. The other two had gone below. The evening was idyllic.

"Sami? I'm curious about something. If you hadn't traveled to Innsbruck, do you think you would have changed your mind about Matt?" The possibility that those two could still get together had been troubling him to the point he had to ask her about it.

"No."

"Yet since the avalanche you've left a door open for him."

She sighed. "Learning of my pregnancy, I realized another little person was going to be totally dependent on me. When I was young, my parents were taken from me. I was sad my baby would also be deprived of a father, so I determined I would be there for my son or daughter every minute.

"But Matt's a great guy and I have no doubts he'd be a great father. Maybe in time I could learn to love him as I should. I'm sure you know what that's like. But if we married, I'm worried he would feel he comes in second best with me because of the baby. That wouldn't be fair to him. He deserves to start out marriage with a woman who doesn't have a history like mine. *No one* has a history like ours, Ric," she half moaned. Her face closed up.

"Maybe I'll change my mind later and get in touch with him. But by then he might have found someone else. I just don't know. For a while longer at least, I've got to find my own way."

Hearing those words, Ric felt as if someone had just walked over his grave. His dream of a week alone with her and the baby had just gone up in smoke. What they were dealing with was too heavy, too serious, for him to live in denial any longer.

"So do I," he ground out. "The air's getting cooler. It's time to go home."

He hoped she would beg him to stay out longer, but she said nothing. With his gut churning, he pressed the button that pulled up the anchor and they headed back to the villa without further conversation.

Eventually they reached the point. By this time Daimon and Mara had come up on deck. As Ric pulled up to the dock, Daimon jumped out to secure the boat with the ropes. Ric helped him. Still hunkered on the pier, he looked down at Sami. She was busy removing the baby's life preserver.

"I've made a decision, Sami." She glanced up at him nervously. "Eliana's waiting for me to call her, but I need your input first before I make that call, because whatever happens from here on out, we're in this together."

Her expression sobered. "In what way?"

"Shall we fly back to Genoa in the morning? Once we're settled in the palazzo, I'll bring her over to meet you and Ric. Or, I can tell her to board her family's jet and fly down here tomorrow afternoon. Which option do you prefer?"

She handed him the baby before climbing onto the pier with the diaper bag. "I'm thankful you've decided to tell her. It's the right thing to do. I think we should face her here where there's no possibility of anyone else being around. As your future wife, she deserves every consideration we can give her. This is going to be very painful for her."

"I agree." Sami's courage and decency made her a remarkable woman.

"She'll be Ric's stepmother," she added. He heard the quiver in her voice. It reached deep inside him. "If it's possible, I want to be friends with her. But I realize that will take time considering the shock she's going to receive."

With those comments he'd just discovered Sami had a goodness in her not found in most people. For their baby to have a mother like her thrilled and humbled him.

"So be it. I'll call her when we go inside and tell her I want her to join me tomorrow evening. I won't indicate the reason until I pick her up at the airport. Until then, I'd like us to enjoy our vacation as long as possible. You'd like to spend time out by the swimming pool tomorrow, wouldn't you, *piccolo?*"

Ric clutched the baby to him, recognizing he only had another twenty-four hours before everything changed.

Sami headed for the villa and went up the stairs to the bedroom where she put the baby down. Ric followed. The baby had fallen fast asleep. After she covered him with a light blanket, she started to rise up and found herself too close to Ric. Instead of moving out of her way, he lifted his hands to her shoulders and kneaded them with increasing restlessness.

His eyes, so black and alive, devoured her features. "If you and I had been taken to the same hospital after the avalanche, we would have been able to get to know each other in the light and hold each other while we thanked providence our lives had been spared. Instead, it's taken all this time for us to finally meet. This is long overdue. After spending today with you, I need to hold you for a minute, Sami, so don't fight me."

He pulled her in to him, not giving her time to answer. The second he buried his face in her hair, she felt his hands rove over her back. Sami moaned and instinctively moved closer to his hard-muscled body. The feel of him, the enticing male scent of him, all were too familiar. The way he touched her and kissed the side of her neck brought déjà vu, sending a river of molten heat through her body. His touch had the power to turn her insides to liquid.

This was like before. She'd could hardly get enough

air then, and she had the same problem now, but not because of being enclosed by tons of snow. This time there was room to stand, and the fragrant air from the flowers growing outside moved through the windows and alcoves of the villa. Once again he'd intoxicated her, filling her with rapture that made her senses spiral and silenced her conscience.

"You're the most naturally beautiful woman I've ever known, Sami. I want you even more than before," he cried urgently before his mouth sought hers in a frenzy of need neither of them could control.

She didn't remember being carried to the bed. Somehow she was there with him, responding to her growing desire for this man who was thrilling her senseless. Every kiss created pure ecstasy. She felt herself going under, deeper and deeper.

"Since the avalanche, I've dreamed about us so many times. To think you're alive… *Sami*—"

"I know." She half sobbed the words. "I can't believe it either." She kissed the scar where the beam had hit his forehead. But in the act of doing it, she was suddenly seized by a cognizance of what was happening here.

When Ric would have found her mouth again, she rolled away from him and got to her feet, just far enough away that he couldn't reach her. She lost her balance and grabbed on to the end of the dresser.

"Don't do this to us. Come back here," he begged. His eyes were smoldering black fires.

She was one trembling mass of desire. "You think I don't want to? But we can't just do what we want, Ric.

It's clear you and I feel an attraction because of what happened during the avalanche and the miracle of meeting up again. But that's all this is. So far we've done nothing to be ashamed of. That's why this has to stop here and now, and never happen again."

He got up from the bed. She thought him even more gorgeous with his black hair disheveled. "So what are you saying?" he said in a voice of ice.

She backed away from him. "I'm saying that in Austria you and I were like two colliding heavenly bodies out in space. But those bodies have long since orbited away from each other despite the pull we've felt today. I suppose it's understandable since we both thought the other was dead."

He folded his arms. "So now that we've discovered we're amazingly alive, what about the next time we see each other and feel the pull?"

Sami took a shaky breath. "We'll deal with it. We *have* to. Yes, we shared one amazing connection together in the avalanche, but it wasn't real life. You have a whole new married life about to unfold. I have my studies."

When he didn't respond, she added, "In January I'm going to get on with my school work. I need a good career to be able to provide for me and Ric."

A tiny pulse throbbed at his temple where he'd been injured. "Where exactly?"

"At the University of Reno. I transferred my credits there when I left California. The nice thing is, the computer engineering department has a program that lets you go to school at night, so I'll be with Ric during the day. I've already arranged for several babysitters who've agreed to trade off helping me nights. It will all work out.

"As for you, you'll be married in a few weeks. After you and Eliana talk things over tomorrow evening, the three of us will sit down and work out a mutually beneficial visitation arrangement for our son. I'm praying that if she's a part of it, then she'll be more accepting of the situation."

Ric moved closer. "You think it's all going to be that simple?" he asked in a dangerously silky voice.

"No," she said, still looking at him. "Do you have a better solution? If so, I'm willing to hear it. But not tonight. I'm really tired after my swim. We all need a good night's sleep."

Stillness surrounded him. "If you should want me for any reason, I'll be in my study downstairs making a phone call."

Please leave now and get it over with. Sami's willpower was nonexistent.

Ric must have heard her plea. In the next instant he was gone.

Sami slept in late. When she came downstairs the next morning, she discovered Mara had served breakfast out on the patio surrounding the pool. There was no sign of Ric or the baby, but his carrycot was there. As she sat down to eat, Ric came through the alcove holding her little darling. Their eyes met.

"Good morning. I'm sorry I got up so late."

He walked over so she could kiss the baby. "That's the

idea when you're on vacation. It gave Ric and me a chance to go for a walk and have a talk together, man to man."

She smiled. "Did you two set the world straight?"

"Of course." He reciprocated with a heart-melting smile of his own.

On the surface, you wouldn't think they had a care, but Sami couldn't take the invisible tension she was feeling any longer. She needed an answer to one burning question. "Were you able to reach Eliana last night?"

He nodded without noticeable emotion. "She'll be arriving at six-thirty this evening."

"I realize she doesn't suspect anything. That makes me nervous."

"If it will ease your anxiety, I did tell her I had something of great importance I needed to talk to her about. It put her on the alert, which was good." He expelled a deep breath. "If there were someone to blame in this... but there isn't." His voice trailed. "You and I clung to life until the last breath. If that was a sin, then so be it, but I won't allow our son to suffer because of it."

"I believe you."

Sami didn't know how she was going to stand meeting Eliana, but she had to go through with it. No doubt Ric's fiancée was an outstanding woman, otherwise he wouldn't be marrying her. But tonight when he would introduce them and they would look at each other, Eliana's eyes would be staring at the woman Ric had made love to in the dark with the result of pregnancy.

Could Sami expect to see any understanding, or would bitter resentment always cloud the other woman's vision?

She looked up at the powder-blue sky. The weather had warmed up to seventy degrees at the pool and was almost balmy. With such brilliant blue water beyond the point, it was hard to believe it was December.

Sami cast a covert glance at Ric, who'd gone over to lie down on one of the sun loungers to play with the baby. He'd dressed in a wine-colored polo and white cargo pants. His well-honed body made it difficult to look anywhere else.

Another sigh escaped. She could only imagine what was going through his mind right now. Once he told Eliana the truth, the word would be out. It wasn't just his fiancée he would have to placate. His family and hers, their friends, everyone who knew and loved him would have questions he would have to answer.

What made this so hard was to realize that a very private act between the two of them—an act even *they* had trouble explaining—would become public knowledge. Because of Ric's prominence, both he and Sami would be the targets of gossip, in some cases malicious. She would hate the notoriety, but she and the baby would be back in Reno where she wouldn't have to be around the paparazzi on a twenty-four-hour basis. Ric would bear the brunt of it.

Of course he'd handle it, but his marriage would suffer. And though she knew he'd go to the greatest lengths to protect their son from being hurt when he was on visitation, it was inevitable the baby would feel it and have to live with it growing up.

Her desire to lift Ric's spirits until Eliana arrived

prompted Sami to get up from the table. "Excuse me for a minute. I'll be right back."

"Hurry. We like your company."

His little personal asides made mincemeat of her emotions. She dashed through the villa and up the stairs for his gift. She'd started making it for his father after finding out she was pregnant. Little did she dream she would be giving it to Ric himself.

Formula wasn't the only thing at the bottom of her suitcase. She opened the lid and pulled out the scrapbook which she'd wrapped in Christmas paper ahead of time. Hugging it to her chest, she hurried back downstairs to the pool.

He was so preoccupied with the baby, he didn't see her coming. "Merry Christmas again, Ric," she called to him, announcing her presence.

He looked up in time for her to hand it to him. "I brought this to give your father for Christmas. I've decided now would be the best time for you to have it."

While he sat up to open it, she picked up the baby and stood there to watch him leaf through the pages.

Sami had put everything in there: pictures of her, her grandparents, more pictures of her sister's family and their parents, the apartment in Reno, the picture the hospital had taken of Ric right after he was born, cards from friends, comments from the pediatrician, more pictures of him turning one week, then two, then three, his room, his crib and baby toys. Everything she could think of to preserve memories for his grandfather.

"Those three photos are the ultrasound pictures. Can

you believe that's our little Ric there? The technician said he had a strong heartbeat and everything looked normal. You'll never know my relief."

Ric went so quiet, she wondered if something was wrong. Then he looked up with those jet-black eyes suspiciously bright. "I'll cherish this forever, Sami." She hardly recognized his voice it was so husky.

Thrilled with his response she said, "When you told me you'd missed the first two months of his life and didn't want to miss any more, I was doubly glad I made this. While you enjoy it, I'm going to put this little guy to bed for a nap."

"Wait— Stay right where you are." He got up from the lounger and dashed into the villa. Not a minute later and he came back outside with Daimon.

"He's going to take a picture of us with my cell phone," Ric explained. In the next breath he came to stand next to Sami and put his arm around her shoulders, pulling her close enough to set off a burst of adrenaline.

"This one's for posterity and will go in the last page of the book. Take a dozen pictures, Daimon. Then we want to take pictures of you and Mara holding him. Before long I intend to fill up a whole new scrapbook with memories."

But when, Ric? Here on the island isn't real life.

After all the picture-taking was done, they went upstairs to put the baby down, then tiptoed out of the room. Sami assumed Ric would use this free time to do the business he'd come to Paphos to accomplish. Nothing could have surprised her more than when he told her he wanted her to drive to town with him.

"I've arranged for Mara to watch the baby while we're gone. I want to show you around the ancient part of the city."

"What about your work?"

"It's getting done."

When? In the middle of the night? How did he do it and still get up with the baby?

"If you feel you have time, I'd love to do some sight-seeing." As long as she could be with him, she honestly didn't care what they did. She was storing up memories before she had to go back home.

"The weather's warm enough to go without a coat, but if you want one, I'll wait for you downstairs."

"I'm fine the way I am."

When his eyes smiled like that, she felt complete. "Then let's make the most of the time."

Within minutes they were driving on the A-6 toward the city they'd passed on the cruiser yesterday. He gave her a running commentary about the origins of the sprawling modern coastal town of 47,000 people.

Once in the busy part of the new Paphos, Ric stopped to buy a stroller for the baby. "We'll need one. It'll be nice to push him around whether we're out walking around or at the villa."

Sami saw a clothing shop and popped in to buy an extra couple of outfits for herself. Everything was decked out for Christmas. Nearby Ric found a sweets shop that sold drinks and *loukoumades*. He bought a sack of the delicious donut balls with syrup for them to eat along the way. "My friends and I used to stuff ourselves with these."

"I can see why. I can't stop with just one."

They drove on. No one was more fun than Ric when he was lighthearted. She became the pushover who went along with all his ideas because she couldn't help herself.

"Ahead of us is Palaepaphos, the old city. It was the island's capital in Greco-Roman times and the main focal point of Aphrodite-worship for the entire Aegean. I'm taking you to see some outstanding mosaics that still remain in the Roman governor's palace."

For the next two hours they explored the remains of everything from villas, palaces and theaters to fortresses and tombs. "Oh, Ric, this is all so incredible."

"Isn't it? I spent all my holidays here, pretending it was my secret world. Come on. I want to show you one more thing before we go back."

Sami dreaded the fact that this time with Ric was almost over. Nothing would be the same after Eliana arrived. If it were in her power, she'd make this time with him last forever.

They soon came to a jewel of an ancient church. "This is the Agia Kyriaki Chrysopolitissa parish church, one of my favorite places. My mother loved it and always brought us here."

"Is it still operational?"

"Yes. They even hold English mass."

She loved its architecture. "There's a very spiritual aspect about the whole place."

His dark eyes fastened on hers. "This city was blessed when Paul of Tarsus visited here in the first century A.D."

Sami reflected on Ric's upbringing. "You were blessed to have a mom you loved so much raise you."

He moved closer to her. "Now you understand why I'm full of gratitude for the way you love our son. Your grandparents did a wonderful job with you."

"Pat and I weren't the easiest children. They'll get a crown in heaven, that's for sure."

While she was caught up with so many feelings she didn't dare express, she was conscious of a clock ticking away. "I think Mara will wonder if we're ever coming back."

Ric's mouth turned up in a half smile. "She hopes we won't."

They started for the car. "Do she and Daimon have children?"

"Yes. Both their married daughters live in Nicosia. They visit back and forth with the grandchildren on a regular basis."

"That makes me happy to hear it." She glanced at her watch and couldn't believe how long they'd been gone. "It's almost time for Eliana's plane to arrive. We need to hurry home."

"Relax. We'll make it."

Ric seemed in no rush. Sami tried to heed his advice, but she was too restless. When they reached the villa, she hurried inside to find the baby. Holding him always calmed her down.

Mara had put him in the carrycot while she was in

the kitchen cooking. Sami entered with Ric to find their son lying there open-eyed and perfectly content until Ric hunkered down to talk to him. The second he saw his daddy, he started crying, wanting to be held. On cue, Ric was right there to pick him up and nestle him against his chest.

Sami burst into laughter. "What a little faker he is. I swear that happens every time with you."

A smile lit up Mara's face. "He knows his *papa*."

"Unfortunately his *papa* needs to get ready to leave for the airport," Sami said. Her gaze shot to Ric. "I'll take him so you won't be late."

She felt his hesitation before he handed the baby over.

"At least Ric still acts happy to come to me. I'd begun to fear he might have forgotten me because of his new infatuation with you."

"Sami..."

Afraid to look in Ric's eyes she said, "I'm taking this young man upstairs. Thanks for everything, Mara."

"My pleasure. He won't need a bottle for a while. I think he's getting sleepy."

"All right then. Let's go change you."

Ten minutes later he'd fallen to sleep. As Sami turned to go take her shower, Ric made an appearance. He looked too gorgeous in a silky charcoal dress shirt and black trousers she hadn't seen before. Her heart pounded outrageously.

"I wanted you to know I'm leaving now."

"I—I'll see you later then." She stumbled over the

words. Fear for what was going to happen had chilled her blood. "I'll pray things go well."

Without saying anything, he went over to the crib and rubbed their little boy's head. "I'll be back, *tesoro mio,*" he whispered.

"What did you just call him?"

"My treasure." His gaze swerved to hers. "When you came to find my father, you brought me the world, Sami."

His words liquefied her insides. "He's my whole world, too." She struggled to keep her voice steady. "Do you have any advice for me for when I meet Eliana?"

A brooding look stole over his handsome face. "Simply be yourself."

That didn't help her. "How old is she?"

"Twenty-five."

A year younger than Sami. "Have you—" She stopped herself, needing to bite her tongue out.

"Have we been intimate?"

"It's none of my business."

"The answer is yes."

Sami had no right to feel wounded by the admission, but she did. Horribly. But she was glad she knew. It put things into perspective. He was a man with a man's appetite and Eliana was his fiancée, after all. Women always dramatized everything.

Well, Sami refused to be like that. Everyone knew that the majority of couples, engaged or not, didn't wait for marriage to sleep together. The fact that Sami hadn't been intimate with a man except Ric put her in that tiny minority.

He darted her a quick glance. "I'll answer the next question you haven't asked yet. I've enjoyed my share of women over the years."

"If Eliana knows that, then perhaps she won't be as hurt when you tell her about us."

His lids drooped over his eyes. "That's a nice thought. Let's hang on to it, shall we?"

"Ric—"

"I should be back with her within forty-five minutes."

Her body trembled. "I'll be ready. What shall I wear?"

He scrutinized her from her hair to her sandaled feet. "You're breathtaking with or without clothes. Put on whatever feels the most comfortable."

After Ric had left the bedroom, Sami stood in the shower paralyzed by what he'd said. How could he reduce everything to its most intimate and personal when he was preparing to pick up his soon-to-be wife at the airport?

Yet, on the heels of that thought, she had to remember he'd been intimate with both Sami and Eliana. The situation didn't fit any scenario she knew of.

Coming to the island had been a mistake. They'd gotten into a false sense of vacation mode. Last night things had almost spiraled out of control. Because of the baby, she assumed that was the reason they'd both subconsciously let down their guard. But one thing was certain. She refused to put herself into such a vulnerable position again.

The only thing to do was get through the next few hours while they all talked, then she'd fly home in the morning. She'd done her part so Ric could enjoy the baby, but now it was over. It didn't matter if he wanted their son with him all the time. That wouldn't be possible. Reno and Genoa were thousands of miles apart. After his marriage and honeymoon, they could talk on the phone and plan how to arrange visitation.

While her mind pored over how she would tell him she was leaving, she did her hair and makeup. After that she opened the closet door and put on her navy blue suit, matching it with a lighter blue silk blouse. The rest of the clothes she'd brought with her comprised a few casual jeans and tops. Sami wanted to look her best. Nothing but the suit was dressy enough for this first meeting with a princess, no matter how casual the surroundings.

When she was ready, she went downstairs and asked Mara to listen for the baby while she walked out to the private marina to take in the view. She hoped Ric and Eliana would arrive while she was away from the villa. Ric could show her the baby before she had to face Sami.

Mara acted delighted and offered to feed him if he awakened. Sami thanked her and stepped outside.

The sun had set an hour ago. Sami presumed Ric would be back fairly soon. Twilight had come on fast and the air was cooler, yet she glimpsed sailboats and cruisers out enjoying the evening. From the corner of her eye she saw a jet climbing in the sky from Paphos airport. Under the right circumstances this time of night could be magical, but all Sami experienced was a heavy heart.

She walked along the path bordering the sand. Everyone knew weddings were for the bride. A bride had the right to expect that the days leading up to her wedding would be filled with excitement. It killed Sami to imagine that because she'd come to Genoa looking for Ric's grandfather, Eliana's excitement would now vanish as if it had never been.

Again Pat's predictions came floating back at her.

Neither Sami nor Ric could change things, but she would go out of her way to appease Eliana in any way she could in order not to do more damage. Lost in thought, she didn't realize she'd been out longer than she'd planned. It had grown dark. She retraced her steps back to the villa and met Daimon coming toward her.

"Enrico sent me to find you."

"I purposely stayed out to give him time to be with Eliana and the baby."

"They've been here awhile. He was worried about you."

"I'm sorry. Where are they?"

"In the living room by the fireplace."

Sami walked inside and made her way through to the front of the house. She peered around the corner to see the couple over on the couch. In the open-necked charcoal shirt and dark trousers, Ric had never looked more appealing. He'd nestled the baby against his shoulder. His little head bobbed, signaling he was awake. Both were heartbreakingly attractive.

Eliana was seated near him wearing a stunning watermelon-colored suit. She had class written all over her and could have been a model for the latest princess doll with her dark blond hair falling in curls over her shoulders.

CHAPTER SIX

"Hello?" Sami called softly to announce her entrance.

At the sound of her voice, Ric's black eyes shot to hers and he sprang to his feet. The way he was looking at her underlined what Daimon had said about him being worried. She hadn't meant to alarm him.

Her gaze strayed to Eliana whose head had turned in her direction. Large amber eyes gave Sami a wintry stare of condemnation. Otherwise her classically Italian features were devoid of animation.

Little did Eliana know she didn't have anything to fear from Sami. But the baby was another matter, because Ric had claimed him. He loved their baby to the depth of his being and intended to be a hands-on father whenever possible.

At the moment his remote countenance was more pronounced than it had been when he'd told her the reason he'd gotten rid of his title. She groaned inwardly for him.

"Christine Argyle, please meet my fiancée, Princess Eliana Fortulezza."

Sami had known he was marrying nobility, but hearing his fiancée's title and seeing her in person at last still took some getting used to. "How do you do, Princess Fortulezza?"

Eliana rose to her feet. "Signorina Argyle," she said and they shook hands.

Ric's fiancée studied Sami without revealing any visible emotion. Though Ric had been honest about his reasons for marrying Eliana, no one could know what was in his fiancée's heart. She'd been trained to maintain her dignity, but now that this ghastly moment was upon them, Sami thought the other woman was awesome.

"Come on," Ric said. "We'll go into the dining room where we can sit around the table to talk." Sami followed them, noting Eliana's tall, slender figure and the three dazzling diamonds of her engagement ring.

The carrycot was still perched on the table. Ric put the baby down in it, then pulled out chairs for her and Eliana. Since her little boy seemed content, Sami sat down without kissing him. She didn't want to get him all worked up and create a fuss.

Mara came in to serve coffee and biscotti. Ric thanked her before she left them alone. His dark, solemn eyes slid to Sami. "I've told Eliana everything that happened last January."

Having said that much, the onus was now on Sami. She cleared her throat and eyed Eliana. "Then you realize that when I went to the police station two days ago, I was expecting, or at least hoping, to meet Ric's father."

"Yes."

This was so painful for Sami, she could only imagine how shocked and hurt Eliana had to be. "I can't tell you how sorry I am to have caused you this kind of grief. I had no idea the elder Mr. Degenoli had died, or that Ric had survived the avalanche." Her voice faltered. "When he lost consciousness, I thought he was dead. Neither of us dreamed we would ever leave our tomb alive."

"So Enrico explained. Did he tell you to call him Ric?" she asked in heavily accented English.

Out of all the questions she might have asked, that was the last one Sami would have expected. "When I realized I wasn't alone in the dark, I asked who was there. He said he was Ric Degenoli. I was thankful he spoke English and told him my name was Sami."

"Sami?"

"My father's name was Samuel. That's how I got the nickname." She leaned forward. "Eliana—please believe me. I have absolutely no intention of ruining your life. I know you're going to be married on New Year's Day. Tomorrow morning I'm taking the baby back to Reno with me."

She purposely didn't look at Ric while she spoke to Eliana. "Once the wedding and honeymoon are over and you've settled into married life, then visitation can be discussed. But be assured my life is in America."

The other woman studied her for a minute. "Enrico tells me there's a man who wishes to marry you."

Sami couldn't fault Ric for telling his fiancée everything. The whole truth and nothing but. No doubt it would make things more bearable for Eliana if Sami were to say that she and Matt would be getting married shortly. But she couldn't, because it would never happen. Sami didn't love Matt with all her heart and soul. In the past twenty-four hours, she'd had that confirmed beyond any lingering doubt.

"There is, but I've decided against marrying him." Her announcement caused something to flare in the recesses of Ric's eyes, whether surprise because she'd been so frank about it, Sami couldn't tell. Eliana didn't flinch. "Perhaps if I give you a little background, you'll understand.

"I was young when my parents died. Though I adored my grandparents, I ached for a mother and father. When Ric was born I made a vow. Since he would never know his father in this life, I would devote my life to raising my precious son to the very best of my ability.

"For the last two months I've thought of nothing else and don't see another man giving my baby the love he'll need." Watching Ric in action with their child had settled the question for her once and for all. Anyone other than his own father wouldn't do.

"How will you live?"

Sami had half expected Eliana's practical question. Ric's fiancée could be forgiven for thinking Sami was out for everything she could get from him. It was time to reassure her on that point.

"Did Ric mention to you that I was in graduate school before I flew to Austria?"

"He said something about it."

"I intend to go back to it. Being a computer engineer will provide me with a good living to help me take care of the two of us and pay back my loans."

"How in debt are you?"

Again Sami understood why she was curious. "By the time I've received my master's degree, I'll probably owe at least $40,000, but I'll pay it back slowly after I'm employed. I'm fortunate to go to a university where I can be with the baby all day and attend classes at night.

"Once I'm back there, I'll email you my schedule. We'll work things out so Ric gets to see his son when it's convenient for you. Do you have any other questions you want to ask me?"

After a few seconds she said, "No."

Then there was nothing more to talk about. Good. Sami couldn't sit here any longer. If Eliana was struggling to hold it all together, she didn't give anything away.

Sami stood up without having tasted her coffee. "If you'll excuse me, I need to put the baby down and go to bed." She went around to lift him from his carrycot. On her way out of the room, she paused for a moment. "I'm glad Ric brought you here tonight so we could meet, Eliana. I wish you two every happiness on your forthcoming marriage."

Even though Eliana and Ric hadn't been engaged last January, Sami had the conviction that the strange circumstances surrounding the baby's conception had driven a wedge that could never be closed. "Since I know you have a lot to discuss, I'll say good-night."

Eliana looked relieved. So was Sami, who hurried to the bedroom, thankful the dreaded meeting was over. Once inside, she hurried upstairs and put the baby down long enough to change and slip into her robe. After that she bathed him and gave him his bottle, needing to feel him close to her.

She still shivered from the look on Ric's face before she'd rushed out of the dining room. It said she hadn't had the last word when it came to her going back to the States. But despite how crazy he was about their baby, he had to face reality. The only way to relieve the tension was for Sami to go home.

As soon as her little cherub had fallen asleep, she put him down in the crib. Afraid she'd toss and turn in agony all night, she took a sleeping pill and turned off her lamp before climbing into bed.

If the drug worked and she fell into a deep enough sleep, she knew Ric would get up in the night with the baby. The experience would give Eliana a taste of what it would be like when it was their turn to take care of him.

While she lay there waiting for needed oblivion, her mind went over the scene in the living room. Sami had given out enough information for Eliana to put her own spin on it. No doubt she believed Sami had come to Italy hoping Ric's father would fund her graduate-school costs. When she'd found Ric alive, that was even better. The count was worth a fortune and would do anything for his son. He'd already proved it.

Surely by now it had entered Eliana's mind that a lesser man with his kind of money could have paid Sami off and been done with the problem without any knowledge of it coming to light. *Not Ric.* He not only loved the idea of being a father, he genuinely loved playing with the baby and seeing to all his needs. You couldn't fake that kind of caring.

Eliana had to be seeing a whole new side to her fiancé. It ought to reassure her he'd be a marvelous father to any children they would have one day. But Eliana would have to get past this obstacle before she could begin to appreciate how exceptional Ric really was.

Still in turmoil, Sami turned on her other side. For the three of them to meet and talk had been the only thing to do, but none of them had come out of it unscathed. Her gaze lit on the baby, who had no idea what was going on. Her sweet little baby… Hot tears trickled out the corners of her eyes.

When next Sami knew anything, she discovered it was after 10:00 a.m. That pill had eventually knocked her out. With her timing off, it meant she would have to hurry to arrange for an evening flight out of Paphos.

There was no sign of the baby. Ric and Eliana must have come in to take care of him. If not them, Mara. With her pulse racing, Sami quickly dressed in jeans and a blouse before hurrying downstairs. She expected to find him with Ric and Eliana in the breakfast room of the villa. Instead the housekeeper was the one to greet her.

"Good morning, Sami. Enrico is at the pool with the baby. I'll serve your breakfast out there."

"Thank you, Mara."

She rushed through the alcoves to reach the pool at the side of the villa. As he'd been yesterday, Ric was seated at the umbrella table, but this morning he was dressed in a pale blue suit and tie. Rather than reading the newspaper, he was playing with the baby, whose animated responses touched her heart. An empty baby bottle lay next to his coffee. Apparently Eliana wasn't up yet.

Ric saw her and got to his feet, the quintessential Genoan aristocrat. *Her baby's father.* Not in a hundred lifetimes could Sami have dreamed up this picture.

"I'm glad you're awake," he said as she approached. "We have to talk. Ric has been looking for you."

Sami leaned over their son. "I think your *papa* is just teasing me to make me feel better. You've been having a wonderful time, haven't you?" She caught his little hands and pressed kisses all over them and his face and neck. After she lifted her head, she turned to his father. "Is Eliana still in bed?"

His eyes roved over her features for a moment. "No. I just got back from driving her to the airport. She flew home in her father's company jet."

Sami's composure slipped. "I'm sick for her, Ric," she cried. "The news had to ruin her dreams. With your wedding so imminent, I don't know how she's handling it."

Lines marred his striking face. "She's not" came the grim admission. Sami's heart plummeted. Ric rubbed the back of his neck as she'd seen him do before. "There's much more to Eliana's reaction than even I had imagined."

"You're talking about the inevitable scandal," she whispered. "I know it will be awful, but compared to a little baby who needs a father and mother, surely she'll come to terms with this in time?"

The lines marring his features made him look older. "The baby plays a negligible part in what's happened."

Sami frowned. "What do you mean?"

"Early this morning I heard from my attorney. The title is now officially gone." His eyes narrowed to slits. "What you said in passing was prophetic. Knowing she'll no longer be addressed as Countess is what has destroyed Eliana's dream. She's demanding that I have it reinstated."

"Did you tell her that's impossible?"

"She doesn't understand the word. As for little Ric, she has no intention of being a stepmother to my child."

"She's saying that now because she wants her own children with you, Ric."

"Not if there isn't a title to bestow on our firstborn son. Her solution to the problem is unthinkable," his voice rasped, igniting her panic.

"What do you mean by that?"

"She won't consider visitation. Either I give up all rights to Ric and never see him again, or the wedding is off. She's giving me until Christmas Eve day to make a final decision. In the meantime she won't discuss this with anyone."

Sami swallowed hard. "She's not a parent yet, or she wouldn't have laid down those rules. Eliana doesn't mean what she said. It was her pain lashing out. You have to give her time. Though the pain's excruciating, in a few days she'll have recovered enough to think more clearly."

"No. She's thinking clearly now. Until last summer Eliana and I only knew each other socially and were never in any kind of relationship. What happened between you and me had no bearing on her, but now she's in a rage because I never told her about you. I explained that I'd gone looking for you and couldn't find you. For all I knew, you had died. Even if I'd found you, I wouldn't have dreamed I'd made you pregnant."

"I had to explain the same thing to Matt. When the doctor told me the reason why I hadn't been feeling well, I almost fainted and had to stay lying down for an hour before I could leave his office. He talked to me about diet and prenatal vitamins, but I hardly heard him for the shock I was in.

"If I hadn't become pregnant, none of it would have come out." Sami shook her head. "Eliana could have no idea how this situation has affected you and me, but it's so hard to explain."

"She doesn't want an explanation. All she cares about is the title."

"Ric—I have to believe that when the worst of her agony subsides, she'll realize she wants to be your wife under any circumstances."

"That's where you're wrong. You weren't raised a princess with specific expectations to be met."

Sami hugged her arms to her waist. "Do you think she's capable of understanding what it would mean for you to give up your parental rights to Ric?"

"She doesn't want to understand, because the baby isn't a factor."

"But he's your son!"

"Eliana grew up in her father's world of black and

white. His daughter is a product of that environment. When he hears about this, he'll demand I get the title back, because he puts his desires above everything else. He'll tell me to pay you off for the child I fathered by some freak accident."

She shuddered. "I've known all along no one would believe what happened to us."

"Certainly not Eliana. When I told her you were in Austria on a working vacation for your sister's travel agency, she's convinced you targeted me when you found out Count Degenoli was registered there. Employing your wiles, you ended up sleeping with me in the hotel before the avalanche struck, and decided to use the tragedy as an alibi to cover our flirtation."

Sami sank into the chair. "Actually I can't blame her for thinking that."

"Nor I. She assumes you came to Italy as soon as the baby could travel in order to extort money from me. Moreover she thinks I decided to rescind the title because you phoned me from Reno and told me about the pregnancy a long time ago.

"Because I was already engaged to her, she assumed I immediately made the necessary arrangements so I'd be able to legally claim Ric as my firstborn, thus cheating her."

"You can't fault her logic, Ric. I'm afraid everyone who learns about us will think the same thing. Do you think Eliana always hoped to marry you?"

"I have no idea." He came to a standstill, gripping the back of one of the dining-room chairs until his knuckles showed white. "Our fathers have brushed shoulders in the same business circles for years, but I didn't consider getting to know her until June of this year. In November I asked her to marry me and we set a date for the wedding."

"She's very lovely. Not very many women in her kind of pain would have handled our meeting with so much poise."

"Interestingly enough, she said the same thing about you."

Sami couldn't look at him. "Unfortunately if Eliana thinks you've lied to her about our first meeting, then she *does* see me as a menace. It wouldn't matter how many times I tell her I won't stand in the way of her happiness, she won't listen."

He cocked his dark head. "Perhaps deep down she does believe it. That's what bothers her more."

"Why do you say that?"

"Do I need to spell it out?" he fired. "Not every woman and man trapped in a situation like ours would have sought comfort as we did."

Again her body grew warm. "I know," she admitted reluctantly.

"I'm still haunted by those feelings and why we acted on them. I can assure you my life hasn't been the same since that experience."

"Neither has mine," she confessed in a tremulous voice. "Maybe it was because we believed our time had run out and we were both single and free at the time to act without hurting anyone else. But the same can't be said of us now."

"No," he murmured. "Since then, we have a marvelous child who needs his mother and father." Without warning he scooped up the baby, laughing triumphantly. The happy sound was a revelation. He alternated kissing and cuddling him close. Ric treated their son as if he'd always been in his life.

Her heart ran away with her. "But everything has changed—"

"I agree. We've all changed. Last night Eliana could feel a certain tension between you and me she couldn't cut through. Don't forget you kissed me back yesterday and the day before, Sami."

"I've forgotten nothing!" When he'd laid her down on the hotel bed in Genoa to talk, her body had come alive again without her volition. Yesterday they'd reached blindly for each other in the bedroom after putting Ric down. She'd only come to her senses at the last second.

He eyed her with a penetrating glance. "I'm glad to hear you say it, because you're not going back to Reno yet. Since you've flown this long way, the three of us are going to stay here and enjoy this time together while Eliana works this out in her mind.

"Maybe the impossible will happen and she'll decide she wants this marriage badly enough to compromise. It'll mean going up against her father, but she knows my terms. Without visitation, I won't marry her."

Sami couldn't stop shivering. "This is all so mean. She's been looking forward to her wedding day since you announced the engagement in November. To defy her father's wishes in order to keep you will be a hard thing, Ric. If she isn't able to go against him, then she'll be forced to call off the wedding and suffer the humiliation of having to undo all the arrangements of a huge public marriage like yours."

"That's where you're wrong, Sami. With my family still in mourning, we'd already planned our wedding to take place in the privacy of the palazzo chapel with only our families in attendance. No reporters will be allowed inside. The news will leak out, it always does, but there'll be no photo ops or press releases, no official reception."

"The poor thing." Tears filled her eyes. "Why didn't you fly back with her?"

"After you left us last night, I told her I'd take her back to Genoa in my own plane this morning and we'd talk to her parents together while you and the baby remained here. She agreed. But when we reached the airport this morning, she suddenly changed her mind and told me she needed to talk to her parents alone first."

That's why he was dressed in a suit. "Why do you think she didn't want you to be with her when she faced them? With you there explaining everything, how could they possibly doubt your honesty?"

"You want the truth?" he rapped out.

"Ric—if we don't have that, we don't have anything!"

"She assumes you and I have slept together since your arrival in Genoa. Last night she asked me not to touch her."

Sami moaned. "Does that mean—"

"It means she slept in the other guest bedroom," he answered.

She bit her lip. "Did she help you with the baby when you got up in the night to feed him?"

"If she heard me and Ric, she didn't make an appearance."

"Obviously she was in too much pain."

He exhaled sharply. "It's commendable how much credit you give her."

"I'm not the woman who has been looking forward to her marriage to you. She's crushed. In the face of what she's dealing with, I admire her more for her honesty, no matter hard it is on both of you."

Ric raked a hand through his black hair. "You're an extraordinary woman, Sami."

"No, I'm not—" she cried. "This is so awful for both of you. I have my own life to go back to, but you two have to wade through so much to make this work!" She buried her face in her hands. "Did you disabuse her about us?"

"In what regard?" he drawled.

"That nothing has happened between us since I came to Italy."

"I wouldn't say that," he countered in a tone that sent little darts of awareness through her body.

Exasperated she said, "You know what I mean."

"Just because you and I haven't ended up in bed yet doesn't rule out what goes on whenever we're near each other." Her trembling started up again. After a pause he added, "Even if I'd assured her we didn't pick up where we'd left off in January, do you imagine it would have done any good?"

Her shoulders slumped. "I should never have come."

"We've been over this ground before," he said in an iron-clad voice. "Don't ever say that again."

She took a deep breath to pull herself together. By acknowledging his son from the start, Ric hadn't given his fiancée a choice. Surely Eliana was aware of his strong will. He wouldn't capitulate. It was up to her to decide what she could handle. No doubt she wanted to scratch Sami's eyes out or worse.

"You need to fly back to Genoa where you'll be close if she wants to see you. I'll leave for Reno on the next plane out of Paphos."

"No. That you *won't* do. For the sake of propriety, she's already set down the condition that you and I stay away from the city until the twenty-fourth."

"Ric—tell me the truth. If she doesn't come around and there's no marriage, then what will it cost you besides the woman you asked to marry you? Don't insult me by pretending this won't shake your world."

He wore an implacable expression. "That's for me to worry about."

"But I *do* worry!" she declared. "My reappearance in your world has done irreparable damage. If anyone should go to her parents, *I* should. I'll ask my sister and her husband to come with me. They'll verify what we've told Eliana.

"If we can convince her parents that I wasn't out to extort anyone or try to break you up, then it's possible they'll forgive you for having a human weakness. Good heavens, they're parents and will have to understand you want to be able to see your son on a regular basis. If

Eliana is willing to accept the baby, then the marriage can still take place."

His smile wasn't reflected in his eyes. "Your reasoning is without fault, Sami. You'd make a very convincing courtroom lawyer. But the crux of the real problem lies in the loss of the title. Eliana has been imagining herself as Countess Degenoli."

"You honestly think she can't get over that?"

"Not her or her father," his voice grated. "She's conflicted at her foundation. It wouldn't matter if you and your family were there to plead my case and win over her parents. She has her own war to fight inside. As I told you earlier, I'm going to find out what's really important to her."

Ric was a wonderful man. A prize. All this time Sami had assumed Eliana had learned to love him more than life. But what if that wasn't perfectly true? What if she loved him with strings?

Since this was virtually an arranged marriage, it was obvious there was a voice inside Ric that had always entertained his doubts about her. He'd gotten rid of his title as soon as he could. Maybe it had been a test. When Sami had asked him if it was such a terrible burden, his answer had left her in no doubt.

While she stood there trying to analyze his psyche, he peeled off his suit jacket and loosened his tie, as if he couldn't wait to remove the shackles of society. "After I've changed, we'll take another boat ride, this time in the other direction."

"What if someone who knows you and Eliana sees us together with Ric?"

"If they do, it won't matter because the person who needed to know the truth was Eliana. By now she's talked to her parents on the phone. If I'm not mistaken, they've already laid out a strategy to deal with the gossip in case Eliana says she wants to end the engagement. Until then, that leaves you and me free to play. When the time comes for us to leave Cyprus, you'll have seen many of my favorite haunts."

Warning bells were going off. "You said you were here to work. If I go home, it will give you the time you need."

His body stiffened. "If you can give me one good reason why…" His voice snaked through to her insides.

"Even if Eliana has set up the rules for this intolerable situation, it's not right for us to be together like this while you're still engaged."

He moved closer to her. "I think the real reason goes deeper than that. You're afraid to be alone with me."

She clutched the baby tighter. "My greatest fear is that your fiancée will always consider me an immoral woman. I felt it without her having to say it. If she's willing to work out visitation so your marriage can go through, I don't want her to hate me forever. Otherwise it could reflect on little Ric.

"To be honest, it hurts me that she doesn't know the real me. For that matter, neither do you. These last few days haven't been an example of real life, Ric. We're still strangers with our own individual lives to lead once I'm gone."

The silence between them was tangible. Finally he spoke. "Then let me get to know my son and his mother better while we have this rare free time together. Since we'll be sharing him for the rest of our lives, why not start this minute?

"You felt strongly enough about Ric's Italian ties to come to Genoa in search of them. Let's not waste your efforts this trip. It's a fact you're here with our son. Until you have to go back, we'll enjoy him. I swear I won't do anything you don't want me to."

If there was one thing she knew about Ric, it was that he'd stand by his word.

"We'll fill our days with fun and laughter. It's been ages for me, and I daresay for you since that's happened."

There was a nuance in his voice. A longing for something he wanted, needed to trust. Her heart ached for him. Between that and his promise to be circumspect around her, his logic had once more defeated her.

She kissed the baby's soft cheek to hide her emotions. "I'll need to let my sister know I won't be coming home quite yet."

A glint of satisfaction lit his eyes for a moment. "There's a seaside restaurant further along the coast with the most luscious purple grapes hanging from the ceiling. You won't be able to resist them. The food just keeps coming. Taramasalata, tahini, kebabs, dolmades, eggs, feta cheese and homemade bread and beer. You'll love it. So will our *piccolo*."

Again the years seemed to have fallen off him. Despite her effort not to feel anything, his excitement was contagious, infecting her. He was right about one thing. For the rest of their lives they'd be parenting Ric. A few more days together while they got to know each other better would pave the way for harmony in the future.

Sami had to be honest and admit she wanted this, too. Knowing what made Ric tick would give her more insight into him when their son was older and wanted to talk about him during times of separation.

She'd had hundreds of talks with her grandparents about the mother and father she never knew. Without their input, her life wouldn't have been as rich. For her baby's sake, she would stop worrying about Eliana for the time being and amass as many memories as possible with his father for the time they had left.

CHAPTER SEVEN

SAMI had done some snorkeling in Southern California, but nothing as exciting as this trip to the sea caves near Cape Gata. Taking advantage of the warm weather, they'd gone snorkeling to different spots over the last two days. In that time she'd become addicted. With Mara and Daimon along, they could all take turns spelling each other off to swim and watch the baby.

Today, after climbing some cliffs, Sami followed Ric around in the crystal-clear waters while he identified new varieties of fish for her. He'd spent a lot of years in these waters and had obtained his SCUBA certification in his teens. This afternoon had been their coolest day; the temperature had only climbed to sixty-seven degrees. It was warm enough to enjoy being in the boat, but her wetsuit felt good once she'd entered the water with her goggles and fins.

Every time they returned to the cruiser for a snack and a drink, Ric asked her if she'd had enough, but she shook her head and rolled over the side to hunt for new species. He stayed right with her. This round he pointed out mullet and a school of colorful perch. What a delight!

But the next time she lifted her head out of the water, she was surprised to see the sun much lower in the sky. Feeling herself getting tired, she made a signal to Ric that she was ready to get back.

Sami hadn't gone far when an ugly-looking brown fish she hadn't seen before swam directly for her. Before she could think, Ric grabbed her hips and pulled her out of its path. When they reached the ladder on the back of the boat, she pulled off her head gear. "What happened out there?"

Ric removed his gear and tossed both apparatuses in the boat. "You barely escaped the sting from the front fin of a weever fish. Are you all right?"

"I'm fine."

For the last while they'd had such a wonderful time swimming in different waters, she'd forgotten he could look that forbidding. Their bodies brushed against each other from the wake of some other boats passing in the distance.

"I've been stung by one before, so it's obviously not fatal, but its poison is stronger than a wasp sting. They sink in the sand to hide. He came in front of you so fast, I almost didn't get you out of the way in time."

Because of his protective instinct, his dark eyes continued to peruse her features, as if he were still doubting her. By now she was feeling fragile, but it was his nearness that had brought on a need for more oxygen.

"Thank you for saving me," she whispered. With their mouths so close, she ached to her bones to taste him. From sunup to sundown she'd had the time of her life playing with him. There was no one more intelligent or exciting.

But so much togetherness had resulted in her desire for him growing out of control. If she gave in to the temptation to press her lips to his right now, then she was worse than a fool. Calling on the little self-control she had left, she turned back to the ladder.

As she hoisted herself into the boat, she wasn't able to escape the touch of his hands on her hips. He might be trying to help her, but they clung to her as if he were having difficulty letting her go. Weakness attacked her body, making it almost impossible to function.

Thankfully Mara and Daimon were there to greet them and provide towels. Otherwise she would have proven Ric right and thrown herself in his arms because she could no longer resist him.

Without looking at him, she dashed down to the galley to remove her wetsuit. After a shower, she changed into the sweats and T-shirt she'd bought in Paphos the other day. Once dressed, she hurried back up to lavish her emotions on the baby, but Ric was holding him.

As she came forward, he gave his son's dear little head a loving kiss before handing him over. The baby immediately snuggled into her neck. "Our son has missed you," Ric observed. "There's nothing like a mother's love."

"I noticed him clinging to you before I came along. He knows his *papa* now."

Her comment produced a light in his eyes. "I think you're right." On that note he helped them into their life jackets and took his time buckling her up. His gaze rested on her. The look of longing in his eyes sent warmth spiraling through her bloodstream. Her desire for him was so palpable, he couldn't help but notice. Yet he still kept his promise not to do anything she didn't want him to do. *That was the problem*.

The other two stayed in the rear of the boat, leaving Ric to take the wheel. He finally started the engine for the trip back. En route he surprised her by pulling into a marina where there was a wonderful seafood taverna. The place featured dancing and bouzouki music. When he asked her to dance, she declined. No more touching.

Ric didn't seem to mind she'd turned him down. He ate up the attention their little boy drew from waiters and patrons alike. Everyone raved over the beautiful baby. Daimon and Ric took pictures. At the rate he'd been snapping photos on their outings, he'd fill that second scrapbook in no time.

After experiencing another halcyon day, they cruised home through the calm blue water. Except for certain breathless moments she was never prepared for, Sami discovered she was comfortable with Ric. Whether they built sand castles on an isolated beach with their son, or walked along in companionable silence, she relished every second with him.

On the ride home, she stayed up in front of the boat with him to shield the baby from the wind, glad for the obvious excuse because she didn't like to be apart from him. Last night had been the worst. After they'd bathed the baby together and put him down after his bottle, Ric got out some maps and talked about their plans for today before he'd disappeared from her room. She hadn't wanted him to go. She'd almost begged him to stay. That was forbidden.

Sami decided he'd left the villa to conduct the vital business he'd mentioned. It had to be then, or early in the morning. She didn't know and didn't dare ask. One thing she was certain of: he continued to see to the baby around four every morning. Mara told her he was always up before she could take a turn. That brought a secret smile to Sami's lips.

Tonight as they neared the point, she verged on panic because it dawned on her they only had two more days left until he had to return to Genoa. So far Ric had honored his promise to keep things under control by including Mara and Daimon in their activities.

Perversely she hoped he would ask her to stay up with him for a little while tonight after everyone else had gone to bed, if only to talk. Even though she knew it wouldn't be a good idea, the realization that there'd never be nights like this again once she went back to Reno tore her apart.

Within minutes he drove the boat to the dock. Before long they entered the villa. Ric carried the baby while Sami followed him with the carrycot and diaper bag. As they walked down the hall past the living room to the stairs, an unfamiliar female voice called to him.

Out of the corner of her eye, Sami watched a stunning visitor with stylish black hair hurry toward him dressed in elegant eggshell pleated pants and a peacock-blue sweater. She resembled Ric. If it weren't for the baby, Sami was convinced his sister would have thrown her arms around his neck. A stream of Italian escaped her lips. She sounded distressed.

"Claudia?" Ric said in a low voice. "Speak English, *per favore*. If I'd known you were coming, I would have met your plane. Is Marco with you?"

"No."

Ric's eyes glittered with emotion, enough to convince Sami something was wrong. "Meet my house guest Christine Argyle from Reno, Nevada."

The introduction proved to Sami he hadn't told anyone about her. Otherwise he would have added something like "You know—the woman I was entombed with in that avalanche."

"How do you do," Claudia responded. Though polite, she was clearly impatient to talk to him alone.

"Sami? This is my only sister, Claudia Rossi. She and her husband, Marco, live near the family palazzo in Genoa."

"It's very nice to meet you, Claudia. We've just returned from snorkeling and are a mess and exhausted. Since you and your brother will want to talk alone, I'll get the baby's bath started."

"I'd rather you stayed." Ric spoke before she could take the baby from him. He turned to his sister. "What emergency has brought you down here?"

"That's what I came to find out."

Ric's brows formed a black line. "Are Vito and Donata having problems again? I'd hoped they were doing better since he's taken over the operations of the company."

Claudia shook her head. "That's not what this is about. Yesterday Eliana called and asked me to go Christmas shopping with her."

His lips formed a thin line. "So this has to do with my fiancée."

"Yes. We had dinner afterward and I asked her how the wedding plans were coming. She told me you would know the answer better than she did. Then she got up from the table and said she had to go home. She walked off without her packages."

"Eliana should never have involved you."

Claudia's gaze flicked to Sami, then back to him. "I didn't know what to do. I've tried to reach you, but you've turned off your phone. I told Marco this was serious and he agreed I should fly down here and find out what's going on."

Ric wasn't at all surprised Eliana had engineered Claudia's visit. She knew how far to go to create an emergency without giving away her secret.

Eliana had been waiting for him to break the silence and tell her he was giving up his son for her and he'd had the title reinstated. But the wait had gone on too long, so she'd resorted to other tactics. By involving his sister when Eliana had promised to keep quiet until Christmas Eve, she'd made a fatal mistake.

Trust was everything to Ric. Without it a marriage could survive, but for all the wrong reasons.

"Let's sit down, shall we?"

When they were seated around the fireplace he said, "Sami and I have a story to tell you. It's a true story."

As the revelations about the avalanche and Sami's pregnancy unfolded, Claudia's worried expression underwent a drastic transformation. "He's really your baby?" she blurted in complete shock.

It *was* so shocking, no one would ever understand what had happened to two desperate people trying to hold on to life eleven months ago.

"*Si.* Already he's the joy of my life. Why don't you hold him, then you'll know beyond a doubt he has the Degenoli genes."

Ric walked over to his baby-hungry sister and put his son in her arms. He undid the quilt so she could see his limbs, too. The movement brought the baby awake. His eyelids with their black lashes fluttered open.

She looked down at him. "*Oh*—you little angel—"

Her cry of emotion was so heartfelt, he and Sami exchanged glances.

Claudia lifted a wet face. "I see the whole family in him. I see his mother in him, too." She smiled at Sami. "He's the most adorable baby I ever laid eyes on."

The second she spoke, little Ric burst into tears, not liking the strange face and voice. He turned, looking for his father. It caused Ric's heart to leap that his son wanted him. He had never heard him cry like that before, and he picked him back up to hold him. Once in his arms, the baby calmed right down.

"Oh, Ric." Claudia laughed through her tears and stood up so she could get another look at him. Already his sister was smitten with her new nephew. She deserved a baby of her own. If it hadn't been for the avalanche, she might not have lost hers.

But if it hadn't been for the avalanche…

"Eliana won't consider visitation."

"What?" With that one exclamation, he knew which side his sister stood on.

"Eliana asked me to give him up by signing away my parental rights. She's given me until the twenty-fourth to tell her my answer. Otherwise the marriage is off."

Claudia's eyes closed tightly for a minute. "If she said that, then she doesn't know the most important thing about you."

Ric was gratified to hear that. "There's something else, Claudia." He told her he'd had the title abolished. "You've always known I find it an archaic custom that should never have existed in the first place. Once the word is out, I'll have made a lot of enemies, but it doesn't matter."

Her eyelids flew open. "How long ago did you petition the court?"

"After Papa's funeral. Two days ago my attorney called and told me it's official. I'm no longer Count Degenoli. The title's gone forever so no one in our family's future will ever have to be hurt by it."

"Does Eliana know what you've done?" she cried.

"Yes. I told her when she came down here earlier in the week. But I've told Mario I don't want this story leaked to the press until Eliana and I have resolved things. I'm not about to embarrass her or her family."

"Of course not. You wouldn't do that." She suddenly threw her arms around him, baby and all. "I'm so glad,

Ric! When Vito hears this, I honestly believe it could make him a new man. He never felt good enough for Papa, and has always felt inferior to you.

"I think it's the real reason he's always had problems, especially since he got back from military service. He hasn't felt as though he fitted in. This will force him to reevaluate his thinking."

"It would be nice if we could be brothers again in the real sense. That's what I'm hoping for."

She hung on to his arm. "Ever since the avalanche, you've been different. What's happened to you and Sami defies description."

"Discovering I have a son has changed my entire world. I've been committed to Eliana, but without being able to have Ric in our lives, I can't marry her if she won't agree to visitation."

"Of course you can't." His sister eyed the baby. "I've learned to care for her very much and am so sorry for this terrible hurt, but if she thought I would come to her defense on this, then she doesn't know me either. I'd give anything to have a son like baby Ric, even if he weren't mine."

Bless you, Claudia.

"By forcing you to choose between her and your child when it doesn't have to be that way, she'll be making the greatest mistake of her life." Her voice shook. "I need to talk to Eliana in person and convince her of that. Maybe I can get her to put back the date of the wedding for a little while longer until she gets over the worst of the shock and can think clearly."

Ric shook his head. "It won't do any good. It's the title she wants back, but that can't happen now." If anyone could succeed, it would be Claudia. But in his gut, Ric had the premonition neither Eliana or her father would give an inch.

"Thank heaven!" She kissed his cheek. "If you and Sami will excuse me, I've got to phone Marco and tell him I'll be flying back in the morning."

"While you do that, Sami and I are going to get our son ready for bed. Tomorrow we'll all have breakfast and see you off at the airport."

His gaze fell on Sami who said goodnight to his sister, then walked out of the living room with him. After they reached the bedroom at the top of the stairs to start Ric's bath, she glanced at him. "She sounded so emotional when she held the baby. Aren't they able to have children?"

"Yes, but in the aftermath of the avalanche that killed our father, Claudia suffered a miscarriage. She'd been two months along at the time."

"Oh, no— That would have been so devastating for her."

"Our babies would only have been two months apart."

Sami made a soulful sound. "The poor darling. To see you with a baby you had no idea was alive has to be bittersweet for her. She needs to get pregnant again."

"I agree. The doctor says it would be the best thing for her, but Marco says she's been fighting it for fear of losing another one."

"Pat had a miscarriage between children. She went

through the same fear before she got pregnant again. It's a very frightening time."

Ric dripped water on the part of the baby's tummy that wasn't submerged. His little legs kicked so hard, he splashed water. He was a miracle. The idea of a permanent separation from him and the mother who had born him was anathema to Ric.

"I saw that fear with Claudia," he murmured, "but tonight that all seems far away. I'm still celebrating the birth of our son and there's no room for sadness right now." He kissed his cheeks. "You know, I think he's hungry."

"I'm sure he is since it's an hour past his usual time. I'll get a new bottle for him and you can feed him."

"After he's asleep I need to talk to you privately, away from the villa. I'll ask Claudia to listen for him. Between her and Mara, he'll be well taken care of while we take a drive to the harbor. It's one of the major attractions I think is best seen at night."

Sami felt all fluttery inside as Ric drove them along the coast road to the city's harbor.

She'd been waiting to be alone with him. Tonight he looked marvelous in a dark green crew-neck sweater and jeans. The estate car smelled of the soap he'd used in the shower. Combined with his own male scent, her seduction was complete, but he had no idea what his nearness was doing to her. Except that wasn't true. She was sure he did, but he wouldn't act on it.

She forced herself to concentrate on the sights out the

window. Tourists from all over the world—lovers, old couples, teenagers—meandered in and out of the colorful shops beautifully decorated for Christmas. The holiday excitement was contagious. Cooking aromas drifted from the restaurants lining the curving seawall. The area was made all the more romantic by the sight of Paphos Castle lit up for Christmas against a dark blue sky.

Ric pulled to a stop on a rise away from the other cars so she could get a good view. "This used to be a Byzantine fort that was rebuilt by the Lusignians, then redone by the Venetians and finally restored by the Ottomans. What you're looking at is one of two towers built in 1222. Sadly, the other was destroyed by an earthquake."

"Being on Cyprus is like living in an ancient open-air archaeological museum. I'm in awe. Thank you for bringing me here, Ric." She clasped her hands in her lap. "I'd be remiss if I didn't thank you for everything you've done for me the last few days, the excursions in the boat—I appreciate how much you've gone out of your way to make this an enchanting time."

"I've enjoyed it, too. More than you know. It's given me time to think about the future. That's what I want to talk to you about. Our lives are going to be connected from here on out. We might as well start laying the groundwork."

Suddenly her pulse sped up. She swung her blond head toward him. "How can you plan anything when you don't know if you're getting married or not?"

"The one doesn't have anything to do with the other.

No matter what happens between Eliana and me, Ric is a part of my life now. I want to talk about how you and I can share our son with the least amount of difficulty."

"There's no such animal, Ric, not when we live on separate continents."

"Then maybe we can change that."

Her heart pounded outrageously. "How?"

He stared at her over his strong arm stretched across the top of the steering wheel. "If you moved to Cyprus."

Sami's eyelids squeezed shut. "You can't be serious."

"Just hear me out. You and Ric would live at the villa. There's a department of computer engineering at the university in Limassol. It's a ten-minute helicopter ride from my house to the campus. With Mara and Daimon here to help, you could get your master's degree and be with our son the same as you would in Reno."

"I don't know Greek!"

"With your brain, you'll pick it up fast and I'll help you."

"Ric—you don't really mean what you're saying."

"Why not? If I'm married, I'll fly down from Genoa every Friday evening after work and fly back Monday morning. You'd have that time to get away, study, travel. Anything. It's a workable solution to our problem so our son sees both of us on a regular basis. We'd bring your sister and family over to visit often. Neither Claudia nor Vito's wife, Donata, would be able to stay away. Donata wants a baby. When Vito sees himself in Ric, he'll want one, too."

"And of course Eliana would be all right with that—"

She was so shaken, her voice was virtually unrecognizable.

"If we're married, then she could either come with me or stay in Genoa. The choice is hers."

"She'd never stand for it."

"Eliana would have to. It would be part of our marriage agreement."

"The idea is ludicrous."

Something flickered in the dark recesses of his eyes. "Can you think of a better one?"

Her thoughts were reeling. "I couldn't just move here—"

"Not even for Ric's sake? How much are you willing to sacrifice to give him a stable home with his own mother and father?"

"That's not fair."

He moved his arm and rested it on the back of the seat. His fingers were within inches of her hair. "I can make it fairer by providing for you and Ric so you don't have to worry about money and paying back student loans."

"You're not my husband!"

"I'm Ric's father," he shot back calmly. "My son means everything to me."

She trembled. "He's my raison d'être!"

"Precisely. That's why we need each other to make this work so everyone's happy. I want to give you and Ric everything. You went through the whole pregnancy alone and have been raising him without help. Now that you've found I'm alive, I'm prepared to do whatever it takes. It's my turn and my right as Ric's father."

"I'm overwhelmed by your generosity, but what you're asking is impossible."

"Not impossible—practical. Flying down here once a week to see Ric makes more sense than for me to fly to Reno on a weekly basis to see him. But I'll arrange it if I have to."

"You couldn't do that—" she exclaimed, alarmed for him. "Your life wouldn't be worth living. You wouldn't have a company to go back to, and your wife wouldn't be able to handle it!"

"Nevertheless it's what I'll do if you can't see yourself moving here. I'll give Vito more responsibility. Claudia's observations about him have given me food for thought."

"But Ric—"

"No buts, Sami. After being trapped together and given a second chance at life, how can we not give our son as much joy as possible? If you can't bring yourself to move, I'll buy a home on Lake Tahoe to be near you. The high elevation makes a perfect setting."

"When were you there?"

"Right before I started college, I traveled to the States with some friends. It's one of the most beautiful lakes I've ever seen. I'll buy a boat for Ric and me to enjoy. But as I said, you have a ready-made home right here on the Mediterranean. Ric will grow up being trilingual, which will be a great advantage to him."

As usual, he had a way of getting to her. She couldn't argue with his logic. He had the financial means to make anything he wanted happen, but he refused to consider the elephant in the room. "Until you know what Eliana has decided, then there's no more point to this discussion."

"I agree. I've told you what I intend to do one way or the other. You have until Christmas Eve to decide what plan sounds best to you," he said on a satisfied note.

He started the car and they headed back to the villa. In the process, he had to remove his arm which brushed her shoulder. The slightest touch sent little fingers of delight through her body. She grasped at any topic to cover her reaction. "Maybe Claudia will be able to make Eliana see reason."

In the darkness of the interior, his expression looked almost savage, sending a different shiver down her spine. "If by that time my fiancée hasn't come to terms with everything on her own, then she's not the person I thought she was."

He sounded so distant, she couldn't pick up on anything else.

"Maybe she doesn't have the capacity to love without qualification. Some people don't. But if growing up as a princess with money and power means so much to her that she can't accept your situation, then that's something else."

Sami had to give Matt credit. Even though the news about her pregnancy had been brutally painful for him, he'd still insisted he wanted to marry her and would love the baby. But that was before she'd discovered Ric was alive and wanted his son.

If she decided to marry Matt now and live in Oakland with him, Ric would buy himself a home there in order to be with the baby. There was no way out. By coming to Genoa, she'd changed destiny.

"In a few days I'll have my answer, Sami."

She bowed her head. "I'm beginning to understand why you did away with your title. More than ever I'm thankful you abolished it. I want our son to grow up having a normal life, never thinking he's better than anyone else."

He exhaled a heavy sigh. "That's the whole idea."

If Eliana didn't love Ric enough to let go of her pride and accept his child, then she didn't deserve him. Having said that to herself, Sami had to admit she'd fallen in love with him. Crazily in love so she could scarcely breathe whenever she heard his voice or saw him enter a room.

"Ric? Tell me something honestly."

"I'll do my best," he said in a slight drawl.

"Was there another woman in your past before Eliana? Someone you wanted to marry?"

His bark of laughter wounded her. "You think my heart's desire spurned me years ago, putting me off women for the rest of my life?"

Her cheeks grew warm. She shouldn't have said anything.

"Don't try to figure me out. You won't succeed. The truth is, I thought I was in love with every woman I got close to. But to my parents' regret, I could never see myself married to any of them." He shifted in the seat. "What about you? Why weren't you married long before now?"

His question brought her up short. "I never met the right one."

"The right one... I wonder if there is such a thing."

"Did your father press you to marry Eliana?"

"He had his hopes, but no." His answer was unequivocal. "I decided to marry her of my own free will, for my own reasons and no one else's."

She hadn't been expecting that revelation. It hit her with the force of the avalanche. His comment put a different slant on everything. After finally deciding to spend the rest of his life with Eliana, she had disappointed him by wanting the title and not being willing to accept his baby. The hurt had gone straight to his heart and meant he was suffering, but he'd never let it show. Sami wished she could shield him from that pain.

"Did your parents have a good marriage?" she asked quietly.

"For an arranged one, it worked remarkably well. Father had his affairs and Mother overlooked them."

That would explain his cynicism.

"I don't know about my siblings' marriages at this stage," he went on speaking. "They were both in love, but these are early days with more difficult times to come. What else would you like to know?" They'd arrived at the villa. He parked the car in the drive and shut off the engine.

"I'm sorry if I've offended you with my questions."

"Offended—" He turned to her. The moonlight pouring through the windshield reflected in his black eyes. "I find it totally refreshing. Nothing's changed since we were caught in the avalanche. I found *you* totally refreshing then, too. For the first time in my life, I was with a woman who knew nothing about me, who couldn't have identified me.

"We took each other as we found each other, Sami. No preconceptions. Whatever came out of you was genuine and honest. I believe that foundation put into motion what happened between us. After spending time with you, it's not a mystery to me any longer."

It wasn't for her either. But she feared that if she stayed in the car another minute, she'd blurt out her love for him. "We'd better go in and check on Ric, just in case he awakened and found us both gone."

"Don't leave yet," he suggested. "Mara would have called me if there was a problem. I thought with this full moon we'd take a walk on the beach. The light brings the dollar fish to the surface. You'd enjoy the sight. I brought a jacket for you."

Heaven help her but she didn't want to go in yet. At least walking would keep her body in motion. Sitting out here in the dark with him amounted to an open invitation to forget rules and beg him to kiss her. But if he did what she wanted, it would be her fault. She wished he *weren't* so honorable, but of course she didn't really mean it.

"As long we're only gone a short while."

"We'll come back whenever you say."

If there were no Eliana, he'd have a long wait.

He reached in back for the black leather bomber jacket and handed it to her. After thanking him, she got out of the car and put it on before he could come around. It was too big, the sleeves too long, but it smelled of him and she loved the feeling of being wrapped in it.

They made their way past the marina, their bodies close together, but not touching. No one else was out walking along the shore. The moonlight made a pale gold path across the water, following their progress. Lights from a cruiser far out from the coast twinkled in the darkness. Sometimes perfection was too perfect. This was one of those times, deepening her ache for Ric.

Keep moving.

"Come look over here, Sami."

She'd been so deep in her thoughts about him, she hadn't realized he'd stopped. When she turned, she saw he was hunkered down close to the water. She walked over.

"Oh—they look exactly like silver dollars!"

"These fish like to come up to the surface at night and moon-bathe."

"How adorable. They look like they don't have a worry in the world. I'd like to do that myself. Where are their babies?"

He chuckled. "I've never thought about it. In summer we'll swim here at night and find out."

He was sounding as though her move to Cyprus was already a fait accompli. "They don't sting?"

"No. Like our son, they're harmless, but not helpless. If they sense danger, they disappear like those heavenly bodies you once compared us to. Amazing how our separate orbits collided again." He stared up at her. "Only this time I can see your hair. Its glow rivals the moonlight. I'm surprised it didn't illuminate our heavenly prison. Once we'd reconciled ourselves to our fate, that time with you *was* heavenly, Sami. Wondrous."

Tears stung her eyelids. "I'll never forget it. Every time I look at Ric, I remember."

"That's why he's perfect, because it was so perfect for us. You thrilled me, Sami."

She was dying inside. "Please don't say things like that and make this harder than it already is," she begged him. "Let's go back and promise not to talk about it again."

He rose to his full height. Ric possessed a virility she had no immunity against. "I promised not to do anything you didn't want me to, but you can't make me promise *that*. You became a part of me. We became parts of each other and it produced our baby. From now on we'll be wrestling with that reality. It's pointless to pretend otherwise."

Sami bit her lip. "So you think talking about it is going to help?"

A grimace marred his hardened features. "No."

Not waiting for anything else he might have said, she started running and didn't stop until she entered the villa. No one was around as she dashed up the stairs to her bedroom and walked over to the crib. Their baby slept soundly. While she looked down at him, examining every precious part, Sami felt Ric's hands slide to her shoulders from behind. She hadn't heard him enter the room. The contact made her feel light-headed.

"I've made a decision." When he spoke, his lips brushed her temple. "We're going to fly back to Genoa with Claudia in the morning. I need to talk to Eliana in person. She should have made up her mind by now. The fact that she hasn't phoned yet seems to prove she doesn't want the marriage. I refuse to play games and wait until the twenty-fourth. Be ready by six to drive to the airport."

CHAPTER EIGHT

AFTER squeezing her shoulders gently, Ric let her go and vanished from the room. Sami stood there for a long time afterward before she started packing. Even when she'd finally put on her cotton pajamas and climbed under the covers to go to bed, she could still feel the imprint of his hands. Talking about the past reminded her how much pleasure he'd given her. If she was going to be haunted by those memories for the rest of her life, she'd go mad.

Sami didn't know when she fell asleep, but it was only ten to three when the baby's crying brought her wide-awake. She turned on the lamp and flew out of bed to pick him up. Since coming to Cyprus, this was the first time she'd gotten up with him in the night. Ric had claimed that job from the beginning.

Though she tried to settle him down, he cried harder. Afraid he was sick, she put him on her bed to change him, but saw nothing wrong. She felt his face and forehead, but he wasn't running a temperature. While she put a clean diaper on him, a disheveled Ric, wearing a brown robe, swept into the room barefooted.

"What do you think's wrong?" He sounded anxious. "Our *piccolo* has never awakened this early in the night."

"He probably had a gas pain."

The second the baby looked at his father, he cried harder than ever. On a burst of inspiration, Sami snapped up his stretchy suit and handed him to Ric. The moment he cuddled him against his shoulder and spoke Italian to him in an incredibly tender tone, the baby quieted down. Every so often a little half sob escaped, shaking his body.

She smiled. "It's obvious there's nothing wrong that his *papa* can't fix."

"Sami..."

"It's true. He's feels safe with you. Every son wants a father like you, but not all sons are that lucky." She walked over to the dresser for another bottle of formula. "Here. While you feed him, I'll go to sleep for what's left of the night."

She turned off the light and went back to bed, assuming he'd sit in the chair as he always did. Instead, he walked around the other side of the bed and lay down on top of the covers, putting the baby between them. "I think he'll be happier if he's here with both of us."

No, Ric—

"He's hungry!"

Sami could tell. The baby made noises while he was wolfing down his formula, provoking laughter from Ric that shook the bed. "After watching you eat, I've decided he must take after you."

"So you've noticed."

Heat spread through her body. She noticed every single detail about him. "It was hard not to when you ordered a third helping of those *mezes* at the seaside restaurant."

"I confess I'm a fish lover."

"They were delicious."

"If Ric grows up here, he'll become addicted. Do you have anything like them in Reno?"

"Not even remotely and you know it! It'll be hamburgers and pizza." The idea of living on Cyprus hadn't left her mind, but she could never do it. It wouldn't be fair to Eliana or their marriage.

And if he didn't marry her?

It still wouldn't be right. In everyone's eyes Sami would be a kept woman. But in Reno, she'd be the head of her own home. He'd be a father who came on visitation, like other divorced fathers. They wouldn't be sleeping together. She'd made her mind up about that, too. Sami hadn't lived her life this long to end up being a man's lover and nothing else, even if that man was the most wonderful man on earth.

She had no illusions where he was concerned. He'd told her he thought he'd loved every woman with whom he'd ever had an intimate relationship, but he'd never wanted to marry any of them. Whatever reason had caused him to propose to Eliana had its underpinnings based on other things he hadn't chosen to reveal.

Sami believed Eliana would break down and agree to anything to be married to Ric. She just needed more convincing, and was waiting for Ric to come to her. Well, her plan had succeeded because he was cutting this vacation short to be with her again. Six o'clock would be here before they knew it.

A loud burp resonated in the room. She grinned. "I heard that. Why don't you put him back down in the crib so you can get some sleep before we leave?"

"Did you hear that, *figlio mio?* Your *mamma* wants to get rid of us."

"I do," she lied.

She felt the side of the bed dip. "Then we'll let you get your beauty sleep. In case you were wondering, you don't need it."

Keep that up and I'm yours forever.

At nine the next morning, Ric's jet landed in Genoa. During the flight Sami had got better acquainted with Claudia, who was a lovely person in her own right. They talked about her miscarriage and Ric's birth. Sami felt that in other circumstances they could be close friends.

A limousine was waiting at the airport to transport them. As Sami glanced around before getting in, she noticed the hood. The special ornament was missing!

Like Pharoah, who'd had the name of Moses erased from every pillar and historical record, Ric had wiped his life clean of its former title. His bodyguards no longer called him Excellency. If all of this pleased him, he didn't mention it. Naturally his thoughts were on the meeting he was about to have with Eliana which accounted for his deep preoccupation.

"We'll take you home first, Claudia."

They passed many of the city's architectural wonders

and eventually reached Claudia's stately villa, one of the Degenoli properties. Sami could tell it was by the gold crest of the ancient seaman on the grillwork of the gate.

Claudia embraced her brother with the promise to get together later. Then she gave Sami a hug. "I can't wait for Marco to meet you and the baby."

Sami grasped her hand. "I'll call you," she whispered out of Ric's hearing. His sister pressed Sami's fingers, as if to say message received. She was a quick study and understood it wasn't an idle remark. After another kiss to little Ric's cheeks, Claudia got out of the limo and ran inside the villa.

Ric told the driver to head to the palazzo. He must have asked him to take the scenic route. They drove slowly through an area Ric pointed out the market of Saint Porphyrius. Local craftsmen displayed their Christmas products along the streets, and squares of the old town were dotted with huge nativity scenes.

Sami loved him desperately for always putting her pleasure and comfort first. She was no longer the same person who'd arrived in Italy fearing a bad reaction from Ric's father, even if she were able to find him. Since discovering Ric was alive, *she'd* come alive. Ric had become her life.

The limousine rounded a corner and climbed toward a beautiful medium-sized palace on the hill. "How beautiful!" she exclaimed to him. "What's its history?"

"Genovans call it the Palazzo Vermiglio. It was built in the seventeenth century. In English it means *vermillion,* so named because of its orangish-red exterior."

"I noticed the unique color right off. The interior must be incredible, too."

"Would you like to see it?"

"Not today, Ric. Remembering your reason for returning to Genoa, don't you know the last thing on my mind is sightseeing?"

"I'll make this the one exception." His playful tone threw her. He could be a tease. She'd seen evidence of it before, but this time she wasn't amused.

"Ric—I'm serious."

"So am I."

The limousine passed through a gate and wound around to the side. When it stopped, several of Ric's bodyguards opened the doors. He got out to help her with the baby.

"We'll go to your room first," he said in an aside before he spoke Italian with the others.

Your room?

Sami moaned. She had to be all kinds of a fool not to have realized this was his home. But the grandeur of it astounded her. How many men born in such circumstances would consider doing away with their title? Seeing where he lived gave her new insight into Eliana's pain.

She looked down at the baby asleep in his carrycot. When she'd told Ric their little boy reminded him of a prince in a fairy tale, she hadn't realized she was only speaking the truth.

"If you've caught up with your thoughts, we'll go in." His low voice curled beneath her skin to resonate through her nervous system.

The men took their things so he could cup her elbow. Bemused, she walked through the doors of the side entrance with him. He introduced her to an older-looking staff member named Mario who spoke in rapid Italian to Ric calling him Excellency. Uh-oh.

Ric guided her to an ornate staircase, not giving her a chance to ask questions. They started up the white marble steps to the next floor lined with paintings and tapestries. Halfway down the hall Mario opened the double doors to a sumptuous suite.

"This is your room, Sami," Ric explained, "and next door is the nursery."

She was so staggered by the opulence, she forgot to walk, and then had to hurry to catch up with him as he strode to another set of open doors. A female staff member he introduced as Sofia was waiting for them.

A cry escaped her throat when she saw the lavish nursery. Her eyes went to the exquisite crib that must have been in their family for years. "This just couldn't be real!"

One of the only grins she'd seen come from him unexpectedly appeared, making her heart leap. "I assure you it's as real as we are. It was made for the firstborn son of the fifth Count Degenoli. Shall we see how our son likes his new room?"

Before she could respond, a disturbance on the other side of the door had her turning around to see a man who was questioning Sofia in Italian. Sami might not understand the language, but she knew an interrogation when she heard one.

"Vito?" Ric called out. "Speak English, *per favore,* and come in."

Another drop-dead-handsome Italian with black hair entered the room. He was the same height as Ric with certain Degenoli traits that were unmistakable. Sami winced when she noticed a scar on the side of his neck. It came up a little above his jawline, no doubt a burn injury from his military experience.

"Vito? I'd like you to meet Sami, born Christine Argyle from Reno, Nevada. Sami, as you know, Vito's my only brother. He and Donata live in the other wing of the palace."

His brother nodded to her, scrutinizing her from head to toe.

"Sami's the mother of my son, Ric, who so far hasn't awakened since we got off the plane."

She could tell the other man was in shock. He stared at the baby, then at Ric. "So it's true what Claudia told me on the phone last night?"

"Every last word." Ric kissed his son's little cheeks again, then picked him up from the cot and put him on his shoulder. "Come take a good look at him and there'll be no doubt."

Vito walked over to inspect the baby. Pretty soon a smile lit up his dark brown eyes. "With that shape of his hairline, he's yours all right. Donata will have a heart attack when she sees him. She's not feeling well this morning, but she'll be up later."

"Would you like to hold him?" Sami asked.

"It's permitted?" He could be a tease like Ric.

"With my blessing. You and Claudia's husband are his only Italian uncles. His American uncle is married to my only sibling, Pat."

He stared at her a moment longer, digesting her words. Then he took the baby and put him against his shoulder the way Ric had done. "What's his name?"

"Ric Argyle Degenoli."

Vito shook his head. "Who would have thought? Monsignor Tibaldi would say when God took one away in the avalanche, he provided another."

"I believe he *would* say that." Ric responded to the dark humor before his gaze slid to Sami's. "I have to say *we* were the most surprised parents on the planet."

His brother's features sobered. "There's only one person more surprised."

"You're talking about Eliana, of course."

"Who else but your fiancée?"

"I'm going over there at noon to talk to her."

His brother handed the baby back to Sami before he looked at Ric. "Answer me one more question. Is it true you got rid of the title?"

"Yes. We're all on the same playing field now. No more firstborns. After centuries, the Degenoli line is free of its nemesis." Sami heard the fierceness in his voice.

Vito must have heard it, too. He looked stunned. "When did you start proceedings?"

"Soon after Father's funeral, but I had to go through a lot of red tape to make it official."

A nerve throbbed at Vito's temple. "Does Eliana know about it?"

"Yes."

He whistled. "*Mamma* always said you played with fire."

Sami's eyes went to the scar at the side of Vito's neck. Both men had them, though Ric's had been hidden.

"She played with it herself by marrying Papa, wouldn't you agree?"

Silence filled the nursery while the two men communicated in silence. Whatever was going on between them was private. Sami and Pat had shared similar moments throughout their lives. Neither of them had to say a word to get what the other was thinking.

There was still a whole part of Ric she knew nothing about. Though it was none of her business, she wanted to know all his secrets and felt deprived.

Vito broke the silence. "I'll be seeing you later, Signorina Argyle." He touched the baby's cheek with the back of his hand before leaving the room.She went over to the crib and laid Ric down. His lids had closed again. "He looks so cute in there. I do believe he's even made your brother baby-hungry."

"For several reasons, the Degenoli family will never be the same again."

Sami heaved a sigh, dreading what was coming. "Are you going to leave now?"

"Not until you're properly settled."

"Consider it done."

"I've never known a woman so easy to please. In case you do need anything later, just use the house phone and press zero. One of the staff will help you."

"Thank you. Now please stop worrying about me. You go on and meet with your fiancée. I have a feeling it will mean everything that you decided to surprise her," Sami's voice shook.

"Not until you and I have another talk first."

She frowned. "Another talk?"

"I saw your face before Vito left. It's time you knew certain facts about my life I hadn't chosen to reveal yet, but the event facing me today has dictated the moment." She had a sudden foreboding she wasn't going to like it. "Let's go in your room so we won't disturb the baby. What I have to tell you will take a while."

Alarmed by his words, she walked out of the nursery first. Ric followed, but he left the door ajar so they could hear the baby if he cried. Whatever he had to say had made her nervous and she sought refuge in the first available upholstered chair.

He remained standing while he leveled his gaze on her. "Eliana's father is from Milan and one of the wealthiest industrialists in our country. He married a Genovan princess, which makes Eliana one, too. For years I've known of her and many other eligible prospects my parents had in mind for me one day. When I turned twenty-one I told them I wasn't the marrying type so they could stop hoping for something that wasn't going to happen.

"They despaired of me, but didn't take me seriously.

Before my mother died, she begged me to stop being foolish and marry Eliana Fortulezza who would make me a wonderful wife and a beautiful one. It surprised me she had a preference. Because she was so ill, I told her I'd think seriously about it in order to bring her peace of mind. But I had no intention of following through. After Mother's funeral, I put it out of my mind.

"Less than half a year after her death, Father and I traveled to Imst for the wedding of my cousin to an Austrian of nobility. I didn't want to go because I knew Father would harp on me about my bachelor status, but he'd had a bad case of the flu and needed help, so I accompanied him. We stayed at the hotel that brought you and me together. The wedding was held in the Maria Himmelfahrt Church."

"I remember seeing it as I was coming in on the train. You couldn't miss it."

He nodded. "Before we went back to Innsbruck for the flight home, Papa wanted to relax in town for a few more days to get back his strength. On the night before the avalanche hit, he broke down and told me he was in financial trouble. That didn't surprise me. Years earlier Vito and I had learned through our uncle in Paphos that our father was an inveterate gambler."

Sami moaned. "That must have come as a terrible shock."

"At the time, you could have no idea. Considering how much money our father had the ability to lay his hands on, it raised terror in our hearts. The family wealth earned over hundreds of years could be like a gift that kept on giving. But squandered long enough if no one stopped him, one day it would come to an end and be the downfall of the family.

"Vito and I confronted him. He laughed and told us to mind our own business. He told me I had no right to question him because I didn't hold the title yet. In the same breath he told Vito he would never have the right to question what he did because he wasn't the firstborn. I'm convinced that rebuke was the reason my brother signed up for the military.

"He was fed up with Father. Already disillusioned by Father's womanizing, Vito didn't want any part of watching our father gamble away his legacy. Unfortunately Donata thought he'd lost interest in her. Vito was so ashamed of our revered father, who had to be the laughingstock of Genoa, he couldn't talk to her about it. The silence on his end did serious damage to their marriage, yet Donata has held on. Vito's luckier than he knows."

"I'm so sorry, Ric."

He threw his head back. "This gets worse. When I asked Father just how deep his problems were, he told me Eliana's father had covered some big debts for him. The mere mention of her father hit me like a bomb blast because it meant he'd needed help from someone like her father who had the kind of money necessary.

"Father had been living in denial for years and now his problems were horrific. He didn't need to spell it out.

The implication was painfully clear. If I married Eliana, those debts would be forgotten."

Sami shot to her feet. "But that's monstrous!"

"Perhaps now you understand my aversion to the title and all it represented. Evidently my mother had known about my father's gambling problem. It suddenly made sense why on her deathbed she'd pushed me in Eliana's direction as hard as she could. She was always loyal to my father, so she wouldn't have come right out to tell me the truth."

"Oh, Ric…"

"I was sickened by his confession, disgusted. Wounded. And still he wouldn't discuss amounts of money with me. He was too cowardly. For him to force me to marry Eliana meant the stakes were astronomical. Nothing less than her father obtaining the title and possession of the existing Degenoli family assets through his daughter Eliana would satisfy the debt.

"Father must have seen the distaste in my eyes because he actually broke down and cried like a baby. I'd never seen him do that before and I realized he was a broken man cursed by two vices that got a stranglehold on him early in life. When he begged me to marry Eliana to save him, I had to get out of the room."

Sami put a hand to her mouth, too horrified to speak.

"As I opened the door to go downstairs, he screamed at me to make that promise to him. He was on his hands and knees and looked so frail he could have been a hundred years old. I finally told him that in time there would be a marriage in the future, but I would do it for the family's sake, not his. That was the last time I ever saw him alive."

What he'd told her was too awful. She loved him so much and felt so helpless in the face of what she knew. "Does Eliana know all this?"

"No. Her father never worries about stooping to criminal behavior to get his own way. He rules her life in what I consider a criminal way and has shielded her because he's been so sure of the final outcome. For a truly greedy man, money isn't enough. He wanted the title to legitimize him once and for all. I'm the target he's been after all this time, which is why he enabled Father to get in deeper and deeper till he had him completely sewn up with no squirming room."

Sami couldn't stop her shivering. "What will he do when he finds out the title's gone?"

"I have a good idea. Rest assured I'm ready for him."

Ric's life was in danger. Sami could feel it.

"But what about Eliana?" she cried.

He sucked in his breath. "Sadly she's a victim of the same system as her father, whose god is money. She's ruled by him. Since June I've done my best to be good to her in order to save my own sanity and make our forthcoming marriage work. But my father's unexpected death put certain dynamics into motion that forced me to act sooner on my promise to him. In the process I hadn't counted on seeing you again in this life."

Another tremor passed through her body. If anything happened to Ric…

"Our emotional connection created a complication that's had a ripple effect. Instead of immediately getting to know Eliana with the goal of marrying her, I spent time looking for you first. Even though Father had died, I knew at one point I had to honor my commitment. But there's another truth to all this. If it weren't for the promise I made to him, I'd still be looking for you."

Ric…

When Sami had been defending him in the hotel room before learning his identity, she'd said he was the most honorable man she'd ever known. She'd believed it at the time and believed it now to the depth of her soul.

"After you and I were buried under the snow, I was positive my father was already dead. While we waited for the end to come, I realized that promise would never be fulfilled. I prayed for Claudia and Vito who'd be at the mercy of Eliana's father once the funeral services were over. He would swoop in and take everything out from under them. It would read like a novel and make headlines felt throughout the country."

She trembled. "But you *did* live through that avalanche." Since then he'd been carrying this nightmare on his shoulders and standing on the edge of a financial precipice.

History had taught her that kingdoms had been lost or won on the promises sealed with lands and dowries. In this case his father's scandalous behavior had cost their family the Degenoli empire. It wasn't fair. It was an archaic, evil system, just as he'd said.

Her thoughts flew back to the day she'd asked him if he were rich. He'd responded with what she now knew was a riddle. The second Eliana called off the wedding, Ric's family would be ruined. Sami couldn't stand it. If she hadn't come to Italy, none of this would be happening. Ric was in real danger now.

He'd told her he had his own reasons for asking Eliana to marry him. Now that Sami understood what they were, she needed to leave the country. If Eliana's father were pushed too far, he might come after the one thing Ric valued above all else. *Their baby...*

At this point there was only one thing to do, but she needed to get rid of Ric first. "After what you've told me, I can't bear for you to be here any longer. Please don't let me keep you. You need to go to her father and work this out."

He gave an elegant shrug of his shoulders. "There might be nothing to work out now he knows there's no title involved in the transaction. We'll see."

"Ric—there has to be some way to make this right."

"That could be asking too much, Sami. You've heard of the sins of the father, and I'm my father's son with a baby and no title."

There might even be bloodshed. Was that why Ric never took a step without his bodyguards?

Tears coursed down her cheeks. "I'd give anything to help you. What are you going to do?"

He looked so grim, she thought he must be ill. "Whatever I have to." His pain-filled eyes devastated her. "What will you do while I'm gone?"

No matter his pain, he was still worried about her. *Put on a face, Sami. Don't let him know.*

"None of us got much sleep last night. I'm going to catch up on mine while the baby has a long nap. Later on I plan to phone my sister and let her know I'm installed in a real palace with the man who refused to be king."

Ric's sharp intake of breath reverberated against the walls. "I don't know when I'll be back. It'll probably be late."

"Take care," she called after him.

CHAPTER NINE

THE second he strode from her room, Sami moved over to the table and pulled out her cell phone to call her sister. Pat wouldn't appreciate being awakened at two in the morning, but this was an emergency. After three rings she picked up.

"Sami?"

"I'm sorry to do this to you, Pat, but I need a favor and don't have time to talk. It's 11:00 a.m. my time. Will you book me on a flight out of Genoa anytime this afternoon or evening my time, leaving for the States? Phone me back when you've got the reservation booked. Love you."

After hanging up, she moved over to the table to use the house phone. When a male staff member answered she said, "Could you connect me with Claudia Rossi, please."

"One moment."

In another thirty seconds Ric's sister came on the line. "Sami?"

"Hello, Claudia. I'm so glad you answered. I'd like to talk to you in person. Do you think we could get together

for lunch today? Maybe we could meet at a favorite restaurant of yours?"

"Of course. I'll come by for you at the side entrance.
Shall we say in a half hour?" Claudia knew something
was wrong and was playing right along. Sami could hug
her for it.

"That would be perfect. Thank you."

She put the phone back on the hook.

Since she was already dressed in her suit and white
blouse, all she had to do was pack the diaper bag with
some formula and diapers she'd need for the flight. She
couldn't take her luggage. That would be a dead give-
away. She needed to look like a mother going out for an
afternoon with a friend.

When it was time, she put Ric in his carrycot. Just as
she was about to walk out, her phone rang. She picked
up. "Pat?"

"It's done. Five o'clock on TransItalia to New York.
You'll connect with a Continental flight to Reno."

"Bless you. Now I've got to go."

She left the suite and walked down the magnificent
hallway with the baby. Several staff people nodded to her.
Claudia's limousine was waiting at the side entrance as
planned. Little Ric was still asleep.

As Sami climbed inside she whispered, "Can your
driver hear us?"

"Not unless I turn on the switch."

"That's good, because I need your help. We need to
devise a plan to get me to the airport without Ric's bodyguards catching on."

"You're *leaving?*"

"I have to. Do you know about your father's gambling debts?"

"A little."

"Then I need to tell you everything so you'll understand." On the drive to the villa, Sami poured it all out. It was time Ric's family knew the terrible burdens he'd been carrying and the danger he could be in. "After hearing what a ruthless man Eliana's father is, I wouldn't put it past him to target our baby as a way to make Ric conform."

"I wouldn't either," Claudia said with conviction. "You're doing the right thing and I'm going to help you. Even if Ric never speaks to me again, it will be worth it when he finds out why you left."

Sami squeezed Claudia's hand. "Ric can't stand for me to take the baby away. After the avalanche, he has this fear he might never see him again. But the situation is too volatile for me to stay in Italy any longer."

"Do you know Vito phoned me before you did? Knowing about the rescinding of the title, he's put two and two together and wants you away from the palace. We both agree you need to be gone until this thing with Eliana is resolved one way or another."

Sami heaved a relieved sigh. "Do you have any ideas how to accomplish this? My flight leaves at five o'clock."

"I've eluded my bodyguards from time to time. Leave this to me." For a moment she sounded like her brother in one of his teasing moods.

Claudia pressed the switch and said something in

Italian to the driver. Then she turned it off. "I told him to take us back to the villa where we'll have lunch and stay until five o'clock when you're due back at the palace. He'll pass that information on.

"When we get to the villa, we'll go inside and have lunch. Then we'll hide you in the back of my secretary's car. Signora Bertelli comes every weekday morning at eight and leaves by three. Her car is parked in the rear near my study. The guards won't have any idea. You can give her your instructions on the way to the airport."

Though Sami was in deep pain, she smiled at Claudia. "You're brilliant."

Ric left the Fortulezza estate for the last time. His business was finished and his agony over. Every asset including money and properties of the Degenoli fortune were now in the hands of Eliana's father.

Thanks to Ric's father, neither he nor Vito had a job, and neither he nor his siblings had a roof over their heads.

At least not in Genoa.

But he'd managed to salvage his mother's assets, enough for all of them to start a new life on Cyprus and be a real family.

He was free. Free in every sense of the word.

His heart pounded like steel striking an anvil. All he could think of was Sami and his son. He climbed in the limousine and told the driver to take him back to the palazzo. Once they arrived at the side entrance, he raced inside and took the steps two at a time to reach the second floor.

"Sami?" He knocked on her suite door. When she didn't answer, he opened it and called her name again. No answer. Her things were still around. He hurried through to the nursery. Ric wasn't in there. Maybe she'd put him in the stroller and had taken him for a walk.

He phoned Mario. "Have you seen our guests?"

"No. She and the baby left with your sister for lunch at her villa around eleven-thirty. As far as I know, they're still there."

"Thank you."

He hung up and called Claudia. All he got was her voice messaging. Frustrated, he phoned Carlo. "I understand Signorina Argyle and my son are still with my sister."

"That's right. Your sister told the driver the signorina would be leaving at five to return to the palazzo." Ric glanced at his watch. It was four-thirty. "She's not answering her phone. Do me a favor and go to the door. I need to speak to her. Tell her to call me."

"*Bene.*"

A minute later his phone rang. "Claudia? I understand Sami's still there. Will you put her on?"

"I'm afraid she's no longer here."

"Then where is she? I'm at the palazzo and there's no sign of her or Ric."

"Listen, Ric—"

He heard her hesitation. A band tightened around his lungs. Whenever Claudia started out a sentence like that, she was afraid of something. "Where is she?"

"A-at the airport," she stammered.

He knew it. "When does her plane leave?"

"Five."

"What airline?"

"TransItalia to New York. Don't be angry. She was afraid Eliana's father might come after your baby and—"

"I know exactly how Sami's mind works." He cut her off. "But I know something she doesn't and everything's going to be fine, so don't worry. I'll tell you all the details later."

He hung up and phoned Carlo. "Get out to the airport and stop the TransItalia flight that's supposed to leave at five for New York. Signorina Argyle and my son are on it."

"But how could they be?" he asked in bewilderment.

"You're dealing with my sister, who knows every trick in the book. I'm taking the helicopter and will meet you there."

On his way to the pad at the rear of the palace he phoned Mario. "Instruct the staff to gather up everything Signorina Argyle left in the suite and have it delivered to my private jet ASAP."

"This way, Signora." One of the flight attendants helped Sami to the window seat in the coach section at the rear of the plane. With so much commotion, Ric was awake. On the flight over, nothing had seemed to faze him, but he was a different child right now and growing fussier by the minute.

As soon as she was settled, she picked him up out of his carrycot and held him close while she patted his back.

"We're going home, sweetheart." She'd cried so many tears, she thought she'd be dry by now. But the baby's tears started hers up all over again.

The plane filled fast. Every seat looked taken. Pat must have pulled a few strings to get Sami on this flight. She couldn't credit that they were really leaving. She felt as if her heart was being torn out of her body.

Knowing Ric, she knew she'd see him again, of course, but he'd probably be a married man when he could find the time to fly to Reno. She had no doubts he'd work out all the complications with Eliana and her father to preserve his family's honor, but nothing between Sami and Ric would ever be the same again.

Visions of their week together played through her mind like a movie, torturing her to death. The final blow came when the Fasten Seatbelts light went on. This was it.

She had to put the baby back in his cot and fasten the straps. He didn't like it at all. She pulled a bottle out of the diaper bag. Once she was strapped in, she held it to his mouth so he'd drink, but he wasn't interested and fought her.

She gave up. Once in the air, she'd be able to hold him and get him to settle down. She let his fingers curl around hers, hoping the contact would keep him preoccupied. The male passenger in army fatigues seated next to the baby smiled at her. "Hi. I'm Gary."

A real live hero from the military. He looked so totally American with his butch cut, she couldn't help but smile back. "I'm Sami. This is my son, Ric."

"He's awfully cute."

"Thanks, but he'd be a lot cuter if he weren't so upset."

Whatever the soldier said back was lost to her because she noticed a couple of Italian men in nondescript suits who didn't look like passengers walking down the aisle toward her. They were scanning the packed plane.

As they drew closer, Sami recognized one of them and gave a little gasp of shock. *Ric's bodyguards.* Her heartbeat took off at a breathtaking pace.

The men reached her row in a hurry. "Signorina Argyle? There was an irregularity with your passport before you boarded the plane. You will have to come with us please on orders of the Chief of Police." Chief Coretti was involved?

The soldier's eyes widened before he got to his feet and stepped out in the aisle to make room. One of the bodyguards took the diaper bag while the other picked up the carrycot holding her baby.

"Good luck," the soldier said as she stepped past him.

She was in too much shock to answer him, because by now another man stood behind the security men. The glint of glittering eyes black as jet was unmistakable.

"Ric!"

He must have noticed her legs start to buckle. The next thing she knew he crushed her in his strong arms. "Hold on to me, darling. Keep holding on and never let go."

"Tell me what this means," she half moaned.

Ric buried his face in her hair. "It means I'm free to ask you to marry me. If you don't say yes this instant, you're in a lifetime and beyond of trouble."

Sami didn't even take an instant before she found his

mouth to give him her answer. After having to hold back for so long, her hunger for him had taken over.

The passengers began clapping. She heard a few wolf whistles. In the background above the din she could hear their son wailing loudly enough to wake the dead, but for once she had to attend to her own needs first.

"I love you, Enrico Alberto Degenoli the thirteenth, but you've always known that."

"Sami, Sami. *Tesora mia.* I adore you."

She heard throats being cleared.

"Excellency," one of his bodyguards whispered. "We need to exit the plane so it can take off."

Sami giggled for happiness. "I'm afraid it's harder for you to get rid of your title than you thought."

"As long as it haunts everyone else, that's all that matters. Give me your mouth one more time."

Three days later she walked down the aisle of the church in Paphos with her new husband, beaming at the small crowd of beloved faces of friends and family members on both sides who'd come to see them married. Their baby rested against Pat's shoulder. When Sami looked at her sister, they had one of those communication moments.

They were both remembering Pat's warning over the phone. *You might be walking into something you wish you could have avoided. Not all people are as nice and good as you are, Sami. I don't want to see you hurt.* Was it only ten days ago?

Pat blew her a kiss. It said, *You were right to look for*

Ric's grandfather. You were on the path to your destiny.
Sami flashed her a brilliant smile.

The doors at the back of the church opened to the sun-
light. What a glorious wedding day! She looked at the
handsome man she'd just pledged her life to. Sami was
so in love with him she couldn't contain it. "Oh, Ric—"

"I know," he said, reading her mind. "We've got to get
each other to ourselves quick."

"Just a few more pictures, then we'll kiss the baby
and go."

Everyone followed them outside. So many hugs and
kisses, but it was clear Ric had trouble letting go of their
son. Sami could be jealous, but she wasn't.

Finally they climbed in the back of the car and Vito
drove them to the harbor where the cabin cruiser was
waiting. As he helped them get on board, he hugged her,
then his brother. Sami heard him say, "I've talked it over
with Donata. She's excited to move here with everyone."

Ric gave him a bear hug back.

When they moved below to the galley, she caught his
face in her hands. "What was that all about?"

"I'll tell you later. First, I need to get you out of your
wedding dress. You looked like a golden-and-white angel
in there today, Sami." He kissed her pliant mouth. "But
will you forgive me if I confess I've been waiting to take
this off you since the second I saw you in it?"

She gave him a playful smile. "I have a confession of
my own to make. For eleven endless months I've longed
to lie in the arms of the man who held me in the avalanche. All we had was each other and very little air

to breathe. I want to re-create that time over and over again, forever."

His eyes burned like black fire, filling her with longing as he carried her to the bed. She embraced him with a love she no longer had to hide.

They lost track of time in their desire to give each other pleasure. Her unseen lover was now her husband, a man whose lovemaking brought her the most ineffable joy. Hours later they surfaced to discover it was night.

She half lay on top of him. Sami rubbed the side of his jaw with her cheek. "Hmm. I feel a little stubble. Do you know I love every single thing about you whether we're in the dark or the light?"

His deep chuckle thrilled her. "It's still not as dark in here as it was that day. I can see enough of you to want you all over again. My appetite for you is indecent."

"Then we were made for each other," she cried.

"Tell me something," he whispered, kissing a favorite spot. "Was that soldier coming on to you?"

She lifted her head. "What soldier? Oh—the one on the plane?"

"Do you know another?"

"No," She laughed because he sounded so possessive. "He thought Ric was adorable and said so."

"Then I guess I forgive him."

"Darling." She kissed him hungrily. "Now tell me about Vito's plans."

He rolled her over to look into her eyes. "With all the money assets including the palazzo and Claudia's villa turned over to Eliana's father, the debt my father accrued is paid up in full."

"I can't believe it took all that!"

"My father's vice was his own undoing, but I don't want to talk about him. The best news is, Vito has agreed to go into business with me and run a new shipping line with the assets from Mother's legacy."

She covered his face with kisses. "I know how much it means for you to be close to him."

"I believe you do. It'll be fun to see if we can build a new Degenoli empire with our own hard work, shoulder to shoulder. Both my siblings are going to buy villas here on Paphos so we can all live together."

"It's perfect, except for one thing. You haven't told me how things went with Eliana."

"That's because her father wouldn't allow me to go near her. After our business meeting concluded, he told me she was spending time at Prince Rudolfo's winter palace in Torino while she recovered."

"That's awful."

"I don't think so. She couldn't handle my having a son, and I don't blame her. Rudolfo's her type and eligible. I think they could even have a good marriage because she'll be marrying a prince. That's much better than a count."

"Ric—" She buried her face in his neck.

"But I don't want to think about any of that again. The only thing that matters is you. You came to Italy as I'd hoped you would, bringing me a Christmas gift that's brought me joy beyond measure. I think I willed you here."

Her breath caught. "I'm positive you did. I felt a force stronger than my own will. Ric and I need you desperately."

"Then prove it to me again, Sami. I couldn't live without you now."

Neither could she without him.

Neither could she.

* * * * *

THE LARKVILLE LEGACY
A secret letter…two families changed for ever

Welcome to the small town of Larkville, Texas, where the Calhoun family has been ranching for generations.

Meanwhile, in New York, the Patterson family rules America's highest echelons of society.

Both families are totally unprepared for the news that they are linked by a shocking secret.

For hidden on the Calhoun ranch is a letter that's been lying unopened and unread—until now!

Meet the two families in all eight books of this brand-new series:

Dear Reader,

There's just something about a cowboy. And there's also something about a man whose heart is so battered that he's going to protect it at all costs. He's going to say no to anything that might even imply love or romance. So when Holt Calhoun walked onto the page I knew he would be a man who knew a lot more about the words *no* and *no way* than he ever planned to know about *yes*. I just knew that he was going to be trouble.

And Kathryn is going to be the worst kind of woman for him. She's very much a *yes* kind of woman. She's a woman who takes on causes, a woman who just isn't going to take no for an answer—at least not when it applies to a cause she believes in. Her heart, now…that's another matter. She's almost as protective of her heart as Holt is of his. Maybe more. Hmm, more trouble…

Then things get worse. Kathryn has a plan—a big plan. And, circumstances being what they turn out to be, there is just no help for this city girl and her cowboy. With Kathryn's big plan in the works, she and Holt are just going to have to mix it up. It's going to get messy. Hearts might be involved. The fact that Kathryn is pregnant and Holt has a secret that makes it difficult for him even to think about babies is absolutely going to come into play.

Too bad that Holt and Kathryn seem to sizzle every time they get near each other. Because—oh, yes—there's going to be trouble. But it's going to be the fun kind of trouble.

I just couldn't wait to jump into writing this story. I hope you enjoy all the trouble, and the sizzle, and the fun.

Best wishes

Myrna Mackenzie

THE RANCHER'S
UNEXPECTED
FAMILY

BY
MYRNA MACKENZIE

MILLS
BOON

First published in Great Britain 2012
by Mills & Boon, an imprint of Harlequin (UK) Limited,
Eton House, 18-24 Paradise Road, Richmond, Surrey TW9 1SR

© Harlequin Books S.A. 2012

Special thanks and acknowledgement are given to Myrna Mackenzie for her contribution to THE LARKVILLE LEGACY series.

ISBN: 978 0 263 89485 1
ebook ISBN: 978 1 408 97158 1

23-1212

Harlequin (UK) policy is to use papers that are natural, renewable and recyclable products and made from wood grown in sustainable forests. The logging and manufacturing processes conform to the legal environmental regulations of the country of origin.

Printed and bound in Spain
by Blackprint CPI, Barcelona

Myrna Mackenzie spent her childhood being a good student, a reader and an avid daydreamer. She knew more about what she wasn't qualified to be than what she actually wanted to be (no athletic skill, so pole vaulting was out; not a glib speaker, so not likely to become a politician; poor swimmer, so the door to marine biology was closed). Fortunately daydreaming turned out to be an absolutely perfect qualification for a writer, and today Myrna feels blessed that she gets to make her living writing down her daydreams about ranchers, princesses, billionaires and ordinary people whose lives are changed by love. It is an awesome job!

When she's not writing Myrna spends her time reading, seeing the latest (or not so latest) movies, hiking, collecting recipes she seldom makes, trying to knit or crochet and writing a blog (which is so much fun!). Born in a small town in Dunklin County, Missouri, she now divides her time between two lakes in Chicago and Wisconsin. Visit her online at www.myrnamackenzie.com or write to her at PO Box 225, La Grange, IL 60525, USA.

CHAPTER ONE

KATHRYN ELLIS closed her eyes and took a deep breath. What she was about to do, seeking out Holt Calhoun when he clearly didn't want to be found…

She swallowed hard. It had been years since she'd seen him and she tried not to envision Holt with his dark good looks and those brown eyes flecked with gold that pinned a person to a wall. The fact that she had once wanted those eyes to pin her, anywhere, was beside the point. She'd been young and naive enough not to understand what she was asking for then. Now she was older, a bit battered and not nearly as naive. She'd learned that a forceful, controlling man was the worst kind of nightmare for a woman like her.

Yet she was voluntarily walking right into the lion's den.

"So walk," she whispered as she climbed from her barely-held-together car and started toward Holt's family home on the Double Bar C Ranch. During the few years she'd lived here, she had driven past the ranch and seen the big white house in the distance but she'd never been inside…or even on the grounds. She'd wanted to be invited in back when she'd been a teenager and called Larkville home. Now she didn't.

But she was going in anyway.

Her heartbeat thudding in her throat, she rang the doorbell and waited, willing herself to stay strong, stand tall, look professional.

But the baby kicked at that moment, and despite the fact that she should be used to such things by now, she splayed one hand over her abdomen and glanced down.

The door opened and she jumped. To her relief and regret, it wasn't Holt but Nancy Griffith, his housekeeper. The woman had kind eyes, but right now she looked a bit concerned.

"I'm sorry. I didn't call ahead, but—" Kathryn cleared her throat, trying not to sound nervous "—is Holt around?"

Nancy smiled at her. "I'm afraid he's not. Since he returned from, well, I guess everybody knows where he was."

I don't, Kathryn thought. Because she had been determined not to be one bit curious about Holt's personal life. *No doubt a woman had been involved,* Kathryn couldn't help thinking. Holt had always had women trailing after him.

"But he's home now, right?" she asked. "I'd heard that he'd returned."

"He's home, but he's not here. Since he came back, he's been so tied up in the office that today he declared he was getting out on the range and nothing was going to stop him."

Including me, Kathryn thought. She'd tried to call Holt several times this week, even this morning. He hadn't picked up. Nor had he replied to her requests for an appointment to see him. She was pretty sure that he knew what she wanted. Maybe he'd heard about it from the mayor. Clearly, he wasn't enthused. She'd been warned not to expect much.

She didn't expect *anything,* but she wanted—

No. Don't go there, she ordered herself. Wanting wasn't

good enough. Another lesson she'd learned too well. If something was going to happen, she had to make it happen. She couldn't rely on or trust anyone else.

"I really need to see him. If he's on the range, could you point me in his direction?" she asked.

Nancy looked stunned. "I— You've been away a long time, Kathryn. I don't know how much you knew of this place, but the Double Bar C is huge and pretty stark in places." Nancy glanced pointedly at Kathryn's car, down at her watermelon abdomen, then up at the sky. The day was sweltering, the sun relentless and blinding as a camera flash.

"I know, but I'll be fine. I'm a runner and these days I keep my phone handy," Kathryn said, ignoring her own misgivings. The ranch might have its stark areas, but the Calhouns had always run it like a well-oiled machine. Communication lines were kept open. "Or…I was a runner until recently. I'll be okay."

Nancy gave a curt nod. "Let me just call Holt." She paused. "I have to be honest. He's not going to like this."

"I know. Besides the fact that he's busy, I've already called six times. If you're going to tell him anything, tell him that I'm—that I'm not giving up. I'll do whatever it takes. Including wandering all over the ranch looking for him."

That wasn't exactly true. She was trying to keep her courage up, to appear determined. Still, she wasn't stupid, and she didn't plan to wander far from the road. But for now, let Nancy—and Holt—think she was a crazy pregnant woman if that was the only way she could get his attention. Frustration and fear were making her a bit desperate. She needed to get as much done as possible before the baby arrived.

"All right. I'll see what I can do." Nancy retreated to

the other end of the room, speaking into the phone quietly. She appeared to be holding her hand over the receiver, too, but even so, Kathryn could still hear Holt's curse when he realized what was happening.

"Just find out where he is." She gave Nancy an apologetic look. "I'll handle the rest. You shouldn't have to deal with my problems."

Instead, Nancy listened to whatever Holt was saying, then directed Kathryn to a seat in the living room. "He's coming."

And he clearly wasn't happy about the situation. Kathryn could see it in the strain in Nancy's eyes.

"Do you mind if I sit on the porch? I'd rather face him head-on. Outdoors. Just in case he throws anything at me." She smiled slightly when she said it, trying to make it sound like a joke, but it wasn't completely. She'd lived her whole life with people who were prone to sudden outbursts of anger. It was always good to have an exit plan.

Nancy gave her a stern look. "Suit yourself, but Holt would never throw anything at a woman. Especially a pregnant one."

Kathryn nodded and marched to a rocking chair on the big low porch. She could tell by Nancy's look that the woman wondered about whatever circumstances had led to Kathryn being alone and pregnant, but she wasn't sharing that with anyone. Not Nancy. Certainly not Holt.

Not that the man would ask. He didn't even want to see her. She was surprised he even remembered who she was.

Maybe he doesn't, she thought. He'd always looked right past her when she was a skinny, lovesick teenager and he was a moody, broody football player who barely said a word to anyone and never even said hello to her.

She'd daydreamed about him being like her, kindred

souls trapped in untenable circumstances with no one to confide in.

Of course, she'd been wrong. He'd simply been a guy who hadn't noticed or cared. And clearly nothing had changed with him.

A lot had changed with her. Except for the fact that she still got tense just thinking of Holt coming down the road, exiting his car and stepping onto the porch.

Which was totally nuts. She didn't have room or the inclination for a man in her world anymore. Especially not this man.

And anyway—a dust cloud in the distance heralded an oncoming vehicle—there was no time to do anything but brace herself. She and Holt were going to talk.

Finally.

Holt threw open the truck's door. He started toward her, big and imposing with a granite jaw and dark eyes that told her she'd pushed him too far.

Kathryn swallowed hard. She reminded herself that she was a full-grown woman, almost ten years older than she'd been the last time she'd seen Holt. And determined to be what she hadn't been then. Strong. Independent. Not affected even by a man as overwhelming as Holt.

"Hello, Holt," she said, rising a bit more awkwardly than she wanted to and holding out her hand in as casual a gesture as she could muster. "Thank you for stopping by." *How stupid. This was his home. And she was acting like a queen expecting him to kiss her hand.*

"Not an issue. I was headed in, anyway," he said, putting her in her place. "Besides, this won't take long."

She blinked. "How do you know that?"

"I know it, because the answer is no," he said, those dark caramel eyes smoldering. "I know why you're here. I *don't* know what the mayor said that led you to believe

that I get involved in causes, but she was wrong. I do only
one thing and that's ranch. I'm sorry you wasted your time,
but I believe it's best to be honest."

Kathryn sucked in a breath and hoped that her knees
weren't shaking. "I believe that, too. And the truth is that
I don't intend to stop being a pest. You'll have to hear
me out."

"I already know what you want. There's no point in
discussing the details."

"Whatever you've been told, it's clearly not everything.
And I intend to follow you around until you listen to the
whole story." It was all she could do to keep her voice from
wobbling. Not just because Holt was so big, with such
broad shoulders, but because he was so…male. The fact
that he was also hostile… Kathryn fought to stay calm.
To remain standing.

"Excuse me?" He frowned, those fierce dark eyes making her squirm inside. She wondered how many women
had ever told Holt Calhoun no. Probably not many.

Probably none. The man looked like the definition of
sex, all long legs, muscles and thick tousled, near-black
hair. He looked like a man who knew how to do things.
And not just ranching things. Things that involved getting naked with a woman.

Which was totally irrelevant…and terribly distracting.
"I mean it," Kathryn said. She frowned back at him, even
if she was mostly upset at herself. Her Holt-crush years
were long gone. She was going to be a mom. She needed
to get her off-track life on track and do right by her baby,
not get derailed by stupid, hormonally driven thoughts
about a man who didn't even want to talk to her and who
reminded her of the bad places she'd been, not the good
places she wanted to go.

"You plan to follow me around?" he finally said. "Lady, do you even know what you're saying?"

No. "Yes. Mayor Hollis highly recommended you."

Holt swore beneath his breath. "Johanna is sharp as they come, but she's dead wrong about this."

"I don't think so. And you can't make me leave. I'm… I'm persistent." Which was such a lie. She'd never persisted with anything. And her ex-husband had loved to taunt her with that humiliating fact. Which might, she admitted, be a big part of why she had to persist with this now.

"This is a ranch," Holt reminded her. "It's big and dirty. There are animals that can break your foot if they step the wrong way or break your body if they fall on you. You are a pregnant woman."

"Yes. I've noticed."

He gave her a you-don't-know-a-thing look. "No following."

"Just give me a few minutes."

He started to say no. She was sure of it, but she stuck out her hand and touched his arm. His blue chambray shirtsleeve was worn. His muscle was firm and warm beneath her palm. Kathryn didn't know what the heck she was doing. She felt reckless and stupid and awkward, as she always had around him, but…

"We've already wasted several minutes arguing. Wouldn't it be easier just to listen to me?"

"I have the feeling that nothing about this will be easy."

So did she. "Just a few minutes," she prompted.

"All right. Let's get this over with. Sit. Talk." He turned a chair backward, straddled it and looked at his watch. "You have ten minutes. No more."

Kathryn swallowed hard and tried to find the right words. For the first time in her life she had Holt Calhoun's attention and she couldn't afford to waste the opportunity. There was too much at stake.

Holt felt like a volcano, bubbling hot and on the verge of blowing up everything around him. What in hell had the mayor been thinking when she'd recommended that he be the one to help Kathryn Ellis? And what was this about, anyway? Some nonsense about a clinic and donors, whatever that meant.

He wanted this conversation to be over, but he'd promised her ten minutes. And just look at her. Despite being heavily pregnant, which brought back terrible memories he didn't even want to acknowledge, she was slender, bone-china fragile, and when she looked at him...

He noticed how her dark blond hair, streaked with a hundred shades of wheat, kissed her delicate jaw, how those big gray eyes looked so anxious. Despite her determined words, this woman looked as if a sharp wind could break her, both physically and emotionally. And then there was the fact that she was pregnant. That made her the last person in the world a man like him should be around. He'd seen her from a distance in town after the mayor had mentioned the situation, so he'd already decided that this wasn't happening. And not just because he didn't want to do what he'd heard she wanted him to do.

"Ms. Ellis," he began.

"I'm Kathryn. You knew me when I was a teenager."

He'd known who she was. Vaguely. A skinny, scared-looking little creature. That's all he remembered. And by calling her by her last name he'd been trying to create distance, to make a point. "Ms. Ellis," he said determinedly. "I'm afraid you've been led astray."

"Johanna said you had business and political contacts that no one else in town has. Is that true?"

"It may be. But it's irrelevant."

"I'm sure you've heard why I'm here."

He knew what he'd heard. The town already had a clinic, so…

"Why don't you just spell it out?"

"I'm trying to get a new medical clinic built in Larkville. And lure a permanent doctor here. To do that, we may need the help of influential people."

"Johanna's the mayor. She has political contacts."

"She's the mayor of a town of less than two thousand. Her influence is limited. Your family name is known by people in high places."

"I don't suck up to them. I don't ask favors. Ever." He glared at her.

"I'm not asking you to—to prostitute yourself," she said, all prim and librarian-like. Her eyelashes drifted down, just a bit before she righted them. Her slender hands were in tight fists. She was clearly nervous. Because she was determined to drag a yes from him or because he was out-and-out scaring her?

Holt wanted to let loose with a string of blue curses. He was rotten at situations like this, at dealing with women with expectations. He'd learned from his mother, his father, from his former fiancée, Lilith, that needing, caring, wanting too deeply, expecting too much, came with a hefty price tag. Emotion could cripple. He knew that. He'd paid that price before and was still paying it. So while he was used to doing all kinds of favors as the owner of the Double Bar C and he did them willingly, he kept things cut and dried, light, easy, uncomplicated by emotions. And he didn't ask for favors himself. He was pretty sure based on what he'd heard that Kathryn Ellis was asking him to break several of his unbreakable rules. *Be the giver, not the recipient. Remain in control of the situation at all times. Never let emotion enter into a deal.*

"You'll have to be more specific than that," he told her. "Just what are you asking me to do?"

"I want you to help me get the clinic off the ground. I want you to help me get funding."

"Which will most likely mean prostituting myself, as you put it."

"Not necessarily. Some people will give out of the goodness of their hearts."

"For a clinic that will only benefit one very small town."

"It's your hometown."

"It's not *their* hometown. You're talking about people who have a million life-or-death causes pounding on their doors every day."

Kathryn blinked. She bit her lip. "I suppose that's true, but...you're Holt Calhoun. You could convince them."

The way she said that made it sound as if he could do anything. And no one knew better than he did how wrong that was. Pain sliced through him like a razor. Easy. Devastating. He slapped the flat of his hand against the porch post. "Dammit. Lady, I may not know much about you, but you obviously don't know me at all."

She looked to the side as if he'd embarrassed her. Maybe he had. Tact wasn't his strong suit. And frankly, he didn't care.

"We need a doctor," she said. "I work part-time in Dr. Cooper's office. He's moving to California to be near his son, and then there'll be no one. And the clinic, if you want to call a two-room building with an examination room the size of a closet a clinic, is crumbling."

"I've heard that it's slightly outdated." But only in passing when Wes, his foreman, had gone in for some minor treatment.

"It's more than outdated. It's inadequate, and once Dr. Cooper leaves, we're never going to be able to lure another doctor here to work in such a tumbledown facility."

"I see. But Austin is only forty miles away and there are doctors there."

She crossed her arms. It made her ample breasts more noticeable, and also emphasized her heavily rounded belly. She was a pretty woman, a delicate one, and her pregnancy only seemed to emphasize that delicate beauty. He could have slapped himself for noticing any of those things. "In an emergency, forty miles might as well be four hundred," she pointed out.

"I see, Ms. Ellis. You're concerned about the trip to the hospital." He did his best not to think of another situation, another pregnant woman. Anger, dark and reckless, filled his soul.

"Stop that," she said. "Stop pretending you don't know my name. And this isn't for me. I'm due to deliver in a matter of weeks. By the time the clinic is built...*if* it's built," she emphasized, turning those big, plaintive eyes on him, "I'll be long gone."

That got his attention. "Let me get this straight. You want to build a clinic in a town you don't even intend to live in. Why?"

"I have my reasons. They don't matter. They're not the point."

And she clearly wasn't going to share them. That was okay. A man like him who never shared his innermost thoughts couldn't blame someone else for holding back. Still, now that they'd slid past the topic of her pregnancy, he could deal with reality. He wasn't the answer to anyone's prayers and he never had been. Head down, he ran the ranch and he did it well. He did what was necessary. But he never strayed beyond that. He couldn't.

"I'm sorry," he said. And a part of him meant that most sincerely. "But it's not happening. I've been away from the ranch for too long." For reasons he wasn't prepared to discuss. "And despite the fact that I have a top-notch foreman and crew, there's a truckload of work to be done. I'm not who you need, and I don't have the time, the inclination or the ability to help you."

"Not even if we're talking life or death?" she asked, emphasizing that fact again. Something in her eyes told him that he'd disappointed her. Well, nothing new there. He was an excellent rancher, but he was also a master at disappointing people who expected him to care too much.

"You've been led astray if you were told to expect this kind of help from me," he said. "I confine myself to small favors, to the doable. I'm no miracle worker."

He stared coldly into her eyes, doing his best to ignore the fear and pain there, the slide of something—a tiny foot, a hand?—across her belly or how she automatically placed her palm over that place.

Her gray eyes pleaded with him, but she said nothing. A sudden, vague memory of a young girl looking at him as if she expected him to answer all her prayers flashed across his memory and was just as quickly gone.

His phone rang, and he deliberately put it on speakerphone. Anything to fill the silence. His foreman, Wes, said, "Holt, that cow with bloat needs seeing to or we're going to lose her. The vet's in the next county and you're the best one to handle something this complicated."

"I'll be there in five." Holt clicked off. He turned to Kathryn. "I have to go," he said. Not *I'm sorry,* or *Excuse me.* The sudden defeat in her eyes made him want to say those words, but that might have given her hope for something that just wasn't going to happen. He wasn't the savior she had hoped he would be, and he wouldn't pretend otherwise.

Her shoulders slumped. She turned toward her rusting car, then turned back. "Off to work a miracle, Holt?" she asked, throwing his "I'm no miracle worker" comment back at him.

"Off to do what I know how to do," he said. "I don't promise what I can't deliver. Ever."

And miracles of any kind were well outside his realm. As he had learned only too well.

Not waiting for her to leave, he strode to his truck. As he drove away in a cloud of dust, a pair of gray, hopeful eyes taunted him.

This time he didn't hold back. He let loose with a string of blue language. Ms. Kathryn Ellis didn't know how lucky she was. Women who got involved with an unbending, emotionally stingy man like him lived to regret it. As he'd been told before.

CHAPTER TWO

OKAY, dealing with Holt wasn't going to be simple, Kathryn thought, back at home. If there was anyone else… But the mayor was adamant that he was the only one in a town this size who had the kind of influence she needed. The Double Bar C was known nationwide. The Calhouns had their fingers in many pies, and Holt was the one who oversaw all of that.

None of that would mean a thing, though, if the man didn't agree to lend a hand. What to do? What to do? And why did it matter so much?

Because she was determined to turn her life completely around and this was the first step. *I came back to my parents' empty house despite the bad memories because I had no money or work,* Kathryn reminded herself. Most of her life had been like that, running from one bad situation and one place to another. But with a baby on the way, she had to do more, to take a stand and become the kind of person a child could depend on. The next time she left somewhere she was going to do it the right way, having left something good behind her, because there was something good ahead of her.

Helping to build this clinic offered her a chance to leave this place on a positive note. On a more major note, it would allow her to use her heretofore useless degree in urban planning and beef up her skimpy résumé. Overseeing the project was the kind of thing that might put a gleam in an employer's eye and finally help her provide a secure future for her and Baby Ellis.

But there was one more big reason. Despite her intent to slip quietly in and out of Larkville, she'd found that with her parents gone, the town was rather charming. She'd made a few friends, some of them her patients. She cared about them, worried about them and understood how scared they were at the prospect of losing their medical care. How could she not try to help? Still, even the best urban planner needed good people helping her. In this case, she had to get Holt's help. How?

Butter him up, she thought. *Flatter him. Play to his weaknesses.* Everyone had weaknesses, didn't they?

Kathryn splayed her hands across her belly as if communing with her child would help her focus her thoughts. "Play to Holt Calhoun's weaknesses?" As if she knew what those were.

Well, maybe she did, a little. During the two years she'd lived here, she'd practically stalked Holt. Other than football, he'd spent most of his time on the ranch. Cows, horses, dogs would be high on his list, she assumed. She hated having to brave the ranch again, but she had no choice. Where else would he be?

"You can do this, Ellis." Her words more bravado than fact. Still, she slipped on her maternity jeans, tennis shoes and a pink top and headed to the Double Bar C. When she arrived, she made a beeline for the stables. A bold move, because she was a little afraid of large animals. She might have lived in Texas, but her parents had been former city dwellers who hadn't liked Larkville. Ranches hadn't been part of her life. Too bad. She was on a mission to rewrite the future, and it all started here. She wasn't running this time.

A snorting, snuffling sound came from her right where a white horse in the corral was tossing its head. It was a beautiful animal. A gigantic animal. And it didn't seem to be too sure about her presence.

Kathryn tried to quiet her nerves. She'd come prepared, knowing that Holt's animals would be a part of this. If she could make friends with this creature quickly, then when Holt finally showed up, he might think she was a natural cow woman, like her better, and he and she might bond over equine details. She had gone online just last night to find some interesting facts. She now knew that there were more than three hundred and fifty breeds of horses and ponies and she knew that horses could walk, trot, gallop and canter.

But none of that mattered right now. Holt's horse was looking at her as if she had horns and a red forked tail. Reaching for what she hoped would be her secret weapon, Kathryn dug into her purse and pulled a carrot from a plastic bag.

"Here, boy." She held out the carrot clutched between her thumb and forefinger. "Look what I have."

The horse lurched toward her a bit, and she jerked back, then stuck her hand out again.

"Don't. Do. That." The deep voice was unmistakable. It came from the barn behind her. "Stop moving. Right now."

Kathryn froze. Holt walked up behind her, and she felt very exposed even though she was fully dressed. Seriously, the man exuded something masculine. He got attention.

But, of course, she was supposed to be the one snagging *his* attention, not the other way around.

"He doesn't like carrots?" she asked.

"He loves carrots."

"I—I see. Or, actually, I don't." She forgot to freeze and waved her hand around as she spoke. The horse followed with his head. He moved closer. Quickly.

Kathryn jumped.

Just then Holt stepped forward, gave a command to the horse and reached out and took her hand, forcing her to drop the carrot in the dirt. She looked at it with dismay.

"Why did you do that?"

"Because I assume you'd like to keep all your fingers. Horses have sharp teeth and massive heads. Daedalus is gentle, but he doesn't know you or understand what you're doing. He wants what you have, but the way you're bobbing around, he'll have to lunge for it, and his teeth might nip you. Or that big head of his might knock you on your rear." Holt shook his head as if he'd had to explain to a child not to cross the street without looking.

"I—" Kathryn felt herself blushing. "Thank you. I didn't realize. I didn't think, I guess."

"But you lived here in horse country." His words were clipped. He looked as if he thought she was lying.

"I only lived here two years, and we didn't have horses. My father came here following a job and he...well, he liked his privacy. He didn't like me making friends, so I didn't have any reason to learn about ranch life."

"And yet here you are trying to feed my animal."

She raised her chin. "Just because I didn't have horses doesn't mean I don't want to know more about them. He's a spectacular horse. And this is a...it's a lovely ranch."

"I like it." He stared her down.

"I'd—I'd really like to know more about ranching."

"Just out of the blue like that? Planning to move to a ranch, are you?" He looked mildly amused. As if he was trying to keep from laughing.

Oh, no. Did he think she was flirting with him, pursuing him?

"No. I'm looking for a job in a city, but odds are my baby will be born here, and I want to be able to tell her a bit about her birthplace." As she said the words, Kathryn realized it was true. She *did* want her child to know something of her history. Because that kind of anchor had been missing from her own life. Her parents had moved constantly. They'd never discussed their lives before she'd been born. They'd never talked much at all without arguing or criticizing their only child for being a disappointment. Her ex-husband had continued the trend. Control by ignoring or criticizing her. Or making her feel that she was being unreasonable or demanding. It had been an effective system. Kathryn had always fallen into line. This time had to be different. She couldn't let Holt's opinion daunt her.

"So you want a history lesson and a tour. And you decided this when? This morning?"

She took a deep breath. "I—no—yes—no. I made that up about thirty seconds ago," she admitted, in part because Holt made her far too self-aware, but also because she just didn't want to get in the habit of lying. Good mothers didn't lie. And, oh, she really wanted to be a good mother.

Holt shook his head again. "If you want a history lesson or information on how a ranch runs, I'll point you in the direction of some books."

"I want more than that."

That had probably been the wrong thing to say. There was always the chance that he knew how big a crush she'd had on him when she was young. She hoped not, but the dark, fierce look in his eyes…the heat that rose within her…

Kathryn took a step backward. She caught her foot on something, a rock or… Suddenly she was slipping.

Just as suddenly, she wasn't. Holt's big hands were on her arms. He was pulling her upward, toward him. Her heart was thundering, her breath was erratic. And then she was free, standing on her own. Trying to act as if she was perfectly fine.

"I'm perfectly fine," she said.

A look of something that might have been amusement flitted across his face and then was gone. "Good. I was going to ask that in a minute." Even though he'd had no reason to ask. She hadn't even gotten near to hitting the ground. His quick reflexes and strong arms had seen to that. But his tone—was the darn man teasing her?

"I—I assumed as much," she said lamely, flustered, not happy that she was letting Holt get to her. But hadn't she always? Had she ever seriously thought they could be a couple when she was a starstruck teenager? She must have been insane. He was the worst kind of man for someone like her. Too intimidating, entirely too physical. His very presence made her feel as if her brain had gone missing. And her plan to butter him up, to humor him? The one that had seemed so right his morning?

It wasn't going to happen. He wasn't a man who craved adoration. If he had been, he would have scooped her up in high school and had all the adoration he could handle. She sighed.

"What?"

She forced herself to look straight into his eyes and not flinch. "I came here intending to schmooze you."

"I see. And how exactly were you going to do that?"

She looked at Daedalus. "Nice horse," she said weakly. "Nice hat."

He almost looked as if he wanted to smile.

Kathryn sighed again. "I'm afraid I'm not very good at schmoozing," she admitted. "I feel totally silly."

"Well, I've been told that I don't know how to accept a compliment, so…"

Yeah, it had been a bad, unworkable idea. "I should go." Kathryn realized that she was still standing far too close to Holt. His sheer size, the breadth of his shoulders, was forbidding. He was quite possibly the most masculine male she could ever remember meeting.

Not that it mattered. Even if she hadn't been extremely pregnant, she was never going to allow herself to think of a man that way again. Especially not a man like Holt. He was the type who could swallow her soul and mangle it, when she had barely escaped her mistake of a marriage with her soul intact. Still, with her retreat she felt her grand plans evaporating. Holt wasn't going to help her. She would have no project to her name, nothing to put on her résumé, probably no means of supporting herself and her child once the clinic closed. And her friends she wanted to help…that wasn't going to happen, either. She was going to fail at all of that. Just because of this stubborn man.

No, that wasn't right. It wasn't him. She was the one who had to convince him to help her. Winning others' cooperation would be a big part of her job if she ever managed to get a job in her field. This was her proving ground.

Kathryn forced herself to look straight into Holt's eyes. "Don't you care about the people of the town?"

He didn't answer that, but his brows drew together in a scowl.

"I see them," she said. "Every day. People who come to Dr. Cooper with serious, frightening problems."

As if she'd said something offensive, his expression turned colder. Without thought, she shoved her hand out and blindly touched his shoulder. Instantly, his muscles flexed beneath the pads of her fingertips. Her hand tingled, her heart took an extra beat. Kathryn jerked back as if she'd touched fire.

The look in his dark eyes was deadly. "Don't make the mistake of thinking I'm going to discuss my feelings."

No, she could see that would be a mistake. "I won't, but—"

He raised one dark, sexy brow, and Kathryn had to work to stay focused. "But what do you think will happen if people don't have a clinic or a doctor in Larkville?" she continued.

"It's not something I've spent a lot of time thinking about."

"Of course not. You're clearly an incredibly healthy man."

He blinked, as if she'd said something shocking when all she'd said—did he think she was ogling him?

Most likely. Women would. *She* had in the past, and if her circumstances and her life and her entire world hadn't turned out the way it had… No, no, no.

"I only meant that you've obviously not spent a lot of time in doctors' offices," she said a bit too quickly.

He didn't respond.

"But there are people who need regular treatments or who need help quickly. If a doctor isn't nearby, they may put off going at all. They might even die. Think about that."

He frowned at her. "I'm thinking," he said. And clearly what he was thinking wasn't anything good. Why, oh, why was Holt the man she had to work with in order to get this thing done?

Holt felt as if he'd been kicked in the gut. By something a lot bigger and more lethal than this fragile woman standing before him. Kathryn wasn't just looking for a favor. He was used to doing small favors. Like it or not, they were part of the ranch's role in the community. But Kathryn wanted more than a small favor. She wanted *him* to ask for favors, and that wasn't his style. The thought of opening himself up that way, begging, burned him like fire. What's more, for a minute he had thought she'd wanted him to discuss his feelings. And he definitely wasn't that guy. He worked, he did his duty, but discussing what he felt—or did not feel—was for other men. Actually, indulging in those deeper emotions was for other men, too.

Still, he looked down into those pretty eyes and realized he could no longer ignore her request for a favor. His father, Clay, had died of pneumonia when he'd refused to see a doctor until it was too late. And his friend and former ranch hand, the one he'd been with these past few months…what if Hank had gone to the doctor and found his cancer sooner?

Holt swore beneath his breath.

Kathryn wrapped her arms around her abdomen as if those slender arms could protect the child inside. That single movement made him remember things, feel raw inside. He didn't like that one bit.

But as if his swearing had unleashed something in her, she changed before his eyes. "Okay, I get it. You're never going to help." Her eyes flashed fire, and suddenly she didn't look so fragile anymore. She looked a bit like a miffed tigress. "I hate to say this, Holt, but sometimes I don't like men very much." With an accusing look, she swung her head and turned to go, her blond hair catching on the pale pink collar of her blouse, exposing her long, slender neck. And whether it was her tigress ways or that beautiful neck, a jolt of physical awareness shot through him.

Don't notice that, he told himself, trying to ignore

the instant heat that her innocent manner and her movement had called forth in him. *Don't think of her that way.*
Kathryn was a woman on a mission, a woman dedicated
to passionate causes, and a woman with a baby on the
way. She wasn't in the market for anything short-lived or
based on physical chemistry alone, while he wasn't open
to anything more. He didn't get involved with women
who wanted too much from him. After Lilith, he especially didn't get involved with pregnant women. The fact
that Kathryn was both passionate and pregnant made her
radioactive. A woman to steer *around,* not get close to.

And yet, here he was, thinking about the long, naked
column of her neck and trying not to think about any more
of her naked. Holt wanted to swear again. He held back.

At that moment, Blue, Holt's German shepherd mix,
wandered near. Blue was big and slobbery with a torn
ear. He looked like a dog who could eat humans just for
fun, and most people kept their distance when they first
met him.

Kathryn bent over and held her hand out to him so he
could sniff and make up his mind about her, then rubbed
him behind his ears just as if he was a cute little puppy.
Blue looked as if he was in ecstasy.

"He's a killer," Holt said, disgusted with Blue, but
mostly with himself.

"I can see that. You trained him to go for the throat?"

Holt raised one brow. "I trained him for a lot of things.
Right now he seems to have forgotten all of them. I guess
you're better at schmoozing than you thought."

She glanced up quickly and evidently noticed him staring at her. A delicious pale pink climbed her throat, making him want to groan.

Kathryn quickly looked at Blue. "No, he just likes to
be rubbed."

"Who doesn't?" Had he really said that? Oh, yeah, he had. The startled look in her eyes left no question. The woman was shocked. Just yesterday he would have been glad. But today she had made him think about things he couldn't ignore. He was going to say yes. The truth was that he couldn't have anyone else on his conscience. He already had a whole lot to answer for, things he struggled not to think about every day, and like it or not, he was going to have to get mixed up in Kathryn's passionate project and do a bunch of things he didn't like.

But two things he wouldn't do. He wouldn't expose his soul, his demons, that part of himself only he was privy to, by letting her know just how she'd talked him into this. And he wouldn't let her be in control the way it had gone down with Lilith.

Time to do a little creative backpedaling. Somehow.

"I probably shouldn't have made that last comment about Blue," he began, not very smoothly.

At his name, Blue's ears perked up a bit, but he was still looking like some lovesick fool, slobbering all over Kathryn's hand. What was it with the woman?

"So you think I should help you get this clinic built?" he asked, stalling while he tried to think of some good idea. She was looking at him as if he'd been the one who'd slipped and maybe hit his head on a rock. And why not? The woman had been all but begging him to help her for days.

"I do. I really do."

"How do I know you're not just some Goody Two-shoes who gets fired up about causes and then drops them to move on to the next one? You just said that you weren't staying."

"I'm not. I'm an urban planner. The jobs I'm looking

for will be in cities and I have a baby to support, but I assure you that I won't run out on this project."

"How do I know that you're truly dedicated?"

She raised that pretty chin. "You could try taking my word on it."

He shook his head slowly, almost sadly. "Kathryn, Kathryn, I'm a businessman. I can't just take your word on things." Even though he did that every day. But she couldn't know that. And anyway, he didn't really know her. There was a good chance she might bolt and he would be left with a mess on his hands.

"And this project will take time away from my ranching duties. I might have to set a few things aside. Like…"

He paused.

"Like…" she prompted.

"Well, like Blue here. He's used to me having time to put him through his paces. What if I don't have time for that stuff?"

She raised one pretty brow. "You're telling me that the only thing holding you back is that you're worried you won't have time to exercise Blue?"

The dog moaned when she said his name as if he'd been waiting for her to do that all his life.

Holt gave him the evil eye. Which Blue ignored.

"A man's dog is his best friend."

"You have friends, then?" she asked, still in full tigress mode.

Holt looked taken aback. "That seems like a snotty thing to say to a man when you've asked him to do you a favor."

She blushed that pretty pink that started somewhere beneath her clothing, and Holt swallowed hard. "You're right. Of course," she agreed. "What if—if you get bogged down and can't take care of Blue, I could, er, put him through his paces?"

"And you think it's my duty to the town to take care of getting this clinic?"

"Just to help. I'll be doing a lot of it, too."

"Ah."

"Are you trying to intimidate me?"

He shrugged. "Is it working?"

"No."

"Good. Because I was really just testing you to see how dedicated you are. So you'll do a lot of the work, you'll walk my dog and you'll—what?"

Kathryn raised herself up to her full height. Despite being shorter than him and very pregnant, she somehow managed to look down her nose at him. "I'll make sure that your town has a first-rate clinic, Mr. Calhoun."

He nodded, then turned to the dog. "What do you think, Blue?"

The dog turned sad eyes on Kathryn and nudged closer, obviously hoping for more of that rubbing. Then to Holt's surprise, Blue gave a little woof. That wasn't like him. He was well trained, and he didn't bark unless there was a reason to bark.

Kathryn crossed her arms. "I suppose you're going to tell me that Blue doesn't think the clinic is a good idea."

Holt wanted to smile, but he managed to refrain. Kathryn Ellis was pretty cute when she was miffed. Why had he never noticed that before?

"Not at all. Blue thinks I should sleep on what you've said and then I'll give you my reply tomorrow." If they were going to work together, he was going to call the shots. He wasn't going to risk a repeat of Lilith.

"I see."

She didn't, of course, but he had to give her credit for being a good sport about the whole thing.

"This isn't a joke," she said quietly.

She was right. "No, ma'am, it isn't. I'll be in touch. Real soon. That's a promise." And for some reason he couldn't fathom, he held out his hand. It was, possibly, the dumbest thing he'd done in a long time.

Kathryn placed her hand in his and he closed his big palm around her much smaller one. As her skin slid against his, he was more aware of her as a woman than he'd been when he was undressing other women.

Quickly, she pulled away. Good idea.

Not like this business of him and Kathryn working together, he thought after she'd gone. That had *bad idea* written all over it. Unfortunately, he was already in. Now all he had to do was tell her. For real this time. Maybe he'd be lucky and she would decide he was a crazy man and find someone else to ask her favors for her.

But he knew that that was a long shot. Kathryn was determined to get her clinic, even if she had to put up with a man like him to get it.

Still, he bet it would be a long time before she would let him shake her hand again. That was a shame. And a blessing. At least one of them was thinking straight. It sure wasn't him. Or Blue.

A short time later his phone rang. It was his sister Jess. His other sister Meg and his brother, Nate, would probably have been in on the call, too, but Meg was living in California now and Nate was still overseas with the army.

"I heard that Kathryn Ellis went out to the ranch today," Jess said. "What did she want?"

He hesitated. "Mostly I think she just wanted to pet my dog."

"I doubt that," Jess said, laughing. "Secretive as ever, Holt? Are you going to help her with that clinic?"

"Haven't decided yet."

"Did she give you her reasons for wanting to build it?"

Oh, no, he wasn't going there. Jess didn't know exactly how much their father had suffered or about the nightmares that kept him awake at night about their father's last days. She certainly didn't know the horrors that his friend Hank had faced and she knew nothing at all of what had gone on between himself and Lilith. "We discussed a few things," he said.

Jess sighed loudly. "You are the most frustrating man. Some day someone is going to get you to open up and talk."

"I talk." They saw each other frequently. But he also kept things to himself, kept things from the rest of the family, as he always had. That was his duty and right as the eldest. He knew that, just as he knew that Kathryn Ellis was not a part of his destiny.

That didn't mean he could keep her waiting forever. By tomorrow she would be pacing the floor and she wouldn't care two hoots about why he was going to help her. She'd just be glad that he was finally saying yes. He hoped.

CHAPTER THREE

THE next day after work Kathryn returned to her house with the almost-peeled-away white paint and the tilting porch where some of the boards were rotted through. Her parents hadn't been able to find a buyer for the house when they divorced so it had sat here neglected and forgotten. She supposed she should be grateful that neither of them was interested enough to object to her staying here. Otherwise, she'd be out on the streets.

She freelanced at the local newspaper and did odd jobs around the clinic a few afternoons a week, but this afternoon she had nothing. The inactivity unnerved her. Not having a full-time job or any solid plan for the future scared her to death, so after lunch she tried to dredge up a positive outlook, donning her I'm-planning-for-the-future attitude. She sent off a few résumés the way she did every day even though she hadn't gotten any nibbles.

Still, she was determined to move forward. So after lunch, she moved out onto the rickety porch swing with a pen and paper and began work on her doctor/clinic list. She tried not to think about the fact that Holt had promised her an answer today and that the answer might be no. She also tried not to remember how it had felt when he'd held her hand. Sensation had ping-ponged through her body. And it had been much hotter than anything she'd felt in high school.

"The man is impossible," she muttered. He could have given her his answer yesterday. That made her think that the answer was going to be no and he was just trying to come up with a way to let her down easy. This was almost like a repeat of high school, with her wanting something from him she couldn't have. The only difference was that this time she didn't daydream about him bending her back over the hood of his car and kissing her with wild abandon.

I don't, she insisted as a hot sizzle went through her. "Because that would be completely inappropriate for an about-to-burst pregnant woman." Not to mention stupid and totally disastrous for someone like herself. She'd learned a lot of lessons during these past few years of being married to a man who was controlling, judgmental and inclined to bursts of cruelty, but the most important went something like this. *Don't get too close to imposing, hard-to-deal-with men like Holt.* James was a larger-than-life, brooding type just like Holt. People admired him and told her that still waters ran deep, but what she'd found was that behind that tough, quiet facade was a man with no soul and a lot of pent-up anger. Faced with that kind of man again, she knew to run. A woman who had been naive enough to fall for a man who hurt her would have to be ten kinds of stupid and something not very admirable if she did it again. But she wouldn't let that happen.

Maybe she could do the entire project herself.

A groan escaped her and she closed her eyes at the impossibility of it all. These kinds of opportunities didn't drop in everyone's lap. This was her ticket to security for her unborn baby, herself and the people of the town who needed good medical care—yet she was already flailing because, once again, she couldn't win over Holt Calhoun.

The sound of boots on pavement made her open her eyes.

As if her thoughts had conjured him up, Holt was crossing the street, heading toward her house. Dressed in jeans slung low on his hips and a pristine white shirt open at the throat, he was like some bronzed cowboy god with that dark hair and chiseled jaw. Instantly and against her will, her body reacted. When his gaze met hers, Holt nodded hello. Without waiting for her to invite him onto the porch, he simply stepped up as if he was used to doing what he wanted and going where he wanted. He probably was.

She struggled to stand so that she would be at less of a disadvantage. Unfortunately, her unwieldy body defied her.

Holt held out a hand as if to stop her. "No need. I just came to tell you not—"

"Holt? Is that you?" A woman's voice had them both looking toward the road. Kathryn peered around Holt to see Mrs. Best, a retired schoolteacher and one of Dr. Cooper's regular patients staring up at Holt as if she adored him. "It *is* you." She sounded delighted. "I haven't seen you since you came home, but I've been meaning to call."

"Good morning, Mrs. Best." Holt's voice was utterly polite, but after his atypical teasing bout with Blue yesterday he had retreated back to strong, silent cowboy mode.

"How nice to see two of my former students together in one place," the woman said. "I don't often, you know. Kathryn was from my last class just before I retired. I remember you had such a crush on Holt back then. It was so cute."

Kathryn wanted to find a place to hide, a tall order at this stage of her pregnancy. She felt her face heating up. "I was very young," she said. She wanted to add the words *and stupid,* but it probably wouldn't do to antagonize Holt when he hadn't given her an answer yet. After all, her goal was to build a clinic, not marry the man. And—fingers crossed—if he said yes, maybe the time spent together would clear away the last skeletal vestiges of his attraction for her. Because she now saw that he was a lot like James. Maybe she'd even been attracted to James because of her leftover crush on Holt. Sweeping him from her soul would be freeing. "I'm not a teenager anymore," she told both Mrs. Best and Holt. "Not so naive."

"Well. Things do change, don't they?" Mrs. Best asked, apparently realizing that she'd committed a faux pas. "It's good that you've grown up. If you hadn't, becoming a mama would probably have done the trick. It's a real responsibility. As a teacher, I saw my share of bad parents. Don't you be one."

If Kathryn hadn't been so scared of messing up as a mother, she might have smiled. Mrs. Best clearly hadn't given up teaching when she retired. Fortunately, she turned away from Kathryn and focused on Holt.

"Holt, I really did need to speak to you," she said. "I hate to mention this, but my fence that Clay built got damaged in the storm and if it's not fixed just right Bitsy gets out. While you were gone, I asked that idiot handyman, Donald, to take care of it, and the next thing you know, my little dog was chasing cars in the road. I've had to keep her in the house since then. I should have known not to trust it to anyone but you." She looked up at Holt as if she expected him to not only do something about her fence, but to restore world peace.

Holt only hesitated half a second. "I'll take care of it, Mrs. Best."

With a smile, the woman turned to go. "He's so good to all of us," she told Kathryn. "Just like his father." For a second she looked as if she might pat him on the cheek. Maybe Holt thought so, too. He had a wary look in his eyes.

Kathryn managed to contain her skepticism. When Mrs. Best walked away, she raised her chin. "So you're not as immune to requests as you seem."

"Fixing a fence is easy."

Maybe. Kathryn wasn't sure it would be easy for everyone. "What did she mean when she said that you're good to everyone?"

He frowned and shook his head. "Not important. Long story."

And one he clearly wasn't going to share with her. The man was certainly living up to that cowboy reputation as a rugged man of few words. It was such a cliché that she almost wanted to laugh.

Almost. Not quite. Holt *was* rugged, and staring up at him from her perch on the chair, she had to look up the entire length of his long, lean body. Pregnant as she was, she was still a woman, and despite her mistakes as a teenager and in her marriage, apparently not immune to Holt's physical charms. She pushed herself to her feet to break the spell and change the view to something less dangerous.

"But you *do* still consider requests for help," she prodded softly. She tried not to hope too hard.

"Depends on the request. Mrs. Best's is something I can do myself. Yours involved begging my friends for favors. I don't beg well. I don't ask for things. Even so, I came to tell you yes."

She blinked. She'd been prepared to argue more, even to plead a little.

"Just like that."

"No. Not just like that. I still don't like this any better than I did, but I'll do it."

"Why?"

"Don't push it, Kathryn. If you've decided you don't need my help after all, I'm better than fine with that."

"No. I want your help. I'll take it. You can't back out now."

His eyes narrowed. "I don't back out. Ever. Once I've given my word, it's golden. Understand?" The look he gave her might have killed a man. But she'd faced worse.

"Do you look at Blue like that?"

He looked taken aback. Then he gave her that maddening, half-amused expression. "Blue and I understand each other. Without speaking."

"My apologies. I'm not a wonderful and psychic dog but a decidedly human woman."

"Yes, I noticed. That you're not psychic. And that you're a woman."

He wasn't really even looking at her body. His gaze didn't drop, but she felt as if he could see through her clothing. Kathryn felt hot. And bothered.

"Okay," she rushed on, irritated that she couldn't seem to seem her reaction to Holt. "I'll draw up some plans, all the things we need to do, and I'll give you a copy so that you know your part and I know mine."

"Why are you doing that?"

She looked up, blinking wide. "I like organization. I make lists."

"No. You're rubbing your back. You're—you're real pregnant."

"Yes. I noticed."

He didn't smile at her sarcastic tone. "You should sit down. You don't need to stand."

Now he was making her mad. "Mr. Calhoun, I don't care to go into the details, but know this. I have been ordered around all my life and I'm done with that. I've thoroughly researched pregnancy, and Dr. Cooper and I have talked. I'm a healthy woman, and I'll let you know if I need to sit down."

He raised that sexy eyebrow that had always driven her mad. "I wasn't giving you an order." His voice was low and somewhat mocking.

"I— Yes," she stammered. "I understand that. My apologies for jumping to conclusions. Of course, you were just being polite."

He didn't answer her. But she didn't sit, either, even though right now her legs were beginning to feel as if they wouldn't hold her up any longer. Her back *was* aching, and if Holt hadn't been here, she would have sat down, but the man had always made her feel weak. She had a bad feeling about what might happen if he knew that she was susceptible to him. It was very important that they keep things on a business footing during the remainder of her time in Larkville.

"Thank you for agreeing to help."

"I won't be available a lot of the time," he warned her. "Now that I'm back at the ranch, I have duties."

"We can meet there."

"I don't think we need to meet."

And she certainly didn't want to meet any more than was necessary, but…

"Humor a pregnant woman," she said, knowing that wasn't fair.

"Just send me a list. I'll do my part. And decide which parts I won't do."

With that, he walked away. For a few seconds, Kathryn wondered what she'd ever seen in him.

Other than that gorgeous body that could still make her squirm. When she woke in the middle of the night having the "Holt dream," the one where he picked her up and carried her to his bed, the one where he came to her wearing nothing but an unzipped pair of jeans, the one where she finally got the chance to plunge her fingers into all that wonderful black hair, Kathryn knew she was going to have to be incredibly careful during her time here.

A man like Holt who could make a bloated, nearly-nine-months-pregnant woman feel desire was far too hot to handle. Good thing he didn't have a romantic bone in his body.

CHAPTER FOUR

THE first place Holt went the next morning was to the hangar on the ranch where he kept his Cessna and his helicopter. There was really no reason to do this. Both were kept in pristine condition, and he wasn't going anywhere. He didn't have any cows to herd out of remote locations. And he had no emergencies to tend to.

While he'd been away, his ranch hands had done their best to keep the place going, but the Double Bar C was big. He had plenty of tasks stacked up. Good. He needed some sweaty, backbreaking ranch work to clear his head and keep away any distracting thoughts of Kathryn. What was it about the woman that made her so tough to ignore? Was it the combination of delicate woman combined with that tigress determination? Or the fact that he could tell that he intimidated her but she still held her own with him?

He swore. Did it even matter? No, it didn't. Because he didn't want it to. They were going to have the equivalent of a "ten-minute business relationship." They were fire and ice, not a good combination. Plus, ranching was all he cared about, all he knew. It was what he was good at, and he wasn't good at relationships. At all. Not that it mattered.

Don't lose track of what's important, he could hear his father saying. *You're in charge of the Double Bar C, the family's legacy. When you're away from the ranch, re-*

member who you are. You represent the biggest concern in the area, and people will look up to you. You have a responsibility to the ranch, and through the ranch a responsibility to the family and the town. The ranch is the one thing that will never fail you. Don't let anything interfere with that. Don't get sidetracked or weak and make foolish mistakes with a woman the way I once did, son. Wanting a woman too much can kill a man.

Holt knew that his father had been talking about someone other than his mother—possibly his first wife—because he saw how his mother suffered for loving his father too much. Sometimes she cried; he remembered her telling him how his father had never really loved her and now he, her son, was becoming another cold, closed-off Calhoun male. She clung to him when Clay was away. He felt sorry for her, but her unhappiness only reinforced what his father had said. Giving in to emotion was a mistake.

That wasn't happening. He'd already made some pretty foolish mistakes. He'd already run into his own weaknesses, and he wasn't doing it again. He'd lost too much. But he didn't want to think about that now.

With a growl, he headed out. Riding across the land, he breathed in the scent of new-mown hay. This was his world, where he could forget his mistakes and just be himself.

So, he buried himself in work, and for the first time in weeks he felt good. Riding up to the house at the end of the day, he knew once again that he was where he needed to be. Just him, a few men, the animals and the land. That was all he wanted.

But when he opened the door, Nancy was waiting. "Kathryn Ellis called three times. I finally gave up and gave her your email address. You might want to check it. She seemed to think there were things you needed to know."

Instantly a vision of soft gray eyes came to him. Pink lips. Luscious breasts.

He fought that image. He reminded himself of the reasons he had to ignore those eyes and lips and breasts. Instead, he marched to his computer and downloaded her message, and the list she'd sent him. And the revised, longer list she'd sent. And two more lists: her part, his part, a timeline. Everything was color-coded. There were links to articles on communities that had built clinics, links to suggested fundraisers.

When he was done reading, Holt had to blink, he'd been staring at the screen so long. He was tired. He was also glad. Kathryn might be pretty and soft, and he might feel the urge to touch her whenever she was near, but she was a finicky list maker.

Good. That made her easier to ignore.

He didn't bother answering. He had his own way of doing things, and he'd already decided what he would and wouldn't do. One thing he wasn't going to do was follow his blasted instincts and kiss Kathryn's pretty pink lips. The irritating woman was clearly emotional about all this stuff, but he wasn't an emotional man. Never had been. Never would be.

And that was final.

Kathryn paced the floor of her house. She checked her email, which meant that she checked nothing. There were no messages from employers and no response from Holt.

For an entire week, she had called. She'd sent emails. She'd mailed him a letter, just to be safe. Nancy had been unfailingly polite, but she was clearly a "Holt woman," loyal to her boss. She didn't want to discuss him, and Kathryn understood that. She wouldn't have discussed Dr. Cooper if someone had been trying to glean information on him.

But enough was enough. The clock was ticking—on two fronts. Baby Ellis had been kicking more and more. Her stomach felt like a giant exercise ball with the exercise taking place on the inside. And several of Dr. Cooper's patients were getting really worried.

"I know it's immature of me, Kathryn," Ava DuShay had said yesterday. "But sometimes when I think of Dr. Cooper leaving, I just see myself running after his car yelling, 'Please don't leave. I'm scared.' Because, you know, I'm old. I don't drive anymore. Getting to an Austin doctor would be near impossible."

Kathryn had tried to soothe Ava, but it was difficult when she understood. And it was infuriating that Holt had told her he would help and now he wasn't helping.

With a sigh of resignation, Kathryn grabbed some papers from her desk, went outside and got in her car. She didn't like getting too far from town anymore. A part of her was half-afraid that her less than dependable car would conk out on a lonely road and she would go into labor with no one around to help.

Still, with two weeks to go, she was probably safe, and she and Holt were at an impasse. He probably thought she would just disappear if he ignored her.

"Think again, ranch boy," she muttered as she drove to the Double Bar C.

She wasn't going to stop at the house, not without making a cursory attempt to find Holt on her own first. It wasn't fair to keep putting Nancy on the defensive, and besides, chances were good that if Nancy called Holt, he would simply give her some placating message and suggest Kathryn go home.

Nervous as she was, with a history of being easily cowed, Kathryn knew she was just going to have to suck it up and do the right thing. If she wanted to be a successful urban developer and a good example for her child, she needed to learn how to deal with adversity and difficult people. Holt was probably an excellent proving ground. But if she'd had a choice, she wouldn't have chosen to practice her negotiating skills on a man who had fueled her fantasies.

Driving over the road on Holt's land, Kathryn felt like a trespasser, but then she heard the sound of men shouting.

"Jackpot," she muttered. She wasn't far from the house. The building was just over the rise, but she wasn't sure her rattletrap vehicle could negotiate the uneven terrain where the voices were coming from without losing some vital parts, so she left her car and began to walk.

Soon she saw a series of pens, some sort of metal contraption and a group of men. There was a lot of swearing and good-natured joking going on. It blended with the bawling sound of animals, and as Kathryn grew closer, she saw that these were calves. Even a greenhorn like her could figure that out. She also saw that Holt, whose height and bearing made him stand out from the crowd, was in the thick of things.

Men were herding animals from one pen to another, into a narrow area of fencing and then into the metal contraption where the calf was caught in place. Then Holt took what looked like a syringe and gave the animal a shot in its shoulder, after which they let the animal out of the contraption and moved it out of the way so the next one could be brought in. It was fascinating, even though Kathryn didn't understand the whys and wherefores. What she understood was that if she waited long enough, Holt would finish and then she could swoop in on him.

She moved closer, intending to stay out of view, but the land was open here, and one of the men saw her. "Holt," he said. "Company incoming."

Holt stopped what he was doing. He glared at Kathryn. She was a good thirty yards from the chute where the men were gathered, but with those long legs of his, he crossed the distance and was standing next to her in a matter of seconds.

"I'm assuming you have a good explanation for why you're standing out in an open field under the blazing sun risking heatstroke and…"

He glanced down at her stomach.

She placed a palm over it as if her puny hand could hide her from his gaze. "I'm in no danger and neither is my baby," she said. "If I went into labor, I'm pretty sure that most of you know something about giving birth."

He looked horrified. She felt a bit horrified herself. It was totally unlike her to say something like that. "Not that I intend to give birth anytime today or anywhere near you."

"That's good to know. But you still haven't given me an explanation of why you're near a big gathering of hoofed animals."

She looked around and saw that in addition to several pickup trucks and four-wheelers, there were a few horses. And, of course, all those calves.

"They're penned."

"Not the horses. And even with the calves, escapes have happened."

"They're…they're babies," she tried to argue.

"Big enough to run you over and trample someone your size if you got in their way. Big enough to hurt you and your baby."

"You're trying to scare me."

"I'm trying to get you to go home."

"I wouldn't be here if you'd answered any of my messages."

"They didn't need answering. I saw your list of what you wanted me to do. I'm doing what I thought needed doing."

"Which isn't all of it if you're saying it that way. And you haven't even told me what you've done. How can we be partners if you don't talk to me?"

He froze. "I'm not good at partnering with people. I like to work alone."

Which was a blatant lie. She pointedly looked toward the men, the ones he'd been working with only moments ago. He shrugged, not even remotely apologetic. "They don't send me fancy color-coded lists like you do, hon."

Kathryn blushed. She was pretty sure he had used that term in order to get the city girl to march back to town in a huff. But the way he said it…she instantly imagined him in a bed half-naked, his arms around a woman after they'd just—

Oh, no, she was *not* going to think of Holt naked. "I don't mind being called 'hon,'" she said, taking his dare.

To her surprise a brief smile flitted across his face. "Good to know. What else don't you mind?"

Okay, so he was better at the sexual dare game than she was, Kathryn conceded, knowing she was blushing. "I'll tell you what I like. I like organization. And clarity. That's why I make lists."

He gave a quick nod. "Fair enough. But I'm not a list maker. I'm a doer."

"You think I'm all talk and no action?" She stared at him pointedly. He stared right back. There it was again, that sudden heat, and the sun had nothing to do with it. Her comment about action felt as if it had sexual undertones, as if she was back to the dares when she was clearly way in over her head with a man as physical as Holt. "I just want to make this happen," she said softly. "I think I've explained why."

"You're afraid that people will die." His voice was emotionless but, for half a second, she saw something in his eyes that looked like…intense pain. When she had told Johanna that Holt had agreed to help her, the mayor had seemed relieved. She'd told Kathryn that Holt had lost his father and a good friend within a short span of time and that he had been with the friend when he died.

"Maybe no one will," she said, not wanting to dredge up bad memories. "But it's still important." She told him about Ava, who couldn't drive to Austin, and he nodded. He knew Ava. No surprise. Didn't Holt know everyone?

He blew out a breath and looked to the side. "I've put a few things in motion. I'm working. Just don't push too hard, Kathryn. I'm not malleable."

If he hadn't looked so frustrated, she might have laughed. Saying Holt wasn't malleable was like saying that grass wasn't purple. "What things?" she asked.

But at that moment, there was a lot of bawling. And yelling. Holt turned around and looked. So did Kathryn. Cowboys were swinging their hats. A calf had managed to get a good kick in. "I'll be in touch," he said.

Oh, no, he was dismissing her. Obviously he had to go. But she might never get near him again. She had to do something. "Wait!"

He turned back to her. And did as she asked. He waited.

"Are you okay?" He looked down at her stomach.

"I'm up here," Kathryn said. "And I'm fine." The man seemed very uncomfortable around her stomach, but she was so much more than a pregnant woman. At least she hoped so.

The bellowing in the background had faded and things were proceeding. "What exactly are you doing here today?" she asked.

"We're vaccinating calves."

"They don't seem to like it."

"It's not their favorite thing, but then cows generally put eating at the top of their favorite things list. Everything else pales in comparison."

"They're cute," she decided, seeing one trying to lick a butterfly off its nose.

Holt looped his thumbs in his belt loops and looked down at the ground, as if praying for patience. Kathryn realized that she was doing this all wrong. She was probably alienating Holt, not winning him to her side. But the darn man made it hard to think straight when he stood there looking so, so Holt-ish.

She probably should leave. Right now. But she didn't.

CHAPTER FIVE

"Excuse me for a minute," Holt told Kathryn. He waved his hat and Dave, one of his men, came running. Holt stepped aside and talked to Dave, who nodded and walked away. In just a few minutes Dave returned with an old black canvas director's chair and a ragged umbrella he had fished out of someone's truck.

Holt unfolded the chair and held out his hand to Kathryn. "I'd feel a lot more comfortable if you sat down," he said. "And got out of the sun."

She nodded. "If it will make you feel better and loosen your tongue."

"It might." It wouldn't. He had never been much of a talker. It was one of his prime flaws, according to the women he had dated. It was definitely one of several reasons everything had gone so horribly wrong with Lilith and why he would never be a father. But he couldn't think about that.

Kathryn sat.

"Don't make the mistake of thinking these are puppies," he said. "One of these calves could drag you if you tried to lead him. Besides, they're not all that cute." Which was a lie. Some of them were very cute. But he didn't want her going all maternal on his animals and getting too close.

Every cowboy had taken a few kicks. A pregnant woman couldn't risk even one.

"*I* think they're cute," she insisted. "And that contraption…" She frowned.

"It's a squeeze chute. We herd the calves through the pens, into the working chute and into the squeeze chute where they're held immobile to keep everyone, including the calf, safe while we give the injection."

"It looks like a torture device." She really was a city girl.

He nearly smiled. "Actually, the calves find being held tight, but not too tight, comforting. If they have room to buck, they work themselves into a frenzy. The chute prevents that. And the injection is given subcutaneously, so it's not in the muscle and is as painless as possible."

"Interesting."

He gave her a look of disbelief.

"No, I mean it. This is all new to me. I'll have stories to tell my child."

Stories. It reminded him of how Lilith, another city woman who had dropped into his life and dropped out again, had told him she'd once envisioned him as a romantic cowboy—but then he had disappointed her beyond belief.

He looked down at Kathryn. In her pale blue dress, she looked ethereal. With that wheat hair and those delicate arms curved around her stomach, she had *angel* written all over her.

The warnings that had been shooting through his brain ever since he'd first heard that Kathryn wanted his help intensified. He wasn't made to commune with angels. Especially since earthbound women had told him that he was the devil.

He leaned forward, placing his palms on the slender arms of the chair, moving into her space.

"This isn't a book, Kathryn. I'm not some romantic caricature of a cowboy. This is my life. It's not yours. So what are you doing here?"

She closed her eyes. One second went by. Two. Then two more. This close to her, he was able to study her pale skin, pink lips, her long eyelashes drifting down over her cheeks. He had no business noticing any of that.

Suddenly she opened her eyes and he nearly sucked in his breath. There was too much feeling shining from the depths of those eyes. That couldn't be good.

"I'm here in Larkville because bad things happened and I ended my marriage, I had no work, I'm having a baby and I had nowhere to go. Until I find a job as an urban developer, I work three days at the clinic and moonlight at the newspaper. As for the rest, I'm not playing games, Holt. I've already explained to you how important this new clinic is. The town needs this, and I need the experience to help me win a position or else I'm going to end up destitute with no way to care for my baby. And yes, I really need your help, but I also need to be the driving force. So I made a plan and I make lists and apparently I'm making a nuisance out of myself."

Her voice was low. There was passion in her eyes. He wanted to move closer. Much closer, and that would be a mistake.

He forced himself away from her. "Why do you need to be the driving force?"

She looked up at him. "I've been controlled by people all my life. Now I'm having a baby, and I can't be that weak person who just gives in anymore. Besides, if I'm going to prove I deserve the kind of job I want, I have to be a commanding force.

"As for me being romantic, yes, I *did* have a crush on you in high school, but so did every girl. Besides, that girl I used to be is gone. I've already done the romance and marriage thing and it was a mistake I don't want to repeat. Don't worry."

"I'm not worried. But I meant what I said. I'm not good partner material. Of any kind. Not romantic. Not otherwise. I have good employees here at the ranch, but there's a hierarchy."

"There won't be a hierarchy with us."

He crossed his arms.

She placed her hands on the chair and stood. Then she crossed her arms, too. "You can't scare me, Holt. I've been scared all my life. Now I'm through with that. And if you want to get rid of me quickly, which I can see you do, then the sooner we get started, the better. I have résumés out all over the country and I'm hoping something turns up soon, but that just means I need to work more quickly on the clinic. Besides, I'm on a bit of a deadline." She smiled down at her stomach.

He blew out a breath and tried not to think about the baby. His chest went tight and he found it difficult to breathe when he thought about babies. Everything hurt, and he wanted to pound his fists into a wall when the subject came up. The fact that Kathryn was pregnant definitely made this whole situation so much worse than it would be otherwise. And the fact that she was so mouthy?

It made him want to kiss that mouth closed.

He scowled.

"Stop frowning at me and give in to the inevitable," she said. "The sooner you do what I want, the sooner I'll go away."

"You know, somehow I don't remember you being this annoying, Kathryn."

To his surprise, she laughed. "You don't remember me at all, do you?"

"A little. You had big eyes and you were very…"

"Intense. I was intense."

"Wistful. And thin. As if a puff of wind would blow you away."

"Well, that certainly won't happen now, will it?"

"You're not exactly a giant." He couldn't help smiling.

"I'm big enough." Somehow he didn't think she was talking about physical size.

"All right, I'll be more cooperative, and I won't ignore your emails and phone calls. And lists. What exactly do you want?"

"For one thing, I want your assurance that you'll be at the town meeting."

"Town meeting?"

She drew a folded-up piece of paper out of her purse. He looked at it.

"It's not my best work," she admitted, gesturing toward the paper announcing that there would be a meeting at the community center on Friday to discuss the clinic. "But when I discovered that we could use the community center Friday and that I could use the mayor's copier, I wanted to get the announcements out right away. I've placed them in every shop and public building."

A note of uncertainty slipped into her voice as he stared at the pristine and very professionally worded bit of paper.

"I'm a little nervous," she said. "When I lived here before, I didn't get to know anyone well. What if people think I'm some city girl overstepping my boundaries? A lot of the people who need the doctor the most are the older ones, but they might not show up at the meeting. For that matter, the younger ones might not, either. This isn't exactly an exciting topic. What if no one comes?"

Holt frowned. He wanted to go back to two weeks ago when he knew Kathryn only as some hazy memory. Now he knew she had a history and fears and a sense of responsibility. She was set on helping Larkville, and the Double Bar C was wedded to the town.

"They'll come," he promised. "And yes, *I'll* come."

"Thank you."

"For agreeing to go to the meeting?"

"And for the lesson on calf vaccination."

He smiled, but as he turned to go, his smile disappeared. She had one hand on her back.

"You're doing it again," he said.

She turned back. "What?"

"Your back? I know you're pregnant, but does this happen often?"

"More often lately, because, well, I'm bigger and it's a bit of a strain. It's nothing."

But after his father and Hank, he knew how nothing could turn into something. "Wes," he called, and Wes Brogan, who was the foreman of the Double Bar C, looked up. "Finish up without me, all right?"

"Not a problem, Holt."

"What do you think you're doing?" Kathryn asked as Holt took her by the elbow and started to lead her toward his truck. He tried not to notice her soft skin beneath his fingertips.

"I don't think you should drive. I especially don't think you should drive that thing you've been driving. I've seen it."

"I'm fine."

Holt counted to ten in his thoughts. "Okay, you're fine. Humor me, darlin'. I just agreed to come to your meeting and I'm all kinds of cranky about that. Those color-coded little lists of yours put me in a bad mood. I'm especially not partial to pink." He made sure his tone was teasing, but he didn't let go of her.

"Are you…are you making fun of me?" she asked as she moved with him. She looked down at where his hand was firmly around her arm. For a second she stumbled.

He caught her more firmly to him, even though that meant she was now wedged up against him and he could feel the curve of her hip. Holt wanted to groan.

Instead, he turned and grinned at her. "Make fun of you? I'd never do that, darlin'."

"Stop that."

"Stop what?" He kept moving her toward his truck.

"Stop doing that sexy cowboy thing. I told you I'm not into cowboys anymore."

"That you did, and I assured you that while you are one very attractive woman, I'm not into relationships, either. On the other hand, I would never forgive myself if I let you drive down some lonesome road in that car and you got stuck out there alone. But I could see you were going to be kind of stubborn about the car and not easy to lead at all. Kind of like those calves."

"A calf?"

Oh, good, she was mad. They were nearly to the truck.

"Only in temperament, you understand. You're a thousand times prettier than a calf. The point is that sometimes the only way to lead a calf is to distract it, even agitate it, and since the last thing you want is a cowboy, I figured that teasing you a bit might get you to be a bit more amenable to me calling the shots on this one thing."

She opened her mouth, no doubt to protest. He leaned closer. She was up against his truck now. He placed both hands on either side of her on the frame of the vehicle. "Get in the truck, Kathryn," he urged. "I know you don't want this, but I have limits. One of those limits is letting people get hurt."

And that was when his teasing ended, because he'd meant every word. "You're in pain. Your car isn't dependable. If you got hurt, it would be on my head. I'm driving you home, all right?"

She shut her mouth and nodded. Her movement sent her body brushing against his, and he wanted nothing more than to touch her. Instead, he forced himself to step away.

"Okay," she agreed quietly. "But if you ever compare me to a calf again, I will go onto the internet and tell the world that you are the least romantic cowboy ever."

Holt couldn't help himself then. He chuckled. "It's a deal, Kathryn." And that was how Holt ended up driving Kathryn all the way back to town.

"I'll have someone deliver your car to you later," he said. "After you see the doctor."

She turned toward him.

"Right," he said. "No doctor in town today. Austin it is."

She shook her head vehemently. "I don't need Austin. I've studied all the books. This pain is uncomfortable, but it's not labor. I'm just having Braxton Hicks. False labor. It will stop."

He swore, all traces of teasing gone.

She winced. "Sorry," she said when he looked at her. "Not a big fan of swearing. I've heard a lot of it."

"Want to explain that?"

"No. It's different with you. Cowboys probably swear a lot."

He smiled slightly. "They might." Then he drove on in silence. They were almost to town when he asked the question that had been bugging him.

"How do you know it's not real labor?"

"Timing. The pain's not regular enough. That's the benefit of working for a doctor. Dr. Cooper keeps up a running commentary. Knowing I'm not close to a hospital, he's made sure I know what to expect and when I need to get to the hospital. It's not yet."

"You still have two weeks?"

"That's the estimated due date."

"Estimated?"

"Could be later. It's my first."

He felt as if a huge weight had been lifted from his shoulders. "Later? Good."

He noticed that she didn't look directly at him. How certain was she about the timing of her due date? It really wasn't his business, was it? None of this was. But…

"So, you're sure you're safe?" he couldn't seem to stop himself from asking.

"You won't have to deliver my baby."

He swiveled his head to stare her down. She had the good grace to look guilty. "I'm joking, okay?"

He still felt like hell.

"Holt?"

"Okay," he agreed, but he knew he sounded grumpy.

"I'm really sorry I made light of you having to deliver my baby. I know that wouldn't top your list of things to do."

"I'm fine."

Which was a bald-faced lie. Despite his teasing her earlier, he wasn't fine. He'd spent a lifetime learning the merits of levelheadedness, measuring his words, keeping his thoughts to himself, never letting himself be ruled by emotion. His parents' situation had been a good example of why those were handy lessons and he'd learned them well. In fact, he'd pretty much had the emotion weaned out of him, and he knew he'd hurt women who had expected what he couldn't provide.

As for Lilith, she'd grown to hate him for not having been that romantic cowboy figure she'd wanted. When she'd gotten pregnant despite taking precautions, she hadn't even told him. Instead, she'd made arrangements to give their baby away. And when he found out…things had gotten so much worse. Hellish. Then, just when he'd settled back to concentrating only on the one thing that never made him feel out of step—the ranch—Kathryn had showed up. Suddenly he was back to staring all his deficiencies in the face, being on his guard. Here was another pregnant woman thinking he was more than he really was.

Thank goodness she was leaving soon. But until then, he wasn't going to have her health or the health—no, the *life*—of her baby on his conscience. And he would not apologize for being a Neanderthal about the whole thing. Kathryn had brought all this to his doorstep. That made him mad as fire.

And he still wanted to kiss her. All night long.

Holt was almost to the house, but Kathryn couldn't help noticing that he was gripping the steering wheel as if he wanted to choke it to death. She probably shouldn't have let him drive her home. She'd promised herself that she'd never let another person order her around. And it hadn't even been his manipulative, sexy teasing that had changed her mind. Frankly, his touch had made her feel embarrassingly wanton for a pregnant woman, so her instinct had been to run before she did something really dumb. But beneath the sexy cowboy act, she could see that he was really worried and that was why she'd agreed to the ride. Holt had faced serious illness and death recently, and the ghosts of those experiences must still be with him.

Besides, much as she wanted to be totally independent and do the breezy "I'm fine, the baby's fine" routine, sometimes being pregnant and alone was terrifying.

And Holt, even when he was annoyed and wishing her in Hades, made her feel as if nothing disastrous could happen when she was with him. Not that she would tell him so. After all he'd been through with his father and friend, he probably didn't need to have her and her baby's welfare on his conscience. She'd tried to relieve him of any sense of responsibility. It hadn't worked. Time to try a different tactic to distract him from her situation.

"Before you leave, I want to talk about the meeting," she began.

He stopped crushing the wheel and looked at her. "You're in pain and you want to discuss a boring meeting?"

"See? That's what I mean. If even you think it's boring and you're one of the chairmen of the clinic committee, no one's going to want to come."

He blinked and bore down on the accelerator a bit too hard. "I am not one of the chairmen of the committee. This wasn't my idea."

"But you're on board now."

He didn't answer that. "I told you they'd come."

She chose not to answer *that*. "I need to find some way to make it fun."

He rolled his eyes. "Will there be football?"

"What?"

"Hon, this is Texas. You may not have lived here long-term, you may not really be a Texas gal, but if you're talking Texas and fun, you're talking football or rodeo or sex."

Kathryn rolled her eyes. "Now you're just mocking me. You know Texas isn't that—that caricature."

"Maybe not, but now you're annoyed and not so worried. Stop trying to make it fun. You're talking about a clinic. You're not offering pony rides. Trust me, they'll come."

"But—"

"Trust me."

"I'm not real good with trust issues. I've been betrayed before."

She felt him glance her way. "You want to explain that in greater detail than you already have?" There was an edge to his voice.

She shut her mouth. She'd said too much, letting that little fact pop right out without thinking. There was too much shame attached to her marriage, and she was sorry she'd mentioned it. "Not a chance."

They drove on in silence. "We still have to discuss your part of the meeting," she finally said.

"*My* part?"

"Yes. People look up to you as a leader in the community. I have friends, but most people will listen to you more than they will a woman who isn't staying. I want you to speak at the meeting."

"I hate public speaking."

"Why am I not surprised?"

"And if you're looking for fun, putting me at a podium will pretty much defeat your purpose."

"Maybe so, but people idolize you. If I don't have fun, I at least have you. You're the star attraction."

He swore again.

"Stop that. When the baby gets here, I don't want her to pick up bad habits."

"Me and the baby aren't going to be tight. We're not going to be anything. We may never even meet."

"I know. That was a knee-jerk reaction. Because you were being difficult."

"Let's be truthful. I'm being a jackass."

"Okay, you are. But I'm not giving up. I need you to speak. Have I mentioned how important this clinic is?"

"I know. People might die if it doesn't get built."

His voice had gone low and harsh.

"Let's not dwell on that part. But please, Holt. Just earlier today, you told me you'd cooperate more and I need you to do this. If you don't give the clinic your stamp of approval, it won't happen. People know I've been after you. If you come and just glower in the background, people will think you're not on board. Then no one else will be, either. This is going to be expensive. We need everyone's cooperation and support. Tell me you'll say a few words to let them know you want this thing."

Holt let out a sigh. "I promised, so I'll do it. Now, will you stop nagging if I speak?"

"Yes."

"All right, then."

"Thank you, Holt," she said primly. "Just so you know, I may distribute a few new fliers with your name on it. Maybe that will bring people in."

"You won't need that. They'll come."

"Why are you so certain? Would you come voluntarily if I wasn't nagging you?"

"I would go to the far side of the earth before I'd show up if I didn't need to be there. But I'm not the people of Larkville. I know them. They'll come to your meeting, even without football."

"Okay."

"Good. Kathryn?"

"Yes?"

"This isn't going to end it, is it? You're going to ask me to do more, aren't you?"

"If you'd really read all my lists, you would know. And you would have already done some things."

"I did some things. I put out some calls to people who might help," he said as he parked the truck in front of her house.

"You didn't tell me that!" She turned toward him quickly, despite her bulk.

"Whoa! Don't do that. And I didn't tell you because nothing has panned out yet. I told some friends who know people who know people in the medical field. That's how it works. Eventually I'll hear something, good or bad."

"Why not go straight to the source?"

"Because that's not how it works."

"You want to explain that?"

"No."

She could see she wasn't going to get any more out of him. And he had been right. The sudden move had made her back ache more. She refused to rub it, though, not with Holt here. This conversation may have made him forget why he was driving her home, but that laser vision that probably made him a good rancher would no doubt quickly have him turning all his attention to her pain if she wasn't careful.

"Don't worry, Kathryn," he said. "We'll get this done."

And over with, she imagined him thinking. She was sure he wanted her out of his hair. Well, she would be glad when they were done, too, because that crush she'd had when she was young didn't seem to have completely faded away.

The thought startled her and she quickly reached to open her door. "Don't move," Holt said. He got out of the truck and came around to her side. When he opened the door, he didn't wait for her to get out. Instead, he reached in, slid one arm beneath her knees and lifted her out.

"Holt?"

"What?"

"What are you doing?" His arms were around her. Her heart was pounding hard.

"I'm making sure you don't nudge anything loose before I get to make a fool of myself at your meeting."

And with that he carried her into her house and laid her on her bed, her body sliding against his. Then he ordered her to stay in bed and left her staring after his departing broad back.

Kathryn was left sputtering. She hadn't even gotten a chance to remind him that she didn't allow any man to run her life anymore. She would tell him next time.

But first she had to try to forget how it had felt to have been held against Holt's chest.

CHAPTER SIX

HOLT swore at himself all the way home. Kathryn was playing serious havoc with his senses. She was going to drive him insane before they were through. These past few years he'd had to deal with losses that still haunted him. He'd learned how destructive emotions could be and he'd faced adversity, but there was something about Kathryn that made him think that she had the ability to really mess him up for good.

He had to stay detached. And when the clinic project was on its way...

Then we're done. Thank goodness. Feeling personally responsible for the health and welfare of an entire town... man, he hated that feeling.

Worrying that Kathryn might start having the right kind of pains in the wrong time and place—*that* made him totally crazy.

Probably because he didn't want her to be his business, or for there to be anything personal between them.

That didn't mean he hadn't noticed how achingly soft she'd been when he'd held her in his arms. And when she'd shifted against him, it had taken all his strength not to lower his head and devour that pretty pink mouth.

Which was just more proof that he needed to be careful. Kathryn would be bad for him, but he would be much worse for her. He needed to maintain even more control than usual.

So stick to what you're good at. Cattle. Horses. Stay away from what you're bad at. Women. Babies. Lilith had told him that someone so emotionally challenged wasn't built for fatherhood, and she'd been right.

There could be no more thinking about Kathryn's lips, he thought as a vision of Kathryn in his arms slipped into his mind, and heat seared him like a brand.

Darn the woman! Or, maybe darn himself. Still, one thing was certain. He would fulfill his promise to speak at her meeting, but his father had been the public speaker, not him. He was fine with small talk, with work talk, but he didn't make heartfelt speeches, so he would do this his way. That would probably plant a solid barrier between himself and Kathryn. Good.

Kathryn arrived at the community center a half hour early, but there were already a number of people there. Jess Jameson, Holt's sister, and her husband, Johnny, were in the front row. As was Jed Jackson, the county sheriff, and his new wife, Ellie, Holt's newly discovered half sister from New York—Clay's daughter from his first marriage. Mrs. Best had snagged an aisle seat and Sarah Anderson, who was in charge of the greatly anticipated Larkville Fall Festival, was just coming in the door. This year the festival was being held in honor of Holt's father, Clay, and was yet another reminder of how beloved the Calhouns were in the town. Ava was also there. She waved and smiled. Kathryn smiled back and noted that Dr. Cooper had, as usual, flown to California for his weekend trips to locate a house. But Dr. Cooper wasn't the only one missing.

Holt was nowhere in sight. As more minutes passed, panic began to blossom inside of her.

Still, she couldn't let anyone see that. Holt or no Holt, the show had to go on. And there was still time. She moved to the front where a podium had been set up and opened her folder of notes. Her plan was to do a general intro and then let Holt do the home-boy routine, talking to the neighbors he'd known all his life in a more personal way than she could. She'd tried to get hold of him several times this week and when that had proved impossible, she had left a phone message for him, outlining his part of the meeting. His only response had been a message he'd left on Dr. Cooper's phone after hours. His exact words were "I got the message."

That alone had been disconcerting. Hearing Holt's deep voice booming out of the speaker when she had expected her usual patients' messages telling her their reasons for needing an appointment had caught her by surprise. She had immediately remembered him carrying her to her house and dropping her on her bed. Suddenly all she could think of was Holt in her bedroom, and to her consternation, she'd blushed.

Unfortunately, she hadn't been alone. Luann Dickens had been in the office and had immediately wanted to know what messages Kathryn and Holt had been sharing. She had looked at Kathryn's stomach as if he might be the father.

"This baby is legitimate, Luann," Kathryn had wanted to say, or "I was in another state and married when this baby was conceived and I have not had nor do I intend to have sex with Holt Calhoun." But neither of those was appropriate when she was Dr. Cooper's receptionist and Luann was a patient. "The message was about the town meeting," she had stammered, then cursed herself for stammering.

"Hey, any meeting with Holt is a good meeting," Luann

had said. "Just as long as you don't get too serious. Every woman wants him. No woman ever gets him. Or if she does, she doesn't get much of him and never for long. He's not into romance." It sounded as if Luann had attempted to catch Holt herself.

"It's business," Kathryn had answered primly. But even she had to acknowledge that there was definitely something about Holt that made a woman think beyond business. She hated the fact that she, who knew better, was just as susceptible as Luann, who was always trolling for men. Maybe they weren't all that different.

But I have to be different, Kathryn had reminded herself. *I can't go around wondering what Holt looks like when he peels his shirt off at night. I have a baby to think about. It can't ever just be about me. I won't be like my parents or my ex-husband.*

Now, remembering Holt's brief message, Kathryn frowned. It was obvious that there were limits to how far she could push Holt just as there were limits to how much time she could safely spend in his presence. With her overactive hormones, she could easily forget to be smart around him.

Now she tried her best to look and *be* smart. But as she glanced through her notes, two things happened. Holt walked in the door, causing all eyes to turn. And right after that, a group of men came in, set up tables in the back of the room and began putting out huge platters of food. Barbecue, coleslaw, potato salad, more. The aroma was enticing, wonderful. Not on tonight's agenda. But the people filing in didn't look surprised. In fact, some of the women came bearing cakes and pies.

What was going on? Kathryn started toward the back where people were entering in twos and threes, but she spotted the mayor and made a beeline toward her. "Johanna, is this courtesy of the town?"

Johanna smiled and shook her head. "This is courtesy of your partner."

Partner? Was that what Holt was? "I didn't know anything about it."

Johanna shrugged. "The only reason I know is because I was in Gracie May's Diner just as they were loading up the truck."

"But..."

"Kathryn, relax. Holt has his own way of doing things. Always has. Always will. And he isn't one to talk about his plans."

Well, that was for sure. Getting the man to cooperate was like trying to drag a mule. Or at least what she imagined dragging a mule was like. The man always seemed to be in control.

And she was a woman who had promised herself she wouldn't be managed by someone like that.

Kathryn turned toward Holt. She had no idea why Gracie May's Diner was serving food at this meeting or why she hadn't been told. What she knew was that if she and Holt were partners, he should be sharing a lot more with her than he had been up to this point.

But when she started in his direction, she quickly found that she was not alone in her desire to talk with Holt. She was still six feet away from him when a man snagged Holt's attention. "Holt, you're just the man I've been dying to talk to. I need some good horse advice," the man said.

"Ed, you don't want me. You want Johnny."

"Yes, I mean to talk to Johnny, too, of course. He's the horse whisperer, but your daddy always helped me out in the past, and the way I see it, you inherited his genes and his horse sense and I wouldn't ever buy a horse without the Calhoun stamp of approval."

Kathryn watched as Holt took a pen and a scrap of paper from his pocket and scribbled something. "All right, I'll find a few spare hours to ride out with you and give you my opinion," he promised the man.

A few feet farther someone else stopped him. Kathryn could tell by the woman's intense expression that she was concerned about something and by the way she walked away looking relieved that Holt had helped her. He made another note on the paper. It quickly became apparent to Kathryn that Holt, who as the quarterback of the football team and a Calhoun had always been looked up to, had now been elevated to the level of Santa Claus. He solved problems. He was the go-to guy for the people of the town. He had been gone for a long time helping a dying man. He had agreed—reluctantly—to help *her*.

And—she looked toward the tables—he had provided food for the masses. Without talking to her. Not that it was a terrible thing, of course, but…

There was no more time to think about it. The clock chimed seven and Kathryn looked toward Holt. He glanced toward the standing-room-only crowd and gave her a look that said, what? Kathryn didn't know, but having those dark eyes turned on her made her feel far too aware that she was a woman.

Too bad. She'd already played that game when she was sixteen, and it had not turned out well. Luann Dickens was right. Holt wasn't a man a woman should be too attracted to unless she was prepared for some serious heartbreak.

Kathryn tucked that thought away. Giving him a slight nod and moving to the podium, she was very conscious of the fact that she had returned to town defeated, divorced and pregnant, and that the few people who knew her by more than sight probably also knew that she was here only for a short time. Nervously, she cleared her throat.

"Thank you for coming." Her voice was a whisper. She cleared her throat again. "I'm sure you know that Dr. Cooper is leaving, the clinic needs rebuilding and Larkville will need a new doctor. We're here to talk about how we can make that happen."

She thought she heard someone whispering that they had come to eat, but maybe that was her imagination.

"It will be costly," she admitted, amid some scowls and shaking of heads. "But it's important." She wanted to list the reasons why, but she knew that a native son would make a bigger impact. Especially if the native son was almost a god to the townspeople.

So, after the briefest of comments explaining the situation, she turned toward Holt. "Mr. Calhoun will explain what we're up against, what our options are and how we can make this happen." That was what she had included on Holt's list when she'd mentioned *his* part. Of course, she had given him many suggestions on things he might mention during his talk.

"Thank you for listening," she ended to polite applause. A few friends and acquaintances, including Mrs. Best and Ava, clapped much more enthusiastically.

"Good idea," Luann said. Warmth stole through Kathryn. When she'd been here years ago, her parents' reclusive ways had set her apart and she hadn't had real friends.

But when the polite applause faded to silence and Holt stepped onto the stage, the crowd went wild. There was hooting and hollering and boot stomping. "You tell us, Holt," some man called out.

Holt had removed his hat and his dark hair shone in the light. Standing on the small stage, his shoulders seemed broader, his legs longer. He didn't disappear behind the podium or take out any paper.

"Not much to say here. You all heard what Kathryn said. She's 100 percent right and that's a fact. We need a doctor and a clinic. You can probably figure out the reasons why. Does anyone have a problem with that?"

Everyone looked around. No one spoke.

"Good. Then we'll do it. I'll help. You'll help. Kathryn will tell you how it's going to get done. If you're uncertain of the reasons why, she has a list that will clear things up for you. Listen to what she has to say because this is important. Then, when she's through and you're all on board, we'll celebrate." He nodded toward the tables in the back. Then he stepped off the stage.

Kathryn looked at him in disbelief. He had been up on the stage less than a minute. He stared her straight in the eye, challenging her. What was she going to do?

What could she do? She couldn't chastise Holt right here in front of his adoring fans. They would probably run her out of town. So, she gave him a tight smile. Then she moved back on stage and began listing the reasons the clinic was needed, using all the arguments she had used on Holt. She told them what would be involved.

"This is a project that the community has to get behind, but it's an important one. You've gotten used to having a clinic—there are those who depend on it and none of us ever knows when it will be our turn. I'm not at liberty to discuss individual cases, but working in Dr. Cooper's office, I've seen people in pain, people who would suffer if they didn't get immediate medical attention." She gave more real-life examples and, despite herself, tears threatened. She fought them back. She didn't want to be accused of using people or trying to gain their cooperation by using her own scary situation as a ploy. Finally, she ran out of arguments. "So, I hope that after you've had a chance to review the facts, you'll all agree to support this project," she ended. "Are—are there any questions?"

One woman raised her hand. "Will Holt be working on this?"

This time Kathryn managed not to blush. She wasn't sure if the woman was interested in him romantically or if she simply believed that Holt could move mountains. Kathryn was no longer so sure that he could move mountains. After all, he hadn't done half of what she'd asked him to do tonight. No way was she answering the question for him.

She turned to him. "Holt?"

He almost glowered at her. "I said I would help. I meant that I would help in whatever way I'm needed."

The woman smiled. "I was pretty sure of that. You always do the right thing."

"That's Holt. Always there to lend a hand or give some good advice," another man said.

Kathryn gritted her teeth. "Well, then, any more questions?"

"Nope," Johnny said. "Holt's on board. That's good enough for me." She wondered if he had been coached to say that, or if it was really true. He *was*, after all, Holt's brother-in-law.

"Good enough for me, too," Mrs. Best chimed in. A chorus of voices agreed.

The mayor stood. "Well, then, if there's nothing more…" She looked at Kathryn, who shook her head. "I'd say that you've all earned a meal."

Immediately there was applause and people began moving toward the back. Holt remained near the front of the room. As if he knew Kathryn wouldn't be happy until she spoke to him.

"You didn't tell me that you were going to bribe them with food," she said.

"Don't sound so prissy, Kathryn. You were concerned that no one would show up, and I told you they would. A little barbecue never hurt anyone."

"I know that. It was actually a good idea, but couldn't you have at least told me about it? Or that you didn't intend to talk about any of the things on my list."

"I think I might have mentioned before that I'm not one to get emotional. This needed emotion. You were the one to supply that."

She sucked in her breath. "I like to think that I'm professional."

He smiled. "You are that. Kind of prissy about it, too."

She frowned at him.

He raised a brow. "Not that there's anything wrong with prissy."

"I like being in control."

"It shows. And you were."

But she was no fool. "They came because of you. Or your food. Or both. And they agreed to go along because you were involved."

He shrugged. "Give them credit. They might not have jumped as soon as you wanted them to jump, but they're not unreasonable people."

"They expect a lot of you. You like being Santa Claus?" she asked.

"As an owner and manager of the biggest money-making concern in the area, I have obligations, and I don't shirk them."

"Is that what this clinic is? An obligation?"

"I have my reasons for doing this. So do you. The people at the clinic. Your baby. Your job."

Kathryn had watched him selflessly giving of his time.

She also knew something else. "But some of my reasons seem selfish."

"No. They're logical. You're human."

"Maybe I'm just scared," she admitted. "A job will keep me from being vulnerable. I can't be vulnerable."

He gave her a long look, and she knew that she had said too much. Fortunately, Holt didn't seem to want to discuss her vulnerable side any more than she did.

"Understood," he said. "And I'll do what's needed, but I won't be what I'm not."

"Which is…"

"The kind of man who operates on an emotional level. So don't expect me to get up on a stage or anywhere else. Don't expect me to share secrets or tell you everything I'm thinking. I never was and never will be that guy."

"All right," she said. And he walked away. Within seconds, the crowd had glommed on to him. She was alone. But then she always had been. That was the way it would be from here on. Her and her baby. She would make a home for them. A life. And men like Holt would never have any say in that world or any power to hurt her.

If truth be told, she was probably the only woman in Larkville who was glad that Holt wasn't an emotional man. It made him safe.

Or at least safer. Didn't it?

CHAPTER SEVEN

HAD there ever been a woman so determined to be strong who looked as fragile as Kathryn did? Holt found himself turning the question over in his mind for the rest of the meeting. She had been upset with him for not letting her in, but he wasn't a committee kind of guy.

Stop kidding yourself, Calhoun. It's not the committee that makes you uncomfortable. It's Kathryn. It was simple, really. He found her attractive. More than attractive. That he could have dealt with, but he also found her intriguing. She'd come back to Larkville a bit beaten up, and here in a town where she'd apparently been an unknown she was going to make her stand, do some good, rebuild her world and rise from the ashes like a phoenix. A phoenix who would soon fly away with her baby and never return.

Remember that, he told himself. He'd already played this scene before. Lost people. Lots of people, but most importantly, a woman. A baby.

And she wanted to be short-term partners with him. No question about it, Kathryn was dangerous. With her passion and her demands, her temporary stature and her baby on the way, she was everything he should be avoiding.

That wasn't happening. He'd given his word. He'd set wheels in motion and he would continue right through to the end. But if he spent too much time in Kathryn's presence he was going to kiss her. He might even lose control and let kissing lead to more. The only way to avoid that was to take a big step back and do his helping from a distance.

That should work. It would at least make sure that no life-changing mistakes were made.

Okay, she got it, Kathryn thought the next day. Holt wasn't going to be led, and he didn't want to spend time with her. That was good, wasn't it? Because she didn't want to spend much time with him, either.

If she did, sooner or later he would disappoint her.

The thought made her smile. *You mean he hasn't disappointed you yet?* she asked herself.

The answer was complicated. He hadn't let her lead him where she wanted him to go, but he *had* produced the results she'd wanted. So she probably should back off, tell him what she was doing and simply wait for him to produce results on his end.

"All right, let's begin," she murmured, staring at the keyboard. There wasn't even any point in wondering if Holt was into social networking. The very thought would probably have those dark eyes turning icy and dangerous. But he was still a businessman. She addressed an email to him. It read:

Results of the meeting. Two hundred people in attendance. All in favor of moving ahead. Now we fundraise. Ideas?

When no response appeared within a few hours, she wrote another. All it said was:

Please?

Five minutes later, she got a response.

Don't do that.

Do what?

Beg. You know how I feel about begging.

I wasn't. I was asking nicely.

I'm not nice. Just say what you want.

I did. You ignored me.

I'm running a ranch here.

I know, but...

All right. You want a progress report. I've contacted a friend who has contacted a friend who is an instructor at a well-known medical college in Chicago. He's sending out feelers. As for the fundraiser, that's outside my comfort zone.

I'll come up with some ideas.

That would be best.

And then I'll run them past you.

You should know that I'll probably say yes to anything.

Even if it's something that might be embarrassing for you?

Are you baiting me?

Maybe she was, Kathryn thought. It occurred to her that even though she was enjoying this time in Larkville much more than the last, and even though everyone in town had been nice to her—they smiled at her on the street, the patients brought her cookies and oohed and aahed over her expanding girth—she didn't really spend any time socializing. Maybe that was because she was afraid of making friends she'd have to leave behind. Her house wasn't that close to other houses because her parents had been sticklers for privacy and they had looked down on the citizens of Larkville. There were empty lots on either side of her and an empty field across the road. Holt was one of the few people she talked to on a regular basis outside of work.

So, yes, maybe she was enjoying this exchange too much. Maybe she *was* messing with him a bit.

She was also starting to experience major pains. Long, undulating waves of pain that made it feel as if her entire body was pulsing, contracting, hurting.

"It'll go away," she thought. She hoped. And it did… until it came back and hunted her down.

She doubled over and panic filled her soul.

Holt waited for Kathryn's response. And waited.

Nothing happened. And he didn't even consider that she had simply decided to be an ass like him and was making him wait. That wasn't Kathryn's way. She was gung ho all the way. If she wasn't responding, there was a reason.

He called her. The phone rang three times. Four. The machine picked up. The beep finally sounded.

"Kathryn, pick up. It's Holt," he ordered.

Silence. Eventually the machine cut off.

He dialed again, and now his muscles felt tight, his heart was pounding the way it had when his father had collapsed. "Kathryn, answer the damn phone. I need to talk about—about the fundraiser." He paused. She still didn't answer. "And I'm coming over. To talk about the fundraiser," he lied.

The phone clicked as the receiver was lifted. "Holt? Don't...don't come. It's not a good time." Her voice was too soft, the words too halting. "It's...it's really..."

Holt heard a distinct gasp and then a moan. "Your back? Braxton Hicks?" he asked.

Silence.

"Kathryn? Talk. Now," he ordered.

He knew something was wrong when she didn't instantly inform him that she wasn't into controlling men like him. "I— Braxton Hicks?" she said. "No. I don't... think so. I don't know." He could hear her breath coming and going. That was bad. Very bad.

"If you don't know, then it's time to go to the hospital and find out."

More silence.

He cursed the distance and the phone and this inadequate way of communicating. "Kathryn?"

"Yes, I will," she promised. "I'll go now." Her voice started to fade and he could tell she was going to hang up.

"Dammit, no! Stop. Do not hang up the phone. And above all, don't get into that car. That's an order. You can't drive. Don't even think about it."

"I— All right, no, I can't drive. I started thinking about this last week, but then...I'm going to go ask Johanna."

"No. You're not. Johanna may be an excellent mayor, but she drives like total crap. And besides, it's too far. Don't move. I'm coming to get you."

"I can't let you do that."

He wanted to ask why, but all this talk was wasting

time. "Watch me. I guarantee I'll have you to Austin in no time."

Then he jogged out to the hangar and jumped into his helicopter.

Holt came through the door looking like one of those guys in a movie, the ones that come walking out of the fog. The ones that come to save the day when all was lost.

And Kathryn was ready to follow him anywhere, because she had never envisioned what this pain would be like. It was like nothing she'd ever experienced. It was eating her alive. And she had to bear it. She had to do everything she was supposed to in order to make sure her baby's health wasn't compromised, but when the pain came in waves, the urge to sink to her knees or to curl up in a ball was fierce.

The thing was, she had tried both, and neither one of them did a thing to cut the pain.

But Holt would get her to the hospital. Just as he'd made sure people came to the meeting, he would make sure she got to a safe place to give birth. Because that was what Holt did. He helped people in the most efficient way possible. His way. Not their way, but the job got done nonetheless.

"Do you have everything you need?" he asked.

She nodded, reaching for a small bag she had packed weeks ago.

He beat her to it, scooping up the bag. "You're ready?"

"Yes." It was all she could get out as the waves of pain returned and she felt herself blanching, being sucked under. Pain that beat her down, threw her around and pummeled her, overwhelming her.

Holt lifted her as if she was nothing. Weightless. His

long strides took them outside and across the street to the empty field. The contraction began to subside.

"This probably wasn't on your agenda today," she said weakly as he placed her in the helicopter and strapped her in.

"Always plan for the unexpected," he said. "That's life on a ranch. This isn't going to ruin my day."

But she could tell that he was tense. His jaw was locked, his words, comforting as they were, were clipped. "I wish I had someone to take care of you while I fly, but you'll simply have to rely on the sound of my voice," he warned.

To her surprise she still had the strength to laugh. A little. "You've never wanted to talk before."

"Anyone can rattle nonsense. It takes practice to be a sullen uncommunicative jackass," he told her. "I'll do my best."

"Did you…did you just make a joke?" she asked. But then the pain returned.

"Be still," Holt ordered. "Breathe. Breathe. Watch me while I fly. Concentrate on me and breathe." The noise of the propeller was loud, but she could still hear every word as he bit them off.

She focused on his hands on the controls. Long, lean fingers. She stared. She breathed. Occasionally a tiny gasp would escape her.

His hands tightened on the controls.

"I'll—I'll try not to do that again," she said.

He swore beneath his breath. "You do whatever you like. If you want to swear or scream or tell me what you really think of me, now would be a good time to let loose. I won't judge you or remind you of it later."

"I don't like yelling," she said. "My parents were yellers. My husband was a major yeller. And—"

"Yes, I've been known to swear the house down when

I'm angry," he said. "So, no yelling. What did you do when all this yelling was going on?"

"Hid. Cowered. Cried. I wasn't equipped to fight back. Or at least I didn't know the right words to make it stop."

He didn't respond.

"Too much information," she said. "More than I should have revealed."

"I don't share secrets. It's not going further than me. You've got no reason to worry."

"I'm not. I'm not. I'm—"

"Almost there, Kathryn. Hang on. Stay with me. Concentrate on me. Tell me, when all that yelling was going on, what did you want to say?"

"Stop yelling. Stop bullying me. I'm a person, too. I count. This is a baby. It's mine, it's yours. How can you not want it? Why are you so angry?"

Kathryn's voice had risen on the last words. She was practically yelling, but she felt the thud as Holt set the helicopter down. Immediately medical personnel appeared. He must have called ahead to let them know they were on their way.

She was placed in a wheelchair. A nurse started to wheel her away. Kathryn looked up at Holt. "I— Thank you."

He nodded and started to walk away. "Will there be someone with her?" he asked the nurse.

"We'll monitor her closely and check her often."

"But some of the time she'll be alone."

"Until it's time for the heavy lifting."

Kathryn thought she heard Holt say something, but the pain took hold again. A few minutes later she was in a birthing room. Holt was holding her hand. "Why are you still here?" she asked.

He ignored her. "Let's do this thing," he said.

She tried to smile. "I'm really grateful. I can see why people see you as the cowboy hero."

"Shut up, Kathryn," he said. And then he kissed her.

The shock, the zing, the utter insanity of it, lasted all the way to the next contraction. Having Holt here was… There was that safe feeling again.

But she could tell by the look on his face that this wasn't easy for him. That kiss had been a prime example of him trying to deal with the craziness of the moment. Holt hated emotion. His jaws were clenched. His big hand was locked around hers like a vise. His tan seemed almost pale.

But he held on and held her. Through contraction after contraction.

Eventually, though, the nurse told her that they were getting to the crucial moment, the part where Kathryn had heard that women screamed out their innermost thoughts. In fact, she'd already let loose with things she shouldn't have. Besides, Holt had borne enough. He didn't need to live through the really intense and emotional stuff. So when the doctor finally came in, Kathryn turned to Holt.

"It's tag team time. Thank you. I'll see you on the other side."

He opened his mouth to say something just as the pain came at her harder than ever. She sucked in a breath, trying to hold on.

"I want you to go. Now, Holt," she yelled. "A man got me into this, and I don't want you or any men in here." It was a total lie, but it did the trick. He left.

Somehow she stopped herself from begging him to come back.

Holt tried not to think about what was going on with Kathryn in the delivery room. Of course, he knew. On a ranch you learned the basics of reproduction at a very early age, but Kathryn was a woman. And she wasn't just a woman in pain. She was a sensitive woman. That much had been revealed during their conversation on the way here.

And though he had meant what he said about not revealing her words or holding them against her, he wasn't going to forget them, either. This was a woman who had been subjected to some situations that were none of his business. He especially didn't want to think about what she had said about her husband. No one knew better than he did that there were two sides to every story. The fact was that she was having a baby and her husband was nowhere in sight. What had happened and whose fault it was, if it was anyone's, was not his concern. But he knew two things.

Kathryn had been hurt and he was just the type of man who could hurt her more and hurt himself, too, if their lives got tangled up together. She was having a baby, and then she was taking that baby and moving to a city, while he wasn't sure if he could ever contemplate having a child again.

Still, during that time he'd been in the labor room with her hand in his—heck, with her lips beneath his—he'd known that hard as it might be to be present for the delivery of a child and all the painful memories that called up, he would have done it. Stayed until the end. He couldn't run. Or leave her alone here.

So Holt waited. And paced. And waited some more.

CHAPTER EIGHT

TIRED but alert after the birth of her daughter, Kathryn mentally thanked Holt and her years of running, in that order. Holt had kept her sane on the trip to the hospital and had gotten her here safely and in time. He'd held her terror at bay during her labor. For the rest, her athletic build had, the doctors told her, made this an easier delivery, if there was such a thing. At any rate, by the time she had decided that, yes, she might in fact want to be drugged, she was too far along. Which was why she was in less pain and wider awake than she would otherwise have been.

That was also why she knew the minute that Holt appeared in the hospital room doorway. He didn't come in, but just stood there filling up the space.

"You okay?" he asked.

"Never better." He was looking everywhere but at her baby. Clearly he wasn't comfortable with babies, so this might be an awkward meeting. A little levity couldn't hurt. "I could climb a mountain."

"Maybe you could hold off on that until later," he suggested.

"Good idea. You might have to rescue me. I *am* a little bit worn out."

"Not surprising. Was it difficult? Were you all right? I could have stayed."

But Kathryn remembered how he'd looked, as if he was being chased by demons. "No offense, Calhoun, but you have quite a reputation when it comes to women. You've probably seen a lot of lady parts, and I wasn't eager to have you see mine under less than flattering circumstances," she teased, wanting to let him off the hook and lighten the tone. "Besides, I was just fine," she lied. At the time it had felt as if her entire body was under attack.

He studied her as if he could determine whether or not she was telling the truth.

"And anyway, I'm perfectly fine now," she told him.

"Which means it was pretty bad at the time." Yes, it had been. At the very end when the pain had made her a little crazy, she had almost asked a nurse to see if Holt was still around, but a woman bent on being independent wouldn't do that, and she had hung on alone.

"Holt, I'm good. Honest."

He looked at her as if he wanted to argue, but finally he blew out a breath. Then he raised that sexy eyebrow. "Lady parts?"

She did her best to look down her nose. "They're mine and I can call them whatever I want."

He touched two fingers to his forehead in a salute. "As you say."

A small noise came from the clear bassinet at Kathryn's side. Holt visibly tensed. He still hadn't looked at the baby, she noticed.

Now he looped his thumbs in his belt loops and glanced to the side. "I'm glad that you're okay." He turned to go, then turned back. "Let me know when you need a lift home. You have my number."

"Holt?"

He pivoted quickly. "Yes?"

"I want you to know that me having the baby doesn't

change anything. As soon as I get back in form, which admittedly might take a week or two, I'm continuing with the project. That race to the hospital taught me just how badly this is needed. Not everyone has a Holt Calhoun, or a helicopter, at their disposal. And I have no idea how much time I have left."

"No rushing things. That's just the drugs talking."

"No drugs. It's me talking."

"But you're tired. We'll discuss this later."

"Are you trying to back out on me?"

He stared her down. "I'm trying to keep in mind that your life has changed."

"It has, but some things haven't. Okay?"

"Okay."

"And, Holt? Her name is Izzy. Short for Isabelle."

His gaze passed over Izzy and landed on Kathryn. "Get some rest, Kathryn. We'll talk later."

Then she was alone with her baby. She looked down into those unfocused, beautiful eyes. "He's not so bad, Izzy," she told her child, kissing her on the forehead. "Don't get your feelings hurt. I'm sure it's nothing personal."

But he definitely didn't like babies. At all.

Holt tried not to think about Kathryn, about Kathryn with a baby or about the baby. He remembered finding out what Lilith had done and his anger when he had confronted her about her plans to give away their child without even having informed him of…anything. She hadn't told him when she miscarried later, either, if that was really what had happened, but he remembered every word she'd said during the argument they'd had when he'd heard about it secondhand. The gist of the message had been that a man like him was so lacking emotionally that she would never want to have a child with him or give birth to a child who might inherit his disposition. And what child would want such a cold man for a father?

He had hated her that day, and had never forgotten her words. There was, unfortunately, truth in them. Because she wasn't the first person who had told him he was cold. His mother, despite urging him not to care too deeply, had in her later years lamented that he was too detached. His father told him that the men in his family probably weren't equipped to offer what women and kids needed. Hadn't other women cursed him for being a cold Calhoun male?

And here was Kathryn, a woman who had already been hurt by other insensitive people. Now she had an innocent baby.

His whole body felt wrong. Chilled. Pained. Maybe he should just tell her that he would donate most of the money she needed. He would finish this thing alone.

But he knew he wouldn't. She'd told him that this was her proving ground. She needed this accomplishment on her résumé. So, what he needed to do was make sure he did his part without overstepping into the tasks she'd laid out for herself.

One thing was for certain. He needed to keep his distance. As much as possible. The woman made him forget who and what he was. And she had eyes that made him want to gaze into them like some idiot with an actual heart.

He cursed his stupidity. And when he got back to the ranch, he took an ax and attacked a pile of wood. It took him hours.

"Are you okay, Holt?" Nancy asked.

He grunted at her.

"Do you want dinner?"

"Can't. Work to do." He kept swinging the ax. *Izzy.*

What kind of a name was Izzy? But he knew. It was the kind of name a romantic, sentimental, wistful woman gave her child. A woman who needed a lot.

He brought the ax down hard, and a piece of wood went flying and nearly hit him on the arm. He almost wished it had. It would be a distraction.

But eventually, the pile of wood played out. And even with all that chopping and smashing, he still couldn't forget what he'd felt when Kathryn had been in pain and so brave.

And he couldn't deny that he wanted to see her again. What was wrong with him? He knew better than to start anything. Or even try to.

I probably just feel responsible for her, he told himself. *If she's struggling to make ends meet, how well-equipped can she be to house a baby?*

Kathryn was tired. Izzy was the sweetest thing on earth. Her heart hurt just to look at her, fearing that something would happen to the tiny baby who seemed like a wonderful but frighteningly fragile gift. What's more, she kept seeing that guarded expression on Holt's face as he'd avoided her baby.

Well, so what? Lots of men—and women—weren't big on babies. No big deal. But between her thoughts of Holt, her worries about Izzy and Izzy's nighttime feedings, Kathryn wasn't sleeping. How did people stand all this stress and responsibility?

"Silly question. They stand it because they love."

Still, she needed to stop worrying and tend to some things. Dr. Cooper was getting by with a rolling group of stand-in receptionists, and her work at the newspaper was flexible enough that her not being there didn't hurt the paper. But she did need to get back to work so she could support herself and Izzy. And she needed to send out more résumés. And stop wondering when she would see Holt again, and…

"I need to just stop. Especially stop thinking about Holt," she whispered. But that wasn't easy. She couldn't help remembering how he had come to her rescue and had taken most of her fears away. Or that he seemed uncomfortable around her now.

She had received an email from him this morning.

Found a potential candidate. Will be traveling to Chicago to talk to him.

That was it. No *How are you? How are you feeling? When can we meet again?*

"He's cut us loose, Izzy." Probably that wild trip to the hospital and all her wailing and baring her soul had disgusted him. *Well, so be it. If that's the way it is, then I'm better off without him.*

But while she'd been recovering, he'd gotten a candidate for the new doctor position. Things were moving, and she had to move, too—on to the next step with the project and her life. She had received a phone interview for a job just yesterday. It hadn't panned out, but it proved that her résumé wasn't totally terrible. Things might happen. They might happen faster if she completed the project. She should finish with Holt. Fast.

Izzy was starting to whimper. Kathryn cuddled the baby close. Just as Izzy had stopped fussing and settled against Kathryn's shoulder, the silence contented and wonderful, the doorbell rang.

Kathryn jerked. Her heart nearly stopped. Then it started thudding wildly. Since she'd lived here, Holt had been the only person who had come to her door.

The urge to look in the mirror was intense. She resisted. For one thing, she knew she had dark circles under her eyes. For another, checking her appearance in the mirror would prove something bad, that she cared what Holt thought of her looks.

She opened the door. And found Jess Jameson standing there. The woman had a slightly sheepish expression on her face. "I'm so sorry I haven't been around sooner, Kathryn. And I—well, the thing is…I should have. Locked into our own lives, we haven't even given you a proper baby shower! But we've gotten together some things now. If that's all right."

Kathryn was uncomfortably aware that this was Holt's sister standing on her doorstep. She shook her head. "Please don't apologize. There's no need. I've had my head down and working, too. I— You really didn't have to do this."

"Of course we did. You've just had a baby! A lovely baby. And your arms are full. May I…bring these in?"

"I— Yes, of course. Thank you." Kathryn stepped back to let Jess in. The woman was carrying two shopping bags.

"I'll just leave them right here," Jess said. "There are some clothes, some diapers and…I don't know what else is in there. And besides baby things, I brought you some of my home-baked treats. My specialty, you know."

Kathryn knew. Jess ran her own bakery and her treats could make a person swoon with pleasure. "Thank you so much. You make the best baked goods I've ever eaten!"

"Well, a woman who's just had a baby deserves to pamper herself a little, I think." Then she looked at Izzy and practically sighed. "She is so darling. Just a little sweetheart. I'm hoping to give my little Brady a brother or a sister someday. And boy or girl, I hope that it ends up with

Johnny's hair. That man has hair a woman loves running her fingers through, you know?"

Kathryn didn't think it would be a good idea to say yes. Jess might think that Kathryn was coveting her husband. Or at least his hair. Worse, she might suspect that it was really her brother's hair Kathryn was thinking about… which was the truth. And was embarrassing. Still…

"Johnny has very nice hair," she said weakly. "But he probably feels the same way about your hair. You might have to have one of each."

Jess laughed as Izzy gurgled happily. She had a nice laugh. And she had brought all these baby goodies. And delicious food from the bakery. And said nice things about Izzy. Tears sprang to Kathryn's eyes.

Immediately Jess looked concerned. "I'm so sorry. Did I come at a bad time?"

"No. You came at a perfect time. Don't mind me. It's just all the hormones. I was simply thinking about how nice you were."

"Oh, hon," Jess said, giving both Kathryn and Izzy a bit of a group hug. "I'm the one who should be crying. I should have come before you even had the baby. We all should have thought of it. We knew you were pregnant, but we just—"

"You knew I wasn't planning to stay. Please don't apologize about not having a shower. I thought there was a chance I might be gone by the time Izzy was born, too. There was no reason you should have needed to help me when I might have been gone before it mattered."

Jess gave her a "get real" look. "That's not the way it works. Neighbors help neighbors even if they're temporary neighbors. I'm going to round up the troops and we're going to help make you a real nursery—even if it's only a temporary one."

Kathryn started. "I have a nursery."

Jess looked surprised. "You do? Let me see. Just so I know what you have and what you don't."

"It's just through here." Kathryn led the way. "But really, I don't expect you to—"

"You *do* have a nursery," Jess said, moving up to the little bassinet. "I thought— He said—"

"He?"

"Uh-oh."

"I assume we're talking about your brother."

"You weren't supposed to know."

"He put you up to this?"

"He might have hinted that a woman with a baby might need some things. He wasn't sure what those things were and—well, you know Holt—he isn't remotely comfortable around topics like this, so he just pushed the button and then acted like he didn't want to talk about it anymore. I completely agree with him, though, on you needing some stuff. You've done great, but if a few of us women put our heads together, we can make things even better."

"I don't want you being pushed into anything, or for anyone to feel obligated. I would hate that."

Jess held up one hand. "You're on the wrong track. Because while Holt may have been the impetus, he was right. And while Holt and I may be different, as Calhouns we share one trait. Once we get something in our heads, we follow through on it. We don't let go. I want to help. I intend to help. Let me?"

"I—Jess, what if I leave next week? I don't know when a job might show up."

"Then we pack up all of your stuff and you move on to your new life. With your new baby things. Come on, Kathryn. It'll be fun. Not just for you, but for me, too. I love shopping for baby things. Okay?"

Kathryn frowned. "I'm really not sure about this."

"You're getting a clinic and a new doctor for us."

"I haven't done it yet."

"You will. I don't really know you, but I know that you've got Holt."

That was a major overstatement. She didn't have—nor would she ever have—Holt.

"Please. Let us give back a little."

"Maybe just a little. For Izzy."

Jess smiled.

"Jess?"

"Yes?"

"I'm not sure when I'll see Holt again soon, but tell him thank you. It was nice of him to do this when he's so uncomfortable around babies."

Jess looked at her. "I'll tell him, but I'll leave out the part about the baby."

"I'm sorry. I didn't mean—it wasn't criticism. Lots of people feel awkward around babies."

"It might be more than that with Holt."

Kathryn raised an eyebrow. And waited. Jess was shaking her head. "I probably shouldn't have said that. My hunch is pure speculation because Holt never discusses his personal life. I know women who have wanted him, but haven't been able to get him. I know women who may have dated him, but don't really have anything to show for it and nothing to tell. I don't know much more. My brother is a complete clam where his emotions are concerned. He's not a talker, not a sharer, and he's been like that all my life. So, all I'm basing my guess on is the fact that he was engaged to Lilith Kingston and then he wasn't engaged anymore. There was a big argument, and some people say that she was cheating on him, that she might even have been pregnant, but I don't know the details. She moved away, and he'll never volunteer that information. He'll probably take it to his grave. But just so you know, I'm sure Holt wouldn't harm a baby."

Kathryn blinked. "I would never think that. It doesn't matter that he's not into babies."

"It does. When a woman has a child, she wants the world to love her baby. It hurts when someone doesn't. But Holt is...Holt. He'll never change."

"I wasn't going to try. We're not that tight."

Jess studied her for a few seconds. Then she sighed. "It's just as well. I was thinking—a whole bunch of us were thinking—that you might be falling in love with him, but I guess it's good that you're not. You're going to leave, and Holt will never go. I'm afraid that he's tied to that ranch more than he ever will be to any woman. Maybe he tells his secrets to the cattle, but he sure doesn't share them with anyone else."

"He's a good man, though."

Jess laughed. "Of course. Holt's the best. He takes care of everyone."

Including me, Kathryn thought after Jess had gone. People had needs. Holt tended to them. He made light of it, but what a burden that must be. She was going to have to make it clear that she was not going to need coddling.

It was time to jump back in with both feet and make it clear that she was in charge of getting a clinic built. *And I'm not even going to think about Holt as a man. At least, not anymore.*

She picked up the phone and dialed. Nancy patched her through. Holt's low, deep, sexy voice came on the line. Immediately Kathryn understood why all those women were always trying to get his attention.

"Something's wrong," he said.

"No. Yes. I just want you to know that I don't want you making me into a pet project."

"Don't have a clue what you're talking about."

She stalled. Felt embarrassed. Then remembered Jess's words.

"Good, then. Just keep thinking that way. I'm an independent woman. I know how to get things and get things done."

"Something get your back up, Kathryn?"

Other than the fact that his voice was making her think of rumpled sheets and things she shouldn't be thinking about?

"No. I'm good. I'm fine. I'm surviving. Not a thing wrong here. I don't need a thing. Nothing. At all."

"Right. Got that. Is that what you called to tell me? That you didn't need anything?" He sounded kind of angry.

"Well. Yes, I did. And one thing more. I'm ready to start up again."

Oh, Lord, that had sounded a bit sexual, hadn't it?

"On the clinic project," she amended. "I want to meet with you. Talk about it. Plan."

Was that a groan?

"Holt?"

"Still here. Kathryn, you just had a baby."

"I'm aware of that. It was two weeks ago. I need to move forward." So that she could move away from Holt and all the disturbing sensations he called up in her.

Silence. Then, "Okay. Let's get this done and over with."

Good. He wanted to end it, too. Why did that not feel good?

"When?"

"I'll be out of town tomorrow. The next day?"

"I'll be there."

"Not in that car."

"Yes."

"Kathryn."

"Holt. It's my life, my car, my world. Soon I'll be gone. I'll be driving all over creation in that car and you won't even think about it because I won't be in your life anymore. Get used to it. I'm driving my own car. It's safe." Well, reasonably safe, but she knew that it didn't look it. "And I have my cell phone. I just have to put some minutes on it."

"What the hell does that mean? Does it mean you don't really have a phone?"

Kathryn bristled. For a second there, Holt had sounded the way James used to when he decided that she wasn't the sort of woman he wanted her to be. The truth was that she couldn't afford a real phone with an expensive plan, but for emergencies, she kept one of those pay-as-you-go phones. Lately, however, she hadn't needed it. She was in yelling distance of the main part of town and she'd barely gone anywhere since Izzy was born. Yesterday the last of her minutes had run out.

"I am a responsible adult and I have things under control," she said. "All right?"

He didn't answer.

"Holt, I know what you do. People come to you with their problems and you fix them. I am not one of those people. I don't need you to fix my life. I just need you to help me with the clinic, but that's mostly for Larkville. I am off-limits," she said. "Is that clear?"

"Crystal," he said, his voice coming out clipped, but still as sexy as ever. "You're off-limits. That's a fine idea. I like it."

She had no idea what he meant by that, and since Holt

hung up immediately afterward, she didn't have a chance to ask.

Not that he would have answered had she asked. Totally frustrating man. She was so glad that the two of them were only going to have to be together for a short time. It couldn't end fast enough for her. She wanted to be contented.

Not in a perpetual state of wondering what it would be like to kiss Holt again.

Holt woke up feeling edgy the morning that Kathryn was supposed to show up at the ranch. The doctor candidate from Chicago hadn't panned out and Holt had sent Kathryn an email to tell her so. He sent out more feelers, made more calls, asked for favors even though he hated doing that.

I can't wait for this to be over, he thought. All his life he had been the guy people turned to. And most of the time he was fine with that. There was a symbiotic relationship between the ranch and the locals, and he was a part of that.

People needed someone they could rely on, and for some reason a rancher seemed to fit their romantic vision of who that person should be. He'd learned to take all the requests in stride. He knew the rules, what to expect, how to play it.

But from the first, Kathryn had thrown him off his game. It was clear she had needs, that she could use some help. It was just as clear that, on a personal level, she didn't want to accept his help. What was a guy to do?

"Forget her," he told the nearest barnyard cat.

The cat seemed to give him the evil eye. Cats were good at that. Okay, he couldn't forget her yet. He had made promises. They had a job to do together. But what he needed to do was to stop thinking of her as a woman.

"Holt." A soft voice sounded behind him, and he pivoted. There she was, dressed in soft blue, a little bundle of baby strapped to her stomach in a cloth carrier. All he could see of the baby was Izzy's pale, fuzzy hair and her little arms and legs dangling from the carrier. Something stabbed at his heart. A mere leftover vestige of his time with Lilith. A reminder that this was not for him, not his path—that he couldn't handle it right, if at all. He looked into Kathryn's worried eyes.

"Ready?" he asked.

She gave a quick nod. "I was a little concerned when Nancy told me that you were away from the house."

He gave her a stern look. "You didn't trust me to stand by my word?"

"No," she said quickly. "It wasn't so much you. I just… I've grown used to being disappointed now and then."

He stared at her, knowing she was thinking about her parents and ex-husband. "I'm not those people." He didn't bother explaining himself.

Kathryn stared straight into his eyes. "I'm sorry. Yes, I know."

"Whatever your parents and husband did to you—"

She shook her head. "It doesn't matter. I'm beyond it and it's no longer important. You're here. I'm here. We have work to do. If you're in, we're good to go."

Clearly, she was not "beyond it" if she'd worried that he might disappoint her, and trust was an issue, but she had finished up her sentence by flashing a big smile, and his breath had whooshed out of him. Already, her eyes were lighting up.

"And just where are we going?"

"I was thinking…I have an idea. Would you mind walking me around a bit of the ranch while we talk? I need to think—no, to *see*—if what I'm envisioning will work."

"It's just a ranch." He didn't want to think why he was so reluctant to show her the Double Bar C, even though he knew. Lilith had always had two complaints about him. One was that a ranch wasn't her style and that parts of it were dirty.

But Kathryn was giving him an odd, probing look.

"What?"

"This is your home, your livelihood, your everything, and all you can say is 'It's just a ranch.' You really are a man of few words."

And that had been Lilith's other complaint. He didn't have any intention of sharing his thoughts or his soul with her.

"Do you need a lot of words?"

She tilted her head, keeping one palm on the back of the baby's head, cuddling Izzy to her. Holt wished he hadn't noticed that.

"I like words," Kathryn finally said. "I like openness. But you and I don't have to be open. We're just business partners, so as long as you're still willing to help with the clinic, I can put up with your fear of communication."

He glowered at her; he might have even growled.

She raised one brow. And then she gave him an impish smile. "I still want to see the ranch."

"A ranch tour? You're on," he said. As he turned to lead her away, their paths crossed and she bumped up against his side. His whole body began to hum, and he realized how much he'd been wanting to touch her. For days.

That was not good.

CHAPTER NINE

Sizzle, pop, ignore that touch. It was just an accident, a nothing touch. Belay all sensation, Kathryn ordered herself, but it wasn't an easy thing to do. With Holt, she was always a bit unbalanced. Half the time she struggled with her desire to kiss the man. The rest of the time she wanted to run as far from him as she could. He made her feel things she had no business feeling.

That was a concern. When she left here, she had to know she could be a world unto herself, not in need of another person's praise, affection, validation or financial support. Because needing people had always been her downfall.

That was why it was so difficult to accept the baby bounty that had come her way lately. Holt's half sister, Ellie Jackson, had dropped off a pretty outfit for Izzy, and she and Kathryn had bonded a bit. Kathryn was suddenly getting to know women she hadn't known her last time here.

Other anonymous gifts had simply appeared on her porch. The thought that Holt might be at the heart of all this wouldn't subside. The fact that he might be practicing his "ruler of the ranch" methods on her made her wary.

Still, even the most independent of people sometimes had to work *with* people to reach their goals.

"Why the sudden interest in ranching?" Holt asked in that sexy, grumpy way of his. She wished he didn't sound so...virile. Especially since she was still trying to forget what it had felt like when her body had come up against his in that accidental touch a moment ago.

Get your mind back on target, she ordered herself.

"Do you have places here where people could stay?" she asked, ignoring his grumpy question.

Those dark eyes were wary. "People? You?"

She felt the blush coming on and quickly turned away and tried to pretend that the horizon held some mystery for her. "Not me. Other people. City people. People who might want to visit a ranch."

"This isn't a dude ranch."

"I know. I'm not suggesting you make it one."

"Good. Because this ranch doesn't just belong to me. There are a number of us Calhouns...and some other siblings, too, as you may have heard."

"How do you feel about your father's other children? You didn't even know they existed a few months ago."

He raised one brow.

There was that embarrassing blush again. "I don't mean to pry, or certainly to imply anything by that. I just— It has to be a shock to find out that you have half brothers and sisters."

"He wasn't married to my mother then, so it's none of my affair. I'm the keeper of the Calhoun ranch. If there are others, none of that changes my role."

Kathryn had a sudden urge to kiss Holt to see if she could get a reaction, to discover if there *were* real feelings lurking under that cool facade, but the heat that quickly rose in her at that thought told her that it would be a bad idea to kiss Holt. Disastrous. He might be made of steel, but she was—unfortunately—human. And steel man or not, she was attracted to him.

She took a deep breath. "I promise not to hurt your ranch."

To her surprise, his lips tilted up in a hint of a smile. "I wasn't exactly worried about that."

"But you said—"

"I was just warning you about what I would and wouldn't allow. Hurting the ranch was never an option."

But she had heard that he might have hurt *women* before, broken their hearts, refused to give them what they wanted from him. That she could believe. Easily.

"Why are you asking me about housing people on the ranch?"

"I want to hold our fundraiser here. Just for a day, or a little more than a day."

"A fundraiser. Here? What kind of a fundraiser?"

"Not a big deal. Just a day at the Double Bar C. Let people see what really goes on at a ranch. Maybe let them get involved a bit. Not a real dude ranch experience, because this would just be for one day and possibly a night. And also because there would be other things going on, too."

He never dropped his gaze from her. She felt as if her clothes were too tight when she had already been doing her best to get back in shape.

"Kind of county fair-ish things," she volunteered without him asking. "Bake sales, animal competitions, maybe a rodeo."

"You want to turn the Double Bar C into a sideshow?"

"Maybe just a very *little* rodeo," she amended. "Because that's the kind of thing that people from the city, people with money, would pay to see. They get to play dress up and pretend they're cowboys for a day. City people like that. And if you show them some info on the clinic and what we're trying to do with their money, they'll like it even better. They might make donations. It always makes people feel good if they can do something good while tending to their own pleasures and fantasies."

That sexy eyebrow of his rose higher.

"Stop that," she said.

"Stop what?"

"Don't play innocent with me, Holt Calhoun. You may not be one for demonstrative displays, but you have a way of making a person feel as if she said something…wanton, when all she—*I*—was talking about was something perfectly innocent."

"If you keep using words like *pleasures* and *fantasies* and *wanton,* we're going to have trouble here." He wasn't smiling now.

And Kathryn *was* feeling rather wanton. Thank goodness she wasn't capable of *doing* anything wanton a little more than two weeks after having a baby. Otherwise, she might be embarrassing herself with Holt even more than she already was.

Needing to anchor and reassure herself, she shifted her hand over Izzy's soft, fuzzy head and the baby made that weak little moan that babies make.

As if he couldn't help himself, Holt's gaze flashed to Izzy and he looked away almost as if he'd been burned.

"I didn't have anywhere to leave her." Kathryn couldn't stop herself from saying the words. "I'm sorry. I know that being around her makes you uncomfortable."

"That's my problem, not hers." The intensity in his expression, the way he never flinched but stared a person straight in the eyes, made Kathryn want to take a step back. Trying to delve into the soul of a man like Holt… what would a woman find?

Heat, she thought. *Power. Passion that had been leashed for a long time.*

A choking sound rose up in Kathryn's throat. "Excuse me," she said. "I need to—to get Izzy out of the sun. I'll be back." She rushed off toward the ranch house, feeling like a coward, but she didn't like the direction her thoughts had turned. Holt seemed to have that effect on her every time they met. Still. She hated the fact that she couldn't seem to control herself around him.

Run, her senses told her.

"Don't you dare," she whispered to herself. "No." She took a deep breath and entered the house.

Nancy was in the kitchen. She looked at Kathryn, studied her for a second. "Did you and Holt fight?"

Kathryn blinked. "No. I just… Holt…"

"Yes," Nancy said. "He's a good man, but not an easy one. Are you leaving?"

It sounded a lot as if Nancy thought that Holt had run Kathryn off. Kathryn quickly shook her head. "No. We have plans to make, but—" she looked down at Izzy and issued a silent apology, feeling as if she was getting in the bad habit of using her child as an excuse much the way her parents had used her "—is there a place I can put Izzy down? I have her baby carrier with me."

"A baby carrier?" Nancy said. "I can do better than that. Come on, sweetie. May I?" she asked Kathryn, holding out her arms.

Kathryn handed over her child. "Are you sure?"

Nancy cuddled the baby close. "We don't get ones this little around here. Brady isn't really a baby anymore. I'm going to enjoy this time. You just go take care of whatever business you and Holt have."

"Thank you," Kathryn said. She could see that Nancy would lay her life down for a child, but it was still difficult to leave Izzy. She dropped a kiss on Izzy's head and turned to go.

"Kathryn?"

"Yes?" she said, turning back slightly.

"I know he's a harsh man in some ways, but a man like Holt, who holds everything inside, doesn't forget or forgive easily. Lilith lived in Larkville when they were engaged. There were rumors that she was pregnant and that he had to find out about that from someone else. There was more, but I don't know how much of it was made up and how much was true. Holt never said, but the way he feels about babies, I think there's a good chance that there was a baby involved. We'll probably never know. He's not a man who opens up. But he's a good man."

There it was. Again.

"I know that," Kathryn said. And she did. She also knew that Holt was a powerful man. Too powerful for someone like her. And now she knew for sure that he had major baby issues. All those were good things to remember. "Thank you again," she told Nancy.

She went outside to find Holt. He was on a ladder next to one of the outbuildings and was hammering on a piece of siding that appeared to be on the verge of coming loose. He turned as she came walking up to him.

"I didn't mean to be gone long," she told him.

"You weren't. I'm just… If we're going to open the gates of the ranch, it should look its best."

She smiled. "You're a pushover, Holt."

"I'm a practical man. Plus, it will be good preparation for the town's Fall Festival."

Interesting. The man didn't really like her idea, but he was willing to go along. Whether it was to move things along and get rid of her or because neither of them had come up with a way to pay for a clinic, she had no idea. Still…

"I won't suggest anything that would leave even temporary damage."

He laughed at that. Actually laughed, a low, hearty, sexy sound. Kathryn found herself staring at him. And he was staring back. "Temporary damage happens all the time, but land is rugged."

Like him.

"Even if it's destroyed by fire or flood or wind, it will eventually recover."

Not like him. Whatever had happened with his fiancée had scarred him. Or maybe he had always been this way. There was no telling, because he wasn't talking.

She looked at that wide, laughing mouth and swallowed. "Okay, but I'll treat it with respect."

"I appreciate that."

"And—"

"What?"

"The day we do this thing…"

"This thing—this ranch field trip, rodeo, bake sale, cowboy school thing," he offered.

"Yes. I'll come up with a name, something better than this ranch field trip, rodeo, bake sale, cowboy school thing," she promised, surprising another small smile from him. "Will it be all right if…that is…will you mind if the visitors bring children and babies?"

He took a step closer. "I'm not an ogre, Kathryn."

She licked her lips. "I know that."

"No. You're not sure."

Kathryn vehemently shook her head. "No, I know you're not. You helped me at the hospital. You help everyone. Whatever happened between you and—and the woman you were going to marry, that hasn't stopped you from doing good."

He swore. Then he swore at himself for swearing. "Has Nancy been preaching at you?"

"Not really. She might have just been worried that I would judge you. I'm not, you know. I'm sure you have good reasons for feeling the way you do."

He didn't say anything.

She sighed. And turned.

He turned at the same time, intentionally or not, she didn't know. What she knew was that suddenly she was standing very close to Holt.

And he was looking down at her.

She looked up.

"You have such trusting eyes," he said. "Don't trust me too much, Kathryn."

She wanted to tell him that she wouldn't, but he was close and very big, very…Holt.

"I won't," she finally managed, and yet she stood on her toes. She placed her hand on his arm.

He leaned in toward her, his lips a mere breath away from hers. Kathryn felt faint. Her blood thrummed in her veins.

"I would be very bad for you," Holt said, his voice a low whisper. "If I did what I wanted to do and kissed you right now."

She stood there waiting, shivering in spite of the heat, aching to have him bridge the gap and touch her.

What am I thinking? she asked herself. *Falling for this man—who doesn't want me and can't even look at my baby—would destroy me.*

She backed away two feet. "It's a good thing you're a man of control."

"That's what I keep telling myself." And then he turned.

"Send me one of those pretty little lists you make of all the things you want to do at the ranch and when you want to do it. Let me know my part," he added as he walked away.

Come back and kiss me, she thought. *Or stand still while I kiss you. That's your part.* But of course she didn't say that. It would have been insanity. It would have started something that could only end badly.

And yet, hours later, she brushed her fingertips across her lips and dreamed that it was Holt kissing her. Just as she had years ago. Some women never learned. Apparently she was one of those women.

CHAPTER TEN

DURING the next week Holt cursed himself for having almost kissed Kathryn and even more for letting her know that he wanted to. Touching Kathryn could only result in disaster. She was leaving; he was staying. She had a baby he didn't even like to think about. She was a woman who had been bullied, and he could be a harsh man. Since Izzy had come along, he'd stopped teasing her. He missed that, but it was smarter not to tease. Teasing led to laughing, sometimes to touching. And touching Kathryn could lead to places he shouldn't go. One or both of them would end up unhappy.

But the memory of her trusting eyes haunted him; he burned to taste her lips. Instead, he settled for a flurry of emails detailing "Come Be a Cowboy Day." He smiled at her quirky name and wrote:

I like it.

She wrote back.

High praise from the man of few words.

Then he asked:

What's my part?

Head rancher. I need you to look stern, distant, a man of the land. Think you can do that?

She was teasing him. Yes, he had missed that. He had half a mind to drive over to her house and tell her so. He resisted. It was hell.

Do you want me to call the guests bad names and tell them I'll tan their hides if they don't do their chores right?

They might like that, but on the other hand we don't want to risk any lawsuits and we want them to shell out their money. Be charming to the ladies (but not too charming; we don't want them to claim you led them on). Make the men think that they're "one of the boys." Teach them tough, gruff, ranch-guy stuff and feed them praise.

Not real good with fake praise.

Too bad. Learn.

He could almost hear her laughing.

I'll make an effort. But I think there has to be more to something of this magnitude than simply acting like the resident cowboy coach. Give me the whole list of what this entire project entails. Everything that needs to be done.

She mucked about.
He prodded her again.

You worked hard enough to get me on board. What's the deal? Why are you holding back now?

She didn't answer right away.

And that was when Holt made an executive decision. He took control.

Kathryn didn't know what had happened. One minute she had been sitting there trying to think of how to tell Holt that her simple "cowboy day" plan had turned into much more than she had intended it to. He wasn't going to be happy to have a ton of people he might have to coddle or suck up to. Heaven knew that wasn't Holt's way. But by the time she had decided to simply dive in, tell him the truth and reassure him that she had everything under control, which she most certainly did *not,* it was clear that he had signed off. A short time later there was a loud rapping on her door.

Her heart started to thud. It was already dark, and she was alone. Of course, this was Larkville, but even in Larkville strangers passed through. She went to Izzy's room, kissed the top of her baby's head and closed the door on the sleeping child who owned her heart. Then she cautiously approached the curtains and peered out.

Holt stood there under her always-on porch light looking like dark thunder. Man thunder. Granite jaw, firm muscles, skin browned from long hours beneath the sun. Instantly, every female instinct she possessed urged her to smooth her hair, stand up straighter, change into something nicer, flaunt what she had.

Forget it, she told herself. *You are not doing that. You tried that when you were young. Now you're smarter.*

Wasn't she smarter? *Please let me be smarter,* she pleaded with herself as she opened the door.

"What are you doing?" he asked, looking anything but happy.

She frowned, confused. "Answering the door?"

"You didn't even ask who was there. I might have been anyone. Someone bent on doing you wrong."

She crossed her arms over her chest. "I saw you through the curtains, so I knew you were safe." What a totally ridiculous thing to say. Any woman could see that Holt wasn't safe. "Aren't you?" she asked weakly.

"If you have to ask that, then maybe no, I'm not." He still looked mad as could be.

She stood in the doorway, blocking the entrance. Kathryn wasn't sure why, but she knew it had something to do with keeping him out here where they could be seen, where things couldn't get personal. "Holt, why are you here? And why did you sign off when we were having a conversation online?"

"I asked you a question about what the fundraiser entailed and you didn't answer right away. You haven't asked me to pull my weight. What's with that?"

"I never meant for you to be that big a part of things. I wanted your help in making connections to people. You've done that—you've given me lists of people who can help. And I wanted your help in locating possible physicians. You've made phone calls, traveled to Chicago to conduct an interview and made more calls. I wanted you to get the people of the town behind the project. You showed up at the meeting. And sent barbecue and even loaned me your ranch. I never meant to worm my way further into your life."

"This is a major project, this fundraiser. You have a child. You have a job. Two jobs."

"The newspaper isn't much."

"That's not what I hear."

She sucked in a deep, panicked breath. James had checked up on her all the time. He'd been jealous, proprietary, ordering her around, telling her who she could and couldn't see, what she could and couldn't do. "You're keeping tabs on me?"

"Nancy tells me that if you have a newborn, you're probably tired all the time. Not getting enough sleep," he said, ignoring her question. "I fought you about signing on, but now…I'm on. I intend to do more."

Kathryn wasn't a short woman but she had to look up to stare fully into Holt's eyes. She did that now, no matter the danger. She pushed her chin up. "I don't like being put in my place."

"Neither do I."

"I've told you my husband was an overbearing man who insisted on running my life. I'm through with that."

"That won't be a problem. You and I aren't married and we don't have a relationship. We're just working together."

But his eyes were fierce, like flames cutting into her. Every cell in her body seemed to be alive.

"Fine. But I'm in charge."

"You told me we were partners earlier," he pointed out in that deceptively quiet voice.

She had, hadn't she? And she was a woman of her word. Kathryn blew out a breath. "Okay. But don't go all Neanderthal on me, okay? James always did that. He thought I was an idiot."

"I don't give half a damn what James thought. And if he said something like that about you to me, I'd probably kick his ass."

"I don't believe in violence."

"Then it's good that you have no interest in me. I have a tendency to use my fists when I get angry."

She blinked wide.

"Not on a woman," he said, gritting his teeth. "I've never hit a woman."

"I knew that."

"Your expression said differently. Did James hit you?"

"No. But he hurt me. That's why I don't…I don't want a man again. I'm far better off without one." Kathryn wondered who she was trying to convince, him or herself.

"Then we're in agreement. We should have no problem. And if I should try to kiss you—and I might try because heaven knows I still *want* to kiss you…don't worry about being a nonviolent person. A good slap won't hurt me, and it might knock some sense into me."

She looked at him more closely then. He wanted to kiss her. He *still* wanted to kiss her.

"You know I'm not going to slap you. I've been wanting to kiss you since the day I first saw you. Every girl wanted you. You were Holt Calhoun, captain of the football team, and I knew you were out of reach, but I daydreamed that someday you would bump into me and kiss me. I was an incredibly fanciful girl. And now—"

She never got past "and now."

"Dammit, Kathryn, you don't tell a man things like that." He moved quickly, smoothly, quietly, walking her up against the wall as he planted his palms on the siding and lowered his head.

"You don't tell me that," he repeated. "Because then I might do this." He swooped in and his mouth met hers. Gently at first and then…not so gently. This was a man who knew how to kiss, and he used all of his considerable skills on her as the kiss became more demanding.

Kathryn stopped breathing. Somewhere in the back of her mind, she thought, *Holt Calhoun is kissing me. And not just to comfort me this time. Finally.* And then she forgot to think as Holt pressed closer. Taking. Nuzzling. Driving her crazy. Giving her the fantasy she'd once wanted so much.

Her whole body felt like blue neon. Bright. Electric.

Every nerve cell sprang to life. She wanted to be closer. Much closer. She reached up and threaded her fingers through all that silky dark hair. A low sigh escaped her.

As if the sound had been lightning cracking overhead instead of a woman sighing, Holt froze. He stopped kissing her. For several seconds, everything was silent and still except for the heavy thudding of Kathryn's heart. Then he reached up, caught Kathryn's hands and stepped away.

"I probably shouldn't have done that. I'm not that young man of your dreams. Don't think I am."

"I don't. I stopped having those kinds of dreams."

"Good. Because I was never that guy and never will be."

"Because Lilith hurt you." Kathryn couldn't say where that thought came from or—worse—why she had the bad idea of saying the words, but they were out and she couldn't take them back.

She wished she could, because if a man could turn to a block of ice, Holt did that now. "No. I was never that man. I don't have that kind of deep feeling inside me. Lilith told me I was a stone. She was right. And at the risk of repeating myself too many times, I shouldn't have kissed you."

She should have let it drop there. Up until recently, Kathryn would have, but she was bolder now. She had to be bolder, and what he'd said...

"So, what? You really do try to turn yourself to stone? Because you can't tell me a man like you intends to go through life never kissing a woman or...anything." She was mad that she stumbled over the ending, but still, she held her ground.

"I never said I didn't kiss women. I said I shouldn't kiss *you*. You're different, more serious. And we have that history. I'm going to try never to touch you again."

Kathryn felt as if cold water had been dashed over her, even though she knew he was right. He was too overpowering for her, and she saw things in him that might not be there. Maybe there was still a part of that younger Kathryn inside her and she still wanted him to be something he never would be.

"I'll help you," she said.

He looked confused.

"I'll help you keep your distance," she clarified. "But we still have to finish what we've started."

"Agreed. Let's do this right, get the town what it needs, get you what you want, wrap everything in a neat package and send you on your way. You're just passing through, and that plan is best for everyone."

It was, wasn't it?

"All right. I'll send you an entire layout of what will be happening at the ranch on the 'Come Be a Cowboy Day,' what will be needed, and I'll divvy up the jobs. You can veto anything you don't agree with, and then we'll talk."

"We probably won't need to do that. Unless you don't give me enough work. Make it equitable, darlin'."

She blinked.

"That's not the first time you've used that term. Are you trying to get the upper hand by using a sexist endearment?"

He looked mildly amused. "Just getting into character for the big do."

But his words had made her recall that she had been wild in his arms only moments before. "I'll do it right this time," she said, half to herself. She was referring to the list, not the kiss. Or was she? "The divvying up, I mean."

"Good." He turned to go. A car drove by, the light hitting the house, just as Holt's boots thumped against the creaky porch. In the background, bothered by the noise or the light or both, Izzy whimpered.

Holt froze like a statue, his broad back stiff. Then he took a faltering step.

"Was…was Lilith pregnant when you left her?"

He dropped his head, rested his hands on his waist. "Leave it, Kathryn."

Okay, she would leave it.

"No. Better yet, don't leave it. This is how it was. You thought I was the dreamy football player. Well, I was a football player, but I was never a romantic guy. I don't even want to be that guy, and I never did. But Lilith hated that I hadn't lived up to her fantasy. Maybe she wanted to punish me for not being what she wanted in a husband or maybe she just didn't want a baby. I don't know. What I know is that she was pregnant, but she didn't tell me. Instead, she made plans to give the baby away. Just like that. No chance for me to even claim my child. I only found out about any of it after a friend of hers confessed the whole thing to me. She and I had a huge argument. She said that I was too cold, too closed off, that I would be hell on a kid and that I was just like my father and any child of mine would probably be at least partly like me. She wanted no part of raising a child like that. Not long after that she told me she had a miscarriage. We were already done by then, but that put a period to everything. And you know what?"

Kathryn waited.

"She was right about me. I'm not ready for any of that and probably never will be. So no fantasy dreams, no romance, no babies," he said. "You have the right plan. Go after your dreams, raise your child, spit in the eye of romance. That's what you need. I need not to have anyone hope I'll be that romantic, giving man. So yes, I kiss women…and things, as you say, but I don't do more. When we're done here, you run, darlin'. You skedaddle away from Larkville as fast as you can. Because I liked kissing you. A heck of a lot. But it would be a real bad idea for us to do that again. There's just no future in it, and you need a future."

She stood there, silently, her mind protesting everything. And knowing he was right. He was dynamite. She needed to be careful around him.

"Agreed?" he asked.

The correct answer was yes. She knew that. She needed to say it, but it was a little-girl answer, a giving-in answer. And despite the fact that he was 100 percent correct in his estimation of what they needed to do, she just couldn't let a man call all the shots anymore.

"I'll think about it."

He swore.

She shook her head. "Don't swear around the baby. And, Holt?"

"What?" The word was clipped, cold, angry.

"Don't worry. There's not a chance in the world that I'll fall in love with you or have romantic expectations of you. That's not who I am anymore, that's not where I'm headed. I might kiss you again before I leave town. But leave town I will. As soon as we're done. So yes, let's get done. Quickly. I have a life to get to."

Now she was done, she thought as he drove away. So why was she shaking? And why did her lips and her arms and her entire body ache?

CHAPTER ELEVEN

As IF that kiss had kicked everything into high gear, things began to take off in the weeks that followed. Kathryn received a request for more information from a company she had sent her résumé to. When the call came, her hands shook. No other company had contacted her, and there was a lot riding on her making the right response. If she did well it would mean leaving here soon.

Her heart lurched suddenly and the world felt off-kilter. "I'm just excited," she whispered. "And I'm concerned because I haven't finished what I started yet."

Yes, that was it. She sat down right then and sent Holt an addendum to the list of activities for the cowboy day. A short time later, he sent back a few terse questions:

This is getting big. You're sure you want it to be this big? And where do you want things to happen? How many people do you need to run things? What do you mean by "ranch things"?

"Well, there's the problem," she admitted. She wasn't quite sure. She didn't want to throw all of this off on Holt. She didn't want to be like everyone else, taking advantage of him. Because just the other day, she had overheard someone in town saying that he was going to ask Holt to help him repair his SUV, and when Mr. Hurdle had been in the waiting room, he had told another patient that if the bank wouldn't give him a loan, he might try Holt. Holt was frequently approached by people in the street. He wrote down their requests and lent a hand whenever he could. It was part of his life here. He was a good neighbor and friend.

Still, unease filled her when she remembered how *she* had hounded Holt. She knew why he had put her off. It was because she had wanted *him* to ask for favors, not the other way around. He might be gruff and grumpy and frustrate a girl to death, until he kissed her, but Holt didn't know how to say no to his neighbors. So, despite his insistence that he share the work of the fundraiser, she was reluctant to put herself back into that category. The truth was that she had pushed him into this whole project, and now he felt obligated.

Kathryn sighed. She tried to think of another way, but Holt could probably tell if she was lying, and the truth was that she needed his help as much as everyone else did. As for his questions, she didn't have all the answers yet, and she knew there was only one way to find those answers.

"Come on, Izzy, sweetie. We have to go see a man about a horse. And a dog. And a bunch of stuff we know nothing about.'

Izzy made one of those cute baby sounds that Kathryn loved.

"I know. He doesn't like you much. I'm sorry about that, love. But he has his reasons, and we're not going to change his mind. Holt is a good man, but he's got a hardshell coating he doesn't want anyone to penetrate." Some men were just like that. Holt might have better reasons than most. She couldn't begin to understand what it must be like to father a child and find out that your child had been on the verge of being given away with no one even giving you a chance to lay claim. And then to lose that child anyway, lose the woman you loved, lose the future you'd planned, all in one fell swoop? All Kathryn knew was that it couldn't be any of her concern. Not if she was smart.

Her dealings with Holt would soon be over. *Thank goodness,* she thought as she made her way to the ranch. Now that she had been kissed full-on by Holt...she wanted to do it all over again.

Holt was wrestling with a calf, a bottle in one hand and the unhappy calf in the other, when a shadow fell over him. He looked up to see Kathryn standing there. She was staring at him as if she'd never seen him before, and he quickly realized that she'd never seen him this way before. He had always been in his big bad quarterback guise or his badass rancher guise whenever they'd met. At least when he hadn't been losing control and kissing her. Or insulting her. That time when she'd been giving birth didn't count, since she'd been out of her mind with pain.

But he didn't like to think about that day.

Now she was looking at him as if he'd turned into a different person. He had a bottle in one hand as he fed the calf and the other hand resting on the calf's furry neck.

"That doesn't look like something the ranch owner would be doing," she said.

He resisted smiling and shrugged. "A rancher can't ask his people to do things he won't do himself."

"Is that rule number one of ranching?"

"Something like that."

"Why are you giving that calf a bottle?"

"His momma died, and he's not old enough to wean yet. It happens. Calves lose their mothers or their mothers can't provide them with enough milk and you have to make sure they get the milk they need. It's easier when the calf is a newborn. Sometimes you can get another cow to take the calf on, or if you have to feed one by hand, they catch on to how it's done in only a few days. This little guy is a bit older so it can take up to fourteen days. He and I are just getting started and he's not real happy, but it's necessary. In a very short time, he's gonna come running for the bottle, no coaxing needed."

"I feel kind of dumb, having lived here but knowing so little about raising cattle."

"We all know what we need to know, I guess. You never had any need to know cattle." And he had never needed to know anything about raising babies. "Where's the baby?" he asked, as if he just couldn't help it. He frowned.

"Don't worry. I don't have her hidden on my body somewhere. Nancy's got her. Now that she's a few weeks old, they're communicating."

"Nancy likes babies." Holt wanted to swear. Everything he said seemed to shout, *I don't like babies!* Which wasn't true. He just hadn't gotten over losing his. He still wanted his child. Maybe someday he'd get his act together, learn how to treat a baby right and have one of his own, but this one was spoken for. She wasn't going to stay, and he couldn't bear the loss of another baby. It was better not to get attached to things you had to give up. "You came about my questions?" he asked, trying to change the subject and forget about the unchangeable past.

"I came to tell you that I never expected you to do so much. I wouldn't have approached you at all if I'd had any connections to people who could help provide a doctor or if I had the kind of pull you do with the people of Larkville."

Holt scowled. "Has anyone here been treating you wrong?"

"Not at all. In fact, I've been gifted with their largesse. Baby items keep appearing on my porch, and I've made friends I never had when I lived here before. I'm grateful, especially since people don't really have any reason at all to be so darned sweet to me. I pretty much drifted through my teen years here without connecting."

"Not your fault. You told me your parents kept you apart from the rest of the town."

"Any ordinary teen would have rebelled."

He couldn't help chuckling.

"What?"

"You sounded downright irritated that you bypassed the rebellious teen phase."

"Did you? Rebel, I mean?"

He had tried to. "I did a few things. Raised some hell. Busted up a car or two. Got drunk." Got a woman pregnant. But by then he'd left his teen years behind. It still galled him that he had messed up that way on so many levels. "Mostly, though, I had to walk the straight and narrow. If you don't take care of your animals, well, ranching can be life or death. You have to time your hell-raising right or everyone suffers."

She laughed at that, and her laugh was soft, musical, enticing. He growled.

"Don't growl at me," she said, surprising him.

"I wasn't."

"You were looking at me when you growled."

He wondered if her jerk of a husband had done stuff like that. "Why'd you marry a guy like that, anyway?"

She blushed, her cheeks turning a pretty rose as she looked to the side. "When I was growing up and things were so bad, I couldn't wait to get away and be on my own.

I floated along for a while just enjoying college and my studies, but when I met James, well, he could be charming and complimentary. And when we got married, he was in grad school and I gave up my own plans in order to take any job I could get to support us. But when I started communicating with one of my former professors who suggested I might want to attend grad school myself when James finished, things got really ugly. James was jealous, he needed adoration, and when I got pregnant…well, I learned a lot about men who need to be in control. They don't like having that control taken from them. My own fault for not seeing it sooner."

"Some men hide things well." It was a warning. To her. To him.

"Well, now I have better and more effective armor than I used to." She met his challenge.

"Do you now?" He looked at her the way a man looks at a woman he wants, and her blush deepened, but she didn't look away.

"You can't scare me into thinking that you're bad, you know," she said. "You're…you're ornery at times, and we want different things from life, but I see what you do. You pretend to be mean, but you're not mean. In fact, you're rather a soft touch."

And she was digging into areas he didn't want anyone to go. "What are you here for really, Kathryn? I've got work to do."

She blew out a breath. "I don't even want to admit it, but you asked me some questions I don't know the answers to. So I'm here to find out the answers."

"Excuse me?"

"You help show me what goes on at the ranch and then I'll tell you what events I want to have. And I'm not letting you do all the work, either," she said. "Thanks to you, I'm getting to know a whole lot more people in the town and I know how to get them to help out. I just need to decide what will work best. I'll make some choices and run them by you. Will you... Can you find some time during this week to show me around? What would be good for you?"

Never would be good for him. He liked looking at her and touching her and just listening to her talk far too much. And she had that cute little baby...

He made his mind go blank for a second. "I can show you around today." Best to get this over with.

She looked at the calf who had finished the bottle. "What happened to having work to do and ranching being life or death?"

"I do, and it is. But I run the ranch now. I hire good people and I have a crew of hands I can call on to moonlight for me when I need to."

"Okay. Just let me go check in on Izzy and talk to Nancy."

He started to tell her that he would just call Nancy on his phone, but he thought she might need to do some "momma" things like feed the baby, things he didn't want to think about. And this would give him time to come up with a plan for the tour.

Instead, he walked her up to the house. Moving beside her, watching the sun catch the lighter streaks in her wheat hair, he breathed in her scent, and his body reacted instantly. That he could ignore...mostly. But when she turned to go inside, she gave him a brilliant smile. "I know showing off your ranch to city girls probably isn't high on your list of things you want to do, but I trust you not to go easy on me."

"Wouldn't dream of it."

She nodded. Then her smile faded a bit and she got a

serious, anxious look in her eyes. "Holt, I have a job interview."

Which meant she might be leaving soon. He tried to ignore the punch to his gut. "That's great. Congratulations."

"Thank you, but it does mean that I need to do as much as I can for the clinic quickly. I don't want to leave this job half-finished. That wouldn't be right."

He started to tell her that he would finish it for her, even though the thought of going on without her made him feel oddly empty, but as he opened his mouth, she spoke.

"In spite of my degree, I've never done anything of this magnitude before and I need to do it right. I—I have something to prove to myself."

"Understood. But even the rancher needs help. Everyone does."

She studied him as if he had just lied to her.

"Says the man who doesn't like to ask people for help."

"I have employees."

"Exactly. They're *employees*. You pay them. They're not doing you a favor."

He gave her the evil eye he had perfected.

She laughed and reached up and patted his cheek. "Just be aware that I may be running full tilt until this is done. While I'm forced to ask people to help with some things, I want to do as much as I can on my own."

"You'll make yourself sick."

She smiled and turned away. "No. But I'll do something important. I'll help people and make a difference. I'll secure my future. I hope."

What was a guy supposed to say to that? "Go talk to Nancy and do what you need to do with Izzy. I'll give you the whirlwind tour when you're done."

A bark had Kathryn turning to greet Blue, who was bearing down on her like a fast-moving tank. She dropped to her knees, which made the dog even taller than she was. Then she gave the evil-looking mutt a big hug. Blue's teeth could take a chunk out of her if he was so inclined. Holt knew that he wouldn't, but Kathryn couldn't know that. She'd only met the dog once.

"Hi, sweetie," she said, receiving a slobbery lick for her troubles.

Holt gave her a look. *Too innocent,* he wanted to say. If this didn't end soon, she would surely make him crazy.

"What?" she asked, a challenge in her eyes.

He started to tell her that nothing was wrong. Instead, he faced her head-on. "I've seen men run when Blue comes at them, but you didn't, not even that first time."

She shrugged. "I guess I figured that even if you wanted me gone, you still wouldn't let your dog eat me."

He didn't say anything.

"I know you think that I'm a bit naive, but I'm not. Not anymore. To prove it, here are the people in town who've won my respect and friendship." She rattled off a small group which concluded with Jess, Nancy and himself. "These are the people I don't know well enough to decide about yet," she said, giving him another list. "And these are the people who make me uncomfortable." There were only two people on that list, both of them bad. Then she raised one delicate, sexy brow. "Am I wrong?"

"I'm thinking about it." But her laughter rang out behind him as he walked away, and he couldn't help but smile. Not that she would know it. His back was to her. He, however, knew one thing. Kathryn Ellis kept him on his toes. And when she challenged him she made him hot. Oh, yes, risky as it was, he was definitely going to kiss her again before she left.

CHAPTER TWELVE

"I NEVER knew this ranch was this big," Kathryn said as Holt drove her around the perimeter and then down some of the interior roads.

"Needs to be. Cattle need a lot of land, a lot of grass."

"And you have horses, too."

"Yes. Enough to do the jobs that can't be done from a truck."

"When can't you use a truck?"

"If you're trying to catch a runaway cow, the truck can go faster than a horse, but it doesn't maneuver nearly as well and there are places it just can't go. Driving a truck, you can't cut back and change directions quickly enough to stay with a cow that doesn't want to get caught. And a horse, once the cow is caught, is more sensitive to the movements of the animal than a truck driver can be. An ATV will do the job, but ATVs, like trucks, can stress the cows more than a horse will. Besides, a lot of cowmen just like horses. We like them on a personal basis, we like the history of them, we don't want them disappearing from the ranch, so there are days, at least on the Double Bar C, when we take out the horses just because it's the right thing to do. A prized truck is great, but a prized horse and a cowboy...that's an unbreakable bond."

"Is that how you feel about Daedalus?"

"He's special," Holt agreed, restraining his praise. He didn't want to get sappy in front of Kathryn. The woman saw way too much.

"I assume you'll be okay with people riding your horses at the fundraiser?"

"I thought that was a given."

"Good. Because I'd like to ride Daedalus. I've never really ridden a horse before."

He stopped the truck. "You're kidding, right? I know what you said about being a city girl and not taking part in Larkville society, but this is Texas, Kathryn. Ranch country. That's practically criminal." He turned the truck toward home.

She saw where he was headed. "Did I make you angry?"

"Yes."

Kathryn sighed.

"What?"

"That's your only response?"

"You asked a question. I answered it."

"You're angry with me because I haven't ridden a horse before?"

"I'm angry that no one, including me, knew that." He pulled the truck up in the drive. "Come on," he said, surprising her by taking her hand again.

Her palm slid against his. She tried not to savor the sensation of touching Holt too much, but this had been one of her teenage fantasies—Holt holding her hand. It felt as good as she had imagined it would, as good as it had the last time they'd touched. And now things got worse. She felt hot. Shivery. All this just from Holt's hand wrapped around hers. What would she do if he wrapped his arms around her and kissed her again?

Idiot. Stop it, she told herself as she tried to turn her attention back to more practical matters.

Neither did she ask where they were going. It was obvious. Or so she thought. When they got to the barn, he went into what she guessed was a tack room and started looking around. "These will have to do," he finally said, giving her a pair of boots that were, she guessed, about a size too big. "These were my mother's, but as long as you can keep them on, they'll be better than nothing."

Kathryn sat right down and put the boots on. She was going to ride a horse. Holt was going to show her how. She grinned at him. He smiled back, just a little. Her heart flipped around.

Easy, she told herself. *Don't react.* But the man was just too potent. She could see why Lilith had been upset that he couldn't open his heart to her. A woman would do a lot to get a man like this to say the words she wanted to hear. None of that excused the heinous things Holt's ex-fiancée had done. But it made Kathryn understand a little. And it made her very wary.

"You've been wanting to do this a long time, haven't you?" he asked.

"I never thought about it too much, but now that I am, I love anything that broadens my horizons. When you spend your childhood and marriage in a vacuum, every new experience is exciting."

Great. A ranch was, for all its acres, a pretty small microcosm. As Lilith had told him repeatedly, she craved the world. Fashion. Excitement. The theater. Anything that wasn't a ranch. Soon enough Kathryn would have tried all there was to try on a ranch. And then?

Then she'd do what she'd planned all along and head off to her new job that could only be done in a city.

Holt saddled and mounted Daedalus. Then he motioned Kathryn over to the fence and held out his hand to her.

She looked at his hand as if it was a rattlesnake. "I thought you were going to teach me to ride, not treat me like a baby."

"Learning to do anything requires baby steps," he said. "You want to ride Daedalus, but he's too much of a handful for a beginner." Still, he knew that part of the reason he was doing this was because he wanted Kathryn behind him, her arms around his waist. And he wanted—for a few minutes, anyway—to stop waiting for her smile, which would be simple if he couldn't see her face. The truth was that he was feeling seriously besotted. That was bad.

In seconds, she had swung up behind him. He groaned inwardly as her hands circled his waist and she nudged up against him, her soft breasts against his back.

"Now we'll take a slow ride until you get used to the motion," he said, trying to keep his voice from going thick.

"Okay." Her voice was a bit whispery. He knew she wasn't immune to him. She had gotten into that kiss the other day with fervor. He was insane for torturing them both this way.

"Let's—let's figure out which things we'll do on the cowboy day," she suggested.

"Good idea." Anything to take his mind off his very bad idea of having Kathryn riding behind him. Together they decided on a few events. Riding, of course. A little roping. Teaching riders to dally and tie on, which he had to explain to her were two methods of securing a rope to a saddle once you'd caught your cow.

"Cowboys tend to be passionate about their favorite method," he told her. "Some parts of the country favor one or the other. Here at the Double Bar C, we use the one that fits the situation. Is that enough events for the day?"

"Not quite. How about some fence mending?" she suggested. "And helping with that bridge you said you were going to repair."

"I'm going to fix the bridge before the guests show up."

"No. People will like it better if they know they're doing a real job, not a made-up one. And since I talked you into this, it's only right that you should get something back."

He had already gotten something back. He was pretty sure that just getting to know Kathryn was going to be the highlight of his days when he thought back on this summer.

They agreed on a few more events for those who were less inclined to the ranching side of things: baking and jam contests, lessons in soap making and other artisan crafts that Holt knew some of the ranchers' wives excelled at. And, of course, the minirodeo at the end of the day, followed by fireworks. But when Daedalus shied slightly at a bee and Kathryn tightened her hold on him, bumping up against him, Holt decided to put an end to this exquisite torture.

"Now alone," he said, switching things around so that he was on the ground and Kathryn was riding single. He led Daedalus around and showed Kathryn how to command the horse to do as she wished.

"I never knew how much fun this could be," she said with a smile. "I wonder if fence mending will be as much fun."

Despite himself, he chuckled "You actually sound as if you're looking forward to mending fences. Think of the unpleasant jobs I could have talked you into if I'd only known."

"Your loss. Too late now," she teased as she made another loop around the corral.

Eventually, though, the time came for her to get down.

Holt held up his arms and she went into them. It was all he could do not to slide her down his body, but that trusting look in her eyes did him in. He had to behave, even though it was killing him.

Her feet had barely touched the ground, however, when she rose on her toes and kissed him on the cheek. Just one kiss. Feather-soft. Sweet. Nothing sensual about it. But it was torture. Not touching her was torture. But so very necessary. He was starting to lose control around her, and wasn't that one of Kathryn's concerns? She wanted to be in control.

"I hope you get that job you're in line for," he said as she put Izzy in her car. He meant it. If he spent too much longer with Kathryn, he was going to do something that was going to leave both of them filled with regret for a very long time. Even after she was gone.

Holt tried to put his head down and just work during the next couple of weeks. The fundraiser was scheduled three weeks from now and there was a lot to do to get the ranch in shape to receive visitors. He'd been in touch with friends and business associates in Texas, Illinois and New York, sending out as big a net as he could in the hopes of tempting one qualified doctor to tiny Larkville. All of that had to be scheduled around the regular ranch duties.

Not that he was complaining about the work. Anything he could do to keep from thinking about Kathryn with her hands on him or Kathryn with her lips on him or just Kathryn was fine by him. There was something about the woman that just drove him mad, and he was pretty sure he knew what it was. During the time he had been taking care of Hank and since then, he had been without any intimate female companionship. Unfortunately, right now there was no other woman that he was attracted to even if he'd had time. But just as soon as all this clinic stuff was over and Kathryn and her baby were back where they belonged, he was going to have to do something about that. As it was, he was half-afraid he was going to grab her and kiss her—or worse—in public, and that wouldn't be good for either of them.

But while he was waiting, he was going to stay away and keep his mind off her as much as possible. At least that was the plan.

Unfortunately, it was difficult to stick to. When he went to town for supplies a few days later, he kept wondering whether Kathryn was at the doctor's office, the newspaper or at home, and how she was managing with the baby. Quickly, he tried to kick those thoughts from his mind.

"Hey, Holt," Gus said when he stopped at Gus's Fillin' Station. "I hear that pretty little gal of yours is creating quite a stir in the town. Got everybody buzzin' and doin'."

Holt's brain had frozen on the words *that pretty little gal of yours*. "You're talking about Kathryn?"

"Who else? I've never seen anybody go at anything with such fire. It sounds like a mountain of a job, but she's always got a smile on her face. She smiles even while she's askin' you to do something, and before you know it, you're saying yes and likin' it, too."

"What exactly is she asking?"

"Oh, you know, would I dress up like a cowboy in full gear for that cowboy thing she's so excited about. And how much will it cost for me to fix her car so it won't break down on the way to the ranch. And will I drive the bus she's borrowing from the school district to bus any of the visitors who need bussing, because she knows she can trust me to get them there safe. And then, besides paying me to fix her car, she promised me cookies and kissed me on the cheek when I said yes, I would dress up and drive the bus."

"She did, huh?" Holt couldn't help sounding grumpy. Or grumpier than usual. Even though it was dumb as hell to be jealous of Kathryn kissing Gus on the cheek. Gus was an old man…but he was a nice man. He had been on Kathryn's list of people she liked. And age might not matter to Kathryn. It certainly wouldn't matter to Gus… or any man for that matter. Kathryn was too damn pretty and she had that smile that made a man feel as if he might burst into flame without any fuel.

He almost growled, forgetting himself. Then he shook himself. Stupid. Gus was his friend, and Kathryn was an exuberant woman. Just because some people—like himself—were shallow and emotionally stunted didn't mean that everyone else was.

"Hey, Holt," Gus said as Holt started to leave. He turned and saw Gus rubbing his neck and frowning the way people did when they were about to broach an uncomfortable subject. Holt quickly considered all the possibilities. Could be a money question. Was the station in financial trouble? Could be an animal question, but that wouldn't make Gus uncomfortable and—

"Hey, Holt, I…uh, I was reading a book on the history of Texas the other day. Thought you might like to borrow it."

Holt blinked. What the— A book? "Sure, Gus. That'd be real nice. Thanks."

Gus scowled. He looked incredibly relieved.

As Holt went on his way, he wondered what that had been about. He and Gus had never had an exchange like that before. They'd never even discussed books or history. Mostly they talked about cars and guns. Maybe horses. But as Holt went about his business in town, a pattern quickly developed. Almost everyone he ran into that day offered him something: cookies, pickles, jam; Mrs. Best brought him a framed photograph of his daddy from when she and Clay were young. And everyone he met—after they had gotten past this awkward gifting stage—had some tale to tell him about how Kathryn had them eager to help her out. The town was a whole lot more excited about Kathryn's cowboy day than they even were about football. That said a lot about the woman. And judging by the talk he'd heard, it sounded as if she was running herself ragged.

Maybe he would stop by her place for a minute—just to make sure she didn't have any color-coded lists she needed to send him. No point in her emailing him if he was here in the flesh, was there? It would save her some trouble.

Unfortunately, his plan wasn't as simple as it sounded. For a town this small, Kathryn really seemed to get around. She wasn't at home, at work or at the SmartMart. He didn't see her at Hal's Drug and Photo, either. And he knew she wouldn't be in the Saddle Up Bar or the Cattleman's Association Hall. By the time he got to the town hall and ran into the mayor, Holt was starting to get worried. "Kathryn?" he asked tersely.

Fortunately, Johanna was used to his ways, and being a woman who knew how to cut to the chase, she simply told him what he wanted. "At the park."

"Thanks."

She moved toward him.

"You're not going to give me anything, are you?" he asked.

The poised, middle-aged, never nonplussed mayor actually looked a bit discomfited. "A bottle of wine?" she suggested.

"Kathryn?" he asked.

"Don't be upset with her. She was just trying to give back, not make you feel uncomfortable." She handed him the wine. He thanked her, somewhat awkwardly.

"Don't worry. I won't make her pay for my embarrassment. Much." He headed out again.

Johanna cleared her throat and he waited. "She's with Izzy." The fact that she even felt compelled to mention it—did everyone in town know that he wasn't good around babies? Had Kathryn told them? He didn't think she would. But he put his head down and set off to find her, wondering what he would say to her when he found her. Telling himself to slap some self-control on before he did something stupid. Like back her up against a tree and mold his body to hers.

Just before he read her the riot act for making people think—for some weird reason—that they needed to give him Christmas presents in the summer.

Put a rein on it, Calhoun, he ordered himself and he thought he was doing pretty well. When he arrived at the park, he came upon an idyllic scene. The grass was green, the sun was shining, the baby was asleep on a blanket in the shade of a tree and Kathryn sat beside her, her blond head bent over a batch of papers on her lap. Holt tried not to notice just how small and innocent Izzy looked. Instead, he turned his attention to Katherine as he moved toward her. His steps were silent on the grass, and he was already standing next to the blanket by the time she noticed him there.

For half a second he thought he saw something in her eyes that made him feel overly warm, but that was probably just his imagination. Maybe just his own wishful thinking because it was gone as soon as it had appeared. She smiled at him.

"You caught me goofing off," she said, her voice low to keep from waking the baby.

He sank to one knee beside her and touched the edge of her papers with one finger. "Do you even know how to goof off? Looks like more lists."

"Some of them are, but my mind was wandering when you showed up. That counts as goofing off."

"Doesn't exactly sound like fun."

"How do you know? In my mind I was in a dreamworld."

He raised one brow. "Doing what? With whom?"

Oh, now he had made her blush. Maybe he had been trying to. She was amazingly pretty when she blushed, and today, tipping her head back, she looked like a woman waiting to be kissed. Or a woman planning on kissing a man. Either way, she looked too damned enticing.

"Nothing like that," she said. "It wasn't that kind of dream. There wasn't a man involved."

Good. "So it was a fun dream, but there was no man involved."

"Exactly. I was practicing affirmative thinking."

"I see." He didn't. "And what were you affirming?"

"I was…it's silly, but I was imagining myself in my own apartment, somewhere in a city. I've just been asked to oversee the redevelopment of an aging part of town, one that needs revitalizing. The people who've hired me know I can do it, because I get results. And what that means is…"

"Lots of money?"

She shook her head. "No. Well, maybe. It means that I can give Izzy all that she needs. I can protect her." Kathryn's voice was quiet but intense. Clearly this was something she worried about. It was the thing that woke her up at night.

Holt's mind went dark. He tried not to think about how alone in the world Kathryn was. He didn't have the right to go there. He didn't even know how to express the confusing, conflicting sensations that were flitting through him. "Good things will happen for you," he said. "Have to. They wouldn't dare elude you. You're a fighter."

"It wasn't all selfish stuff I was thinking about, either," she said as if wanting to protect your kid was even close to selfish. But he knew what she meant. The apartment. The job and accolades. "I was imagining Ava DuShay calling me. She's the lady who's most worried about Dr. Cooper leaving. She was telling me that she loved the new doctor and the clinic and that now she wouldn't have to worry about her son coming back to Larkville and putting her in a home."

"Mrs. DuShay worries about that?"

"Yes. Her son lives—"

"In Dallas. Yes, I know Buddy. He's an ass. A bigger ass than I am."

"Well, I know you wouldn't be putting her in a home if she was your concern."

"Damn straight I wouldn't." He frowned.

"I probably shouldn't have mentioned that," she said. "You're looking fierce."

"I'm thinking that I need to talk to Buddy when he comes to town next time. Maybe move his nose to one side of his face. Making his momma worry like that."

"I think she might worry more if you punched Buddy. He's her son, and she loves him no matter what. You can understand that, can't you?"

He stared at her. She knew darn well he wasn't a sensitive guy. He didn't *want* to be a sensitive guy. He didn't want to *feel*. Feelings brought trouble and everything bad that had ever happened to him had been a result of out-of-control emotions.

"Anyway, she isn't going to have to worry about that," he said, ignoring his thoughts. "We'll get a doctor. You'll get that phone call. And you'll get that job, too. Anyone can see that you know how to get things done. I must have met twenty people today telling me about what they were doing for their part of the fundraiser."

"Yes, they're excited, aren't they?" she asked. "*I'm* excited, too. This is going to be so much fun! Everyone's going to have a great time. I talked to Nan and she says that the Bunk'n'Grill is booked solid. I asked her to see if she could find some more places to put people. Nan's on it."

He smiled in spite of himself.

"What?"

"Did you promise her cookies?"

She looked guilty. "I promised I'd teach her to braid beads in her hair. She likes quirky things like that. But she would have done it without. Nan doesn't need bribing. No one here does. I just— They're all working so hard, I want them to know I appreciate it."

"You're not even going to benefit from the clinic."

"You know I will. I'll get to talk about it in job interviews and, more than that, I'll just know I helped make it happen. My point is, people are capable of doing a lot of things they might not think they're capable of doing if they don't have you to run to. I'll bet they all got along when you were out of town."

"So you *are* the elf?"

"Excuse me?" Oh, weren't those gray eyes pretty when she opened them that wide?

"You know what I mean, Kathryn," he said, his voice

low. "I have a pickup truck full of food and other gifts. What's that all about?"

"People always take their problems to you. They…love you, just like they did your father. I just thought maybe they might not have thought about how much work taking care of them is and that they might, maybe, possibly, want to show you that they appreciate you in some way other than simply saying how great you are. Speaking of which…" She turned to rummage in her bag.

He saw what she was going to do and automatically, without thinking, he put his hand over hers. He tried to ignore the softness of her skin and how his own flesh reacted to this simple touch. Kathryn froze and turned to him.

"Not you," he said, his voice tight. "You've been doing all the work. You don't get to do the payback thing."

"You saved me and Izzy. I never paid you back for that."

"Sure you did."

"How?"

But he got stubborn. *You lived. You're safe,* he thought. That was her payback to him. But he would never say that. That was delving into territory he didn't want to and wouldn't traverse. Especially now.

"I'll let you give me some of Gus's cookies."

"How do you know I wasn't going to give you cookies?"

He chuckled then. "I guess I don't. Just don't give me anything. I don't want payback."

She crossed her arms. "Are you going to tell me that you turned all those people down?"

He frowned. "No. I didn't. I wanted to, but I didn't. It would have created problems."

"It would have hurt their feelings."

"Yes."

She smiled. Brilliantly.

"What?"

"You turned down my gift. That means you consider me an equal, a partner, because you didn't worry about hurting my feelings."

"You have too much sense to take anything I say or do to heart. We've discussed this before."

"You're darn right. You and I are…friends. We don't have to stand on ceremony." Suddenly she gave him a strange look. She had risen to her knees and crossed her arms. There was a stern look in those gorgeous gray eyes. Kathryn looked at his pocket. "I see you have another of those little scraps of paper, those *lists*," she emphasized. "Who asked you to do what today?"

Holt felt like a kid who had gotten caught passing notes at school. He was half tempted to cover his pocket with his hand. "There's not much on it."

"And you say that you don't make lists…" she drawled.

"Your lists would make my lists ashamed to be called lists." He pulled the slip of paper from his pocket. "Not a single color code in sight and only two items on it."

She took a look. "These are both things they could figure out on their own. Not that I can talk. I've asked you to do more for me than anyone else has. Thank goodness that, as I told you, I'm done asking you for things."

"I know what you said. You're telling me I'm expendable." For some reason, that ticked him off. All his life he'd been following in his father's footsteps, being everyone's go-to guy and—yes—he seldom admitted it even to himself, but there *had* been times when he'd wished he could step out from under the weight of all that responsibility for a while. But now? Here with Kathryn telling him she didn't want his help?

She looked totally surprised. "I've…offended you?"

"No. I'm not offended." He was…he didn't know what in hell he was.

"I just wanted you to know that I realized I shouldn't have pushed you so hard. You made the calls, you gave me your ranch to more or less destroy, you lent me Nancy when I needed her, you gave up your time, you even gave me riding lessons and you made sure Izzy was born safely. I came back to Larkville determined to declare my independence and make it on my own. Asking you for so much…I took too much help from you. I should have stood on my own feet more."

"Who told you that?"

She was shaking her head, looking sad and lovely. "I didn't need to be told. Growing up, I was powerless, but when I married…I take credit for making that mistake. James might have been a controlling man, but I was the one who married him and allowed that to happen to myself. That's why I have to be my own person and be much more proactive."

"You *are*."

"Good. I can't be that woman again. When I got pregnant with Izzy—I had been sick and I neglected to take a couple of my birth control pills—James flew into a rage. He didn't want her. That's when I knew I had to leave him and I had to change. So immediately asking you to help me was not the way to go."

He shook his head.

"What?"

He was as angry as any man could be inside. At himself. At her stupid ex-husband. At any man who made a woman feel guilty for not agreeing to be under his thumb. But he smiled. "If you think you seemed dependent when you asked for my help, you're wrong. You were persistent. Stubborn. Annoying."

"I was scared."

"Could have fooled me. You were bold. A dog that wasn't going to let go of a bone. You were ready to fight me for what you wanted, to make it clear that I was being a stubborn idiot. And you were right. I had the contacts. This is my town, these are my people, they're my responsibility. And you wouldn't take no. That's not being dependent, and you know it."

She blew out a breath. "I know it. And I'm proud that I was able to walk away from James and of my part in trying to make this clinic happen. But that still doesn't make it right that I and every person in town over the age of eighteen comes to you to solve all their problems. That has just got to stop."

"No."

"Holt…"

He gave her a "don't go there" look.

She grumbled something under her breath.

"What?"

"I said that you're a damned stubborn man."

"That I am. Deal with it, hon."

"You can't tell me you're always fine with everyone leaning on you. You fought me tooth and nail."

"Because you asked me to do the asking. I sure as hell don't like that." But she was right. There were days when he wanted to feel free to say, "I don't have time today." So why was he arguing so hard? He knew why. Because if he admitted it, she would stop asking him for things. And then he'd have no reason for these intimate little conversations.

His blood ran hot thinking of the word *intimate*. His blood ran cold thinking of ending his time with her.

"I know you don't like asking," she agreed, and she looked up at him. Suddenly he wasn't thinking about her ex-husband or the clinic or the town. He was thinking about *not* asking. Just doing exactly what he wanted to do.

Holt reached out and slid his hand beneath her hair. He cupped her neck, drew her closer. Now they were body to body, her breasts to his chest, her thighs against his, and he was staring down into her eyes. Then his lips were on hers, on all that berry softness, feeling the pressure of her mouth as she returned his kiss and made him burn. He pressed closer, took more. Any second now he was going to slide his palm down her curves, take as much of her as he possibly could. Right here in a public place.

"Hell." The single word came out too loud.

Then he heard a small sound, just the slightest of sounds, a tiny whimpering. He froze. Kathryn practically leaped away from him. Izzy was stirring. The baby who ruled Kathryn's world, her reason for living, her reason for most of what she did. Soon it would just be Kathryn and Izzy.

Holt withdrew his hand and moved away.

Kathryn sat down on her heels. "I'm sorry," she said.

"For what?" he asked as nonchalantly as he could given the fact that his body was still aching for her.

"Don't do that."

He didn't pretend to misunderstand. "You think I'm going to blame you for not wanting to roll around on the ground with your baby right there?"

"Some men would." He could imagine who she was talking about. He wanted to tell her that he wouldn't be like that. He wanted to make her promises. How idiotic was that? It wasn't going to happen.

Instead, he reached into his pocket and pulled out a slip of paper.

"I don't understand." She took it as he rose and started to walk away.

"It's a list of three potential doctor candidates," he told her. "They'll all be here at the fundraiser."

And then he took off. Fast. Giving her the list of candidates was, after all, what he'd really come to do, anyway, wasn't it? He surely hadn't come to tell Kathryn that she made him crazy, that he found himself remembering her behind him on that horse, that he thought of touching her all the time.

He definitely hadn't come here to kiss her.

CHAPTER THIRTEEN

HOLT wasn't even out of the park when Kathryn's cell phone rang. She answered it, hung up, grabbed Izzy and started running. She must have been making a fuss because Holt turned around.

"Kathryn, what's wrong?"

"Nothing. Everything. That was the town of Skyridge, Illinois, calling. The city manager has been called out of town and he wants to push the video interview to now rather than two days from now. I have to get home, change clothes, set up the computer with the camera and… and…" She looked at Izzy. "I have to get Izzy to Johanna or Gracie or Mrs. Best. Fast. What if Izzy started squealing or crying while I was in the middle of the interview? I hate dropping her off on someone or feeling like I'm getting rid of her, but—"

"Give her here," Holt said, and he held out his arms.

Kathryn stopped babbling. She stared at him.

He glared at her. "Don't say anything. Don't argue. You don't have time to talk about it. I won't hurt her."

"I'll try to make it short," she said, reluctantly giving Izzy over to him.

"Make it what it has to be. This is your moment. Now go. Call me when you want her back."

She leaned forward, kissed Izzy, said, "I love you,

baby," and then sprinted toward her house. She tried not to think about how Holt had avoided all things Izzy up until now. She was 100 percent certain he wouldn't let anything harm the baby, but she wasn't so sure about Izzy's effect on him. This was a man who had known he had a child on the way and had had that child taken from him forever.

The stress of worrying about what was going on between Holt and Izzy made Kathryn's smile too tense, her answers falsely bright. Her mind wasn't on the interview and she was faking it. Ed Austen, the interviewer, had a million questions, but he seemed particularly interested in the clinic and the "Come Be a Cowboy Day." "Sounds like a winner," he said.

"I hope so," Kathryn said, her mind still wandering to Izzy and Holt. Then she realized what she was saying, what she was doing—or not doing—and she sat up straighter, looking directly toward the screen. This was her baby's future. She couldn't waste it. Worrying wouldn't change what was going on with Holt and Izzy. "We're at capacity right now," she said, sitting up straighter, "and everyone is ready. This fundraiser should give us a good start on beginning our work on the clinic."

"And what if you leave? Who will make it happen then?"

Kathryn didn't even hesitate. "Holt Calhoun, Johanna Hollis, the mayor." She rattled off the names of several other people. "Almost everyone in the town, really. They've all gotten into the spirit of things. But Holt's the one who's helped the most. He'll follow through." She owed him for that. She hoped he had found someone at Gracie's or Johanna's to babysit Izzy. As soon as she had the thought, she was sure that he had. Holt got things done. He would find a capable sitter.

Kathryn breathed a sigh of relief and settled in to give

the best interview she could. But the second it was over, she didn't even bother to change back into her more casual clothes. Instead, she bolted out the door and headed straight for the mayor's office.

"Holt? Izzy?" she asked Johanna when she didn't see either him or Izzy.

"Not a clue," Johanna said. "Is there a problem?"

"Oh…no." *Maybe*. Kathryn started to head toward Gracie May's Diner when she remembered what had almost flown past her in her haste to get to the interview. Holt had told her to call. She did that now and realized that she could hear his phone ringing. He was still in the park not fifty yards away. He had his back up against a tree; he was holding Izzy up and making raspberries on her little belly.

Kathryn's heart stopped. Her brain stopped. Her mouth…maybe it fell open. She wasn't thinking about herself that much. What she *did* think about was how Izzy was laughing and clutching great fistfuls of Holt's hair. And pulling. Her hands might be tiny, but Kathryn knew how hard they could clutch at things. That had to hurt.

The strangest thing was that though Holt was clearly amusing Izzy, he was holding her as if she were a piece of delicate glass. And he wasn't laughing back. He wasn't reacting.

Until Izzy, in her excitement, spit up all over his shirt.

Most people who had zero experience with a baby would have gasped or yelled or held the baby away from them. Holt didn't do any of those things. He just stared down at his shirt as if he'd never seen it before.

Izzy had stopped laughing and was cooing quietly, happy and blissfully unaware that she had done anything wrong or had probably killed any last hope that Holt would ever like babies. He still hadn't looked up and Kathryn moved closer, ready to scoop Izzy up and offer to clean Holt's shirt.

He slowly raised his head and chuckled. "You little booger," he said, but there was no anger in his tone. "I guess you showed me not to blow raspberries on you. Of course…maybe that means I hurt you. Hell…I mean, heck…I should have known better. What's a rough cowboy like me doing trying to play with somebody as tiny as you are, anyway? You look like you'll break if the wind kicks up a notch. Are you okay?"

Izzy just stared at him with those big blue eyes. She looked at him as if he was an alien life form she wanted to study, as if she was fascinated with this big, deep-voiced creature. Then she blew a wet bubble and made a little fizzy baby sound.

"Is that a no?" he asked.

Kathryn had to smile. "Relax. You didn't hurt her at all," she said, stepping in. "Looks like she did a number on you, though."

"I have other shirts."

"I'll wash that one for you."

"No, you won't. It's fine."

She wrinkled her nose. "Other people might not think so."

"Other people can go straight to…they can just mind their own business."

"She was laughing," Kathryn said. "Really laughing."

"I might have taken the raspberry thing too far."

"She got overly excited. It happens, but she hasn't laughed yet. The books say that's still kind of an advanced skill at her age, and not every baby is there yet. I thought you were going to take her to Johanna."

"I never said that." He stared her down. "I figured I couldn't do too much damage if we didn't move around."

"I was gone a long time. What did you do?"

He shrugged. "We sat and talked."

Kathryn raised an eyebrow.

"I held her on my lap and told her ranch stories. It was pretty boring. She went to sleep. She snored a little."

"I know. It's cute, isn't it?"

He gave her a look. "Don't think I've changed."

"You didn't want to like her."

"I still don't want to like her."

"But you did well."

"I managed. I'm not asking for a gold star." Izzy was batting at Holt's shirt. Her hand was about to go in the mess. "You better take her." He handed the baby over, rose to his feet, peeled his shirt off. "I hope your interview went okay."

Kathryn tried not to stare at all that bronzed skin and muscle. She hoped she wasn't breathing noticeably faster even though her heartbeat had kicked up. "It did, I think," she said, trying for an airy tone. "I mean, the job is an entry level, but that's to be expected. That's what I want, and it sounds…interesting." But definitely not as interesting as Holt's bare chest or his biceps.

"Well, we should go, Izzy. Thank you so much, Holt."

To her surprise, he smiled. A nice, easy smile. "You're staring, Kathryn."

And she was blushing, too. She was tempted to cover her hot cheeks with her hands, but she was holding Izzy. "Well, yes. Yes, I am. If I took off my blouse, I'm sure you would stare, too."

She had been trying to be bold and a bit audacious, but the steamy, smoky look that Holt gave her…

"Darlin', if you took off your blouse I'd want to do a lot more than look."

With that, he took his stained shirt and turned toward

his truck. "I probably shouldn't have said that, but I'm not sorry. It's just the way it is. I'll see you at the fundraiser, Kathryn. I'll have my best host manners on by then." He walked away.

Oh, no, he was not going to make her blush like that and then get the last word, as well. "Make sure you have a shirt on, too," she called.

To her dismay she saw that Luann Dickens was across the street. She was laughing.

"That wasn't the way it sounded," Kathryn said lamely.

"Yes, it was, Luann," Holt said, his voice deadpan.

Luann let out a hoot, Kathryn gave her a frustrated look, and she turned toward home. "That man is…frustrating," she said.

"That's because you want to kiss him," Luann said, close enough now that her voice was much lower. Still, Kathryn turned around to see if Holt had heard.

"He's gone," Luann said. "You can't kiss him now."

But I did want to kiss him again. I wanted to do more than kiss, Kathryn admitted to herself. And it was more than just a physical thing. Holt, despite having his child ripped from him, despite having lost so many people in his life in a few short years that he had to be protecting his heart like mad, had still sacrificed his own fears and feelings to play with Izzy. How could you not love a man like that?

You couldn't. *I do love him,* Kathryn thought. And that was just too damn bad. Because she couldn't have him. She could never have him. Holt, despite being forced into action with Izzy today, was emotionally unavailable. He was unavailable in every way and just as off-limits to her now as he had been when she was young. Only then she'd merely had a crush. Now every bit of her longed to be with him. Always.

Too bad. You'll have to settle for your day at the ranch and then hope that a job comes through soon, so you can get out of here before he realizes that you've fallen for him. He wouldn't like hurting her. She wasn't going to let him know.

Once she was gone, she would tend to her broken heart. Alone.

Holt was up long before sunrise on the day of the "Come Be a Cowboy Day." There was so much to do today that he shouldn't have had any time to think, but that didn't stop him. He was, he admitted, seriously messed up.

Kathryn had become too much a part of his life lately. Her parting words to him had him living in a constant state of suppressed desire, her insistence on bravely pushing ahead on this project when he knew that she'd been nervous, and he'd been mean and uncooperative, had won his admiration and…something he didn't want to think about. Her insistence that she and everyone else pay him back for things he'd never expected payback for made him feel something he didn't understand. And that little baby, laughing at him… Kathryn smiling at him…

"Stop it. There's no point in all this." He had work to do. Kathryn had a life plan that was going to take her to Illinois, or if not Illinois, somewhere else. What would an urban developer do in Larkville once the clinic was done?

Besides, he didn't want her to stay. He didn't want to…feel. Because feeling led to bleakness, pain, loss. He couldn't help remembering the faces of all the people he'd lost these past few years: his parents, Hank, Lilith, the baby… No man would voluntarily step into that kind of hell again. "And I'm not going to," he told Daedalus as he did a final inspection of the barn and corral to make sure they were cleaned up to company standards.

"I believe you." Wes's voice came from Holt's right. "The point is, do you believe you?"

"What are you talking about, Wes?" Holt asked, angry because he'd been caught talking to thin air. "Don't you have something to do?"

Wes held up his hands. He smiled as he backed away. "I've got tons of work. That little gal of yours has given me a whole list. As for what I'm talking about—not a clue. But then you're the one that seemed upset. Something wrong?"

"Yeah. Something's wrong. I've got a whole town full of people and a bunch of tourists showing up here today. Why shouldn't there be something wrong?" Holt asked, grumpier than ever.

Of course, none of those things had anything to do with what was bothering Holt. And he suspected Wes knew it the way the man chuckled as he pulled out his color-coded list and walked away. Everything that was wrong centered around Kathryn.

And everything that was right did, too. What was he going to do about that?

Keep my head down, do my jobs, help her make this day a success and, above all, don't touch her. Don't tell her that she's getting to me. Don't dare do anything that will have her worrying about me once she's gone. Because once she was away from here, he wanted her happy. Blissfully happy with Larkville and him just a fading image in the rearview mirror of that rattletrap car of hers.

CHAPTER FOURTEEN

KATHRYN arrived at the ranch with her heart in her throat. This was a big day in more ways than one. She had received another message from Skyridge already, requesting more information. She might be on the verge of getting a job. That was a good thing, but it also meant that she would be leaving Larkville sooner rather than later.

Suddenly leaving here seemed much more real than it had before. And she wasn't ready. Not just because this time around she'd gotten to know people in Larkville and had made friends, but...

Don't. Don't think of Holt, she ordered herself. If she thought of Holt, she would hurt. And today she had to stand beside him as his hostess. She had to do Larkville and the Double Bar C proud and help win over the benefactors and the doctor candidates. Being sad wasn't allowed.

Taking a deep breath, she pasted on a smile and removed Izzy from her car seat. "Come on, sweetie. You're going to meet some other babies today. Luann and Mrs. Best have a nursery set up. Let's go find some toys."

Izzy's response was to coo and pat Kathryn's face. She kicked her little feet and then grabbed for the red scarf Kathryn was wearing around her neck. By the time Kathryn had untangled Izzy's fingers, kissing her chubby little fist, they were at the porch. Holt was there, and other people were beginning to spill out the door. To her surprise, Holt took Izzy from her and looked her baby in the eyes as he held her in front of him. "You're lookin' good, Iz," he told her. "Nice...whatever that thing you're wearing is called. That kitten on your tummy is real cute. Play nice with the other kids so your momma won't worry today, okay?"

Izzy wrinkled her nose in her best baby smile. Then she bucked a bit, kicked her tiny feet some more, rounded her lips and made what seemed like a half-formed blowing motion. A bit like the raspberry Holt had given her yesterday. It was probably just a coincidence, probably just an accident, but Holt tilted his head and squinted. "Yeah, you're your mother's daughter all right. Always asking me to do things. Okay, then. You and me. Later. One raspberry. Maybe two. But no spitting up milk like yesterday, all right? A cowboy needs his dignity." But his voice was gentle as he passed Izzy over to Mrs. Best.

He turned to Kathryn. "Looks like we're all here and everyone has their lists." Was that a smile on his face? If it was, it quickly disappeared as he mentioned to everyone that their guests would be arriving soon. He had flown several groups in last night, and Gus would be bringing them on the bus. "Any last words or last-minute things you want done before we begin?" he asked Kathryn.

She shook her head, trying not to think about how much was riding on this day. "Just...be yourselves. You've made me feel welcome. You all know your skills better than I ever could. Just be prepared to answer a lot of questions, and if you don't know what to say, send them to me or Holt. Depending on what the question is."

"We'll send the men to you and the women to Holt. That should win them over. They'll all leave here in love,"

Dave, one of Holt's hands, said. He winked at Kathryn, and she laughed.

Holt gave him the evil eye. "The only thing we want them to fall in love with is Larkville and ranch life."

Dave laughed, clearly taking no offense at Holt's cranky tone. "Yes, sir, Holt. We'll show them the best we've got. Ain't that right, boys?" The other men agreed and began to move off to their assigned tasks. Nancy had told Kathryn that the men would walk through fire for Holt just as they would have for his father. There was a mutual respect between the rancher and his cowhands born out of a common background, a love of the land and the sometimes harsh circumstances nature sent their way.

Once everyone was gone, Kathryn looked up at Holt. "Can we walk? I'd like to see Daedalus before the frenzy of the day begins."

To her surprise, he took her hand and she held her breath for a minute, just savoring the feeling of his big palm cupping hers. No doubt she shouldn't indulge herself, but this might be one of the last times she got to do this with him. "I better watch myself," he said. "It wouldn't do for me to get all riled up and grumpy when we have guests. I saw you looking at me that way."

"What way?" For a few seconds, Kathryn's heartbeat started galloping wildly. Did Holt suspect that she had feelings for him beyond simple attraction? Because she would hate for him to know that. When she left here, she wanted to leave proud and tall. Holt's equal, his partner. If he even suspected she was in love with him, he'd get that stern, sad look in his eyes and start telling her what a jerk he was. And that would mean he was trying to let her down easy, that he felt sorry for her. She'd—she would lie to his face and deny she even thought of him as a man before she let that happen, and she hated lies.

Holt was studying her. Waiting. She shook her head. "You managed to get a whole group of people to come here from all over the country. I'm not worried about what they'll think if you get a little grumpy. Most of them will probably fall right in with everyone else and think you're just that cowboy of their imagination, the romantic über-masculine guy with a generous dollop of testosterone in his soul. You being cranky would probably just entrance them more."

He didn't answer. She looked to the side. His lips were twitching.

"I don't believe it. You're laughing at me."

"Sorry, Kathryn, but you sounded just a tad put out that I could behave badly and people would give me a pass because it fits their image of the Hollywood cowboy."

She chuckled. "Well, it seems very unfair that if a woman got grumpy and started giving people deadly looks, no one would sigh and think she was fulfilling some romantic fantasy of theirs. They'd probably give her a wide berth or make insulting and sexist wisecracks."

"No. If it was you, they'd probably be too busy trying to figure out how they could get back in your good graces. You're going to win some hearts today, Kathryn. Dave was right. I'll tell him so. Eventually. I don't want him to get a big head. Not when he's got chores to do. He's leading the bridge crew today. I'm a bit worried about that one and the fencing crew. It seems wrong subjecting people with soft hands and a desire for fun to hard labor."

"I'm not worried. Men who spend their days in suits like getting a chance to pretend they're brawny tough guys who get to swing things, hit things and make things. And everyone here is going to schmooze them to death. We all want good things to happen. I can't imagine anyone walking in here and not feeling welcome."

As they moved toward the corral, Blue followed along, letting Kathryn trail her fingers on his fur. Daedalus whinnied when he saw them, and Kathryn reached in her pocket and pulled out a carrot. Placing it on her palm she held her hand perfectly still until Daedalus took her offering with almost microprecision. "I don't think he would have ever hurt me even that first time. I think you were just mad at me for showing up that day."

"Could be. I have a temper."

"I noticed. It's not an evil temper, though. You turn it on yourself more than you turn it on anyone else. I just tried to corner you that day."

"You *did* corner me. I was stuck with no way out the minute you made up your mind to begin this project."

"I didn't know it."

He smiled. "I hadn't admitted it at the time, either, but I knew that you were trying to force my hand. And before we begin today, I want to thank you. You've done a good thing, a big thing. I don't know when I've seen everyone here so excited. Today is big doings for a town the size of Larkville. They're beginning to really care about the clinic and to believe it might happen."

"I hope it does. It still might not. It's difficult getting doctors to move to small towns when they can command better money in cities."

"Then I guess we'll just have to offer them something they can't get in a city."

She smiled. "Cowboy charm?" she teased.

He doffed his hat and bowed over her hand. "I aim to please, ma'am." His lips touched her skin, making her feel hot and terribly aware that she was a woman having her hand kissed by the most wanted cowboy in the county.

Just then the bus came down the road and Gus climbed out and escorted everyone off the vehicle.

"Showtime," Holt said.

"Places," Kathryn agreed. They both made a beeline toward the bus. And with that, "Come Be a Cowboy Day" began.

The ranch was a beehive of activity. Gus was showing the kids the animals. They were chasing chickens, corralling cats and dogs and milking cows. There were craft workshops, roping sessions, work crews. Holt and Kathryn had taken a group of riders out, but it was a large group and each of them had their assigned visitors. Holt knew he might not get a chance to spend any time with her until tonight when all the groups would converge for dinner and a dance.

Instead, he tried to focus on his group. He kept up a running commentary about the ranch and the town and the advantages of being within driving distance from Austin while he watched Kathryn do the same with another subset of the group. She had her head thrown back and she was laughing as she spoke. She looked good on a horse. No one would have known that she had only had one lesson. If he didn't know better, Holt would have wondered if she hadn't whispered some sweet nothings into Daedalus's ear. That horse seemed almost as besotted as the members of her group, both men and women.

"This isn't the way it is most of the time, is it?" a voice asked.

Holt turned to see one of the doctor candidates coming up beside him. "You mean the ranch?"

"The ranch, all of it."

Holt shrugged. "I wouldn't say that. It's just a bit compressed. The way it would be if you made a time-lapse of ranch life. Plus, the weather cooperated and there's no mud, so these are ideal circumstances. You disappointed?"

He didn't want to have to tell Kathryn that another candidate was dropping out. One of the three had failed to show up. Now this. Having this man asking such pointed questions had Holt worried, so he might have sounded just a bit cranky in spite of his promise to tone it down.

"Am I disappointed?" the man asked. "Nope. Just making sure I know as much as possible. I've spoken with Dr. Cooper, of course. Ms. Ellis put me in touch with him, and he's given me a good idea of what his practice entails, but anyone who signs on to take the job—if it's offered—will have to live here."

"It's a good place," Holt said.

"Ms. Ellis said that, too. I'd really like to get to know her better."

"She's not part of the package."

"I—"

Dammit, why had he put it that way? "By that I merely meant that she's planning to move away very soon."

The man didn't answer, and Holt glanced toward him. To his surprise, the guy, Lee Sullivan, was smiling. "You have a thing for her, don't you?"

No. No. No. Yes, of course. Who wouldn't? "It's not like that."

"Which probably means, 'Mind your own business.' I don't blame you. I'm half in love with her myself and I've barely met her."

Half in love with her. Half in love with her. The words skimmed through Holt's mind the rest of the day. It wasn't as if he hadn't already thought the same thing and pushed it aside. It was just that this day, that guy, her job situation, all served to keep Kathryn's impending departure on his mind constantly. He dreaded having to say goodbye, and he hated that he even cared. But that couldn't matter. He had spent a lifetime submerging his emotions. He wasn't going to let them start leading him around now. Especially not when it would upset Kathryn to know that his interest in her was more than merely physical. And way more than merely friendship.

With the greatest of effort, he tamped all of that down. And waited for the night when he hoped he could dance with her. Getting close to her might be difficult in this crowd of admiring males.

Kathryn had cleaned up and changed into a white blouse and a blue skirt with a bandanna at her throat. She still had several hours of being on camera, of having to woo people, and all she wanted was some time to spend with Holt.

That was wrong. This was something she had started and it was important. Under ordinary circumstances she would be happy. The day had been going great once she'd accepted the fact that they were down to only two doctor candidates. But when she had turned on her cell phone that had been turned off, she found a message. Ed Austen's voice said, "Congratulations! The job is yours if you want it. Come out Monday? We'll put you and your daughter up in temporary housing until you can find your own place. Call me."

She hadn't called. Not yet. And she hadn't told Holt. This day was for Larkville and for him. This day was to be their first triumph. She wasn't going to inject her own personal plans into it.

And the truth was, she didn't want to think about leaving Holt. Not today. Instead, she found her smile. She entered the room where Ellie Jackson was giving everyone dance lessons. Ellie was a former ballet dancer from New York, and while ballet might be her usual game, she clearly knew her Texas two-step, too.

Kathryn found a place near the back of the room and

within seconds Holt was there. Her chest, which had been fine all day, felt suddenly tight. "You want a progress report?" she asked.

"Only if you want to give me one. What I want is a dance partner."

"I'm afraid I'm not very good at this."

"That's why you have Ellie. And me." And he swirled her into his arms and into the dance. She stumbled. "Easy," he said, his hands on her to stabilize her. "It's a triple step, then another, then two singles. That's right. We're just going to keep it simple at first. We'll dress it up when you're comfortable."

"Holt?"

"Yes?" His palm was at her waist, the warmth of his touch seeping through to her skin. She felt flushed and achy. Surely anyone could see how he was affecting her.

"I may never get comfortable," she said. Not with him holding her. But then he was twirling her, guiding her and she fit with him, moved with him. He moved toward her, he turned her in his arms. And she followed as if she had been dancing with him all her life.

"Hot. Very hot," Luann said as she glided past, her duties with the little ones turned over to Mrs. Best. Kathryn couldn't have agreed more. She felt very hot, and perfect.

"Okay, a dip, just for fun," Holt said, and he dipped her back over his arm at the end of the song. His face was over hers, his lips were so close. She was… Oh, my word, she had been reaching out to pull him even closer. Instantly, she scrambled and nearly fell. Holt righted her immediately.

"May I cut in?" one of the benefactors asked. "I can't promise you anything like that, but I won't embarrass you too much, I don't think." He was an older man, a very nice man who had lost his wife and who was still sad.

Immediately Holt and Kathryn separated. She smiled at the man even as she was completely aware of Holt moving away from her. Asking other women to dance. And she accepted dances from other men. That was the way the rest of the evening went.

And this was how the rest of her life would go. She and Holt had had their time, and now she had a job. They would both move on. Their time together was over.

Could a man be more frustrated than he was right now? On the one hand he should be ecstatic. The young doctor from the trail seemed interested in the town and maybe the job, they had raised a lot of money and everyone had had a good time. But every time he had tried to get close to Kathryn, some other man had stepped in to take his place. And he'd had to let him. Them. All of them.

After that first dance, he hadn't gotten close to her again and now she was standing in front of him telling him…

"I'm going home on the bus with Gus."

He blinked. "I can drive you."

She shook her head. "No."

"You want to explain that? Have I been channeling that jackass husband the way I've done so often with you? Made you angry? Pushed you?" Wasn't he pushing her now by asking all these stupid questions that were really none of his business?

Again, she shook her head. She looked tired. He felt like a beast for prodding her. "No, I just…I have to think, and I don't trust myself to think straight with you there. You make me want to do risky, unwise things."

"And you don't like that."

"I like that too well, but tonight I can't. I have to return a phone call. From Illinois."

Then she was gone, and he didn't know whether the phone call had been good news or bad. It had been obvious that she wasn't in a sharing mood. She was withholding crucial information from him. And it was her right. This wasn't like Lilith. This was Kathryn, and she had every right to tell him nothing at all if she so desired.

And there wasn't a thing he could do about it, was there?

CHAPTER FIFTEEN

KATHRYN looked around her at her little house and tried to decide what she should do. She had asked Mrs. Best to take Izzy, but she hadn't told her why she needed time to be alone.

In truth, there wasn't a good reason. She had called Ed Austen; she had done the only thing she could do. By rights she should be ecstatic.

And I will be, she promised herself. This was what she had set out to do. Get a job in her field. Become independent. Make her own little family. It was perfect.

Except…

When the knock came at the door, she knew it was Holt. She had been less than forthcoming with him last night. Because she was afraid she might do something stupid. Like cry. Or get clingy. She'd been tired and not completely in control of her emotions. There had been a very good chance that she might have done something emotional, something they'd both regret.

But it was morning now. She should be fine. Had to be fine.

She opened the door. And looked up into those dark eyes. She wasn't fine.

"I just came by to…see how you thought everything went yesterday."

Kathryn nodded. She wanted to sock him on the arm. He was so obviously making that up. "It went well. Fantastic. Don't you think?"

"Me? Yeah. Great. I think we'll probably bag that young doctor. And we pulled in enough… I've got some architects in mind and—hell, Kathryn. I don't want to talk about the clinic."

She waited.

"The phone call," he said. "Yes or no?"

"Yes." Her voice sounded too weak. "Yes," she tried again. "I start Monday."

He let out a whistle. It sounded very nonchalant. Her heart felt very rocklike. She wanted to kick some of the piles of stuff she had been trying to organize and sort for the trip. "Monday?"

"I couldn't say no. It's a good opportunity."

"Yes, it is. I'm happy for you. You can do and be all those things you wanted to."

"I know. Isn't it great?" She tried so very hard to dredge up a brilliant smile and a convincing tone of voice. The last thing she wanted was for Holt to know that when she left here she left…in love with him. This was a man who piled responsibility on himself. She didn't want him to feel responsible for her. Or to feel guilty when he heard her name. *Light. Keep it light,* she ordered herself.

"I'm going to miss all the good stuff, the plans for the clinic, the groundbreaking," she told him, trying to keep her smile brilliant. "Send me—send me lists."

"Right. Sure thing."

She had motioned him to the couch. Now she stared down at him. "You're not going to, are you?" And why should he? He didn't owe her anything. She shouldn't even want him to contact her. It would only open the wound over and over.

"I—Kathryn, no, I'm not going to send you lists or anything else," he said, shaking his head. "When things end, they're done. I don't look back."

That felt like a blow, and yet she tried to put herself in his place. He'd faced so much. A weaker man might have gone crazy.

"I shouldn't ask, but is that because…I know you've lost a lot of loved ones…"

"No point in remembering."

"Even the good memories?" She didn't wait for him to answer. "Holt, I want to be a good memory. Someone who makes you smile when you think about her. You say that you're not a sensitive or emotional man. But I've seen how patient you are with Mrs. Best and how mad you were when Ava DuShay's son wasn't treating her right. You may have a responsibility to the people of Larkville, but all those things you… I'm just not buying that it's all out of duty or that you're some emotionless robot. You care what happens to people. They touch your heart even if you don't say the words. Why do the words matter? You show them instead. So don't put me on your 'do not remember' list. Remember me just a little. We've been friends, haven't we?"

He reached up and took her hand, pulling her down beside him on the couch. "Don't you ever give up?"

"Yes. Yes I do. Sometimes, but—"

"Shh." He drew her onto his lap. He kissed her, a long, sweet kiss. "Don't you want to know what I'm doing?" he asked.

"You're kissing me. I'm kissing you, too."

"I'm making some good memories," he whispered against her mouth.

She smiled against his lips. Her heart was still filled with pain, but she wove her way around it, over it, under it. The pain would wait. Now she was with Holt. "Let's make more memories," she said. "Izzy is at Mrs. Best's."

"We're alone? No one's going to cut in and ask you to dance?"

"Just you. Dancing with me. We'll begin where we left off last night. Where was it?"

"I think it was…here," he said, sliding his palm around her back. "And then here." He gently touched her lips.

"And this was where we were headed," she whispered, and she leaned into him, kissing him more deeply. She placed her palms on his shirt. "Open the buttons for me."

He never stopped kissing her, but in seconds she was able to push his shirt wide. He slithered out of it.

"We could dance better, closer, without these," he said, removing her blouse and then her jeans. As he turned with her, rolled with her, danced with her, they did away with the rest of their clothes. Then he took her in his arms and danced her into her bedroom. He laid her on the mattress, he braced himself above her. "When you're gone, I'll send you whatever you ask for," he whispered.

"Send me you. Now," she said.

"With pleasure," he agreed.

And he was right. Kathryn had never been loved so well. She knew why, too.

Because Holt knew how to love in many ways even if he didn't actually love her. And also because she actually *did* love him. Desperately. Hopelessly. Now wasn't the time to think about or regret that. She would have a lifetime to get over loving Holt.

She didn't hesitate. She had no desire to hold back, because these would be her last memories of him. She wanted them to be perfect.

So when they finally awoke, she kissed him once more,

loving him with all her heart. "Don't stay," she said. "I have to get ready. I have to pack and leave."

Within moments he was gone. Forever. Only the thought that she had a child to take care of kept her from collapsing.

Holt rode Daedalus for miles. And then for more miles. He paid no attention to time or the weather. He could have ridden forever but a man's horse shouldn't have to bear the grief of the man.

Eventually, he came back and stopped by the creek. This had always been one of his favorite places. Today it was empty, and his heart wasn't here.

"She's almost gone, boy. You won't see her again and neither will I," he said. "I wish I had some way to change things so that what she needs and wants could be here. I wish I had the words to make her want to stay, but that's never been me. Not good with words or matters of the heart. Lots of disappointed people, lots of loss. People think I'm something because of the Double Bar C, but I'm not so much. Kathryn, now, she's something. She knows how to get things done, how to make people want to do the things she wants. Her and her lists." Those silly, sweet lists. She drove him mad with them. She made him smile.

If he hadn't been in so much pain, he might have smiled now. As it was, smiling wasn't an option today.

He hadn't even said a word when he left last night, the last time he would ever speak to her.

Don't feel, he remembered his father saying in a rare moment of introspection. *Feeling makes you weak and brings you trouble. Don't ever say anything that will let anyone see into your soul and give them power over you. Just work. Love comes and goes, but the ranch is a lasting legacy. That's all that matters in life.*

Don't you dare cry, Clay had said when he got hurt.

Pick yourself up and move on, his father had said when his dog died. *Don't feel. Don't feel. Don't let yourself be blinded by passion.* The words echoed through his mind.

Holt got up and began trying to outwalk the litany running through his head. *Don't feel. Don't feel.* He'd followed that directive all his life. It had crippled him to the point where his throat froze every time he even thought the word *love.*

But I love her. Holt lurched, bumping into Daedalus, who sidestepped and whinnied.

"Sorry, boy," Holt said. "Look what I did. Just thinking the words messed me up. How could I ever tell her?"

Maybe he didn't have to. The thought came to him in all capitals, in bold. What had Kathryn said? That the words weren't important because she knew that he cared about people?

Maybe so, but that seems way too easy. That's like giving me a pass to be a total jerk.

Besides, for the first time in his memory, he *wanted* to love and to say the words. He wanted to let his heart out of its cage and be able to tell the woman he loved that he cared. And not awkwardly, either. Kathryn was a woman who liked words, no matter what she'd said. Otherwise, she wouldn't work for a newspaper and fill up reams of paper with her lists.

You'll mess it up. You'll say the wrong thing. You might even yell and act stupid. And what's the point, anyway? She's going. She's going.

And maybe that was the point exactly. She was going without knowing that she was loved beyond belief. She wanted him to have good memories of her? He wanted her to know that she had changed him in a way no one ever had before. He wanted her to know how much she mattered, to give her what all the people she'd loved had withheld from her. Too bad he wasn't an eloquent man.

Still, he intended to make the effort.

Kathryn was crossing the park on her way to the SmartMart. She needed some last-minute items to tide Izzy over for the trip and her mind was so…no, it was her *heart* that was the problem. She kept forgetting things.

But this was absolutely the last trip to the store. She had her bags in the car, she'd said her goodbyes to everyone in town and there was nothing left to do but go. And try to get over Holt. Because she hurt. She was a mess.

You shouldn't have trusted him. The thought slid in. *He hurt you the way everyone else has.* But no, that wasn't true. He had warned her from the first that he wasn't a man a woman should love. He had tried to protect her heart, and everything he did, everything he was, was honorable. He was the most trustworthy man she knew. He had given her back what she had lost: trust, faith in herself and in others. It wasn't his fault that he didn't love her the way she loved him.

Stop thinking. Stop feeling. Go, she told herself. So, she got the things she needed from the store, she put them in the car and put Izzy in her car seat. She took one last look around and turned to go, fighting the tears in her throat. She reached for the car door handle. *Go. Go now before you break down right here in public.*

"Kathryn, don't. Don't go." Holt's voice sounded behind her and she whirled, almost into his arms. "Don't go *yet*," he clarified.

"What's wrong?" There had to be something wrong. He had left hours ago, and Holt was, as he'd said, a man who never looked back.

"I lied," he said. "I *do* look back. I *do* remember. And

I regret. I think of the things I wish I'd said, and you'd think that would help me the next time, but it doesn't. So I live with the fact that my father and I never shared our feelings, I probably didn't give my friend Hank the proper goodbye he needed and if I had been able to tell Lilith what she wanted to hear, our child…well, I don't know, but maybe the ending might have felt less brutal. Now here you are, and you matter…the most. I can say the unimportant things, the grumpy things, I can discuss minor issues, I can even offer you mundane compliments. But to express what's in here—" he tapped his chest "—it's awkward, dumb, not anything anyone would want to hear."

For a second she started to say that she would, but that might sound as if she was pressuring him. "Holt, when I came here I didn't trust anyone, not even myself. I was running scared and bluffing my way through, trying to look capable so no one would see how frightened and unsure I was. Everyone I had cared about had betrayed me and criticized me. And then there was you. You didn't sugarcoat anything and you didn't even cooperate half the time, but you were true. You had your principles and your rules and you stuck to them no matter what. You were—*are*—the most trustworthy man I've ever met. Knowing that you existed, that there was one solid, steadfast person in the world I could depend on, come flood or fire, changed me, inspired me to have faith in myself and helped me become more than I'd ever been. So there's nothing you could ever say that I wouldn't want to hear, no matter how awkwardly it was phrased. But I want you to know that you don't have to say anything."

"Kathryn. Hell, Kathryn, I didn't even say thank you for last night."

Her heart lurched. She managed a smile. "Yes, you did. You didn't have to say the words. You *showed* me." And then she just couldn't help herself. She rose on her toes and kissed him. Just once.

He groaned. He kissed her, too. Just once. Then, reaching into his pocket, he pulled out a folded sheet of paper. He handed it to her and she unfolded it. It was color-coded.

The code for *Physical* was yellow.

You make my knees weak. I wake up every morning wanting to kiss you; I go to sleep each night wanting to hold you. The scent of your hair makes me think of…sunshine and fields of roses. When you grow old, I'll still love looking at you, because your beauty comes from the inside.

She didn't read it out loud because she could already see that Holt was squirming under her scrutiny of his prose. She moved on to blue for *Other*.

You make me want to be a better man than I am. You drive me crazy with your demands, but I seem to like being driven crazy because I look forward to seeing you. Every day. You have a beautiful, sweet baby girl I adore.

Kathryn had to stop reading for a minute while she wiped her eyes. Then she looked down again. There was just one thing more.

I am so happy for your success. I want you to be happy forever, and I want you to know that I will love you all the days of my life.

Her face nearly crumpled. "For real?" she asked.

"It's on the list, isn't it?" he asked, drawing her to him

and whispering against her neck. "Lists don't lie. At least ours don't."

"I liked the color-coding."

"Two seemed kind of skimpy, but I was afraid you would leave before I finished. Besides, this was my first time. I don't have any practice in writing love letters."

"I'm glad. I wouldn't want to think of some other woman reading about how you love her."

"That won't happen. You're the one, the only one. All the days of my life," he repeated. "Now. What time do you have to be in Illinois?" His voice sounded thick.

"You're not asking me to stay?"

He hesitated. "I don't want to stand in your way. You worked hard to get your degree and to get this job."

"And I'll get another one. Closer to home. Closer to Larkville. Austin's close. If I make a big enough nuisance of myself, maybe they'll like me and give me a job."

"Maybe they'll love you," he said, and he kissed her nose and then her lips.

"Just as long as you do."

"I definitely do love you, Kathryn."

"Do you want to know how much I love you, Holt?"

"I hope it's a lot. I hope you'll agree to marry me."

"I think it was written in the cards. Or at least it was written." She reached into her purse and pulled out a folded piece of paper. "When I was cleaning out boxes for packing today, I came across this. It was written years ago and I was pretty young, so I'm sorry for the girlish cursive and the purple ink."

She opened the yellowing sheet of paper where a much younger Kathryn had written "I love, love, love, love, love…"

The words went to the end of the page where Holt's

name was printed. And in the header of the paper, she had written "Kathryn Calhoun. Mrs. Holt Calhoun."

"How could I not marry you?" she teased. "It says right here in bright purple that my name is Kathryn Calhoun."

He laughed out loud. "Darlin', how did I miss you back then?" he asked.

"It doesn't matter. You've got me now."

And he swept her into his arms. He had her.

EPILOGUE

On a sunny blue-sky day in August, three months after Kathryn had walked back into Holt's world, Kathryn and Holt embarked on their next project together: their wedding. The Double Bar C had never looked so festive. There were white and pale blue ribbons and flowers everywhere. Daedalus even had pale blue ribbons braided into his mane as Kathryn, dressed in a white dress and perched precariously on a sidesaddle, met Holt at the juncture where they were to begin the procession.

As he mounted his father's stallion, Storm, he smiled at her. "I hope you know that only the fact that I love you more than I love my dignity or my horse's dignity is getting me up on a horse that is decked out in ribbons."

Kathryn's heart filled to overflowing. "I hope *you* know that I love you enough that I would have married you in a mud hut with no ribbons, flowers or guests."

"I do," he said. "But I want people to know how much I care. You deserve only the best."

"Well, I've got the best. The best cowboy. The best man."

"Ah, I see you're still delusional, love. Well, let's ride, then." They turned their horses in the direction of their eager audience.

The people of Larkville lined a rose-petal-strewn path

that led to an altar at the edge of a grassy field. They cheered as Holt and Kathryn passed by.

When the two of them reached the altar, Wes and Dave led the horses away, and Holt turned to Kathryn. He kissed her.

"Not yet," someone shouted and everyone laughed.

"I love you," he said.

"Not yet for that, either," someone else said.

Kathryn kissed Holt. "I love *you*."

"Would someone please get these two married already?" a third person called out.

So the ceremony began. It was short and sweet with the only holdup being when Blue delivered the rings and wanted to lick Kathryn to death. The pastor had barely said the last words before Holt swept Kathryn close. "Thank you for waiting for me," he said, as his mouth covered hers in a kiss that took Kathryn's breath away. Then he kissed her again, softer this time. Sweeter, but just as nice. All Holt's kisses were nice.

Eventually, however, he set her back on her feet, and they smiled at each other as the recessional music began.

Holt held his arm out to Kathryn, but she shook her head. "Not yet," she said quietly. "Gus?"

Gus, who was seated in the front row, stepped forward. He was holding a book.

Holt raised an eyebrow. "You want me to read? Now?"

Kathryn took the book. "Not exactly. I just… Remember the day everyone was giving you gifts and you wouldn't take mine? This is it. I researched the history of the Double Bar C, and everyone contributed photographs and stories. It's made so you can add more pages. Things about your parents and Jess, Megan and Nate only you would know. And your new brothers and sisters." She smiled at Ellie, who smiled back.

Holt looked down. He blinked. Then he took Kathryn's face in both his hands and kissed her, hard. He smiled at his sisters, who were beaming, and at Nate, recently home from the army, who gave him a silent nod. Then he turned to Ellie. "I would love to know more. To know *you*. All of you."

Ellie blinked back tears. "I'm going to love getting to know you, too."

In the brief moment that followed, Kathryn leaned toward Holt and whispered, "I didn't want to put anything about your baby or Lilith in there without talking to you, but I want you to know that he—or she—is going in there. I know you wanted that baby and grieved its loss."

Holt didn't speak for a minute. When he did, his voice was thick. "Thank you. I *did* love that baby and I hope you know that I love Izzy heart and soul. I consider her mine."

She smiled. "You're going to be such a good daddy if you don't spoil her silly. She already adores you."

He grinned. "I intend to spoil all our children silly. I mean to love them like crazy and tell them so every day, but I'm never going to love anyone the way that I love you."

"We can't hear you," someone yelled. "What are you talking about?"

Holt and Kathryn turned to face all of Larkville. "We're talking about making babies. Kathryn wants to get right on it," Holt said.

"Now?" Wes asked, laughing.

"Just as soon as Holt quits talking," Kathryn teased. "This man just loves to talk and make long speeches."

Everyone laughed, and Holt smiled at his wife. "You're going to pay for that, darlin'."

"I certainly hope so, love," she said. "Here's my first payment." And she launched herself into his arms.

The people of Larkville went wild. Holt Calhoun had finally found his voice, his love, his future and his reason for living.

A sneaky peek at next month...

Cherish™

ROMANCE TO MELT THE HEART EVERY TIME

My wish list for next month's titles...

In stores from 21st December 2012:

❑ Suddenly You – Sarah Mayberry

& His Larkville Cinderella – Melissa McClone

❑ Fortune's Cinderella – Karen Templeton

& Fortune's Valentine Bride – Marie Ferrarella

In stores from 4th January 2013:

❑ The Cattleman's Special Delivery – Barbara Hannay

& The Surgeon's Favourite Nurse – Teresa Southwick

❑ A Home for Nobody's Princess – Leanne Banks

& The Prince She Had to Marry – Christine Rimmer

Available at WHSmith, Tesco, Asda, Eason, Amazon and Apple

Just can't wait?

1212/23

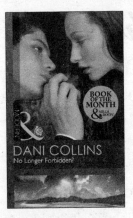

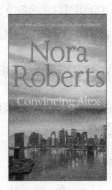

Have Your Say

You've just finished your book.
So what did you think?

We'd love to hear your thoughts on our
'Have your say' online panel
www.millsandboon.co.uk/haveyoursay

- 🌹 Easy to use
- 🌹 Short questionnaire
- 🌹 Chance to win Mills & Boon® goodies

Visit us Online

Tell us what you thought of this book now at
www.millsandboon.co.uk/haveyoursay